THE HORSE KNOWS THE WAY

BOOKS BY JOHN O'HARA

JOHN O'HARA

THE HORSE
KNOWS
THE WAY

Over the river and through the wood
To grandfather's house we'll go;
The horse knows the way
To carry the sleigh,
Through the white and drifted snow.

—Thanksgiving Day,
by Lydia Maria Child (1802-1880)

RANDOM HOUSE · NEW YORK

FIRST PRINTING

© *Copyright, 1963, 1964, by John O'Hara*

All rights reserved under International and Pan-American Copyright
Conventions. Published in New York by Random House, Inc., and
simultaneously in Toronto, Canada, by Random House of Canada Limited.
Manufactured in the United States of America
by H. Wolff Company, New York
Library of Congress catalog card number: 64-7751

Of the twenty-eight stories in this book, four first appeared in
The New Yorker, and thirteen first appeared in *The Saturday Evening Post*.
The remaining stories are herein published for the first time.

FOREWORD

For a while, at least, this will be my last book of short stories. I know that Mme. Schumann-Heink, Sir Harry Lauder, and W. Somerset Maugham have made frequent farewell appearances that followed farewell appearances, and I have qualified my announcement by saying "for a while." I am also perhaps overconscious of the fact that at my age, fifty-nine, a man had better not be too sure that he is going to finish anything he starts. Suddenly—it seems suddenly to me—I find myself referred to as the "granddaddy" and the "old master" of the short story field. Those are direct quotes, and they have as much actuarial as literary significance. I think it was a character of Bugs Baer's whose doctor said, "You're all right, but don't start any continued stories," a prognosis that is as dismal as the governor's refusal to answer the telephone the night before the execution.

It is going to be difficult to resist the temptation to go on writing short stories—for me more difficult than it is to write them. Magazines buy nearly all the stories I write, and they pay me well. Those that are not acceptable to the magazine editors eventually get printed in my short story collections (and have as good a critical record as the stories that were turned down or, in a few cases, were not even submitted). A story that I sold to *The New Yorker* for five or six hundred dollars many years ago has brought me around thirty thousand dollars in movie options and the end is not yet. I could live nicely on my income from short stories and nothing else, even without movie options and television sales, and my taxes would not be so devastating. There is also a temptation to play it safe in my war with the academics and the critics, since they have a hard time rapping the stories and are driven to complaining against "the kind of people" I write about.

(Excuse me for just a minute while I tell a little tale on a London critic. He roasted my novel *Elizabeth Appleton* in a thousand-word review, and throughout the review he kept referring to Valley Spring College, which mystified me as my fictional institution was called Spring Valley. But then I found out that in that particular edition of *Elizabeth Appleton* the writer of the jacket blurb had made the mistake of transposing Spring and Valley. In the book itself there is hardly a sequence of five pages that does not mention Spring Valley. The jacket blurb mentions Valley Spring once. You *never* get used to that kind of reviewing.)

But how safe is playing it safe? Thirty years after the publication of my first novel I have been given the Award of Merit of the American Academy of Arts and Letters, the highest honor of my professional career. It was given to me for the *novel,* not for the short story. It may seem to have taken the Academy a rather long while to get around to it, but they voted me the Award at a stage in my career when my stort stories were being praised and my novels deplored. That Award has made a hell of a difference to me. It was given to me in spite of the fact that I had resigned from the National Institute of Arts and Letters three years earlier. It was a complete surprise of a kind that I badly needed, how badly I did not realize until I was able to think about it.

Now the members of the Academy (who are not what I contemptuously refer to as the academics) did not play it safe. They gave me an honor that had previously been given to Theodore Dreiser, Thomas Mann, Ernest Hemingway, and Aldous Huxley, and to no one else. What do you do in a case like that? You say "Thank you," of course, when you want to say, "Here, take a quart of my rather tired blood." If you are me, you cry a little and you rush to tell the people you love, and you wish that some others could have known about your good news. Perhaps what there is of them in you *does* know. But then when this emotional crisis has passed and is replaced by the joys and vexations of Art, you find that you have a new fear of the temptation to play it safe. You have something, and good people have told you that you have it. They have not said that you owe them anything; they have satisfied their artistic obligation for what you have done, and they want to get on with their own work. Nevertheless you have an obligation to the something that is not all you and is not all Art, but is that which does make cowards of us all, and hence the fear.

I have work to do, and I am afraid not to do it.

JOHN O'HARA

Princeton, New Jersey
Spring 1964

CONTENTS

CONTENTS   (x)

THE HORSE KNOWS THE WAY

ALL TIED UP

One day Miles Updegrove, who did not ordinarily notice such things, noticed that Earl Appel came to work in a pair of loafers. They were not twenty-five-dollar loafers, they did not have tassels, they were not even polished. They were exactly the same kind of loafers that Miles Updegrove wore around the house on Saturdays, when he did the chores that piled up during the week. They were Miles Updegrove's version of the canvas sneakers his father had worn when he did his chores around the same house. Seth Updegrove would never have worn his sneakers to the bank; Miles would never wear his loafers to the bank; and he did not like to see Earl Appel come to work in loafers any more than he would have liked Earl to appear at the bank without a necktie. True, Earl's shoes did not show from his post behind the counter. Also it was possible that Earl was having his regular shoes repaired, and the loafers were a substitute. Miles, moreover, was a man who believed in keeping his distance from the members of the bank staff, and to speak to Earl Appel about shoes would be a violation of his own rule. Nevertheless when Miles Updegrove attended the next Monday meeting of the directors he made a point of checking on Earl Appel's footwear, and, as he feared, Earl was again wearing the loafers. A week later, again after the directors' meeting, Miles Updegrove was disturbed to see that loafers apparently were Earl Appel's regular shoes. They may have been polished once since Miles first noticed them, but they still looked out of place in a bank.

Miles thought of preparing a memorandum to the bank staff. In 1955 a memorandum to the male members of the staff had taken care of a problem of a somewhat similar nature. "It has been called to our attention," Miles then wrote, "that certain of our staff have recently been afflicted with attacks of 'five o'clock shadow,' a malady that in these days of a growing percentage of women customers does not add to the tidiness or prestige of The Bank. Upon inquiry we have learned that in order to achieve punctuality in the morning, several of our staff have formed the habit of shaving the night before, no doubt a continuation of a custom originating during army or navy service. It is our earnest hope that the habit will now be discontinued as several complaints have been received." The memo was signed "M.B.U., President, For the Board of Directors," and Miles took some pride in it because it combined firmness with a light touch, and it was completely successful. The offending night-before shavers—two others besides Earl Appel—obeyed the directive, and there never again was a complaint against five o'clock shadow.

This, however, was a different situation. (Actually, of course, there had been no complaints by women customers on the score of unshaven tellers. That had been an inspired detail that happened to coincide with a then current campaign to attract women's savings accounts. It was Miles Updegrove who noticed that the younger men's beards were heavier than the middle-aged men's in the late afternoon.) Earl Appel had almost no occasion in the course of his work to come from behind his counter and let the customers see that he wore loafers. It was not a problem that could be handled as the beard problem had been. Earl Appel was the only man who wore loafers to work, and a memorandum to the staff would be too pointedly directed at him. And yet something had to be done, or said, for although it was true that Earl Appel did not often have business on the public side of the counter, he did walk to work every morning, he did have lunch every noonday at the Y.M.C.A. cafeteria, and he did walk home every afternoon. In other words, he was seen, and everyone knew he was an employee of the bank.

"It gives such a bad impression," said Miles Updegrove, one evening at home. "A man too lazy to lace his shoes in the morning."

"Speak to him about it," said Edna Updegrove.

"When? I only go there twice a week, regularly."

"But you're president of the bank," said Edna. "What's to stop you going in any time you feel like it?"

"You don't understand, Edna. My father always told me, he said the cashier is the one to handle the personnel relations. Pop didn't say personnel relations, and now we call the cashier the manager, but that was the general idea."

"Then have a talk with Fred Schartle. Tell *him.*"

"I thought of that already, but if I say something to Fred he's going to get touchy. He'll take it like it was a criticism of his personnel relations. You know. Him not noticing it that Earl Appel comes to work every day wearing sport shoes. A person has to be very careful with Fred. You won't find a better manager of our size bank in the State of Pennsylvania. Absolutely as reliable, sound, as they come. But don't criticize."

"You don't have to be afraid of Fred Schartle. The other way around, would be my guess," said Edna Updegrove.

"Oh, I guess I'm not afraid of Fred Schartle. I guess nobody would think that. However, though, he's apt to be very sensitive if somebody trespasses on his territory. That time when we talked about voting a bonus for Clara Slaymaker. Remember Clara suggesting some little gift for new women customers?"

"Well, I don't remember, but go ahead."

"Yes, Clara suggested some feminine trinket or other. To go with every new savings account of ten dollars or over?"

"No, I guess I forgot about that," said Edna.

"Well, anyhow we put the ad in the *County News* and we got about forty-five new women customers, all told."

"What was the prize, I wonder," said Edna.

"Some kind of a plastic something or other. They ran us under two dollars each wholesale. I gave you one."

"Oh! Those picnic sets. I remember. They weren't much good if you left them out in the hot sun. Not that I blame Clara for that. I think they were made in Japan. I'm almost positive."

"What difference does it make where they came from, or what they were?" said Miles Updegrove.

"Excuse me, but you don't have to ask the whole neighborhood," said his wife.

"Well, you get me sidetracked on things that don't matter," he said. "I was trying to tell you about Clara Slaymaker and Fred Schartle, how touchy he is."

"Go right ahead."

"I will," said Miles Updegrove. "So at this meeting somebody had the idea that we vote a special bonus for Clara. Not anything big. In the neighborhood of fifty dollars, or maybe a week's pay. Fifty dollars, as I remember it, because it wasn't even a week's pay. Clara gets seventy-five, now, but I think she was only getting seventy then."

"Goodness, I didn't know she got that much. That's what my father got when he was superintendent of schools. Three hundred a month."

"Yes, but how long ago was that? Earl Appel gets a hundred and a quarter, plus the Christmas bonus. You ought to see our salary list. It would hand you a few more surprises. Very few years Fred Schartle doesn't make over ten thousand, *with* the yearly bonus, that is. But he was dead set against a special bonus for Clara. Nothing personal against Clara. But he didn't want us to be the ones that recommended a bonus for individual members of the staff. That kind of recognition should come from him, was his argument. They were his people, and he was supposed to know more about them than the directors did. Well, he was right, Fred. Maybe Clara did suggest the picnic sets for new women customers, but if that entitled her to a fifty-dollar bonus, then others were entitled to as much or more. Like it was Earl Appel that probably saved us a heck of a lot of money when he heard we were considering a branch bank out on Northampton Turnpike, the old Northampton Turnpike near the Zellerbach farm. We thought it'd be a good place for a branch, there at the intersection of the Northampton Turnpike and the Lehighton Road. But according to Fred, he was told by Earl Appel that some big outfit from Philadelphia were thinking of putting up a huge supermarket about a mile or so down the Turnpike. How Earl found that out, I don't know, but he was right. In other words, if we'd of gone ahead and put a branch bank at the Lehighton intersection, we'd of been a mile away from where the business was. Out in the cold, so to speak."

"Yes, I can see how that would be," she said.

"So if we were handing out special bonuses, Earl Appel was more entitled than Clara Slaymaker."

"I should think so," she said.

"With that information most people would have bought some land in the neighborhood, but Earl was either not smart enough or more likely carrying a debt load that was as much as he could carry. We don't like our people to go beyond a certain limit. It varies with different individuals, but our policy is a bank employe shouldn't obligate himself to more than one third of his weekly pay. And Earl Appel is always pretty close to that figure."

"How do you know?" she said.

"How do we *know?* Listen, if somebody like Earl Appel runs up a bill or buys anything on time, it's Fred Schartle's *business* to know. He watches them like a hawk. We never fire anybody if we can help it. It isn't good for the bank to have it get around that we fired somebody."

"You mean good for the person," she said.

"For him either, but it isn't good for the bank. People always want to know why So-and-so was fired, and nine times out of ten they don't believe the explanation. That's why we have to keep people on when we'd just as soon let them go. We give them a strong hint to quit, go look for another job. But firing them is another matter entirely."

"Well, now," she said. "Are you thinking of firing Earl?"

"Did I say that? No, I certainly did not."

"No, but that's what you inferred," she said.

"That's what *you* inferred. You can never get that straight about inferred and implied, as long as I've been married to you."

"All right. Hinted at. I think you want to fire Earl," she said.

"Well, to tell you the God's honest truth, I wish he'd resign. I don't like a man that's too darn lazy to lace his shoes in the morning."

"Well, in fairness, if it's gone that far you're duty bound to say something to Fred," she said. "Did Fred make any money on the supermarket thing?"

"Good heavens, no. That would have been a real estate speculation, one of the things we're most against."

"Then Earl's entitled to some credit for not speculating," she said. "What have you got against Earl, in addition to coming to work in sport shoes?"

"To be honest with you, I don't know. I wouldn't like to think it was anything personal. He's been with us now nine years in September, ever since he got out of the army. The Appels are all fine people."

"Except for Dewey, the one that married my cousin Ruth Biltzer. I couldn't say much for him. But he was only distantly related to Earl."

"About a third or fourth cousin," said Miles Updegrove. "Dewey was supposed to be shell-shocked from World War One. That's what they said. But I can remember from when I was little, before World War One, Dewey Appel drove the ice wagon for Noah Klinger, and they used to say you could get a cheap drunk on just from his breath. But Dewey was only a third or fourth cousin of Charley Appel, Earl's father."

"Hung himself, finally," said Edna Updegrove.

"No, you're thinking of Sam Klinger. Dewey Appel shot himself. Sam Klinger was Noah's brother, the hunchback, and *he* hung himself. But Dewey Appel shot himself with a .22 rifle."

"You're right. I was thinking of Sam Klinger. Goodness, do you remember that?" She put down her mending and looked back in her memories. "When I was going to First Street school, little Sam Klinger used to scare the life out of us. He was always there in the afternoon when school let out, and all our parents told us to never go anywhere with him. The boys used to throw stones at him. Yes, he hung himself, and Dewey shot himself. That was it. I guess I was going to High then."

"No, you were away at Normal, and I was still going to Muhlenberg, a junior or a senior, but I heard about it."

"That's right. I had a letter from Mom."

"Soozenserp," said Miles Updegrove.

"What?"

"That was the saying. He committed soozenserp. Anybody

that hung himself, they used to say he committed soozenserp. I guess it was slang."

"Good grief! I haven't heard anybody use that expression since I was ten years old. How did you happen to think of it?"

"I don't know."

"Soozenserp," she said. "High German?"

"I doubt it. *Süssen* means sweeten in High German, but that wouldn't have anything to do with suicide. Sweet syrup? I don't know. Maybe it had something to do with taking poison. But I can remember we kids saying somebody committed soozenserp, whether it was poison or like Sam Klinger or Dewey Appel."

"If Pop was still alive, he'd know. He collected all those odd sayings."

"Yes, some of them pretty odd for a school superintendent to collect, I'll say that much."

"That was because when he retired he wanted to work on his Pennsylvania Dutch dictionary."

"It would have got him locked up if he put in some of those expressions."

"Oh, it was just an ambition of his," she said. "Mom threw all those notes in the stove, a couple of desk drawers-full. Pop's penmanship was terrible, for a schoolteacher. You could hardly decipher it. You never would have thought he had so much education. My, my. When you think of all that education. Even my cousin Ruth Biltzer graduated from Normal, and a lot of good it did her, married to Dewey Appel. A few dollars once in a while, substituting at First Street school, but he took it away from her to buy drink. Look at me. I had the equivalent of two years in college, but I don't know anything."

"What are you supposed to know?"

"What am I supposed to know?" she said.

"Yes. I'm a college graduate, with a bachelor of arts degree, but I make my money digging cement. I don't need a college degree for that. Pop didn't have a college degree, not even a high school diploma, but look how much he made."

"That's just what I'm saying," she said. "I got my certificate from Normal, but I never made any use of it."

"That's because you married young."

"And a man that was well off. But if you wouldn't have been well off I would of got a job teaching, and there would of been an altogether different story."

"I don't understand what you're arguing about," he said.

"I don't either. *Yes* I do. I was thinking my education went to waste, and how my father scrimped and saved to put us through school. My mother would think it was sinful, the money we spend. That trip to California. Twenty-five dollars a day for a room in a hotel. Just the room, no board."

"It'd be twice that now. But it's our money, and we didn't go in debt to pay for it. Now they don't think twice about going in debt for things. That's why we have the personal loan department at the bank. The big money-maker out at the Turnpike branch is the personal loan department, all those young couples."

"Thanks to Earl Appel," she said.

"How, thanks to Earl Appel? Oh, because he steered us away from the Zellerbach farm. Well, yes."

"Did you ever thank him for that?"

"Me personally? No, I just got through telling you, those are the things that Fred considers his territory."

"Did Fred thank him?" she said.

"Sure he did. I wasn't there, but I'm sure Fred Schartle wouldn't just take the information without saying thank-you for it."

"But no bonus," said Edna Updegrove.

"Why should he get a bonus for a thing like that? Earl works for the bank, doesn't he? Don't we pay him his salary every week? If the bank lost a lot of money on a bad location, Earl wouldn't get his bonus at the end of the year."

"Oh, he got a bonus at the end of the year?" she said.

"All employees of the bank get a bonus at the end of the year, if we vote one. But we couldn't vote one if we had a bad year. The bonuses come out of profits, don't forget."

"Oh, out of profits, eh? I see," she said.

"You don't see, but I'd be surprised if you did. Women never take the trouble to understand about banking."

"Clara Slaymaker does," said Edna Updegrove.

"No. She's pretty dumb. When she retires we won't replace her. All she ever knew was bookkeeping, and we got machines for that now. We could run the bank on half the number of employees we have now."

"Then why do you keep her?" she said.

"Because she and Walter Fertig are the last ones left that my father hired. If it wasn't for that they'd have been let go when we put in the new equipment. Sentiment. If it was me, I would of let them go, but Pop said take care of Clara and Walter, and I said I would. But I don't have any sentiment where certain others are concerned."

"Meaning Earl Appel," she said.

"Meaning anybody that don't have enough respect for their job to come to work in moccasins. I never had to tell Walter Fertig to put on shoes, or shave in the morning. It makes my blood boil."

"Yes," she said. "Well, then you better find some way to get rid of him."

In the succeeding two or three months, on his twice weekly visits to the bank, Miles Updegrove was aware of his mounting antagonism toward Earl Appel, but considerably less aware of the fact that it showed. Although he left personnel problems to Fred Schartle, it had always been his custom upon visiting the bank to stop and say hello to Walter Fertig and Clara Slaymaker, and while so doing to greet by their first names the other members of the staff. "All they want is for you to say hyuh to them," his father had once remarked. "But that much they do want." Miles did not realize that his growing dislike of Earl Appel was compelling him to abandon a habit that was almost a tradition, and when the fact was called to his attention he was disturbed. It was Fred Schartle who mentioned it.

"There's one other thing I've been meaning to ask you, Miles," Fred said one Friday afternoon.

"Why sure, what's that?" said Miles.

"It's kind of hard to bring it up."

Miles Updegrove smiled. "Only one thing could be that hard," he said. "You want to borrow some money. How much, and what for?"

"It isn't money, though," said Fred. "Money-wise, I'm contented. But one of our fellows, Earl Appel, came to me a week or two ago and said something that I thought he must be getting what they call a persecution complex."

"Who's persecuting Earl?"

"Well, now don't get me wrong, Miles. But what it comes down to is he thinks you are. Not persecuting him, but that you don't like him. He said you stopped speaking to him, but you speak to everybody else."

"As far as I know, I speak to everybody every time I come in the bank. If I see them. I can't speak to those I don't happen to see, but as far as I know . . ."

Fred Schartle hesitated.

"What is it, Fred? Come on, say it."

Fred Schartle shook his head. "Then I guess it's unconscious," he said.

"What is?"

"Well, since Earl mentioned it to me, I noticed every time you came in you always talk to everybody but him. A couple times you walked right past him. Once he even held the gate open for you and you didn't say anything to him. The gate that—"

"I know where the gate is. I could find my way around this place blindfolded," said Miles Updegrove. "I didn't know I was supposed to do a curtsey when somebody held the gate open for me. I often hold the gate open for this one and that one, depending on if I get there first. But I don't remember anybody telling me I was a nice fellow for that. That's a thing you do, whether you're president of the bank or a junior like young Bob Holtz, just starting out in the business."

"Well, it isn't only holding the gate open," said Fred Schartle. "It's when there's three or four staff people gathered together and you say hello to all but one. And if it's the same one several times, I feel it my duty to all concerned to inquire if there's any particular reason."

"Fred," said Miles Updegrove. "I hired you, and then I promoted you over some that had seniority on you. I was saying to Edna a little while ago, there isn't a better manager of our size bank

in the entire State of Pennsylvania. I honestly believe that, and I'm
as proud of your fine record as anything I ever did for the bank.
But when you come to me with some story about a bank employee
having a persecution complex, then I have to remind you, Fred,
you're not perfect. Nobody's perfect. Not even you, Fred."

"I never—"

"Just let me finish what I have to say, *please*. That expression
you used, persecution complex, I know where it comes from. It
comes from nowadays I understand certain big banks in Philadelphia and I'm sure New York—New York, I'm *sure*. They employ
full-time psychiatrists, and every time John Smith makes some mistake they send him to the doctor for a mental checkup. Maybe he's
sneaking a couple drinks in the lunch hour, or has designs on
some young woman in the filing department. I was out to Denver a
few years ago and heard all about how some of those big banks
have these so-called head-shrinkers. Oh, I know what they call
them, and head-shrinkers is a good name for them. The bankers'
convention in Denver. I was sitting next to another country banker
like myself, and he said to me, 'Mr. Updegrove, I'm beginning to
think we're in the wrong business.' He said we ought to turn our
banks over to the head-shrinkers, if we can't fire a man that's undependable. Stop this wet-nursing of undependable young fellows
before the whole banking structure falls into a state of collapse.
And I'll tell you quite frankly, Fred, I don't take to it when a good
reliable manager like yourself talks to me about persecution com-
plexes. I've always backed you to the hilt, even when I didn't entirely agree with you. Personnel problems are your territory, and I
won't touch them. But when you graduated from Temple University
they didn't give you an M.D. degree. You were trained in com-
merce and finance, and if Earl Appel needs help along those lines,
mental, then maybe I can speak to the board, or *you* can, and we'll
see what we can do. Maybe a leave of absence. Maybe we'll just
have to let him go. I don't know, Fred. I honestly don't know. And
that's all I have to say for the present."

"For God's sake," said Fred Schartle.

"Hmm?"

"For Christ's sweet sake," said Fred.

"Now, Fred. Remember who you're talking to."

"Remember? I don't have to remember."

"Oh, yes you do," said Miles Updegrove. "You're on the verge of saying some things you may regret a long, long time—"

"But I'm quitting. I resign," said Fred.

"That's one of them. But be careful what else you say. Because regardless of what you want to get off your chest, I'm the one that will have the last say, Fred. Remember that. And you damn sure better remember it. You're not going to walk out of here and into as good a job as this, just like that. You may be out of work for quite a long while. I know I wouldn't hire a manager that wanted to turn my bank into a mental institution. You go home and talk to your wife, and I'll be here Monday as usual."

"You think you have me all tied up."

"Well, haven't I? The bank holds your paper. The question is, Fred, when I think it over am I going to *want* to have you all tied up? I don't fly off the handle as quick as some, but don't go too far with me. Goodnight."

Miles Updegrove drove home and had his usual two ounces of whiskey and listened to Edna through dinner. The Philomatheans, her old literary society at Normal, were having a get-together dinner in the spring. "What do they want to have a dinner for? The Philos went out of existence back there in the Thirties somewhere. You never go to your A.T.O. dinners, so I don't see why I should go to this. Still, it's kind of nice to have them go to all this trouble. And I have my pin yet. We were all Philos. My father, two sisters, and me. All Philos. Oh, how we hated those Keystones. They were full of Catholics, the Keystones. A Catholic couldn't get into Philo when I was there. I wouldn't let a fellow carry my books if he was a Keystone. Paul O'Brien. No, *Phil* O'Brien. That doesn't sound right, either. He was from the coal regions. It *was* Paul. I understand he was a judge later. Me refusing to let a judge carry my books because he was a dirty Keystone. But a Catholic, too. Now I don't hardly mind them at all. I just found out those Bradleys are Catholic, and they've been here almost a year."

"What Bradleys?" he said.

"Out past the country club, on Heiser's Creek Road. He's some electrical engineer."

"Oh, that Bradley. No, he's with the light company but he's not an engineer. Assistant district manager. They won't be here long. Five years and they get transferred. A friend of Fred Schartle's, and *he* won't be around here much longer either."

"Oh, for goodness' sake, Miles. I knew there was something worr'ing you. Some other bank stealing Fred away from you. More money, eh?"

"Nothing of the kind," said Miles Updegrove. "My mind isn't made up for sure, but I don't know why I should keep him."

"You mean you're firing him, Fred Schartle? When was it —last summer you said you never fired anybody. It must be serious, a man you had such confidence in. It isn't—you didn't catch him in some kind of a shortage, I hope."

"Not a shortage of money. Although I'll have a look at his figures before I let him go. No, as far as I know now, he's clean. But I just found out that Fred Schartle considers himself an amateur head-shrinker. That's slang for psychiatrist."

"Fred Schartle?"

"All this time I gave him a free hand with the employees, his idea of how to handle them was to see if they had a persecution complex. Well, are we running a bank or a mental institution? If Fred wants to run a mental institution, that's his privilege, but—"

"Somebody at the front door? Who would that be at this hour?" said Edna Updegrove. "Sit still, I'll go." She went to answer the doorbell. He remained at the dinner table, straining to recognize the voice of the visitor but unwilling to make an appearance. The first intelligible words he heard were Edna's. "You don't want to talk to me, Dorothy. You better save it for Mister. We're just finishing our dessert." Dorothy was the first name of Fred Schartle's wife. Miles got up and went to the front room.

"Good evening, Dorothy," he said.

"Oh, Mr. Updegrove? What did he *say* to you? He came home around seven with some wild story. All I can get out of him was that he—"

"I'll leave you two be," said Edna Updegrove, and left them.

"Sit down, Dorothy. Have a cigarette if you wish to. Would you care for a cup of coffee? We were just having some."

"Nothing, thank you, Mr. Updegrove. He was like a wild man. I never saw him act like that before."

"Did he have anything to drink?" said Miles Updegrove.

"Yes, I'm sure he did. He wasn't staggering or anything, but he was an hour late, and I guess he had one or two. Yes, he did. Not when he came home, but before. But, oh, please tell me what he said. All I could get out of him was you and he had some kind of an argument."

"I'm sorry you had to be subjected to this, Dorothy," said Miles. "Yes, Fred and I were having a discussion about bank matters, and then all of a sudden out of a clear sky he started abusing me. Using strong language and making personal remarks that I couldn't tolerate."

"*Did* he quit? *Did* he resign?"

"Yes, he did," said Miles Updegrove.

"Oh, God," she said. Her hands dropped from the arm of her chair and the weight of them seemed to cause her torso to crumple. For the moment she had nothing to say.

"Can I get you a drink of something?"

"Water? Could I have a glass of water?"

He called to his wife. "Edna, would you bring us a glass of water for Dorothy?"

The woman opened her handbag and took out a pack of cigarettes. "I think I *will* have a cigarette," she said.

"Yes, have one," he said.

"Would you care for one?" she said.

"No thanks," he said. "I never use them. A pipe is all I ever smoke. Sometimes a cigar."

"Here we are," said Edna Updegrove, with a glass of water. "Is there something else I can get you? A cup of coffee?"

"No thank you. I just—my throat felt dry."

"Of course. Now if you want anything else, just call. I'll be in the kitchen, so call loud in case the dishwasher's going." Edna Updegrove departed.

"She's such a wonderful person, Mrs. Updegrove. So well liked all over town," said Dorothy Schartle. She sipped the water. "I'm all right now. My throat got suddenly dry."

"Yes," said Miles. "Well, I don't know what else I can tell you, Dorothy."

"What did he say when he resigned? Why? What reason did he give you?"

"Reason? Oh, he didn't give any reason. He took exception to certain things I said about personnel matters. I guess that was it. But there was no call for him to fly off the handle that way. Frankly, I left the bank before he could say a lot worse."

"It's so unlike him," said Dorothy Schartle.

"Yes, I guess it is. In fact, I just finished paying him a compliment a few seconds before he started in on me. That's why it's so hard to understand. But maybe you can explain it."

"How?"

"Well, I don't want to pry into anybody's personal affairs, but being's you came here, and you're naturally worried about him—have you noticed anything unusual about Fred lately?"

"No, I haven't," said Dorothy Schartle.

"Nothing worrying him? How is he sleeping?"

"Well, I guess he could use more sleep. He wakes up pretty early. Daylight, most of the time. They say you don't need as much sleep as you get older, but Fred's only forty-three."

"I always got my seven or eight hours when I was that age, but we're all different, I guess."

"He wakes up around six o'clock and goes down and has a cup of coffee. He drinks a lot of coffee, that I will say."

"Too much coffee isn't good for you. He has a cup of coffee at six A.M. And then I guess you give him his breakfast."

"Yes, with the children. He likes to have breakfast with the children before they're off to school. He usually walks to the corner with Phyllis, our youngest. She takes a different bus than the other children. The older two take the high school bus. Then he comes back to the house and gets the car."

"So I guess he has one or two cups of coffee at breakfast—"

"Two, as a rule," she said.

"And I know he always takes another cup at coffee break, at the bank."

"Yes, and at lunch," she said. "Do you think it's the coffee?"

"Oh, I wouldn't say. It may be something else entirely."

"Not that I know of," she said.

"What does he do for recreation?"

"Well, he has his carpentry. He has all these drills and lathes and all. Woodwork, you know. He just got finished making a birthday present for Earl Appel. A cigarette box."

"Earl Appel? I didn't know they were such friends."

"Well, not very close, but Earl has the same hobby. Woodwork. It's a sort of a rivalry, you might say. Last year Earl made Fred a stand for an ash tray. We have it in the family room. Earl does more complicated things than Fred."

"Is that so?"

"Oh, yes. Earl built all the cabinetwork for the Appels' hi-fi."

"Uh-huh."

"Earl got Fred innarested, in the first place."

"What else does he do, for pastime?"

"Fred? He takes walks."

"He and Earl Appel?"

"No, no. Sometimes with the children, sometimes by himself. On Sundays he usually gets up around ha' past seven and goes for a walk."

"Do the children get up that early on Sunday morning?"

"No, Sunday mornings he goes by himself. He goes up over Schiller's Mountain and down the other side and home by way of the county road."

"That's a good ten-mile walk," said Miles Updegrove. "Nobody with him, huh?"

"No, all by himself. He likes to be by himself," she said. "He says he sees plenty of people during the week."

"And doing this woodwork he's by himself, too, I guess."

"Oh, yes. I used to sit there with him, but the saws and the lathes make such a noise. I can feel it in my teeth. Not that he doesn't like to be with the children and I."

"But he has these times when he likes to be alone," said Miles.

"Yes," she said.

"How is his temper when he's home?"

"Well—he's very strict with the children."

"How is he with you, Dorothy? If you don't mind that question."

"Well, we've been married now almost twenty-one years. I guess we're just like any other married couple. You take the good with the bad."

"But you're satisfied the way things turned out," he said.

"Why, yes, of course. Except like tonight, my goodness. When a thing like that happens, I don't know what comes over him."

"A thing like that? What else was there like that?"

"Oh, when he loses his temper over something. But that's personal."

"And then he likes to be by himself," he said.

"He's not the only one. I want to be by myself, too," she said. "Mr. Updegrove, what's going to happen? We have our home isn't paid for yet, and our eldest daughter wants to take a course in textile design. The boy wants to go to the Air Force Academy. That's free, I guess, but nothing will be coming in. We have some saved up, but we don't want to touch that."

"I don't know, Dorothy. Fred was very positive."

"Where does he get any right to be positive?" Now she began to cry, and only words, not sentences, were intelligible among her mutterings. Such words as ". . . positive . . . right . . . children . . . me . . . nice home . . . selfish . . . whole life . . ."

"Maybe I ought to get Mrs. Updegrove to come in," said Miles.

"No, no! Please don't. I don't want her to see me like this," said Dorothy Schartle. "I'll be all right." She stopped crying.

"I don't know what to suggest, Dorothy," said Miles Updegrove. "I told him I'd see him Monday, but naturally you can't expect me to have much to say. He just as good as threw his job in my face, and nobody's indispensable these days."

"But I know him, Mr. Updegrove," said Dorothy. "I know what he'll do. He'll go for one of his walks tomorrow afternoon—"

"Did he say anything about coming in tomorrow?"

She hesitated. "I'll be truthful with you. He's drunk. He won't be in tomorrow. He can't take more than two drinks and never could. He'll be sick all night and tomorrow he'll be no good for work. No, he won't be in."

"Saturday morning. One of our busiest days. But I guess it's better if he doesn't come in, for his sake as well as the bank's."

"Let me talk to him. He wouldn't listen to me tonight, but I know how he'll be tomorrow and Sunday. If I talk to him will you let him come and see you, Mr. Updegrove? Please?"

"I told him I'd see—"

"Not Monday. Sunday. Here. I know how to handle him, Mr. Updegrove. I really do."

"Maybe you do, but I don't."

"You won't have to when I get through talking to him. Just let him come here and apologize, and tell him you're willing to forget about the resignation. You're a *good* man, Mr. Updegrove. You'll do that, please? It takes a big man, and you're that."

"An apology won't mean much without good intentions behind it," said Miles Updegrove.

"I promise you, Fred Schartle will never give you the slightest trouble, ever again. I'll say the same thing to you that I'll say to him. If he ever causes any more trouble, I'll leave him. I'll go back to my parents in Quakertown, and the children with me."

Miles Updegrove tapped his fingers on his knee. "Well, if you're so sure that it will do any good—all right. He can come in Sunday after church. And if I'm convinced—"

"You will be! You will be! I promise you. And I'll never forget this as long as I live. I'll never stop thanking you."

"Well, let's wait and see what happens Sunday," said Miles. He put on a smile. "But I have a feeling that Mrs. Fred Schartle has a great deal of influence over Mr. Fred Schartle. The hand that rocks the cradle rules the world, they say."

Dorothy Schartle rose. "Thank you very much. Will you tell Mrs. goodnight for me? I don't want her to see my eyes all red."

"You run right along, young lady. I'll say goodnight for you, and see you to the door," said Miles Updegrove.

He stood in the vestibule until Dorothy's car moved out of the driveway. He turned off the porch light and went back to the kitchen. "Well, how much could you hear?"

"Hardly anything, from back here," said Edna Updegrove. "But she was in a state, I could see that."

"Yes. Well, the upshot is he's coming here Sunday noon, to apologize."

"Oh, Miles, we won't *be* here Sunday noon. We're going over to Amy's for the christening."

"I can't help that, Edna. This is bank business, and Amy isn't any relation."

"No, but it's her first granddaughter," said Edna. "Oh, well, you're just like your father. You and that bank."

"I want to see what this young fellow has to say for himself," said Miles Updegrove. "A great deal depends on that. Is there any more coffee?"

"I threw it out, but I could make some fresh."

"Never mind," he said.

THE ANSWER DEPENDS

They wonder how we can sit and watch ourselves in those old movies on television. Doesn't it embarrass us to be reminded of the awfulness of the bad pictures, and embarrass us in a different way to see the inferior quality of our pictures that were supposed to be good? Our makeup was so awful, the lighting was so unprofessional, the cutting so jumpy, the direction so unimaginative when it was not artily intrusive, the dialog so dated, the stories so untrue to life. They laugh, the younger ones, and kid the clichés and ask us why we don't buy up those old pictures and burn the negatives. One of them said to me last week, "Come on, Bobby, you have enough money stashed away. You can afford to buy back a thing like *MacKenzie of the Royal Rifles*." Well, I have not got enough money to buy back *MacKenzie,* but even if I had, I wouldn't buy it. Yes, I am momentarily uncomfortable when my grandson sees me as a gallant young subaltern—wearing too much lipstick and too much eye-shadow. Only too well do I know what he is thinking: his grandfather must have been a swish. His manners are just good enough to keep him from coming out and saying so, but he looks at me on the TV screen and then at me, there in my den, and in his mind are serious doubts of my virility. I, on the other hand, cannot banish those thoughts by revealing to him that at the time I was making *MacKenzie of the Royal Rifles,* his grandmother was sulking in our North Canon Drive mansion because I was away on location with Doris Arlington. I cannot tell the boy that his grandmother had every good reason to sulk. I would not tell him that I very nearly did not go back to his grandmother, that

Doris Arlington and I went from the High Sierras location to a cruise in a borrowed yacht that had nothing to do with the making of *MacKenzie of the Royal Rifles*. "My boy," I could but cannot say to him, "if Doris Arlington had been a better sailor, you would not be alive today, and neither would your father."

We don't see what *they* see in those old movies. The news and sports and the weather are finished, and the night's movie comes on. Sometimes it is a picture I never heard of, sometimes it is a picture in which I had the male lead. Most often it is a film that stars men and women I used to know, and frequently I am able to recall the giant première at the Chinese or the Egyptian or the Carthay Circle. The pra-meer, they pronounced it. That was the year I had my first Duesenberg. That was the year I had my first Rolls. That was the opening that Lowell Sherman came to in a broken-down flivver—but there I am confusing fact with scenario. Lowell Sherman did that in a film called *What Price Hollywood?* Someone else did it in real life. Who was it, who *was* it that came to a world pra-meer in a broken-down flivver? I remember Connie Bennett in *What Price Hollywood?*, the Brown Derby waitress in a starched, ballooning-out skirt. It was a good, good picture. Gutsy, with a suicide ending. But who actually did drive the flivver to a grande luxe opening? I can remember Connie singing "Parlez moi d'amour" in the film, but why can't I recall the actual driver of the actual flivver? I make a note to telephone Bill Powell in Palm Springs. He'll remember. But by the time the night's picture is finished I forget to telephone Bill.

Oh, we would never do anything to keep those old films off TV. It would be like burning a diary. It would be worse than burning a diary. I did burn a diary before I went to the hospital a few years ago. No one else knew that I had kept the diary, no one in the world. It contained no written-out names, but there were a few people who would have been able to make pretty good guesses as to identities and events, and their guesses would not have made anyone happy. The doctor said my operation would be merely exploratory, which is what it turned out to be, but he was quite pleased that I seemed to be so calm. "Most men your age put on a good act, but you're not a bit worried," he said. I told him I had great confidence in him and let it go at that. I didn't want to tell him that I had prepared for the operation by burning a diary. Surgeons are such hams, every bit as bad as we are, every bit as hungry for a little applause. And at my age my doctor is almost a companion, if not exactly a friend. I have no friends who are also companions. Bill Powell is in Palm Springs, Dick Barthelmess was until recently in Southampton, Ned Revere has his farm in upstate New York, Jack Paisley has returned to England. They are all far removed from my little ranch in the San Fernando Valley. But I don't really miss them. I could move to New York and join the actors' clubs, take up bridge and pool, and sit in the club bars with men who would do to me what I would do to them—interrupt my reminiscences with questions of fact or because I had been talking too long. I know those clubs, I used to belong to them in my movie-star days because membership in them spruced up my biography in *Who's Who;* but I seldom went near them, and when I did I always came away depressed and re-determined never to end my days in them. I don't need clubs, and I certainly don't want my recollections to be interrupted by other retired actors who think their memory is more accurate than mine.

I get very good reception on my TV set at my ranch. Day or night I can go to my little den and sit alone. My family and my neighbors know that my doctor has told me to stay out of the sun, and they think I am "making the best of it." Well, I am, but not in the way they believe. I am having a very good time. Every old movie, whether it was a super production or what we used to call a program picture, takes me right back to the exciting days when I was on my way up, or to those later days when (according to one magazine writer) my face was on some screen in some part of the world every hour of every day, when I was making fifteen thousand a week and spending at least half that. I bought suits twenty at a time, ordering them from swatches, and many of them I gave away without having worn them a single time. I once owned a speedboat that I never even saw because I was too busy to go to Catalina. Now, of course, I am limited to a stationwagon and a black sedan, neither of them in the five-thousand class, but a couple of weeks ago I was watching an old film about a monarch in a mythical kingdom, played by Jack Paisley. There was a scene in which Jack is riding through a village in the royal town car. The car runs over a child, and a revolution starts. I had forgotten about that film, but I recognized the car. It was my car, a Rolls with a Barker body, and I had lent it to Sidney Gainsborough, of Gainsborough Pictures, as a personal favor, for that picture. I think he paid me a thousand dollars a day, although I had not asked him for any money. They kept the car on the Gainsborough lot for three or four weeks while making the picture, and I recall that the money they paid me was more than the car had cost me new. That was how we did things in those days, too. The strange thing was that it made sense, according to Sidney, to rent my car instead of waiting a whole year while the Rolls and the Barker people built a car new. That was how we thought in those days, too. We who remember those days are not mystified by the cost of making pictures, even forty-million-dollar pictures. I was never paid a million to make a picture, but I made a million a year for six or seven straight years, and Tom Mix made much more than I did. This Taylor girl, by the time she gets through paying her taxes, will wind up with a lot less than Mary Pickford put away, and don't you forget it. In fact, I wouldn't be surprised if when she reaches my age, she has less than I have now. I spent it freely, but I didn't spend it all. Ronnie Colman, Warner Baxter, Bill Powell, Dick Barthelmess, Jack Paisley, Ned Revere and I held on to enough to give us security. Even Ned Revere, with five ex-wives, won't die broke on that farm of his up near Cooperstown, N. Y.

Good old Ned, the rascal. This present wife of his was an acquisition of his post-Hollywood days, and I don't know very much about her, but she must be a pretty good sort. Ned had that automobile accident ten years ago that left him rather badly crippled, just when he seemed about to be embarking on a new career on Broadway. He got those excellent notices in one play that folded after three weeks, and some young fellow who had never seen him in those comedy movies wrote a play especially for Ned. I would never have thought that Ned would strike anyone as the type to play a broken-down old politician in a Southern town. I had known Ned so well that the ravages of time had not been particularly noticeable; to me he was a good light comedian who was getting older, as I was getting older. But to the young playwright, seeing him for the first time, he was the perfect actor to play an unprincipled old buzzard who had always been able to get by on his charm. To some extent that was true of Ned himself, in real life, but it had never occurred to me that anyone would get that impression of Ned so strongly as to want to write a play about it. Ned understood it, though, and he told me when he went into rehearsal that it was going to be very difficult to overcome the temptation to play himself instead of the character as written. It was especially difficult, he said, because he was a native Southerner and after all those years of stifling his accent, he was being encouraged to lay it on thick. He was genuinely apprehensive, and for the first time in his life he was thinking of someone else, in this case, the young playwright who had such confidence in him. He wanted to be good for the playwright's sake. Well, as everyone knows, he was. The notices were unanimously favorable and there was praise for all concerned; for Ned, for the playwright, for the supporting cast, the director. Then Ned was injured in that smash-up of his taxi and a mail truck, and the only luck Ned had was that he came out of it alive, plus the fact that he met the lady who eventually became Number 6. She was in the hospital at the same time, and they would meet in their wheelchairs in the sun room. She was a widow, fully aware of Ned's matrimonial record, and inclined to be moralistic about it. But besides being moralistic she was sympathetic toward the afflicted, as moralistic people are sometimes apt to be, and Ned was at his lowest ebb. He had a good deal of pain during a series of operations, and was pessimistic as to his future. His old ebullience was gone, and she began to think of him more as a discouraged invalid than as a much-married movie actor. He in turn began to realize that she never said a word about her own illness, which was cancer, and that she was giving him a lesson in courage. She invited him to visit her at her farm near Cooperstown, repeated the invitation when she was leaving the hospital, and he found after she left that he missed her companionship so much that when it came time for him to leave the hospital, he went to Cooperstown and stayed.

I hear from him once in a while. He has one of those golf carts that enables him to get around in good weather. I have a standing invitation to visit him, but it is one I shall never accept. It isn't only that Cooperstown is too far away. In fact, in a manner of speaking it is much too near. Ned Revere, dependent on a golf cart to get him around, is not Ned Revere in a Stutz Bearcat or a Mercer Raceabout, as he always was when we were making silent films. When the talkies came in we bought the newer cars; Ned persuaded me to buy my first Duesenberg. He doesn't even remember that, and I will not go all the way to Cooperstown to get into an argument over it. He wrote to me a couple of months ago, and I saved his letter, although I don't know why I did. It is so full of misinformation that it is practically a classic.

Dear Bobby [he wrote]: I suppose you saw in the papers that Dick Barthelmess has passed on. The ranks are getting thin. I had not seen Dick in recent years. He spent most of his time on Long Island. Am told he had seven operations and was down to 110 lbs when he died. Was always fond of Dick in the old days. Sent me a wire on opening night of *The Blighted Magnolia* & had tickets for the night after I had my accident with the taxi and the mail truck. He was one of the first to send me flowers to the hospital. Dear old Dick, a real gentleman & a fine actor.

I caught you on TV the other night, the late show. It was *Lord of the Forest* the one in which you played a civil engineer who wants to build a big dam & the girl threatens to shoot you when she sees you surveying the timberland. If they show it in California don't look at it. You will want to cut your throat. It wouldn't be hard, either, as you go around in all kinds of weather with your collar open and your chest showing as if you were a sweater girl. It is not the worst picture I ever saw but it will do till a worse one comes along. All I could think of watching that picture was you and Edna Blaine, who played the girl. My wife was watching the picture with me & she said you seemed to be really in love with the heroine. "I'll say he was," I said to her. I told her about how you and Edna sneaked away after the shooting was finished and went off on a cruise in Sid Gainsborough's yacht. But you were seasick from the minute the yacht left the dock and Edna got so fed up that she made the captain turn back after you were only gone two days. Still, you were quite a chaser as long as you stayed on dry land. I saw another of your pictures *MacGregor of the Royal Rifles* with you and Doris Arlington. She was just a kid at the time, everybody was after her, including yours truly, but she was really stuck on you. I was always surprised you didn't marry Doris. I guess you would have if you had to. Then some new kid came along & you palmed Doris off on Jack Paisley, a lousy trick to pull on any girl. I don't watch TV very much. They are always reviving our old pictures & there ought to be some kind of a law like invasion of privacy to keep them from digging into our past. I guess one good thing is that the young people today think we are all dead. The young fellow who manages our farm, a young Cornell graduate, worked for us two years before he discovered that Edward J. Revere was the Ned Revere he saw on the late show. I guess if the truth be told I always hated Hollywood. They kept me doing those damn comedies till I could never get a decent part in anything serious. I was in my late fifties before I ever got a chance to show I could act & then it was Broadway, not Hollywood, that gave me the chance. I was never cut out to be a comedian. I should of left Hollywood thirty years ago and concentrated on the legitimate stage, maybe doing a comedy now & then like Alfred Lunt but mostly sticking to dramatic roles. Well, it is too late now and there is no use being bitter . . .

No use being bitter, he says. Poor Ned. I see him on the late movies, and it is true that those comedies were not worth remembering (although they made money for everyone connected with them). But I pay so little attention to the dramatic content of our old pictures. I don't try to follow the plot lines of Ned Revere's films. In a few minutes after one of his pictures has begun to roll, I am in a daze of recollection, of remembering Ned as a gay companion; irresponsible, Quixotic, romantic, attractive to men as well as to women, and with no illusions then as to his stature as an artist.

He himself often said that his pictures were all the same picture, based on the foolproof formula of boy meets girl, boy loses girl, boy gets girl. I confess that I may have envied him a little in those days. I had to work so hard to create a new character in every new picture, whereas Ned, with his perennially youthful countenance and those sure-fire parts, could show up at the studio with absolutely no preparation and let the director do the thinking when any was necessary. I remember a discussion with Jack Quinlan, who directed so many of Ned's films, silents and talkies. Ned's mind, Jack said, was like an old-fashioned schoolboy's slate. You wrote something on it, then you rubbed it out and wrote something else. Ned was never bothered by subtleties or nuances, and I don't suppose he had ever read a book in his life. He had a perfect light-comedy face, as Jack pointed out to me. Regular features, a small straight nose, a fine head of hair with a widow's peak, and an awkward grace that was natural and could not be copied by anyone else in the business. There was absolutely no difference between Ned on-screen and off, and the smart directors like Jack Quinlan never tried to make Ned do anything or say anything that required discipline or invention on Ned's part. It was his naïveté that got him into so many marriages. He might just as reasonably have married five other girls instead of the five he did marry. He merely happened to have proposed to five girls who accepted his proposals. He had a daughter by his second wife, his only child, but she grew up with her stepfather, took her stepfather's name, and probably has not heard from Ned in more than thirty years. I doubt if Ned ever gives her a thought. Certainly he never used to mention her to any of us. Come to think of it, I can't recall his ever mentioning his mother either. I suppose you would call him a man with no emotional ties, who never inflicted his problems on us because he had none. His lack of them, of course, made him an ideal companion for the rest of us, who may have had a tendency to exaggerate our emotional involvements. You could tell him anything, he would listen, nod at the right places, and forget what you said. I told him, for instance, that Doris Arlington had been seasick on Morris Spitzer's yacht, but he will believe to his dying day that I was with Edna Blaine on Sid Gainsborough's yacht. Sid never had a yacht, but he did have

Edna Blaine. I don't know who is better off: me at my TV, with memories as fresh as the news in the morning paper; or Ned, scornful of those pleasant and profitable days, and with the lingering bitter taste of that one success on Broadway. Who is better off? Why I am, of course, unless you put the same question to Ned Revere.

ARNOLD STONE

Hemphill & Stone offered only plays that had stood the test of some time. The test had not necessarily been a long run on Broadway; in the Hemphill-Stone repertory were some comedies that had not done well in New York. But they had proved themselves over the years in productions put on by the half dozen Hemphill-Stone companies that were likely to be playing at any given moment in the Middle West and the East. There was nothing experimental about the Hemphill-Stone selections, and they never, never did Shakespeare. The late Arnold Stone has said, as far back as 1905, that Shakespeare was for colleges. He said he had lost his shirt on Shakespeare—not true, but he had indeed lost money on the few occasions that one of his leading men had coaxed him to put on *Hamlet,* or one of his leading ladies had seduced a production of *Macbeth* out of him. In 1905 he established the policy: no more Shakespeare. By that time Arnold Stone was immune to the blandishments of leading ladies. Only an occasional soubrette or ingénue, not the Lady Macbeth type, could get anything out of him that way, and Arnold Stone made all the decisions.

There *was* no Hemphill; it was just a name Arnold Stone happened to like, that he thought would add a little class to his enterprise. But the ghost partner came in handy as a taker of blame. "Hemphill ain't only my ghost, he's my goat," Arnold Stone was fond of saying to his intimates. When Arnold Stone changed his mind about something, or forgot something, or wanted to bargain on a tentative basis, he would invoke the support of Harold H. Hemphill. It will never be known how many actors and theater owners, in towns and cities east of the Mississippi, have wanted to kill Harold H. Hemphill with their bare hands. "Arnie Stone had me all signed up, or just about," the actors would say. "I gave up my room at the hotel, and spent six hundred dollars on new wardrobe. Twenty weeks' booking, sure. Then that bastard Hemphill vetoed it. Nothing Arnie could do. Hemphill is the money man, the son of a bitch. Out of his own pocket Arnie reimbursed me for a hundred dollars of what I spent on wardrobe, that's how embarrassed Arnie was. But if I ever see that Hemphill, I don't care where it is, right in the middle of the Hunting Room of the Hotel Astor, I'll go right up and punch him in the nose." More than one actor and actress had stormed into the Hemphill & Stone offices, in a Seventh Avenue building just south of Times Square, and demanded to see Hemphill. "He isn't in," Miss Shapro would say. The indignant ones would push past her and find no one else in the office. On their way out Miss Shapro would say, "Now're you satisfied?" And Arnold Stone once said to an actor, "Bobby, I happen to see that letter you wrote my pardner, Hemphill. I took the liberty of doing you a great big favor. I put your letter in my pocket, and here it is. You should know better than write that kind of a letter to a manager. He could take a lot of umbrage from reading a letter like that. You'd never work for him again."

Twice a year Arnold Stone would take a business trip. The first would be to call on the theater owners to tell them what he had lined up for the next Hemphill-Stone repertory season. It was a pleasure, that trip; meeting his old friends and haggling with them over terms and coming away with signed contracts. The second trip was his inspection trip, to see how each company was holding up. But on this trip he had to listen to the theater men's complaints, the actors' bellyaching, and he would see things on his own that he did not like, such as bored leading ladies walking through their parts and leading men hamming it up unreasonably. He would also catch the owners in discrepancies between their reported grosses and the real grosses. On these trips he would arrive in a town without giving advance notice of his coming, and stay out of sight until curtain time. He knew the seating capacity of every theater that he did business with, and he would climb the

stairs to the peanut gallery—the groot, it was called in some towns
—and look down at the balcony, the boxes, and the orchestra, and
be able to guess what the take should be. It would then be necessary to have an unpleasant talk with the owner and the box-office
man. "Stealing a few dollars from me ain't gonna land you in the
sneezer," he would say. "I'd have a hell of a time proving anything,
specially me against you in the local court. But why do you want
to rob me? It ain't good business to rob me. For a few miserable
dollars you take a chance on all next season, and listen to what I got
lined up. *Within the Law, The Little Minister, The Great Divide,
Polly With a Past, Alias Jimmy Valentine.* You got Emma Dale
Renwick this season. I got you Emma Dale because she got a big
local following. But you try my patience and the only time you ever
see her in this town again she'll be playing the Orpheum. I'll let
you keep what you stole so far, but don't try that again on Hemphill
& Stone. Don't try *that* again." He would then have to have a talk
with Emma Dale Renwick, who had loafed through a performance of
Enter Madame that night, and he would have to tell her that he had
received reports that she was losing her local following, and no
wonder, the performance she gave tonight. Trouble and tears everywhere he went on those inspection trips, and he dreaded them more
and more each year.

By 1920 he could call himself a millionaire, not all of it made
through his theatrical enterprises, but the hard cash for his real
estate speculations had come from the hard work he had put in
in selecting the right plays and the right players for his repertory
companies. He got the Broadway hits as soon as they were released for stock presentation because he had a good reputation
among the playwrights' agents. He made a study of the popularity of certain actors in certain towns; he could not explain why one
town would go to see Emma Dale Renwick reading out of the
Sears, Roebuck catalog, and a town a hundred miles away would
stay away from her like she had the smallpox. He lost money in
some towns, where they would not go to a theater to see The Cruci-
fixion with the original cast. Some towns did not like Emma Dale
Renwick, some towns did not like the theater, some towns wanted
Officer 666 every season without fail, and there probably were some

towns that liked Shakespeare, although Arnold Stone had not discovered them. Some towns would support two burlesque houses all year long and if Sothern and Marlowe were booked there, they would only do enough business to justify a split week. And so Arnold Stone had no desire to raise his social standing by engaging Sothern and Marlowe, or to try to do rep in a vaudeville town, or to stuff Emma Dale Renwick down the throats of Wilkes-Barre, P A. Dan Frohman could do his Shakespeare and Bill Brady could make the decisions for Grace George; Arnold Stone would do things his way and head for his second million.

It was always a serious thing when a local owner or manager had to send for Arnold in mid-season. Most of the houses into which he booked his rep companies were locally owned and managed by the owners, who had a lot at stake. Few of them ever felt quite at home with actors; they were business men who for one reason or another happened to be in show business. They could get along all right with Arnie Stone, who likewise was a business man in show business but who also fully understood performers. In his early days in show business he had put on costume and makeup to play bits—waiters, Indians, sailors, second halberdiers —and probably could have eked out a living in the acting end, but he had not been infected by the itch to perform; he would always give up a chance to play a minor role if he could get a job selling delicious richly coated milk-chawklit-covered imported awmonds with a surprise gift in each and every package As a candy butcher he always made more money than as an actor, and indeed he made some of the money from actors, to whom he would lend ten dollars at a dollar a week interest. It was not the hazardous sideline for him that it was to other men who lent money to actors; he was there, in the theater, a few feet away, when the company manager handed them their weekly salary. He made sure he was there; he understood actors. And he was not unsympathetic to them merely because he had not become one of them while he was young, or because he found them vacillating creatures when he got older. "Like they say, scratch a Russian and you find a Cossack," he once said. "Well, scratch an actor and underneath is a show-off kid." He tried, and with much success, to maintain friendly relations with actors. (Here, of course, he owed a lot to Harold H. Hemphill.) Even when it became necessary or desirable to break off more intimate relations with actresses he took a gentlemanly pride in remaining their old and discreet friend. He had no stauncher admirer than, for instance, Emma Dale Renwick, unless it was Rosalind Chatfield-Leigh, his only two Ladies Macbeth. It was distressing, therefore, to be summoned to the Gibbsville, Pennsylvania, unit of the Hemphill & Stone Production Company in the summer of 1921.

Gibbsville was much the smallest in population of the cities visited by Hemphill-Stone companies, but the census figures were deceptive. It was the county seat, surrounded by boroughs that brought the area population close to 100,000, making it larger than Wilkes-Barre or Reading. It was a pretty good show town, with vaudeville (three-a-day), six moving picture houses, a lyceum program, Chautauqua, Ringling Brothers, the Miller Brothers-101 Ranch, the Denishawn Dancers, the Philadelphia Orchestra, college glee clubs, traveling light opera, and one-nighter road shows all doing generally profitable business from year to year. Arnold Stone had played it twice in his youth, although the theaters he had played—the Academy of Music, and the Loughlin—were destroyed by fire before he returned to the town with a Hemphill-Stone unit. The owner-manager of the Globe, a theater built in part on the insurance money from the Academy fire, was a man named Harry Lang, who had lived most of his life in Gibbsville but to most of its citizens was as remote as if he had been an absentee owner. To the actors who played his theater Lang seemed, contrariwise, like a man who had never once left Gibbsville. He did not have a sign that read, "Don't send out your laundry till we see your act," but in all other respects he was the kind of manager whom actors feared. He never wasted time in the amenities: he neither welcomed nor bade godspeed to the hundreds of actors and actresses who had played the Academy or the Globe. Any messages he had for them were passed to them through Kelly, his head stagehand, or Mary Hogan, his secretary and box-office treasurer. No matter how big the star—and some big ones came to his theaters on their tours of the provinces—he had never been known to send a box of posies to her hotel room. No matter how many bows a song-and-dance man earned or how many encores were demanded of an accordionist, Lang never bothered to telegraph the good news back to the artist's bookers in New York. The artist had to do that himself. A monologist might have the audience splitting a gut at his comedy routine, which he had painstakingly peppered with allusions to local people and places (the chief of police, the cheapest hotel, the nearby insane asylum), but Lang, standing in the back of the house, reacted no more or less favorably than he did to a dog-and-pony act. "How was I, Mr. Lang?" the artist would say.

"Hello," Lang would say, pretending not to have understood the question. A hello was often more than some performers got in the course of nine performances in three days.

But Harry Lang had great respect for Arnold Stone. He automatically respected any man who had made a million dollars in any line of business, and he was in ignorance of the fact that Arnold Stone's million had been made in real estate speculation. He therefore believed that Arnold Stone had made his million in the precarious business of putting on stock-company productions, and this entitled Arnold Stone to even greater respect than the average business-man millionaire. Harry was, for him, ecstatic that day in the winter of 1918-1919 when Arnold Stone, whom he knew only by reputation, called on him at the Globe and talked about putting on six weeks of stock. Harry Lang usually said no to everything that originated with anyone else, but against Arnold Stone he offered no resistance. This man, this successful millionaire about his own age, quickly proved that all the legends about his business acumen were justified. He knew more about the Globe than anyone but Harry Lang and Mary Hogan, and it would have been useless to argue against him. "You close for these six weeks anyways," said Arnold Stone. "One week you got the painters in, the carpenters, but the rest of the time you don't make a nickel. Your taxes and your insurance you gotta keep on paying. My proposition is, you offer famous Broadway plays with star actors at a dollar top, fifteen cents in the groot. A brand-new different play every week. You won't sell every ticket, but you'll sell enough tick-

ets so we both make a few dollars." Arnold Stone knew that vaudeville did not draw in the summer; the good acts laid off, and the
others were so awful that the audiences stayed away. But for some
reason—possibly because of a different kind of audience, which
did not patronize vaudeville—repertory companies sometimes
made money. This might be the case with the Globe, where money
had been made with road companies of established plays and play-
lets that presented top stars.

The two men shook hands on a deal, and the summer seasons
of 1919 and 1920 were profitable. Their winter meetings were
pleasant. Arnold Stone suspected that Mary Hogan was stealing a
little, but he refrained from complaining to Lang; he had only to
see Lang and Mary Hogan in the box office together to guess that
she was Lang's mistress and presumably had been so for a long
time. She was now well up in her forties and Lang was past sixty,
but they had that look of being used to each other. She had a neat-
ness about her that told Arnold Stone that she was capable of han-
dling a love affair in the same orderly fashion that was typical of
her spruceness of attire and her ledger entries. Her pince-nez
spectacles left little bruises on the bridge of her nose, but her skin
was remarkably unlined, her figure well corseted, her stockings
silken, and Arnold Stone was sure she did not miss a word of the
conversations between him and Lang. She was much too carefully
giving the impression of not eavesdropping. She was Lang's lady
friend, and to accuse her of stealing a few dollars was not worth the
risk. It could even turn out that what she was stealing was stolen
for Lang. And Arnold Stone was inclined to be tolerant of Lang
because he had met Lang's wife, a disagreeable woman whose tiny
eyes were almost hidden in her fat face. He had met Mrs. Lang just
once, when she entered the box office during a business conversation and with no preliminaries said, "Give me fi' dollars for
Leonard."

"I'm talking business," said Lang.

"I know you are, but I'm in a hurry."

"Introduce you to Arnold Stone," said Lang.

"Oh, Arnold Stone of Hemphill? Well, this *is* a pleasure," said
Mrs. Lang.

"Likewise," said Arnold Stone. He did not rise.

"Heard so much about you from Harry," she said. "Harry, will you let me have the fi' *dollars?* Leonard's up at the corner, with the other kids, and the trolley'll be along any minute. It's the school picnic."

"Fi' dollars to take along on a school picnic? What's he doing, *giving* the picnic?"

"Don't you want your son to be popular? Fork over," she said. She snatched the bill Lang handed to her. "Please to meet you, Mr. Stone. Come for supper."

"I appreciate—" said Arnold Stone, but she was gone.

"I won't invite you for supper," said Lang. "You're better off eating at the hotel, that I promise you."

"Anyway I couldn't accept your invitation, much as I appreciate the thought. Owing to a previous engagement."

"I know. Your previous engagement said was it all right if she didn't stay for the curtain call tonight. I told her it was all right."

"I know," said Arnold Stone. "Just as long as she don't think she's a privilege character. I got other privilege characters."

"Like a sailor, one in every port," said Lang.

"Not every, but pretty near," said Arnold Stone. Miss Hogan went right on working, and Arnold Stone understood everything.

But he did not understand anything but the urgency of Harry Lang's telegram summoning him to Gibbsville in the summer of 1921. Like all telegrams originating in small towns, the message from Lang was worded discreetly. "Important you come soon as possible discuss cast problem," it said. Lang was not one to waste his money on a long-distance telephone call, or, possibly, to trust telephone operators any more than he trusted telegraph operators. Arnold Stone telephoned the Globe on his arrival in Gibbsville, and was surprised that it was neither Harry Lang nor Mary Hogan who answered the call. Lang, however, got on the wire and said he would be at the hotel in ten minutes.

"First of all, let me ask you a question," said Lang. "Where did you get that Jerome Wellington from? What whorehouse did you pick him up out of that he was pimping for?"

"Jerome Wellington? Jerome Wellington?"

"Yes, Jerome Wellington. Don't stall me," said Lang.

"I had to think a minute. The young juvenile lead. Why, he was a chorus boy in a couple shows and he had a couple walk-ons. A very handsome sophisticated young fellow with a complete wardrobe. Riding togs, swallowtail, all his own wardrobe. What did he do to get you all so upset?"

"You'll find out."

"If I live long enough, or you do. What the hell's the trouble, Lang?"

"He made off with twenty-five thousand dollars. Him and Mary Hogan."

"Your lady friend?"

"Yes, God damn it. Over twenty-five thousand. Maybe closer to thirty-five. All the cash in my two bank accounts. The week's take for last week, and some Liberty bonds I kept in my safe. Monday morning I went in my office and no Mary Hogan. She has to be there early Monday morning to go to the bank with the Friday and Saturday receipts. But ten o'clock, eleven o'clock, and finally twelve noon and no Hogan. And her phone don't answer all this time. Then I started looking around in the safe and I couldn't find a God damn cent. Yeah. I found six dollars in pennies. But nothing above a nickel. Cleaned out of all the cash and the Liberty bonds, five of them."

"Then you called the banks," said Arnold Stone.

"Like hell I did. I didn't want this to be all over town."

"Ah, how smart of you, Lang. Congradgulations."

"I went and saw my lawyer and I got the loan of two thousand dollars from him, on a personal loan. I couldn't write a check on my bank accounts, because they would of known I didn't authorize the withdrawals."

"How did you know she cleaned out the accounts?" said Arnold Stone.

"If she cleaned out what was in the safe, the small stuff, she wasn't such a fool that she'd leave the bigger stuff, in the banks. But just to make sure, I got my lawyer to call one of the banks and they gave him the information."

"How did he do that?"

"How did he do that? Easy. Called a fellow he knew and like he was expecting it he said did Mary Hogan close out the Globe account, and the fellow said yes she did, Saturday morning. To think of the nerve of that whore, selling tickets here all Saturday matinee and evening, and all my cash in her satchel somewhere. Did you ever hear of such a thing?"

"No, not exactly," said Arnold Stone.

"How did you know she was sleeping with me?"

"That was only a guess," said Arnold Stone.

"A clever guess. Nobody else ever guessed it. Little Irish girl, came to work for me twenty-two years ago the first of June. We fell in love with one another and kept it secret all these years. She wouldn't marry a Jew, but she didn't care if I did."

"Then you were married twice?"

"Wife Number One passed away, then I married again, the present one."

"Was Hogan true to you all this time?"

"I never had the slightest doubt. She used to knock down a few dollars every week. That I knew, but she was entitled. But sleeping with? Nobody but me, of that I'm so positive I could bet on it."

"And you're not a betting man," said Arnold Stone.

"I wouldn't bet on the fourth of July coming after the third, but I'd bet on that," said Lang.

"Well, she cleaned you out of your cash and some bonds. Her and Jerome Wellington. What's wrong with sicking the dogs on them? The police?"

"It'd come out about me and her, and I don't want my wife and son to find that out. I raised him very strict, my son, and it don't look like I'll have another. If it came out about me and Mary, my wife is liable to get my theater and my son, and where would I be?"

"What I want to know, Lang, why did you send for me?"

"I wanted to talk to you about something. I wanted to get your advice. But that ain't all. Your help is what I want, too."

"Financial, you mean?"

Lang nodded. "I'm down to two thousand dollars capital, that I got the loan of from my lawyer. You're a rich man."

"I'm listening."

"How much would you say this theater of mine is worth?"

"Oh, anywhere from twenty-five to fifty thousand. That depends on if you're talking about real estate or a theater that's making money."

"I make money. You know that."

"I do, and you got a nice, fireproof modern theater."

"Including the latest in movie projection machines," said Lang.

"Uh-huh. But what do I want to own a theater for? I'm in New York City, and I'm over sixty years of age."

"I don't want you to own the theater. All I want is you to loan me twenty thousand with the theater for security."

"You own it outright?"

"Free and clear. No mortgages. I don't like to pay interest on anything. I like to collect interest. Near all my bills I get a discount for cash within ten days. That's why I had so much cash in the banks."

"You must have good credit then."

"The best. But I can't go to the banks and tell them my cashier run out on me. I can tell you, an out-of-towner, but I can't tell the bankers I been doing business with all my life."

"Supposing I was to let you have the loan of fifteen thousand."

"It would have to be twenty. I want it to look like I was putting that money back in the two bank accounts. It'd have to be twenty."

"Well, say twenty. What's in it for me?"

"Fifty dollars a week guaranteed interest for fifty weeks. In other words, a total of ten percent interest on twenty thousand, even if I repay the twenty thousand in six months. If I go over the year I keep on giving you fifty a week till the principal is paid back. That sounds like a pretty good proposition to me."

"To you, Lang. But how it sounds to me is what counts. You put up the theater for security, but what's the time limit on that?"

"Eighteen months, but don't you worry, you'll get the principal back long before that. I don't want to keep on paying interest, not at those rates. You won't get terms like that anywhere else, but I have to pay high interest because I don't want it to get out that Mary Hogan robbed me."

"I'll have to talk to my pardner, Hemphill."

"No, I don't want you talking to *any*body. I don't know Hemphill. This is strictly between you and I."

"It's a lot of money, twenty thousand dollars. I was thinking for that much cash I ought to get a ten-year contract to put on Hemphill and Stone productions on the same terms we got now."

"Arnie, that's taking advantage."

"Maybe it is, but Hemphill is going to find out some day, and he's going to say what was I doing making deals behind his back. By rights he ought to be in on every theatrical deal I make, win or lose. I gotta have something to show him that I was looking out for the firm."

"All right, I give in," said Lang.

"You give in? I don't know if it's you giving in or me giving in," said Arnold Stone.

They wrote out an agreement with pen and ink on hotel stationery, then summoned the manager of the hotel to witness their signatures without showing him the body of the contract. This concluded, Arnold Stone wrote out his personal cheque for $20,000 and caught the night train back to New York. Later the next morning the Gibbsville bank telephoned him to verify the signature on the cheque, and he assured the bank that it was authentic and that he had already instructed his New York bank to that effect. He had lunch that day with the good appetite of a man who has combined a good deed with a safe and potentially profitable investment. It was particularly enjoyable when he recalled his frame of mind upon being summoned to Gibbsville. He had gone there expecting trouble and not knowing what kind of trouble.

The blow that killed him fell three days later. Miss Shapro opened his office door and closed it behind her. "There's a man out there says he's a detective, from Gibbsville," she said. "Schroeder, his name is. He has a badge."

Arnold Stone trembled. "Let him in and close the door, and as soon as you close the door get my lawyer here right away."

Schroeder, in a tight-fitting double-breasted Palm Beach suit, entered Arnold Stone's office and showed his badge, which was in a leather case. "District attorney's office, Lantenengo County, Mr. Stone."

"Have a seat," said Arnold Stone. "What seems to be the trouble?"

"Well, like it often happens, it comes in pairs. Did you see or hear from Harry Lang since you left Gibbsville three nights ago?"

"Not a word."

"Uh-huh. The cheque you gave him, Mr. Stone. What was that for exactly?"

"Exactly twenty thousand dollars."

"I meant in payment of what?"

"It was a loan."

"Do you have a note or anything on that order?"

"I have, but that's private business, Mr. Schroeder."

"Yes, so far. I'm only here to ask questions for the time being. Principally I want to find out the whereabouts of Harry Lang. You have any information on where he would be?"

"No, none. Why?"

Schroeder studied him silently for a moment. "Mr. Stone, we're on the same side in this matter, or I'm very much mistaken."

"On what matter? So far you didn't say anything much."

"You want to be on the side of the law, don't you? I understand you're a reputable business man."

"I am always on the side of the law, but what's this beating about the bush? Spill it, Schroeder."

"All right, I will. We have good reason to believe that Harry Lang has rooked you out of twenty thousand dollars, along with some other people. Does that make you wish to cooperate?"

Arnold Stone found breathing difficult. "How cooperate—if it's true. Tell me the whole story, get to the point."

"Harry Lang has flown the coop. He borrowed a certain amount of cash from two banks, he wrote two good-sized cheques, sold a diamond ring belonging to his wife and other articles of jewelry, plus some bonds belonging to her he took out of the safe deposit box, plus various small amounts of cash he borrowed from

merchants, like fifty dollars here and fifty dollars there up and down
Main Street. We don't know how much he got all told, but it comes
to over twenty thousand dollars, not including the twenty thousand
he got from you, and not including closer to thirty thousand his
cashier, Mary Hogan, got away with a week ago. We have reason
to believe they planned this together and are together right now.
There's warrants out for their arrest, and I'm glad to say the New
York authorities are fully cooperating with us, Mr. Stone."

"I'll cooperate. But right off the bat, you're wrong about one
thing," said Arnold Stone.

"What's that?"

"The Hogan woman ran off with an actor. A fellow by the
name of Jerome Wellington."

"That's where *you're* wrong, Mr. Stone," said Schroeder.
"She only took him as far as Philly. He was a cover-up, or else she
just ditched him, we don't know for sure. You oughta know him,
Mr. Stone. He was one of your people—"

"My people?"

"You hired him, didn't you? Lang didn't hire him."

"Oh, that way my people. Yes, I hired him," said Arnold
Stone. "A cheap actor."

"And a queer. You knew he was a queer, didn't you?"

"Listen, I started trying to find out what actor was a queer
and what one wasn't—this is show business, Mr. Schroeder. I don't
know who's a queer and who isn't, and I don't care. But I guess
Wellington was more one than some others. So?"

"Well that's the part we don't understand," said Schroeder.
"How Mary Hogan got innarested in him in the first place."

"You want me to do your detective work for you?" said Arnold Stone. "Well, all right. Some queers aren't all queer. Some
can satisfy a woman, especially a woman in her middle age and she
got a little money. You want my theory, my theory is the Hogan
woman got Wellington to run away with her, all right. Give him a
few dollars and make out like there was gonna be plenty more.
That was the cover-up. They get as far as Philly and she ditches
him. That'd be easy for her. She gives him a hundred dollars to go

out and buy some clothes, and when he comes back—no Hogan. She's on her way to meet Harry Lang."

"That's about the way it happened, from what we know. You're a smart man, Mr. Stone."

"Am I? I ain't as smart as Harry Lang, that took me for plenty. I got his paper, that entitles me to his theater maybe, but it'll be a long time before I get ownership of that. A long time. And I don't want his God damn theater."

"I'd like to have a talk with Mr. Hemphill. Is he in?"

"There ain't no Mr. Hemphill."

"Dead?"

"There never was no Hemphill. He's a figment of my imagination. I'm Hemphill and I'm Stone."

"Isn't that a sort of a funny way to do business?" said Schroeder. "Why would you want to have the name Hemphill on your door, on your stationery?"

"Because I'm a crook. What the hell kind of questions are you coming here and asking me. It's no business of yours what name I do business under. If I called myself Broadway Theatrical Productions would you ask me these kind of questions? Well, I call myself Hemphill and Stone."

"Calm yourself, Mr. Stone. Calm yourself."

"Yeah, calm myself. You as much as accuse me of being a crook. If I was a crook would I be as big a chump as that, to get robbed of twenty thousand dollars by a small-town hick from Gibbsville P A? I'm worth over a million dollars, Schroeder. Over a million dollars. I don't bother with petty larceny."

"You can't seem to make up your mind whether twenty thousand dollars is a lot of money or petty larceny."

"Will you just get out of here and leave me alone? Will you kindly do that, please?"

"All right, Mr. Stone. But would you be willing to come to Gibbsville and make out a complaint against Lang?"

"On what grounds? If Lang sends me fifty dollars by the end of the week, I got no charges against him. I don't think he *will* send me fifty dollars, but so far I got no cause to have him arrested."

"You're absolutely right, I guess," said Schroeder. "But if it turns out that he did steal your twenty thousand dollars, will you be willing to come and testify?"

"We'll cross that bridge when you find him. I'll bet you never find him."

"We'll find him, all right. He won't get far."

"You want to bet me? Him and that Hogan woman, they're the first ones ever outsmarted me in my whole life. A couple of hicks from Hicksville. No, I won't testify. Arnold Stone on the witness stand, testifying under oath how a couple of hicks swindled him out of twenty thousand dollars? No, I changed my mind. I won't be the laughingstock of Broadway."

"Well, like you said, we'll cross that bridge when we come to it."

"We just came to it, and I refused to cross it," said Arnold Stone. "I don't care if I never cross the Pennsylvania state line the rest of my life. You can't make me testify. Now will you please go away, Mr. Schroeder?"

"Yes, I'll go, but I'll probably have to come back."

"Don't have anything personal against you, Schroeder, but I won't testify, that's all there is to it."

"I'll give you a chance to think that over," said Schroeder. "Your lawyer may advise—"

"That reminds me, where *is* my lawyer?" He called out: "Elsie! Miss Shapro! Did you get Arthur Yeddin?"

Miss Shapro appeared in the doorway. "Mr. Yeddin's in court and won't be back till five o'clock."

"When you need them," said Arnold Stone.

"So long, Mr. Stone."

"Yeah. Yeah, yeah, yeah," said Arnold Stone. He did not watch Schroeder's departure. "I don't feel so good."

"A glass of water, Mr. Stone?" said Elsie Shapro.

"A glass of water maybe," said Arnold Stone. "Ooh, ooh, ooh-ooh-ooh. Elsie!" He fell out of his chair and lay on the floor.

The only medical assistance she could think of was a dentist in the building, and he, in his white coat, came to the office. "He's had a stroke," said the dentist.

"I could *see that,*" said Elsie.

"All I can do is phone an M.D. There's a urologist across the street."

"Well, do something for God's sake, the man's dying."

"I wish I could think of the man's name, the urologist," said the dentist.

Arnold Stone did not die that afternoon, but his life was rapidly ending. He could not go to his office again. Elsie Shapro visited him every day in his apartment at the Marie Antoinette, brought him his mail and took dictation of the letters he was writing to wind up the affairs of Hemphill & Stone. "I'd leave the business to you, Elsie, but a woman couldn't handle it," he told her.

"Thank you, Mr. Stone, but I wouldn't want it anyway."

"I got my sister in Baltimore, her son could have it but he's in medical college."

"I know. Mrs. Cohen's son. Who's putting him through medical college if not you? Who supported the entire Cohen family if not you?"

"Well, your only sister. I'm taking good care of you, Elsie. You know that, don't you?"

"I do know that, Mr. Stone, thank you very much."

"I don't have to tell you to invest it carefully. No quick get-rich-quick schemes, nothing like that. You can live comfortable the rest of your life. Be satisfied with five thousand a year, don't try to stretch it to ten."

"Don't you worry about that, Mr. Stone."

"I was thinking of adding a codicil."

"Another codicil? You got a lot of codicils as it is."

"Yeah, but I got a lot of money. Make a note of it for Yeddin. A codicil. Two thousand dollars to Father Duffy over on Forty-second Street."

"Why him?"

"Oh, he's a nice man. And what he done in the war. But he gives money to actors, I know he does. Ones that need it. Put him down for twenty-five hundred, tell Yeddin. No, what's twenty-five hundred? Put him down for five thousand."

"It's your money," said Elsie Shapro.

"It's the only enjoyment I can get out of it now, thinking of the surprised look on their faces. Like Father Duffy, when they tell him I left him five thousand dollars. 'Arnold Stone? You sure? I didn't hardly know Arnold Stone, just to say hello to.'"

"You ought to have a better reason than that for leaving a man five thousand dollars," said Elsie.

"You tell me a better reason," he said. "Five hundred dollars to Jimmy Pacelli."

"Who's that?"

"Used to be my barber."

"Jimmy at the Astor House? That one?"

"That's the one."

"He died a couple years ago. You sent flowers."

"Oh, did I?"

"Yes, you did, and you were glad when he retired, so you wouldn't have to go to him any more. You said he was rough. Rough hands."

"Now I remember. Uh-huh. Yeah, he had rough hands. You wouldn't think a barber would have rough hands, all that hot water all day. But he did."

Elsie Shapro would duly report these conversations to Arthur Yeddin, and once a week Yeddin would appear in Arnold Stone's suite at the Marie Antoinette with the codicils properly drawn. On one such visit, early in the fall, Arnold Stone said to him, "While I got you here, Arthur, put down the name of Mary Hogan for twenty thousand dollars."

"Mary Hogan. I know that name. Where do I know that name from?"

"No, you never heard of her, Arthur."

"I'm sure I have, Arnie."

"No, I never told you about her. I had her in a couple shows. Binghamton, two-three summers ago. Wilkes-Barre. She was never much on Broadway, but she was a big draw in Wilkes-Barre. She was a particular friend of mind for a couple years. Beautiful woman."

"Where does she live now?"

"Oh, you can get that information from Elsie," said Arnold Stone.

Arthur Yeddin dropped in to see Elsie Shapro. "Arnie suddenly remembered another one, but this one's for twenty thousand. Who is Mary Hogan?"

"Mary *Hogan!*"

"I know the name from somewhere," said Yeddin.

"I'll say you do. That's the cashier in Gibbsville. Ran away with the owner, Lang."

"Could there be another one, an actress?"

"No, don't you see, Mr. Yeddin? The boss is gradually losing his mind."

"Oh," said Yeddin. "That's going to be a problem."

"I can see that, all right," said Elsie.

"He has you down for a hundred thousand."

"And you for twenty-five," said Elsie.

"It's quite a problem," said Yeddin.

"I'll say it is," said Elsie.

"My, oh, my."

"You're right," said Elsie.

"Some of these bequests, you know, they're entirely proper. I mean, the trust fund for Mrs. Cohen, the sister. And Mount Sinai Hospital. Federation. This, that, and the other. But then we come to this Mary Hogan. She's a fugitive from justice, warrants out for her arrest."

"Not to mention, I told you he wanted to leave five hundred dollars to a dead barber," said Elsie. "I stopped him from doing that."

"A good thing you did, or it'd be in the will right now. That wouldn't look good in there. That would look just as bad as Mary Hogan, if somebody wanted to break the will. Mrs. Cohen, for instance, or her son."

"Or her no-good husband."

"Well, I don't know anything about him, but the sister could easily break this will if the dead barber was in there and Mary Hogan. Anybody could, that knew what we know. It's a tremendous problem, Elsie."

"I can see that, Mr. Yeddin."

"We have to look at it from all sides," said Yeddin.

"I'll say we do," said Elsie. "From *all* sides."

"These charities, for instance, in the event of Mrs. Cohen breaking the will, they wouldn't stand to get anywhere near the money Arnie has them down for. Could be they wouldn't get anything, these hospitals and philanthropic organizations. Not a thing. In an out-of-court settlement sometimes the various parties agree to a lesser amount, just to keep the thing out of litigation, you understand."

"Yes, I know."

"But for instance now, if it went to court. If I was on the opposite side of the fence, counsel for Mrs. Cohen, the sister, I'd be pretty sure to make something out of Hemphill. Harold H. Hemphill."

"Oh, yes, I see."

"I'd subpoena you, Elsie Shapro, and make you testify that deceased carried on a pretense of having a partner named Hemphill when in fact no such person ever existed. That you were frequently called upon to lie regarding the existence of said Hemphill. That on various occasions you pretended over the telephone that said Hemphill was busy on the other wire. I heard you pull that one more than once myself."

"Under orders, sure."

"Therefore, it would be my contention that said Arnold Stone behaved in a strange, eccentric fashion over a period of years, finally culminating in the last will and testament that could not have been the work of any sane person, et cetera et cetera. Furthermore, the loan of money to the fugitive Harry Lang is additional evidence of a deteriorating mental condition, resulting in bad judgment in business matters also indicating impairment of the mental faculties."

"My goodness, Mr. Yeddin," said Elsie.

"In plain and simple language, Elsie, this will could be broken by any lawyer that knew half of what you and I know."

"I don't doubt it," said Elsie. She waited for him to go on, but for the moment he merely looked at her. "It's beginning to sink in, Mr. Yeddin."

"What is, Elsie?"

"Well—I don't know for sure."

"Just say what's in your mind," said Yeddin.

"Well, I wouldn't like to see all those charities lose this money."

"Uh-huh."

"And it's probably too late to get the boss to start a whole new will."

"Which would probably be a worse will than the one we have now, don't forget."

"So—we don't do any more about this will."

"Are you suggesting that we ignore this new codicil?"

"Well, we could type one up and get him to sign it, but we don't have to add it to the rest of the will. I'd need some will paper, if you wanted me to do it."

"I can get the paper all right, but of course you'd have to do the typing. I wouldn't like to have that done in my office. And there's this to consider, Elsie."

"What, Mr. Yeddin?"

"If we stall around a little, it may not be necessary."

"Yes, he don't look so good, I'll say that. And maybe he'll forget about Mary Hogan—but don't be too sure about that," said Elsie. She sighed. "I wish I would of been born a pretty woman. He certainly did take a fancy to pretty women. But then I guess if I'da been pretty he never would of hired me in the first place."

"And a lot of pretty women wish they had a hundred thousand dollars, Elsie."

"Well, I guess I'm entitled," said Elsie. "Not that he didn't always treat me right, Mr. Stone. Mr. Stone was always very good-hearted."

"And you can look at it this way, Elsie. If he had all his faculties he'd realize we're only doing the right thing."

"Oh, I believe that, Mr. Yeddin," said Elsie.

AT THE WINDOW

The first thing to go was the gilded-horse weathervane on top of the barn. From an upstairs window Moore had been watching it as it spun crazily, clockwise and counter-clockwise, resisting the wind and going with it. The ornament was a rather ugly thing, resembling—unintentionally, Moore was sure—one of those quarter horses that are raced in the Southwest, with a body that was too long and legs that were too short. Nevertheless Moore was sorry to see it go. In the last fifteen minutes he had come to forgive it its ugliness and admire its spirit, as though it were a real animal and putting up a struggle against the gale. Then the rod snapped, and the whole weathervane was carried away.

"There goes our horse," said Moore.

"What horse?" said Helen Moore.

"The weathervane," he said.

"Is *that* what you've been watching?" she said. "I thought you were sitting here brooding about the trees."

"I am. But I got fascinated by the weathervane," he said. "I wonder how old it was."

"It was here when we came," she said.

"I know it was. And that'll give you an idea of how it's blowing out there."

"I don't need that to tell me," she said. "All I have to do is listen."

"All the storms we've had since we moved here, but this is the one that finally blew away the weathervane. I hope we'll be able to find it."

"*I* hope we'll still *be* here," she said. "There's no electricity. The stuff in the refrigerator's going bad, and everything in the deep freeze. The water pump. I've been filling pots and pans with water, while you've been up here watching a weathervane. I just hope the wind doesn't come along and blow away our bottled gas."

"The wind isn't coming from that direction," he said. "I'm afraid we can expect to lose some trees, though."

"Yes, and the radio said to expect possibly four inches of snow."

"Are you worried?"

"Well, not yet," she said. "I mean, we have plenty of food in the house, and we can cook it. And there's lots of firewood down in the cellar."

"If it snows we'll have plenty of drinking water."

"Don't worry, it's going to snow. The phone is on the blink, and our only communication with the outside world is the radio."

"One-way communication, at that," said Moore. "There! The first snowflakes. God, they're big. Look, you can hardly see the Williamses'."

"I notice they've lit a fire."

"Oh, an hour ago," said Moore. "They must have lit theirs as soon as the electricity went off."

"Well, they have to have a warm room for old Mr. Williams. Now you can hardly see their house. I don't think I've ever seen so much snow come all at once."

"Every year I talk about getting a Delco and one of those little tractors."

"What's a Delco?"

"An electric power plant."

"Oh, that's a Delco?"

"There are different makes. The first one I ever knew of was a Delco and I call them all that. Isaac Hostetter. He was a farmer in our valley when I was a boy. He was the first one to have a tractor, too. The other farmers thought he was out of his mind. He was, a little, I guess. He went into deep debt to buy all sorts of modern equipment. The most modern thing most of them had was a De Laval. A cream separator, operated by hand. We had one. I used to crank it, sort of like winding the dasher when my mother made ice cream. Didn't I ever tell you about old Isaac Hostetter?"

"Maybe you did, I don't know. I guess there won't be any mail today."

"Oh, I doubt it now," said Moore. "I doubt if they'd start out in this weather. Last year we didn't get any mail for two days, remember?"

"Twice. Once for two days and another for three. No, I guess that was the year before when we didn't have mail for three days."

"Well, there's no use of their starting out and then getting stuck somewhere. How would you like to have Mr. Andrews as our house guest for two or three days?"

"The postman Mr. Andrews? Not very much," she said. "Why?"

"Well, if he got stuck in the road anywhere near our house, what else could we do but invite him to stay?"

"Oh, in that case of course we'd have to have him. We couldn't turn him away," she said.

"Actually, of course, he's not a bad fellow. Just a bit of a bore to talk to. And he's a talker."

"Now you can just about make out our barn."

"Imagine if we had cows?" said Moore.

"And you had to feed them?"

"Not only feed them. *Milk* them. If you were a real farmer's wife you'd have to do the milking twice a day."

"No thank you," she said.

"That's the way it used to be, when I was a boy."

"Your mother didn't have to milk cows."

"No, but the farmer's wife did. Mrs. Stroub. Pretty soon we won't be able to see our fence," he said.

"I hope it'll be there to see when this is over," she said.

"Isn't it strange what the wind does? It'll blow down a tree that's stood fifty years, a deeply rooted tree. But a tin mailbox stays right there. And a big thing that you'd think would make a good target, the tool shed, it hardly seems to shake. But my little weathervane with the horse on it, away it goes."

"Oh, I guess it's a lot like life. When your time comes, you go too."

"Uh-huh," he muttered. "I never get tired watching the snow-flakes. Do you ever try to pick out one snowflake and watch it all the way to the ground?"

"Yes, I have," she said.

"Really? We've been married thirty-three years and that's something we never knew about each other."

"You can't expect to know everything about a person, no matter how long you live with them. I wouldn't want to know everything about a person. And anyway, how could I? Every day you live you add something new to yourself."

"And lose something, too, I suppose," he said. "Think of the things we forget about ourselves. Mentioning old Isaac Hostetter, I remember something that happened fifty years ago, at least, and I haven't thought about it in all that time, till just now."

"I don't think you ever mentioned him to me before," she said.

"Oh, I must have mentioned him, years ago, but not lately."

"It's an unusual name. I'd have remembered it," she said.

"Yes, but there were a lot of unusual names, unusual to you when we were first married. Hostetter. Hochgertel. Fenstermacher. Womelsdorf. Wynkoop. Zinsendorf. Just thinking of names in our valley."

"How did a Moore get in there?"

"I must have told you that story," he said. "A farmer by the name of Billy Poffenberger. He ran up a big bill at my grand-father's store and for two years he didn't pay anything on account. He finally told my grandfather that he could have the farm for a receipted bill and a thousand dollars cash. It was a good farm, only Poffenberger'd let it go to hell, so my grandfather made the deal. He left it to my father in his will."

"I knew your father inherited it," said Helen Moore.

"To show you what neglect will do, it took my grandfather most of five years to get the property back in shape. I guess he must have spent quite a little money on it, but it was worth it. When my father died my mother sold the farm for forty thousand dollars, that's with everything on it. The livestock, the implements, and so forth. She had the house all fixed up nicely. Our house, that is.

Jake Stroub, our farmer, he'd never spend any of his own money on their house. They had another house on the other side of the barn, he and his family. They kept it clean, but they didn't even have a picture on the wall. All the walls were bare. They used to have a calendar in the kitchen, and that was all. A farmer has a hard time getting along without a calendar. I don't remember their ever having a clock, but they always had a calendar. The Swedish Haven Bank gave out calendars every year, and every farm in the valley had one. The one thing you'd see in every kitchen. We had one in our kitchen, too, but that was natural because my father was a director of the Swedish Haven Bank. A funny thing was, we were never there much in the wintertime. We didn't usually open up our house till around Easter. My mother said it was too gloomy during the real dead of winter, and of course we kids had to be in school in town. But as soon as we opened up the house around the first of April, one of the first things my father always did was to hang the bank calendar in the kitchen. I can remember him tearing off January, February, and March, and every year he always said the same thing. 'Well, that winter passed quickly,' he'd say."

"Yes, he had a good sense of humor," said Helen Moore.

"I guess he had to have, to put up with me," said Moore.

"And I guess your mother wasn't too easy to get along with," said Helen Moore.

"No, I guess she was pretty neurotic. That's what they'd say about her today. Neurotic. I suppose they would have called me a juvenile delinquent."

"Well, that's what you were, weren't you?" said Helen Moore.

"Oh, I don't deny it," he said.

"No, don't deny it to me," she said.

"I never have, have I? You can't say I ever pretended to be any better than I was, Helen. That's one thing I never did."

"No, I guess if you'd have tried to be a hypocrite I never would have married you," she said.

"I never had any use for a hypocrite," he said. "I had one or two friends of mine, and I don't have to tell you who they were. But they were getting away with murder, only because they never got caught. But no matter what I did, I always got caught at it sooner or later. You take now for instance, Johnny Grattan. The night I had my accident, Johnny'd been driving the car and he almost went off the road a couple of times, so I made him change places with me. The result? When the truck hit us, he was sound asleep, dead drunk, in the back seat, and *I* was the one that was pinned behind the steering. But it could have been Johnny that lost his arm instead of me."

"I don't see how that makes him a hypocrite," said Helen Moore.

"Well, it doesn't make him a hypocrite exactly. But in a way it does. I mean, he pretended he was sober enough to drive, but he wasn't. That's the way he was, you know. He was always putting up a big bluff. Always bluffing. Oh, sure. He could drive the car. A whole bunch of people on the porch of the Sigma Nu house, and I started to get in behind the steering, but no. Johnny had to show everybody how he could drink twice as much as everybody else and still drive. He lasted to the other side of Allentown, and then I had to take the wheel."

"Well, which is worse? For forty years he's blamed himself for what happened to you," she said.

"Now that's what I call being a hypocrite. He blames himself, but he has both arms. And I wonder how much sleep he lost over me."

"He never took another drink," said Helen Moore.

"So he says," said Moore.

"Well, you *know* he didn't, Frank."

"Sure. Sure. Good for him," said Moore. "Let's move back to Swedish Haven so we can see more of John L. Grattan, the non-drinker."

She suppressed her reply. "Well, this isn't getting my work done," she said. "Do you want anything?"

"Do I want anything? What, for instance?"

"Well, I thought I'd spend the rest of the morning in the attic, sorting out things for the rummage sale."

"The attic? Do you know what it'll be like up there? You'll freeze to death."

"Oh, I have my big thick sweater. I won't be cold. And if it does get too cold, I'll stop. But I promised the committee I'd be ready when they sent the truck."

"This snowstorm will put everything back at least three days," he said.

"Well, I'm more than three days late. I should have done this a week ago. There's coffee in the glass pot. You may want to heat it. I put the milk and cream out on the windowsill. It'll keep just as well there as in the refrigerator."

"We used to have a box to keep things in during the winter. It was just outside the kitchen window, and you could keep meat and vegetables there. It opened from inside the kitchen. We ought to have one of those."

"Yes, that'd be a good idea. I suppose we could get a carpenter to make one."

"You know damn well I couldn't," he said. "You need two hands for that."

"All right, we'll ask Mr. Rosetti. But first let's find out how much he's going to charge us. Not like the last time, when he charged us eighty-five dollars just to fix a few feet of fence."

"Well, he knows I can't do it."

"Oh, Frank, will you stop?" she said. She left the room, got her sweater and retired to the attic.

She did not remain there long. It was a hard cold in the attic, with the sound of the wind beating against the roofing, and the power failure keeping the room in just enough darkness to make her chore difficult. She gave up and descended through trapdoor to ladder to the second-story guest room where her husband was still sitting at the window.

"I couldn't get anything done," she said. "No light, and my hands got cold. Would you want an early lunch?"

"I don't know what came over me," he said. "How long is it since I bellyached about my arm? I don't do that often, do I?"

"No," she said.

"One thing leads to another," he said. "I got on the subject of Johnny Grattan and before I knew it I was back there forty years ago. Forty years, that's a good solid block of years."

"Well, let's hope it's out of your system," she said.

"It'll never be out of my system altogether. It gave me a good excuse for being a bum."

"Oh, you're not a bum, Frank. That's silly," she said. "They should have made you get an artificial arm, then you could have done certain things and you'd have gotten used to it, so that when those new ones came along, the World War Two arms, you'd have been ready. I don't know, maybe you could still learn to use one of the new ones. They say they're marvelous."

"No, I couldn't learn to use one now. I'd only get discouraged, and I'm bad enough as it is."

"Only when you're feeling sorry for yourself. Then you can work yourself into such a state that you can be a disagreeable son of a bitch."

"Well, I don't enjoy it when I'm that way."

"I should hope not," she said. "How would you like some soup and a sliced chicken sandwich for lunch? I have the last of that chicken. Or I could fix you some cold cuts with a hot soup? I have some ham and liverwurst."

"The cold cuts," he said.

"I'm going to give you a steak tonight. We had three left in the deep freeze. If they get the electricity back on soon—but I'm not counting on that."

"No," he said. "I guess they'll try to have it on for tonight, but I wouldn't count on it much before dark."

"Old Mr. Williams must be miserable."

"Do you know what the Eskimos do with their old people? They put them out in a storm and they just fall asleep and never wake up. It seems to me a very sensible way."

"Are you suggesting that that's what they ought to do with Mr. Williams?"

"Not seriously, no," he said. "But this would be their chance, wouldn't it? And the Lord knows, Mr. Williams isn't getting much enjoyment out of life. He's over ninety."

"His mind is all right, though," she said.

"For a man over ninety. But he hasn't got much control over

himself. He's practically helpless, and he's nothing much to look at. One of the funny sights is to see that old man, born right after the Civil War, shaving himself with an electric razor."

"Well, he won't be able to use it today."

"Oh, he probably doesn't have to shave more than once or twice a week. I'm thirty years younger than he is, but I notice a shave lasts me longer than it used to."

"He must be a problem in weather like this," said Helen Moore.

"Yes. Well, he's clinging to that last spark of life," he said. "And I guess they have enough firewood to keep him warm. I imagine they have him in their livingroom."

"Yes, I would think so. He doesn't sleep upstairs any more. They more or less turned their diningroom into a bedroom for him."

"I didn't know that," said Moore.

"Oh, last year," she said. "They had that lavatory in the hall, so all they had to do was bring down a bed from upstairs. Once a week they take him upstairs and give him a bath. That's the part I wouldn't like, giving an old man his bath. But Rachel doesn't complain. She's very fond of the old man."

"Well, that was the understanding, you know. He put up the money for the farm, on condition they'd give him a home. I guess they never expected him to last *this* long, though. That was twenty years ago."

"Yes, he got his money's worth. But Rachel doesn't look at it that way."

"It's still coming down," he said. "I think the wind has let up a little. Slanting. I noticed one little spot behind the tool shed, no snow on the ground at all. Just that one little spot. But I'll bet you there'll be two feet of snow there tomorrow, if not before."

"Well, let's hope it fills up all the reservoirs. We don't want any more water shortages next summer."

"No. Just think if we farmed this place," he said. "I mean if we had to depend on it for a living. Tom Williams told me last fall, I forget how much he said he lost last year. He about broke even on the dairy end, but he lost on the sweet corn and his potatoes. And Tom's a pretty good farmer. He uses all modern methods and reads up on all the latest information. But if you don't get rain at the right time and in the right amount, you can be the smartest farmer in the country and for all the good it does you you might as well stay drunk."

"Tom doesn't drink," she said.

"I didn't mean *he* might as well stay drunk. Anybody. Although you're wrong about Tom not drinking. Once or twice a year Tom ties one on that lasts four or five days."

"Oh, he used to, but not any more," said Helen Moore.

"Have it your way, but I happen to know better. The difference is, now he goes away, and I know where he goes. He and his brother, from Wilkes-Barre, and one or two friends of theirs go up to a shack they have in the Poconos. To go deer-hunting, they say. But last year Tom took a case of bourbon with him and it was all gone when he came back. Figure it out for yourself. Twelve bottles of whiskey. Four men. Four days. That's pretty good drinking for a man that doesn't drink. I could have gone with them. He invited me. Just bring some money, he told me. They play poker. I almost went."

"What stopped you?" she said.

"Well, if you think back, that was when you just got back from the clinic that time. You were waiting to hear from the doctor."

"Oh," she said. "Well, I'm glad you didn't go. Thank you."

"What the hell? I knew you were worried."

"You didn't say anything," she said.

"Neither did you. But it was a natural thing to be worried. And I probably wouldn't have had any fun. I don't like to be around a bunch of men when they're drinking and they have a lot of guns around."

"Why do you have to spoil it? You do something nice, and then it's as if you were ashamed of it," she said.

"Well, I don't know," he said. "Maybe I would have gone, and maybe I wouldn't. I don't know."

"You *would* have," she said.

"Well, I usually win at five-card stud," he said. "But then

somebody gets a little drunk and they start all those fancy varia-
tions. Seven-card high-low, wild cards. Takes all the pleasure out
of it for me."

She kissed him.

AUNT FRAN

Mary Duncan heard her husband stomping his feet on the front porch, heard him kicking his shoes against the porch rail, and then there was the complaining squeal of the front door being pushed inward. She did not look up from her letter-writing. "Is the game over?" she said.

"No, there's about ten minutes left in the last quarter, but I began sneezing, so I came home. G.H.S. is ahead, eighteen to six." He took off his trench coat and hung it on the clothestree in the hall, then came in the front room. "Look, I just wanted to show you. Wringing wet." He held out a knitted Balaklava helmet.

"Well, don't wring it out here," she said.

"I just wanted to show you," he said.

"And you ought to get those shoes off," she said.

"My feet are dry. These shoes held up. A very good buy, although I didn't think so at the time. I paid fifteen dollars for them in 1917. That was when we wore shoes with leather puttees. Then we all had to get boots, before we were shipped overseas. Thirty-five, the boots were. They lasted me most of the time in France, then after the armistice I got a new pair to come home in. Sitting in the attic. If I knew somebody that rode horseback I'd give them away."

"Give them to Jimmy Malloy," she said.

"He has a pair, and anyway I don't think my boots would fit him."

"Well, then keep them. You wear them on Decoration Day."

"I didn't wear them last Decoration Day. I didn't go in the parade. Who are you writing to?"

"Aunt Fran. I'm trying to tell her we won't have room for her this Christmas. Take that wet cap out in the kitchen and wring it out. And maybe throw it away."

"You knitted it for me."

"I know I did."

"I get a lot of use out of it. Skating. Gunning."

"All right, don't throw it away. But please don't have it dripping all over my rugs. And go on upstairs and dry your hair, or you'll catch more cold."

"I'll dry my hair on the roller towel."

"All right, do as you please," she said.

"And I'm going to have a shot. Do you want one?"

"No thanks. I have to finish this letter," she said.

"A good slug of whiskey might inspire you."

"It might inspire me to tell Aunt Fran to go some place else for a change. Why does she always have to come here?"

"She doesn't have to. Why do I go to a high school football game, in rain and snow and mud?"

"Search me. Look at your trousers. They're soaking wet. I think you'd better go on upstairs and take off everything."

"I will if you will," he said.

"Oh, stop that kind of talk on a Saturday afternoon. It isn't becoming."

"I wasn't in earnest, for cripes' sake," he said.

"Get some dry clothes on and then maybe I'll have a highball. I got some ginger ale yesterday. It's in the pantry next to the preserves. The shelf on your right. You know what you ought to do is take a hot bath."

"Hell, I used to sleep in places that were worse than that field."

"Yes, but you haven't lately and you're seven years older. Go on, act sensibly and let me finish this darn letter."

She could hear him running a tub and moving about, and she went on with her letter to her aunt. She forgot about him until he reappeared, wearing white flannels, a crimson sweater with a white letter G, and a pair of sneakers. He handed her a highball. "You look like a cheerleader," she said.

"I couldn't button the top button of my white flannels, but everything else fits me."

"The sweater fits you quick," she said.

"A little quick, but I can still get it on."

"It's not the same sweater you had in high school, is it?"

"No. They used to give us coat-style sweaters."

"That's what I thought."

"I bought this one myself. Six bucks."

"When you were coaching. I remember."

"Coaching the backfield." He sat down and stretched his legs. "You finish your letter?"

"Finally," she said. "Do you want me to read it to you?"

"To correct your grammar?"

"Oh, when *you* can correct *my* grammar. No, to get our stories straight. 'Dear Aunt Fran. I am writing you this far ahead in order to make it possible for you to alter your plans in case you were planning to visit us this coming Christmas. As you know, we would always love to have you over the holidays but this year both children have invited school friends to visit them. Junior is bringing a boy from Seattle, Washington, who will not be able to go to his own home for the holidays and Barbara is inviting a girl whose father and mother are missionaries in China and she does not expect to see her parents for two more years.' "

"That sounds as if Barbara didn't expect to see *her* parents for two more years."

"Shut up. It does not. 'Barbara is also having two other friends for the Christmas festivities, namely the club dance and the Assembly and another dance being given by Judge Choate's daughter Emily. Therefore we will have a houseful with two girls sleeping in the guest room.' "

"Is that true?"

"Well, Barbara asked me if we'd mind having this girl from Scranton that has a crush on Bobby Choate. He asked her to go to the Assembly and she has no place else to stay. And Emily Choate's dance is only two nights before. To continue. 'Bill and I hope you

THE HORSE KNOWS THE WAY

will be able to visit us later in the winter when things have quieted down and there is more room.' Then some stuff about the people she knows in town, and love from you and I, Mary. All right?"

"Well, I hope so. We don't want her to cut you out of her will."

"She can't. Grandpa established a trust fund, and when she dies the principal goes to me."

"I know that. But she never spends any more than she has to and she must have saved some out of the income."

"I'm not worried about that," said Mary. "It's just that I don't want to hurt her feelings."

"Yes, and I guess it can get pretty lonely around Christmas, an old maid living in a hotel. But she has your other sisters to invite herself to."

"She never has, though. She's always come here. And I will say I was glad to have her when you were away in the army. A grown person. Those two Christmases you were away, the children were just the wrong age. I couldn't let them see I was miserable. They were so proud to have their father a captain, and at that age they got used to having you away. But if I would have shown any signs of how I felt, they would have started feeling sorry for themselves, too. So I was glad to have Aunt Fran to talk to. And cry a little."

"Then for cripes' sake let's have her," he said. "We can put cots in the attic, or something."

"No. We can't. I've made up my mind. I'm very fond of Aunt Fran and all that. But now it's the children's turn. You can't go on all your life doing things for the older people. The time has to come when you must start giving preference to the younger ones. Aunt Fran's had her life, but Barbara and Junior are just starting out. I may sound heartless and cruel, but if Aunt Fran has to spend Christmas in a hotel, that's not our fault. It isn't, Bill. She could have made more of her life. She always had enough money to live nicely and do what she wanted, and I'm not going to let sentiment spoil our children's Christmas."

"No, I can see you're not," he said.

"Well, whose side are you on, anyway?"

"I don't know. She may not be around much longer. In her

late sixties. And the kids have all the time in the world ahead of them."

"No, this is the time when they store up memories, and the parties this Christmas are going to be the best this town ever had."

"You and I didn't have a country club to go to."

"No, and more's the pity. My parents wouldn't allow me to go to the Assembly till I was twenty. Chicken-and-waffle suppers. Sleigh rides. Picnics. Heavily chaperoned."

"But we got married, Mary. And I like those memories, even if you don't seem to."

"Don't twist what I say. I like those memories, too, but our children will have different ones. And I'm not going to let Aunt Fran deprive them of them."

"All right. No use getting all het up about it. Let's forget Aunt Fran." He sipped his highball and lit a cigarette. The telephone rang. "I'll get it," he said, and went out to the desk in the hall.

She heard him say, "Oh, hello, Joe," and thereafter she paid no attention. He was on the telephone about five minutes.

"That was Joe McGonigle. He promised to call me. Guess what happened. You won't believe it. You know when I left, the score was eighteen to six, favor of G.H.S. Well, then they fumbled and Reading recovered for their second touchdown, making it eighteen to twelve. Reading kicked the extra point. Gibbsville then received and I'll be damned if they didn't fumble again. You know, wet ball, a day like this. And Reading recovered and went for a touchdown in two plays. Maybe he said three plays. Joe's still so excited he can hardly talk. That made it Reading nineteen, Gibbsville eighteen. Then Reading made that extra point and it was Reading twenty, Gibbsville eighteen. Well then do you know what happened? Gibbsville returned the kickoff to Reading's thirty-yard line, a hell of a run by young Dvorshak on that sloppy field. Then with about two and a half minutes left to play, Dvorshak kicked a field goal from the forty-yard line, and it was Gibbsville twenty-one, Reading twenty. Why didn't I stay? You know Dvorshak's that kid that when I was coaching the backfield, I taught his older brother how to dropkick, and his brother taught him. But forty yards on that sloppy field, and the ball must have weighed ten pounds. *I'm* going to have another drink. How about you?"

"Yes, I'll have another," she said.

"He's a fine kid, too, this Dvorshak. I wouldn't be surprised if he went to Notre Dame. There's a whole family of them. Five brothers. One went to Fordham. One to Villanova. One to the University of Maryland, and one to Pitt. The one I coached went to Fordham. But I think this one is headed for Notre Dame."

"Have you got any stamps in your wallet?" she said.

"Yes," he said. "You want me to get you one?"

"Please," she said. "No hurry."

THE BONFIRE

Kitty Bull said the final goodnights to the children, the final "no, no more stories" to the older two and paid a silent visit to the baby's room (for she firmly believed that a one-year-old can sense a break in his routine even when he is asleep). The cook and the maid were at the early movie in Southampton. The Bannings and their guests—a noisy cocktail party—had taken off for a dinner party in Wainscott, leaving all the lights on in the house next door but leaving, too, a merciful silence. The ocean was reasonably subdued, pounding the beach at long intervals and with only enough force to keep you from forgetting that it was there, that it had been angry most of the day and could be angry again.

She kicked off her Belgian slippers and went out and stood on the top of the dune. There was still enough light for a visibility of five miles, three miles, six miles. Make it three miles. It was about three miles to the Inlet, and she could see two white dots that would be fishing boats heading for the Inlet in a race against the coming darkness. The sand squishing through her toes made her wish she could run down and go for a brief swim, but she could not leave the house so soon. This was the first half hour, when Jeanie might be naughty and find some excuse to call her. She would pay no attention to the first call, and Jeanie might give up; but sometimes Jeanie would be insistent and repeat her call, louder and often, and disturb the other children.

She thanked God for the children. She thanked God . . .

Now she could not see the white dots and she would have to suppose that the fishing boats had got inside the Inlet. The visibility, whatever it had been, was now to be estimated in yards, not miles, and far far out, where the horizon had been, there were three twinkling lights, the riding lights of three other fishing boats that she had not seen before. They would be out there all night and if she got up early enough—five o'clock in the morning—they would still be there, but at six o'clock they would be gone. They were professional fishing boats, bunker boats that filled their nets, loaded up, and returned to Islip or to Baltimore with catches that would be converted into some kind of fertilizer. That, at least, was what Jerry had told her years ago. Five years ago. Six years ago. *Seven* years ago, when they had first come to this house. Could it be seven years? Almost a fifth of her life? One wave, heavier than all the others had been, struck the beach like thunder and she picked up her slippers and went inside.

In her bare feet she went upstairs and stood outside the children's rooms and listened. There was not a sound from them. She opened the door of the baby's room. She could not see him, but when she caught the rhythm of his breathing she closed the door and went downstairs again. The first half hour was more than gone, and for a moment she thought of going for a swim; but that was something she had promised Jerry never to do. Never go in that ocean alone, but especially at night. He had never permitted her to go in alone at night even when he was there in the house, watching a ball game on the TV. It isn't a question of how good a swimmer you are, or of keeping your head, he had told her. Naturally you would have sense enough to conserve your energy, and try to keep the lights of the beach cottages in front of you. But who could see *you* in the dark? Never go in alone at night, he had said; and then one night a year ago, a little tight and just arrived from the hot city, he had broken all his own rules. He had stopped for dinner at Rothman's on the way down, and you did not stop at Rothman's if you were alone, but she guessed whom he had dined with. It was not a clever guess. It was not a guess at all. It was an assumption based as much on instinct as on the things she had heard. "I feel as if I'd been dipped in oatmeal," he had said.

"You've been dipping in something stronger than oatmeal," she said.

"A few. Not enough to do any damage. I'm going for a swim."

"I can't go for a swim. Dr. Mando said not to for a while."

"That's all right. I just want to dunk."

"Why don't you just take a shower?"

"Because I want to go in the ocean! My God, Kitty."

"Well, you're always the one that says—"

"I'm *not* planning to swim to *Brazil*. If you're going to make a federal case of it, I won't go in. But my God, Kitty."

"Oh, go ahead," she said.

She could have stopped him. For a year she had told herself that she could have stopped him, and many times during the second half of that year she had wondered why she had not stopped him. She had given in to him and to his irritability and his stubbornness, but had there not been some irritability, some jealousy, on her part? Four days later they found his body near the Inlet, confirming his identity through his dental history, an X-ray photograph of a shoulder he had broken in college, and physical measurements that matched his in the Navy files. It was he, all right, beyond any reasonable doubt, and it was not necessary for her to look at him. His mother and father had been perfectly wonderful, and so had his brother. The only unpleasantness had been created by his sister, when he had been dead six months.

"You don't mind talking about Jerry, do you, Kitty?" said Edna.

"Not a bit. Why?"

"Well, because he was always against going in the ocean at night. It was so *unlike* him."

"Your father brought that up. Your mother did too."

"I know they did, and you tried to stop him. I know that, too. But can you think of any reason why Jerry would do such a complete about-face? I mean, he was my brother and we were very close."

"I know."

"I adored him. I really did."

"I know you did, Edna."

"But I wasn't blinded to his imperfections," said Edna.

"He had a few. Who hasn't?"

"Yes, who hasn't? Francine Barrow, for instance. You know what she's saying, of course."

"Yes, I do. But I didn't expect you to repeat anything Francine Barrow said. Jerry didn't commit suicide over Francine Barrow. He didn't commit suicide over anyone or anything. He was quite tight that night."

"You might have thought the cold water would have sobered him up."

"It doesn't always work that way. In fact, almost never. Haven't you ever been to a beach party where there was a lot of drinking? I haven't noticed that going in the ocean sobered them up. Quite the contrary, in some cases. I remember one night when you were tight and you went in and came out without your bikini."

"I've never been allowed to forget that," said Edna.

"Well, I only bring it up now to show that cold salt water doesn't necessarily sober you up. Jerry himself said you were really bagged that night. And you were."

"I'm perfectly willing to change the subject, if that's what you want to do, Kitty."

"No, I'd rather have this out. I knew about Francine. It started the last few months I was having the baby, and it continued for the same reason after the baby was born."

"Did you quarrel with him about it?"

"We had some minor quarrels, not over Francine. Although I suppose that was at the bottom of it. I didn't like it. You wouldn't like it if Mike slept with someone else while you were in the midst of having a baby. My first two pregnancies were fairly simple, but not this one. I was having a hard time, and Jerry wasn't much help to my morale. I've always thought Francine was one of the worst tramps on Long Island anyway."

"So do I, for that matter."

"Well then why do you help her spread that story? Jerry did not commit suicide. I would have known if he'd had any such intentions. The only reason he came down that night was because he was playing in a tournament at the National the next day. That was on his mind, not committing suicide."

"All right, Kitty. I'm satisfied. I'm sorry I had to bring this up, but I had to."

"Yes, I suppose you did," said Kitty, and the weariness in her voice surprised her. Acute grief had gone and now there was weariness that she had not suspected, and it remained with her for many months. It was much worse than the acute grief. The doctor had told her that she need not worry about having the strength to recover from her pregnancy and take care of the children. Nature is very reliable, he had said; when something like that happened to you, a shock, a dramatic episode, Nature responded. But when the acute grief began to wear off and the postponed weariness set in, that was the time to be careful. She went to see him, and because he was a good man she told him about her sister-in-law's conversation.

"I was afraid there'd be something like that," he said. "She hit you with it at just the wrong time. I'm going to send you up to the hospital for a G. I. series."

"Is that the barium thing? I haven't got an ulcer."

"Let's make sure," said the doctor.

She saw him again in a few days. "Now you can be glad I made you swallow all that barium," he said. "There's no sign of an ulcer."

"I knew there wouldn't be," she said.

"Did you indeed?" he said. He smiled.

"Well, I was right, wasn't I?" she said.

"Gloating, hey?" He had a pencil in his hand and he began sketching on a prescription blank.

"Now what, Dr. Mando? I always know there's something when you start drawing those little pictures. Are they my insides that you're drawing, or just anyone's?"

"You're pretty fresh. I think you're greatly relieved at my good news."

"Well, why shouldn't I be? I'd *hate* to have an ulcer. But come on, Doctor, what's on your mind?"

"*You* are, Mrs. Bull. Four cigarettes just since you've been here. I'm sure your internist has spoken to you about them. I *know* he has, because we had a conversation this morning. He had the first look at your X-ray pictures, you know."

"Yes, you two keep me up in the air like a shuttlecock."

"Badminton," said the doctor.

"Don't tell me I'm not going to be able to play games."

"No, that isn't what's on my mind. You can start swimming any time you feel like it, and golf or tennis, if you're planning to go South."

"I'm staying in New York, but there are places where I can swim and play squash."

"Exercise will be good for you. Dr. Randolph will tell you that, too."

"Fine, and now you tell me what's got you drawing those pictures."

He put down his pencil and sat back in his chair, his hands folded across his chest and reminding her of a spiritual adviser. "Is there any chance that you might be getting married fairly soon?"

"No," she said. "Is there any reason why I shouldn't?"

"On the contrary, there is every reason why you should, from my point of view."

"I haven't thought about it, at least not very much. And there's no man in the offing. Some day I suppose I will. Some day my prince will come." Suddenly, inexplicably, the sound of her words made her burst into tears. The doctor bent forward and gave her one of his large, hand-rolled handkerchiefs.

"Good Lord," she said. She dried her eyes and blew her nose.

"Mm-hmm," the doctor muttered.

"May I keep the handkerchief? I'll send it back to you," she said.

"Of course," said the doctor. He opened his desk drawer and took out a silver cigarette box. "I keep these out of sight nowadays. Have one?"

"Thanks," she said. He lit it for her. "I remember that lighter," she said.

"Yes, it's quite a beautiful piece of workmanship," he said. He looked at it and put it back in his pocket, and resumed his clerical attitude.

"It was the words of that song," she said.

ery strange if you weren't. I've known you pretty well these last six or seven years."

"Well, what do you suggest?" she said.

"I suggest that you start going out a little bit."

"In the hope of meeting some man," she said.

"Naturally."

"And having an affair with him, even if I don't fall in love with him?"

"You may have to wait a long time before you'll admit that you're in love with anyone."

"Yes, you're right," she said.

"In fact, you could conceivably go through the rest of your life without falling in love again."

"Yes," she said.

"Your husband left you three children, and the circumstances of his death. No other man will be able to make that deep an impression on you. On your life. On your memories. So don't expect anyone to."

"You didn't like my husband, did you, Dr. Mando?"

"That's not a very nice question to ask me, young woman. And I'm not going to answer it. But if he were my own son I'd still give you the same advice. You're in your early thirties and most of your life lies ahead of you. That includes having children, if you want any more. And you should, or these nice children you have now will become something that they shouldn't."

"What's that?"

"Walking reminders of your husband, of course. Making it impossible for you to start your new life. I hope you'll meet an interesting man and marry him and have children right away."

"I don't think that's going to happen," she said.

"It won't if you don't give it a chance," said the doctor. "Well, when do you want to see me again?"

"When do *you* want to see *me*?"

"In about three months. Miss Murphy will give you an appointment."

"Not till then? That's the longest I've ever gone without seeing you. Aren't you going to miss me?"

He smiled. "Yes, as a matter of fact I will. But it'll do you good to stay out of here for a while. Save you money too."

"You're such a lovely man, Dr. Mando. You really are," she said.

"Of course I am," he said. "My patients are nice, too. Some of them."

"Me?"

"Go on, young woman. There are women waiting," he said. "And I have to clean out this ash tray."

There was no "interesting" man at any of the small dinner parties she went to. Among the new men there were the pitiers, depressing fellows who acted as though Jerry had died last week; there were the others who were so determinedly cheerful that they seemed to deny that Jerry had ever lived at all. Among the men she had known in the past there were the instant patriarchs, contemporaries of Jerry's who took it upon themselves to plan her life for her; and, not surprisingly, there were two who were ready to move into her life. One of them was a dirty talker, who had never talked dirty to her while Jerry was alive; and the other was Edna's husband, Mike, who had always looked at her from the edges of groups with a dumb lechery that he now expressed in terms of love. "I think you've always known how I felt about you, Kitty," he said.

"Not exactly," she said. It was malicious, drawing him out, but she had not forgiven Edna for her inquisition.

"Maybe not exactly, but you must have had some idea," said Mike.

"Some idea, more or less," she said.

"Invite me to dinner some night. Just me."

"Without Edna?"

"That's the general idea," he said. "I suppose you're going to say that's impossible, but it isn't."

"But it is. If I invited you alone, there could only be one interpretation of that. There isn't any other interpretation."

"Oh, I see. You mean that you'd be the aggressor?"

"Not only the aggressor, but—well, yes, the aggressor. The troublemaker."

"Would you go away with me? If we went in my car, I'd be the aggressor, if that's what you object to. What I'm trying to tell you is—we've gotten sidetracked with this aggressor talk. I want you to see me without Edna, without anyone. To get used to me. And if I can convince you—to marry me."

"Oh."

"I know you're not all that anxious to get married again so soon. But it would take time in any case. Unfortunately people don't just say 'I've had it' and end a marriage that way. But I've been in love with you for a long time. We would have had this conversation sooner or later, even if Jerry had lived."

"I wonder," she said.

"You needn't. He kept you pregnant most of the time or I'd have spoken up sooner."

"That was very considerate of you, Mike."

"Is that sarcasm?"

"Not at all," she said.

"The week after next I'm going to Pinehurst. Come with me. I'm taking my car because it's more convenient. I'm making stops on the way down and then circling back through West Virginia, Ohio, and Pennsylvania. I'll be in Pinehurst for three days, a business convention, and you probably wouldn't want to do that, but you could join me when the convention's over, and we could have the better part of a week together. The most I'd have to spend with my business acquaintances would be two or three hours a day, and you like to read. What do you say?"

"Oh, you know what I'm going to say, Mike. How could I nip off for a week, leaving three small children and telling the nurse that I'd be at such-and-such a motel?"

"You're so practical," he said. "What if I sent Edna away, that is, gave her a trip abroad?"

"I don't know. Yes, I do know. I think that when I'm ready

to do anything in that department, I *am* going to have to be the aggressor. I'm the only one that will know when I'm ready—and I'm not ready now."

"That Jerry. He's still got a tight grip on you, hasn't he?"

"Or I have a tight grip on myself. One or the other, or maybe both."

"When you loosen up a little, will you let me know? I'm serious. You can trust me, you know."

"You mean if I just wanted to have sex?"

"Yes. Don't you ever want sex? You've had a lot of it. With Jerry, I mean."

"And for seven years with no one else. So, when the time comes—I'm awfully tired of the word—but I'll be the aggressor. I much prefer 'on the make.' "

"You'll never go on the make, Kitty."

"Except that I did with Jerry. I wanted him, I went after him, and I got him. And I've lost him."

She would have been more abrupt and far more cruel with Mike if she had not realized, midway in the conversation, that the conversation was useful to the clarification of her problems. Mike was in no sense a stimulating man, but he had helped her to see that the next man in her life would have to be one she chose. Whimsically she told herself that she owed something to Mike for his collaboration, and in that mood she thought of inviting him to spend a night with her. But he was a clod and he would be around again and again, believing himself to be in love with her and upsetting the lives of too many people. Nevertheless she felt better for having come even that remotely close. Very tentatively, a toe in the water, she was back in life once more.

It was enough to go on for a while, and there were other things to keep her busy. At home there were the children, uncomprehending of the mystery of death or, in the case of the baby, petulantly demanding that she keep him alive. The older two were forgetting about their father. Kitty put a cabinet-size photograph of Jerry in a silver frame and set it on a table in the livingroom of the New York apartment. It was two days before Jeanie noticed it. She stood in front of the picture for a moment, and Kitty waited for her comment.

"That's Daddy," said Jeanie.

"Yes. It's my favorite picture of him. Do you like it?"

"I guess so."

"But not very much," said Kitty. "What is there that you don't like about it?"

"He's so serious, Mum."

"And that's not the way you remember him? Well, that's because when he was with you and your little brothers he *wasn't* very serious. Nearly always laughing. Little jokes and so forth."

"Didn't he have jokes with you too?"

"Oh, yes. Lots of them."

"Tell me one," said the child.

"A joke that he told me? Well, let me think. A joke that he told me. There was one that Grandfather Bull told him. About an oyster?"

"Tell it to me."

"It's sort of a riddle. What kind of a noise annoys an oyster? Do you know the answer?"

"What?"

"A *noisy* noise annoys an oyster."

"Oh, that's old."

"It sure is. See if I can think of another. Most of his jokes with me were about people. I'll think of some and write them down so I won't forget them. And I'll see if I can find a picture of him smiling. Where shall we put it, if I find one?"

"I don't know. Over there, I guess. Mummy, can I watch TV after supper?"

"Nope. Before supper, yes. After supper, off it goes."

The older boy, Timothy, was only three, cheerful and strong and increasingly able to take his own part when his sister bullied him. The Irish nurse would say to him, "You're the man of the house, Timothy."

"I yam not a man. I'm a boy, silly."

"You'll be a man soon enough, then."

"You're silly, Margaret. You're silly, silly, silly. You think a boy is a man. *You're* a man. You have a moustache."

"For that somebody gets no pudding this supper."

"It isn't pudding, it's junket, and I hate junket. So yah!"

And there was the baby, now old enough to follow her with his eyes when he was serene and to scream for her and only for her when he was not.

There was more money than she had expected, and many more lawyers to see. There were certain financial advantages to be gained by a delay in settling Jerry's estate. "This could drag on for another year at least," said her lawyer. "But we want it to. Now for instance, Mrs. Bull, there's the matter of your husband's insurance. He carried a lot of insurance, much more than young men usually do nowadays. But he could afford it, so he did. The interesting thing here is that we've been arguing with the insurance company about the circumstances of your husband's death. We feel that accidental drowning may change the picture to your advantage. On the other hand *they* feel—I have to say this—that the possibility of suicide alters the picture in their favor. The medical examiner's report said accidental death by drowning, but the insurance company is trying to inject the element of suicide, not because they think they can get away with it, but maybe in the hope that we won't collect anything extra, like double indemnity. Give and take, you know. That's their position. But they know perfectly well that we're prepared to go to court. And by prepared I mean that you have enough money without insurance to not have to make a quick settlement. By the way, who is a Mrs. Barrow? Francine Barrow? She wasn't at your house the night your husband lost his life, was she?"

"No. She was a friend of his. And mine, I suppose. My husband had dinner with her early that evening, over on the North Shore. But she wasn't in our house. She's never been in our house."

"No, I shouldn't think so. In a very roundabout way we found out that the insurance company is basing its whole argument on some story of hers."

"Well, she's a congenital liar, among other things."

"That's a good thing to know," said Mr. Hastings. "You understand, Mrs. Bull, that if we collect a large amount of insurance, it'll go a long way toward paying your inheritance taxes. In fact we may come out a little ahead of the game. You'd have no objection to suing the insurance company, I hope?"

"None whatever," said Kitty. "Especially if Mrs. Barrow is on their side."

"When Mrs. Barrow understands a little better what could happen to her in court, she may not want to testify. I know if I were her lawyer I'd tell her to think twice."

"She doesn't embarrass very easily, Mr. Hastings. In plain language, she's a tramp."

"It's a curious thing, though, Mrs. Bull. There's something about a courtroom. The austerity of the furniture. The flag. The judge's robe. The strange language. It produces an atmosphere that's the next thing to a church, and it's intended to. And a woman like this Mrs. Barrow, although she may be shameless in her everyday life, when she gets in court a remarkable change comes over her. They fight like the devil to stay respectable. The insurance companies have very good lawyers. None better. And I seriously doubt that they'd want her to testify. In short, Mrs. Bull, her lawyer will advise her to shut up, and the insurance lawyers won't want her. But I have to give you the whole picture, to explain why we're moving so slowly."

"I'm in no hurry," said Kitty.

"That's good, that's fine. I'm sorry you have to come down here so often. I could save you some of these trips. There's probably a notary public in your neighborhood."

"I like coming down here. It's almost that same atmosphere you just described, the courtroom. And it makes me feel useful, as though I were doing it for my children. Although I'm not."

"Yes you are," said Mr. Hastings.

"Well, maybe I am," she said. "But doing things for them is the same as doing them for myself. It's what I like."

She put on a sweater and went out again and sat on the top of a dune. There were stars but no moon and down the beach at someone's cottage—she was not sure whose—there was a sizable bonfire and moving about it, like comical figures in some pagan rite, were the members of a beach picnic. They were too far away to be recognizable, even to be distinguishable as to sex. It seemed to be a fairly good-sized party and she was glad that the noise they would make was no closer to her house. It was a party of the young, that much she could determine by their frenetic activity. A great deal of running about, chasing, and, as she watched, two of the figures picked up a third figure by the hands and feet and carried it to the ocean and dropped it in. This might go on all night. It was at the McDades', the only cottage in that section that would be having that kind of party for the young.

The young. *She* was young. She had been a young wife, she was a young widow, and people like Dr. Mando continually called her "young woman." She would still be young, really, when those children now asleep in her cottage would be having beach picnics like the McDades'. She was old to them now, as a parent is old to all young children; but to Jerry's father and mother she was so young that they had worried about her ability to cope. She was too young to have been invited to any of the Bannings' noisy parties. She was only four or five years older than some of the members of the McDade picnic. Angus McDade was twenty-six, George Lasswell was twenty-six or seven. Harry Stephenson had been one of Jerry's favorite golfing companions. They would all be at the McDades' picnic.

Something got her to her feet, and she knew what it was. She denied it angrily, then admitted it so that she could dismiss it. It was a word that had first come up in her conversation with Mike, and the word had stayed with her. Aggressor. Well, she was not quite being an aggressor if she was being drawn to the beach bonfire like a moth to a flame. They would be nice to her, they would offer her food and drink, and they would admire her in the ways that she was used to being admired. She would sit with them and drink beer out of a can and smoke a cigarette and in a little while they would start singing and she would sing with them. She would only stay a little while.

She kicked off her slippers. It would make her seem more like one of them if she arrived in her bare feet. She walked down to where the sand was hardest, at the dry edge of the beach that was not being licked by the tide. She turned and headed toward the bonfire, and she was almost very sure of herself, and her step was light. She did not feel that she was leaving footprints on the hard sand.

It was a long way, and she could make out the figures before she could hear them. She was so close to the ocean that its sounds were all she could hear for the first fifty yards, the first seventy-five yards, the first hundred. And then the voices began to penetrate the sounds of the ocean. She walked on and the voices grew more distinct, the voices of young women and young men, a harsh and frightening chorus of people who did not want her. She stopped to listen. Now she could hear baritone derision and alto contempt and soprano coquetry answered by the baritone derision, and though they were ignorant of her existence they were commanding her to stay away.

She turned and for a terrifying second her eyes, so long focused on the bonfire, looked into blackness. She could not move. Then she looked up at the sky until she could see a star, and then there were more stars and to her left were the lights of the cottages on the dunes. She ran all the way home.

THE BRAIN

A certain type of man gets a certain type of headachey look about him long before his headaches become more or less chronic. In the case of Robert Ammond, vice-president of Ammond & Stepworth, publishers of technical books for the electrical and mechanical engineering professions, the look preceded the incidence of migraine headaches by about fifteen years. In his late twenties Robert Ammond began wearing glasses full-time, but already he had a fixed, intense, squinty look in the triangle between the tip of his nose and the extremities of his eyebrows. He seemed to be concentrating all the time, especially during those moments when it could be presumed that there was no call for concentration. Gazing out a train window, standing on the first tee while the foursome ahead of him got under way, sitting in the company box at the Yankee Stadium while one team was taking the field and the other getting ready to go to bat, Robert Ammond gave every appearance of having his mind on one of the hard problems in an A. & S. textbook. The truth was that Robert had had a liberal arts education and was in the advertising department of A. & S., and he could not have solved a problem in high school physics, although he had passed physics with a little to spare. Nevertheless people gave Robert credit for concentrative powers. He remembered every card that had been played during a hand of bridge, and his post-mortems were exhaustive. He was very good at reciting the complete casts of old movies. No one challenged his memory for baseball statistics. "I wouldn't take your money," he would say when someone offered to bet him on who had the record for the most putouts

in World Series play. Such demonstrations of a head for figures and
a powerful memory were of course supported by the concentrative
look, and there was hardly any doubt that Robert deserved the
routine promotions that were given him in the A. & S. organization. "Fellow's smart as a whip," they said. *"His* name didn't
have to be Ammond," the only possible inference being that Robert's younger brother George was in the organization only because his grandfather was its founder. George was in the production department, with the title of vice-president, but the work was
done by a plant superintendent and a couple of foremen. George
was a good-time Charley who was always put in charge of the
A. & S. exhibits at the engineering conventions and acted as host
in the A. & S. suite down the hall. He had early symptoms of
emphysema at the age of thirty, but he could stay up all night with
the best of them. His untimely death at age thirty-eight left Robert
the only direct descendant of the founder still in the organization,
and while ownership and control of the company had passed on
to the vast Wycherly Enterprises, Robert apparently was set for life,
at $30,000 per annum and bonuses. Wycherly Enterprises did not
sign that kind of contract, but Robert Ammond and his friends
were far from worried. Robert, as well as his friends, took the position that a contract carried with it certain disadvantages for a man
who could reasonably count on twenty good years ahead of him.
The electrical and mechanical field was wide open, and family
pride would not tie him down if for instance a Wycherly competitor should decide to organize a new publishing house. The
Ammond name was one of the oldest in the trade, and Robert had
no contractual obligations to prevent his going on the board of a
brand-new outfit.

To that extent Robert Ammond did begin to concentrate. That
is to say, he began to give a great deal of thought to the possibility
of a new publishing firm. Wycherly (which was headed by a man
named Dennis Brady, from Chicago) had put all its own men in
the top jobs at A. & S., which was to be expected, but at the end of
two years Robert Ammond had not been put on the new A. & S.
board, which was definitely not expected. During those two years
Robert had been bereft—temporarily, he believed—of his vice-

presidential title and he had been functioning with the title of advertising manager. He continued to use—and to use up, as he put it—his old stationery, which proclaimed him "Vice-President in Charge of Advertising," but only in personal correspondence with friends in the advertising business and in such trivial communications as letters to his alumni weekly. He had about a thousand sheets of the old stationery still to be used up when he was visited one afternoon by a fellow called Spencer, who was known as Mr. Brady's troubleshooter.

Spencer did not customarily make appointments, nor did he for his visit to Robert Ammond. He opened the door of Robert's private office—unannounced by Miss Hathaway—and poked his head in and said, "May I come in?" He was wearing his perpetual grin.

"Why, hello, Spencer. Yes, come right in," said Robert.

"Thank you," said Spencer. He sat down without shaking hands or taking any other notice of the fact that this was his first visit to Robert's office. "Minor matter, and not important enough to put in an inter-office memo. But Mr. Brady is a stickler for form in some things."

"Oh, really?"

"Yes. In as big an organization as Wycherly, the uh, the uh, precise position of one man vis-à-vis the other members of the organization has to be stated and maintained. Do you know how it works in the federal government, for instance?"

"You mean where they give a man a classification number, and that determines whether he rates a Chevy or a Buick?"

"Exactly. Who gets pictures on the wall, who gets a leather easy chair and so on. I see you're familiar with that. Good. That makes it easier for me, and *you* won't misunderstand."

"Let's have it, if it's something I've done."

Spencer took a deep breath, and put his fingertips together. "I only want to call your attention to the fact that since the reorganization, you have not yet been made a vice-president. I stress that *not yet*, thereby not ruling out the possibility that you'll get your old title back. However, for the present, Ammond, you're not actually a vice-president in the Wycherly organization."

"No one knows that better than I do, Spencer."

"I'm sure of it. And yet I have here in my pocket, let's see, here it is. This is from the Princeton Alumni magazine. It seems to be a letter you wrote, fairly recently, and it gives your title as Vice-President in Charge of Advertising."

Ammond laughed. "I can explain that easily enough."

"Before you do, I also have a Xerox copy of a letter you wrote to a man in one of the big advertising agencies. It's a personal letter, nothing about Wycherly Enterprises or Ammond & Stepworth. Nevertheless, it was written on old stationery that has your name and your old title."

"A small economy on my part. I never use that letterhead in business correspondence."

"I know you don't. Before coming in here I took a sampling of your recent files."

"Boy, you are thorough."

"You bet I am. That's my job." For just a brief moment the perpetual smile all but vanished. "This may seem picayune to you, Ammond, but what's actually happened here is not so damned lintpicking at all. By that I mean, the Wycherly organization is very, very big, as you well know. And getting bigger all the time. And unless we have well-defined policies concerning certain things, we're going to have inefficiency and confusion. You don't know it, but you have an opposite number in a smelting operation we own in Montana. Personnel might decide to have you and him switch jobs. We do that all the time, and it often works out very well. Not always, but by the time we're ready to move, we've studied the various factors pretty carefully."

"I hope you're not going to ask me to transfer to Montana, because I might have a little to say about that."

"The point is, if the Montana man came here and discovered that he was being swapped for a Wycherly vice-president, he might get off to a very bad start. Do you see why this isn't lintpicking? The Montana man would want a promotion to vice-president before we were ready to give it to him."

"Uh-huh. And the vice-president wouldn't want to be downgraded," said Ammond.

"Well, in actual practice we don't do much of that. We buy up the rest of a man's contract, if he has one, or we turn him loose. A downgraded man is a sorehead, and he's no good to anybody, least of all himself. If a man is to be downgraded, that is, if a man reaches a stage where we have to lift him out of his job, we want to be as fair as we can. We'd much rather fire a man than demote him. He can put himself in the executive market and maybe even better himself. Some men, of course we may come across a special situation where a man ought to take a long leave of absence. We have a talk with him. Personnel. Psychiatrist. Medical man. Marriage counselor. We may talk to his wife. We're not all that inhuman, you know. We have fifteen men right now, men in grades above the one you're in, who are on temporary leave of absence, trying to straighten out one problem or another. And of course we're always helping men to place themselves with other organizations. And always on the lookout for good men who want to leave other organizations. We steal, just like the rest of them. Well, I have to be in Chicago in two hours from now. Glad to've had the chance to talk to you."

"I'll see that those letterheads are destroyed."

"I wish all my chores were as easy as this one. Tonight I'm having dinner with four United States senators."

"In Chicago?"

"No, no. In Washington. I'll only be with Mr. Brady a half an hour."

"I feel strangely honored to take up so much of your time. Four U.S. senators. I'd like to meet Mr. Brady sometime."

"So would the senators, face to face across the table in the Caucus Room. My chore is to try to persuade them that that would serve no useful purpose, and I'm licked before I start, especially in a presidential year. They want Mr. Brady, and they're going to get Mr. Brady, and he'll be completely cooperative. But I have to make it a little hard for them. Not telling you any secrets. It'll be in all the papers the day after tomorrow."

"Are you thinking of firing me, Mr. Spencer?" said Robert.

"The only man not facing that possibility is Mr. Brady himself. How's that for an equivocal answer? So long, Ammond."

One of the most difficult tasks Robert ever had was to give Miss Hathaway the order to destroy the remaining stock of old letterheads, and she was sympathetic. She was always on his side, always saw his side of every question, and she had become indispensable. If she had been just a little less plain, perhaps just a little less devoted to her mother, she could have been, might have been, more to him than merely his secretary. For things at home were going through one of those periods of strain that can develop in any marriage. Yolanda Ammond, with both children away at boarding-school, had more time on her hands, but she could not find the time to do things she wanted to do because she was not sure what she wanted to do. She had become, for example, a lingerer: she was the last to leave ladies' luncheons because she had no place else to go. She engaged in long conversations with the people in the markets and in the shops, and she despised them because they were always having to excuse themselves to go wait on another customer. Yolanda was a retired pretty girl. Twenty years earlier she had been the prettiest girl in all The Oranges, or anyway a strong contender for the title. She had retained much of her girlhood prettiness, but no one retains it all, and in some cases, like Yolanda's, the prettiness of girlhood is anomalous in a woman of forty. A hostile acquaintance described Yolanda as an overgrown midget, which some women in their circle of friends took as an oblique reference to Yolanda's intellect. She was *not* a brain, and some of Robert's admirers thought it unfair to make any comparison between her mind and his. The extremely fair among their friends, who were aware of the imperfect state of relations between Yolanda and Robert, said it was a pity that Yolanda had no resources to fall back on, but Robert had always been so far ahead of her mentally that he had never taken the trouble or had the patience to develop that side of her, such as it was. You had only to look at the two of them together—Yolanda with her empty, pretty face, and Robert deep in thought—to see that this marriage had been headed for trouble from the start. Yolanda was no good at bridge, just as bad at canasta, and a pigeon at gin rummy. It took her three months to read *Peyton Place,* and after all that work she confessed her disappointment in it. She said she did not know whether it was well written or not, but the stuff in it was no worse than some of the things she knew about friends of hers, if they wanted to be truthful about it.

Sympathy was not entirely on Robert's side. Not only was it felt that he could have tried a little harder to interest Yolanda in the things of the mind, but he had not always been fully appreciative of the job she did in running the household and bringing up the children. Robert took an awful lot for granted, and he did not seem to realize what a lot of work went into having a neat, attractive home and kids who were a credit to their parents. A man like Robert Ammond, prominent in the publishing business, thinking up new ideas and dealing with those scientists, could probably be darn hard to live with. And one thing you had to say for Yolanda: although she was still pretty and had a nice figure, she did not play around. Two cocktails was her limit, and if any of the boys got the least bit out of line, Yolanda knew how to put a stop to it, and did so. Robert, on the other hand, was not *all* intellectual. Edna Watlinger had accidentally opened the coat closet one night at a party at Peggy Stuart's and found Peggy and Robert in a very compromising position, to say the least. And there were other little stories here and there that would not have amounted to much if they had been about anyone else, but they certainly proved that Robert Ammond was not perfect. Not that Robert had ever gotten involved in a big thing with any other girl, but he certainly was not perfect.

Other marriages had weathered worse storms than this, and as far as their friends knew, the Ammonds' difficulties had not reached any crisis. Nothing that could be called dramatic. It was what might be called a familiar American situation, in which the wife found herself with not enough to do, and the husband was so intent on business that he did not find the time to rectify matters before they got worse. This belief, this diagnosis, as it were, was so strongly held by the Ammonds' friends that no one could believe the real news about Robert. But it was true. Robert Ammond, surely one of the brightest men around, had been fired.

As it happened, Stan Musgrove was the only man among the Ammonds' friends who was in a position to get close to the story.

Stan was in Research at an advertising agency, and he had never had any direct business contact with Robert Ammond. But when a thing like this happened to a friend of yours, you wanted to know more about it. Robert would only say that he had been fired and ask to change the subject, but it was plain to see that that mind was turning the subject over and over, and his friends were sure he would come up with something pretty good. Meanwhile, however, his friends had to have *some* information, and Stan inquired around until a perfectly credible story had been pieced together. It was incredible, but Stan insisted that his best contacts would vouch for its authenticity.

According to Stan's version, Robert had had some unimportant tangle with Dennis Brady's chief troubleshooter, a man named Spencer. It started over nothing, as those things will. The Wycherly crowd had asked Robert to do some kind of survey of some mining properties that Wycherly owned in Colorado. It was not to be a scientific, or engineering survey, but a study of executive personnel. Robert protested that it was not his kind of work, but Spencer tried to persuade him that that was the way they often did things in the Wycherly organization. The outsider with the fresh point of view. But when Spencer mentioned that Robert would probably have to spend two or three months in Colorado, Robert turned down the whole thing, flat. Spencer was quite disappointed, because he had to go back to Dennis Brady and report failure. Robert, being no fool, perceived that this could mean a loss of face for Spencer, and that Spencer, who was a sort of high-powered errand boy, would bide his time and at the right moment, no matter how long it might take, would give Dennis Brady a bad report on Robert. Any man with a responsible job is bound to make some mistakes. John J. McGraw never fined a ballplayer for a fielding error; McGraw's theory was that the man was in there trying, and it was the same way in business. You did occasionally come up with a real blooper.

Well, according to Stan Musgrove, Robert had the thing all figured out, as he would with that analytical mind of his, and so he quietly and carefully and methodically went about the business of interesting various individuals in an idea he had. The idea was simply to start a new publishing house, just as his grandfather had done. He lined up some pretty good men, men who were not too old to be set in their ways and not so young that later, when they went to the money men, they would be turned down for their youth and lack of experience. Bolger Brothers, who had about the same kind of setup as Wycherly Enterprises, were a natural for the financing of the new publishing firm, and one of the fellows Robert had lined up had a very good in at Bolgers'. Some family connection. But the fellow must have spoken too soon, and certainly without Robert's authorization, because the leak could almost positively be traced to Bolger Brothers. And that cooked it.

Apparently Spencer flew to New York one morning in time to be sitting in Robert's private office when Robert arrived for work. Robert's secretary tipped off Robert that Spencer was waiting for him. Her name was Hawthorne. Miss Hawthorne. Had been with Robert for fifteen years, and she was one of those really loyal secretaries that every executive dreams about. In any case, Robert went in and found Spencer sitting at his desk and actually reading his mail. The argument started right away, and it could be easily overheard. They made no effort to keep their voices down.

"What the hell do you think you're doing?" Robert said.

"I'm reading the company mail," said Spencer. "What's it to you?"

"It's this to me, if you don't get the hell out of here, I'll resign."

"You have resigned," said Spencer. "All you have to do is put your signature at the bottom of this letter." And Spencer handed him a letter of resignation, all written out, with all the details about its being his understanding that the resignation was to take effect as of above date, that same day, and that he agreed to accept one year's salary as final payment and in return for his discontinuing his efforts to organize a publishing company in direct competition with the firm of Ammond & Stepworth.

"I won't sign this," said Robert. "That's more like a confession than a resignation."

"Then you'll take what you get, which is the absolute minimum," said Spencer. "You're fired, as of nine-thirty-five this date.

The inkstand belongs to you, and those family photographs. The rest is ours, so beat it."

And that was Stan Musgrove's version, not necessarily accurate in every small detail, but all from pretty reliable sources. Miss Hawthorne, Robert's secretary, stayed on at Ammond & Stepworth because she had this mother she supported, and anyway Robert would not need a secretary until he made up his mind about what he wants to do next. Yolanda has been taking a course in typing, and at least that gives her something to occupy her time. Their friends say they are not really so terribly badly off, except for Robert and his migraine headaches. He ought to take it easy for a while.

CAN I STAY HERE?

The famous actress went to the window and gazed down at the snow-covered Park. The morning radio had said there would be snow, and there it was, an inch of it settled on trees and ground, and making her warm apartment so comfortable and secure. She would not have to go out all day. John Blackwell's twenty-one-year-old daughter was coming for lunch, and would probably stay an hour and a half; then there would be nothing to do until Alfredo Pastorelli's cocktail party, and the weather had provided an excuse for ducking that. As for dinner at Maude Long's, any minute now there would be a telephone call from Maude. Any minute—and this was the minute.

"Mrs. Long on the phone, ma'am," said the maid.

"I'll take it in here, Irene."

"Yes ma'am," said the maid.

"Hello, Maudie. I'll bet I know what you're calling about."

"Oh, Terry, have you taken a look outside? I just don't think it's fair to ask George and Marian to go out in weather like this. I could send my car for them, but that'd mean O'Brien wouldn't get home till after midnight. And he's been so good lately."

"So you've called off the party. Don't fret about it, Maudie," said Theresa Livingston.

"You sure you don't mind? I mean, if you'd like to come to me for dinner, just the two of us. We could play canasta. Or gin."

"Maudie, wouldn't you just rather have a nice warm bath and dinner on a tray? That's what I plan to do, unless you're dying for company."

"Well, if you're sure you don't mind," said Maude Long.

"Not one single bit. This is the kind of day that makes me appreciate a nice warm apartment. Oh, the times I'd wake up on days like this and wish I could stay indoors. But would have to get up and play a matinee at the Nixon. That's in Pittsburgh, or was."

"Yes, it's nice to just putter, isn't it?" said Maude Long. "What are you going to wear?"

"Today?"

"Yes. I always like to know what you're wearing. What do *you* wear when you're just staying home doing nothing?"

"Well, today I'll be wearing my black net. That sounds dressy, but I'm having a guest for lunch. A young girl that I've never met, but her father was an old beau of mine and she's coming to see me."

"That could be amusing. Could be a bore, too."

"I can get rid of her, and don't think I won't if she turns out to be a bore."

"Trust you, Terry. Well, let's one of us call the other in a day or so, and I'm sorry about dinner."

Having committed herself to her black net, Terry Livingston reconsidered. In fairness to John Blackwell she could not give his daughter the impression that his actress girl friend had turned into a frump. Not that the black net was frumpish, but it *was* black net, and something brighter would be more considerate of John, and especially on a day like this. "I'm not going to keep this on, Irene. What have I got that's brighter?"

"Your blue silk knit, ma'am. With that you can start breaking in those blue pumps."

"I wonder what jewelry. This young lady that's coming for lunch, I've never seen her, but her father was one of my biggest admirers, back in the Spanish-American War days."

"Aw, now ma'am."

"Well, it wasn't World War Two, I can tell you," said Theresa Livingston. "And not too long after World War One."

"Try her with one good piece," said Irene. "I always like your diamond pin with the squiggly gold around it."

"With the blue silk knit, do you think?"

"If you wear it over to the one side, casual."

"All right. You've solved the problem. And I suppose I ought to start breaking in those pumps."

"They've been just sitting there ever since you bought them, and the old ones are pretty scuffed," said Irene. "Will you be offering her a cocktail, the young lady?"

"Oh, she's old enough for that. Yes. Let's put out some gin and vodka. They drink a lot of vodka, the young people."

"And I'll send down for a waiter at one o'clock."

"A little earlier. Have him here to take our order at one sharp."

"I won't promise he'll be here. That's their busiest time, but I'll try. In case you may want to get rid of her, what?"

"The usual signal," said Theresa Livingston. "At two-fifteen I'll ask you if you've seen my cigarette holder. You pretend to look for it. You find it and bring it in and remind me that I have to change for my appointment."

"Where is the appointment supposed to be?"

"Three o'clock, downtown in my lawyer's office."

"Just so I make sure," said Irene. "I made a botch of it the last time Mrs. Long was here."

"Oh, well, with Mrs. Long it didn't matter. I wonder if I ought to have some little present for Miss Blackwell. Her father was very generous to me. Some little spur-of-the-moment gift that I won't miss."

"You have any number of cigarette lighters that you don't hardly ever use."

"Have I got any silver ones? A gold one would be a little too much, but a silver one might be nice."

"You've one or two silver, and a couple in snakeskin."

"The snakeskin. Fill one of the snakeskins and put a flint in it if it needs it. I'll have it in my hand. A spontaneous gesture that I'm sure she'll appreciate, just before she's leaving. 'I want you to take this. A little memento of our first meeting.'"

"I'll pick out a nice one. Snakeskin or lizard, either one."

"And you'll see about the drinks? Tomato juice, in case she

asks for a Bloody Mary. Now what else? We'll have the table in the center of the room. I'll take the chair with my back to the light. At this hour of the day it doesn't make a great deal of difference, but she's young and she might as well get the glare. You listen to what I order and be sure the waiter puts my melon or whatever on that side of the table."

"Yes ma'am."

"When she gets here I'll be in my bedroom. They'll announce her from downstairs and I'll wait in my bedroom. You let her in. She'll naturally turn right, I imagine, and you tell her I'll be right with her. I don't like that picture of President Eisenhower where it is. Let's take it off the piano and put it more where she can see it. I don't suppose she'd recognize Moss Hart, so we'll leave that there. Dwight Wiman? No, she wouldn't know who he was. She might recognize Noel Coward's picture, so we won't disturb that. That's a wonderful picture of Gary Cooper and I. I must remember to have that enlarged. Gary. Dolores Del Rio. A writer, his name I forget. Fay Wray. That's Cedric Gibbons. He was married to Dolores Del Rio. Frances Goldwyn. Mrs. Samuel. Dear Bill Powell and Carole Lombard. There we all are, my first year in Hollywood. My second, actually, but I have no pictures of the first time. That was a Sunday luncheon party at Malibu. Look at Gary, isn't he darling? He wasn't a bit interested in me, actually. That was when he and the little Mexican girl, Lupe Velez, they were quite a thing at that time. You know, I haven't really looked at that picture in ages. Certainly dates me, doesn't it? And this one. Do you know who that is? I must have told you."

"I never remember his name."

"That's H. G. *Wells*. One of our *great* writers. Not one of ours in the American sense. But British. I think he was out there visiting Charley Chaplin or somebody. They all went to Hollywood sometime or other. Never mind. I made a lot of money in pictures, and people heard of me that never would have if I'd confined myself to the theater. Well, this isn't getting into my blue knit."

"You have over a half an hour," said the maid.

They went to the bedroom. Irene laid out the blue dress, and produced three cigarette lighters. "You don't want to give her the one with the watch in it," said Irene. "I took notice, the watch is from Cartier's."

"No, I'll take this little thing. I think it must be lizard. Quite gay, don't you think? And doesn't go at all badly with my dress. I haven't the faintest idea who gave me this one."

"Just so it wasn't the young lady's father."

"Oh, no. Not John Blackwell. Downstairs, in the safe, that's where I keep his presents. Or at least I've had most of them reset, but he never gave me any cigarette lighters. He's president of the United States Casualty and Indemnity Company, and his father was, before him. One of those firms that you don't hear much about, but I wish I had their money. Baltimore. Did you ever hear of a horse called One No Trump? A *famous* horse. I'm not sure he didn't win the Kentucky Derby. This girl's father owned him. I'll tell you another little secret to add to your collection. For when you write your memoirs. Mr. Blackwell, John, always wanted to name a horse after me, but of course he was married and I was too, at the time, and we were both being *very* discreet. I just wonder how much this girl today knows about me. Anyway, John knew he couldn't actually call a horse by my name, but he had a very promising filly that he thought would win the Kentucky Derby. Only one filly ever won the Derby, you know. A horse with the unfortunate name of Regret. So John wanted to name this filly after me, but instead of giving it my name, he gave it my initials. He called it Till Later. T.L. That was our secret. *One* of them, I might add. Oh, dear, I think of all the little lies we told to protect other people. Including this girl that's coming today. *There.* How do I look?"

"Let me just smooth the skirt down over the hips," said Irene.

"It has a tendency to crawl up. I wonder if I ought to put on another slip?"

"You'll be sitting down most of the time. It's not very noticeable. Here's your pin," said Irene.

"Right about here, do you think?"

"Yes. Maybe about an inch lower."

"Here?" said Theresa Livingston.

"Just right."

"There. Now we're ready for Miss Evelyn Blackwell."

"She ought to be here in another five minutes."

"I hope she's prompt."

"She will be, if she knows what's good for her," said Irene.

"Well, if she's anything like her father. He had the best manners of any man I ever knew." Theresa Livingston lit a cigarette, had a couple of looks at herself in the full-length triplicate mirrors. She was alone now; Irene was in the kitchen. Being alone was not bad. Ever since she had rated her own dressing-room—and that was a good many years—Theresa had always insisted upon being alone for the last five minutes before going on for a performance. It gave her time to compose herself, to gather her strength, to be sick if she had to be, to slosh her mouth out with a sip of champagne which she did not swallow, to get ready for the stage manager's summons, to go out there and kill the sons of bitches with her charm and beauty and talent. Perceptive of Irene to have realized that this was just such a time, if only for an audience of one young girl. Too perceptive. All that prattle had deceived Theresa herself without for one minute deceiving Irene. *115094*

She wanted to remain standing so as not to give the blue silk knit a chance to crawl up, but after ten minutes she was weary. The buzzer sounded, and Theresa heard Irene going to the hall door. It was the waiter with the menus. Loyally Irene was annoyed by the young girl's lateness. "Why don't you just order for the both of you?" said Irene. "Or do you want me to?"

"I'm not terribly hungry," said Theresa. "You order, Irene."

"Yes. Well, the eggs Florentine. Start with the melon. The eggs Florentine. You won't want a salad, so we won't give *her* one. And finish up with the lemon sherbet. Light, but enough. And you'll want your Sanka. Coffee for her. How does that sound to you?"

"Perfect. And it'll take a half an hour before it gets here. She certainly ought to be here by then."

"If she isn't, I'm not going to let her come up."

"Oh, well, traffic. She'll have *some* good reason."

"What's wrong with the telephone? She could of let us know," said Irene. "I'll give him the order and then *you're* gonna have a glass of champagne."

"All right," said Theresa.

"We'll give her till ha' past one on the dot," said Irene.

It was ten minutes short of one-thirty when the girl arrived. "She's here," said Irene. "But you'll have to judge for yourself the condition she's in."

"You mean she's tight?" said Theresa.

"She's something, I don't know what."

"What is she like? Is she attractive?"

"Well, you don't see much of the face. You know, the hair hides the most of it."

"What makes you think she's tight?"

" 'Hi,' she said. 'Hi. Is Miss Livingston at home? I'm expected. Expec-ted.' I said yes, she was expected. Didn't they call up from downstairs? 'Oh, that's right,' she said. 'Oh, there's Ike,' she said. 'Isn't he cute?' Ike. Cute."

"Oh, dear. Well, let's get it over with," said Theresa. "Tell her I'll be right out."

"I'll tell her you're on the long distance," said Irene.

"It might be a good idea to stay with her. Keep an eye on her so she doesn't start helping herself to the vodka. Is she that type?"

"I wouldn't put it past her," said Irene. "I wouldn't put anything past this one. And remember, you're supposed to be going downtown and see your lawyer."

"Yes, we won't need the cigarette holder bit."

Theresa Livingston allowed a few minutes to pass, then made her brisk entrance, and saw immediately that Irene had not exaggerated. The girl stood up and behind her lazy grin was all manner of trouble. Theresa Livingston gave her the society dowager bit. "How do you do, my dear. Have you told Irene what you'd like to drink?"

"She didn't ask me, but I'll have a vodka martini. I might as well stick with it."

"Irene, will you, please?" said Theresa Livingston. "Nothing for me. I've ordered lunch for both of us. Save time that way, you know. The food is good here, but the service can be a little slow."

"I know."

"Oh, you've stopped here?"

"No, we always stay at the Vanderbilt, but I was with some friends in the What-You-Call-It-Room, downstairs."

"I see," said Theresa.

"I guess I was a little late, but I got here as soon as I could."

"Well, let's not talk about that," said Theresa. "Why don't you sit there and I'll sit here. I was so pleased to hear from your father. I hadn't realized he had a daughter your age. Did you come out, and all the rest of those things?"

"Oh, two years ago. The whole bit."

"And from your father's note I gather you've given up school. Are you serious about wanting to be an actress?"

Irene served the cocktail, and the girl drank some of it. "I don't know. I guess I am. I want to do something, and as soon as I mentioned the theater, Daddy said he knew you. I guess if you were a friend of Daddy's you know how he operates. If I said I wanted to be in the Peace Corps he'd fix it with President Johnson, or at least try."

"Well, I don't know about that, but your father was a very good friend of mine when we were younger. Not that I've seen him in—oh, dear, before you were born."

"Oh, I know that. It's been Mrs. Castleton ever since I can remember."

"What's been Mrs. Castleton?"

"Daddy's girl friend."

"But your father and mother are still married, aren't they?"

"Of course. Mummy's not giving up all that loot, and why should she? Could I have another one of these? I'll get it, don't you bother."

"Well, yes. You may have to finish it at the table."

"Do you want to bet?" The girl took her glass to the portable bar. "First Mummy said they'd stay married till after I came out, although why that's important even in Baltimore. But then I came out, and nothing more was heard about a divorce. If Aunt Dorothy wanted him to get a divorce he'd get it, but being Dorothy Castleton is still a little bit better socially than being Dorothy Blackwell. And they're all old."

"Yes, we are."

"I didn't mean that personally, Miss Livingston."

"I don't know how else you could mean it, considering that I'm the same age as your father and mother. I don't know about Mrs. Castleton, of course."

"Same age. All in their late fifties or early sixties, I guess. Anyway, not exactly the *jeunesse dorée.*"

"No. Well, Baltimore doesn't seem to be very different from any place else, does it? And meanwhile, your father asked me to have a talk with you about the theater. Which I'm very glad to do. But *you. You* don't seem to have any burning, overwhelming desire to become an actress."

"I couldn't care less, frankly. It's Daddy that as soon as I mentioned the theater—"

"How did you happen to mention it, though?"

"How did I happen to mention it? Well, I guess I said I wanted to do *something,* but when it came down to what I could do, we exhausted all the possibilities except riding in horse shows and modeling."

"So naturally you thought of going on the stage."

"No, I didn't. That was Daddy's idea. This whole thing was his idea. I think he just wanted to name-drop that he knew you. I have no delusions about being an actress, for Christ's sake."

Irene went to the door to admit the waiter with the rolling table.

"You would have lost your bet," said the girl. "I won't have to finish my drink at the table."

"Well, then, it isn't a question of my using my influence to get you into the American Academy or anything like that," said Theresa. "I must say I'm relieved. I certainly wouldn't want to deprive a girl of a chance that really cared about the theater."

"Forget it. I'm sorry I wasted your time, but it wasn't all my fault. Daddy's a powerhouse, and when he gets an idea he keeps after you till you give in."

"Shall we sit down? Why don't you sit there, and I'll sit here," said Theresa.

They took their places at the table, but the girl obviously had no intention of touching her melon. "Would you rather have something else?" said Theresa. "Tomato juice, or something like that? We wouldn't have to send downstairs for it."

"No thanks."

"We're having eggs Benedict," said Theresa.

"Eggs Florentine, ma'am," said Irene.

"Don't worry about me," said the girl.

"Have you had any breakfast, other than a vodka martini?" said Theresa. "Why don't you have a cup of coffee?"

"Where's the bathroom?" said the girl.

"Will you show her the bathroom, Irene?"

"Yes, ma'am."

"Just tell me where it is, don't come with me," said the girl.

"Through that door, which leads to the bedroom. And the bathroom you can find," said Theresa.

"The eggs Florentine," said the girl. "Eggs anything." She left the room quickly.

"I hope she makes it," said Irene.

"Yes," said Theresa. "I think you'd better move this table out in the hall. Leave the coffee. I'll have some myself, now, and you might make some fresh, Irene."

"You're not gonna eat *any* lunch?"

"No."

"Nine dollars, right down the drain."

"I know, but I'm not hungry, so don't force me."

Theresa had two cups of coffee and several cigarettes. "I think I ought to go in and see how she is," she said.

"You want me to?" said Irene.

"No, I will," said Theresa.

She went to the bedroom, and the girl was lying on the bed, clad in her slip, staring at the ceiling. "Do you want anything, Evelyn?"

"Yes," said the girl.

"What?"

"Can I stay here a while?"

"Child, you can stay here as long as you like," said Theresa Livingston.

CLAYTON BUNTER

There was neither excitement nor rejoicing over the death of Clayton Bunter, and certainly no one carried out the threat, heard so many times over the years, to commit certain acts of desecration on his grave. It is possible that Clayton Bunter, by taking a long time dying, extended the potential drama of his passing until nothing was left of it, so that he was allowed to leave this world almost unobserved, just like any other sick old man. The quiet departure of a man who had been so roundly hated was curiously disrespectful to him, and he would not have liked it one bit. Several months after Clayton was laid to rest the newspapers published the information from the Orphans Court that appraisals had been concluded and that the total value of the estate was just under $800,-ooo. "The son of a bitch wasn't even a millionaire," was the rather weak comment in the barber shops and cigar stores, and so real was the citizens' disappointment in the size of the Bunter fortune that the comment became his epitaph. They hurried to forget him, and no one talks about him today.

And yet Clayton Bunter during the first quarter of the century was regarded, not unjustly, as something of a financial wizard, a shrewd guesser in real estate transactions and a clever trader in the stock market. Although he was not even the twentieth richest man in Gibbsville—he probably did not belong among the top thirty—he was more conspicuous than most of the rich men because of his eccentricities. To begin with, there was his mode of dress. Other rich men wore cheap suits and wore them threadbare, but Clayton, having paid twenty dollars for a suit, would never again subject it to the presser's iron. He understood as well as any man with an extensive wardrobe that sponging and pressing shortens the life of a garment. It was not true that Clayton refused to sit down because he did not want to wear out the seat of his pants. He had another reason for wanting to remain standing, a painful one, and he did not like to be kidded about it. In general, though, he was not disturbed by disrespectful or insulting remarks, whatever they might pertain to, or whoever made them. Only on Sunday and on Monday morning when he attended his bank directors' meeting, would he wear a collar; the rest of the week he went without collar and tie, and his flesh rolled over the neckband and all but hid his brass collar-button. During the warm weather he went without coat and vest, but he continued to wear long underwear. He would roll up his shirt sleeves and tuck in the neckband, and all day long he would stand under shopkeepers' awnings, fanning himself with his straw hat and soaking his underwear with his sweat. It did not pass unobserved that he always started the week with clean underwear that got progressively soiled by Saturday.

With the coming of cold weather Clayton would put away his straw hat and get out his fedora and his rubber overshoes. He wore rubbers not so much as a protection against the damp as an economical protection for the soles of his shoes. Except in severe cold he wore a fireman's rubber coat, one of several gifts from the man who handled his fire insurance.

Clayton was a fat man, whose dimensions were no larger than those of some men who were called stout; but no one ever called him stout. He was fat. He would have been fat if he had weighed twenty pounds less than his two hundred ten. He was on his feet most of the time; owing to the already mentioned ailment he was seldom at his desk for long periods. But it was also a part of his disposition to be moving about, to be where he could see people, watch them, talk and listen to them even though the things they sometimes said were insulting. "I don't consider it an insult when I can buy and sell a fellow, when all I have to do is get a dispossess and he'd be out in the street. Water off a duck's back," he would say. He was often insulted by men, particularly young men, who were ignorant of the fact that he was their landlord. He operated

behind numerous business names, all representing holdings of
Bunter & Company, some of them better known than others, and
some not identified with him at all. These latter were the nominal
owners of Clayton's slum tenements, among the worst in town.
Clayton's refusal to proclaim his possession of his filthy firetraps
was not out of a sense of shame, but merely precautionary. He did
not wish to be bothered with his tenants' complaints of leaky roofs
and falling plaster; even more he dreaded the wrath of tenants
whom he had had dispossessed. He did not like to part with the
fees he paid his collectors, but he knew, from having tried vainly,
that you can't get something for nothing in this life, and the collectors contributed to his peace of mind.

But it would be a mistake to think of Clayton as an unhappy
man. Miserable, perhaps; but not unhappy. He lived with his wife
and his older sister in a red brick marble-stoop house in a neighborhood of red brick marble-stooped houses that he owned and that
his wife and sister dominated. Laurie, his sister, and Florence, his
wife, were lifelong best friends, and as a team they kept 752 West
Market Street spotless, from attic to cellar, from windowpane to
stove lid. Their cleaning work was never done because women's
work is never done. On Sundays, when dust gathers just as much as
it does on other days, they put aside their mops and dustrags, but
they noticed things that they would have to get started on on
Wednesday, after the Monday washing and the Tuesday ironing.
They took turns with the cooking of supper, the big meal of the
household day, and they shared the preparation of Sunday dinner.
Clayton did not come home for the noon meal on weekdays, but
supper and Sunday dinner were planned to please him, and he in
turn pleased them by being a good eater. He would compliment
Laurie by eating two platefuls of her sauerkraut, pork, and knepp,
and still have room for two wedges of Florence's shoofly pie. (All
three Bunters were of English and Welsh extraction, but their church
was the German Lutheran and their kitchen was Pennsylvania
Dutch.) Sauerkraut was the Saturday night fixture on the Bunters'
menu, as firm as Clayton's full hour in the bathtub, when, contrary
to legend, Clayton would soak and scrub away the week's grime and
be ready to start the new week bright and early on Sunday morning

with a fresh union suit, put on his collar and tie, and accompany
his wife and sister to divine service.

The women would walk arm in arm, in step, and Clayton
would go along as a kind of outrider on foot. After church the
Bunters would walk home together at a somewhat more leisurely
pace, the women stopping now and then to exchange greetings with
parishioners of other denominations while Clayton stood aside like
other husbands and brothers and let the women do the talking. If,
as infrequently happened, the women's conversation threatened to
be overlong, Clayton would take out his watch and say, "The roast,"
and in simulated alarm the women would end the conversation
and the Bunters would proceed homeward. The Bunter women did
not need any reminder from Clayton; they knew precisely how long
a cut of beef or lamb ought to remain in the oven; but they liked to
linger (with *some* acquaintances) to give Clayton the opportunity
to be the dominant male, which in turn gave them the opportunity
to be the dominated females. It was a harmless fiction that deceived
absolutely no one. The Bunters never had any guests in their house,
but everyone knew that the sisters-in-law, although proud of Clayton's business head and pleased to make him comfortable, ran the
household at 752 without the slightest interference by Clayton.

It was, in fact, an ideally happy ménage, with no member of it
having cause for envy. Laurie had her consanguineous relationship
as her claim on Clayton, and Florence performed her wifely duties
according to Clayton's dwindling demands. Clayton was corre-
spondingly pleased that he was able to provide a home for his sister
while at the same time providing company for his wife. The basic
marital relationship gave Laurie no cause for jealousy since she
regarded Clayton's needs as a male weakness that was better ad-
ministered to by Florence than by some woman who would fill the
house with children. Florence, submitting to Clayton's spasmodic
urges, never gave Laurie reason to suspect her of taking advantage of her position. The topic was not discussed in detail,
but Laurie had been given to understand that Clayton himself
regarded his urges as a weakness, and Laurie was almost positive
that she could tell better from her brother's diffident manner than
from any indication by Florence when he had yielded to his desires.

Laurie admired Florence's dignified fortitude at such times, and was if anything a little embarrassed that it was her brother who had imposed on her friend. But these were no more than minor crises, having neither great nor lasting effect on the happiness of the ménage. Florence hardly seemed to notice them, and for Laurie it became less and less a problem to hide her gratitude from Florence. Her gratitude was a practical thing; she knew, as Florence did not, that Clayton was the owner of several houses that were of ill repute, and without Florence he might have been compelled to patronize the dreadful places. Laurie remembered only too well that their father taunted their mother with his boasts of visits to such houses. He had come very close to being found dead in one, and all her life, but especially in Clayton's young manhood, Laurie had been apprehensive for the first sign that Clayton would follow in their father's footsteps toward Railroad Avenue. But when she was seventeen or eighteen Laurie realized that she had an almost ready-made solution to that problem: Florence. Florence was in and out of the Bunter house every day, and Clayton, then about thirteen years of age, liked to be with his sister and her friend. He liked to be with them when they made fudge, he held up willing hands when they were winding balls of yarn, he would sit on the back porch and help them shell peas, he ran errands for them in rain and snow. He asked to sleep with them when Florence spent the night at their house, and Laurie remembered her father's boisterous consent, "Sure, let him! Do him good," and their mother's weary refusal. Boys her own age began to take an interest in Florence Cutshall, but they were discouraged by Florence's insistence on their finding a boy for Laurie, an impossible condition. Consequently Florence emerged from the bloom of her teens into the plainness of her early twenties without having formed any attachment that threatened Laurie's plan. When Clayton reached twenty-one, already stout and looking older than his years, and making money in real estate since his graduation from Gibbsville High, he asked Laurie if she thought Florence would marry him, and Laurie said yes, but to postpone his actual proposal until their father died. Laurie did not want Mr. Bunter to say some dreadful thing that Florence and the Cutshall family would not be able to forgive. Bunter died, obscenely delirious to the end, and his wife died a few days later from —Laurie believed—the effects of listening to the terrible things Bunter had said to her on his deathbed. The doctor said she died of a stroke.

Laurie had the house ready for Clayton and Florence on their return from Niagara Falls. In the busy first days of showing Florence where everything was and helping with the housework she put off making her speech about finding a room elsewhere, and the speech was never made. She became indispensable as unpaid houseworker and companion to her sister-in-law, and steadily and soon the friends, now relatives, had a pattern for their lives that was to endure for a quarter of a century—until the death of Clayton Bunter, who was only the third party to their arrangement. The sisters-in-law did not need any outside friends; they did not need Clayton except as the payer of bills; but he did not get in their way, and he was useful as the excuse for their devotion to their house and the pleasure they got out of their teamwork.

Except on Sunday morning they did not care how he looked or how he smelled. They wanted him nice for church, but he was a man, and on weekdays, taking care of his business affairs, he had a right to look as he pleased. As his fortune grew—they were aware that it was growing, without being told how much—they became more resistant to any change in themselves and in him.

"You two want to buy an auto*mo*bile?" he said one evening.

"An auto? What for?" said Laurie.

"You can't drive," said Florence.

"No, I can't, but if George Wizmer can learn, I sure can. I went for a ride with him today. He just bought a new Haynes. Electric lights. Doors in the front. Self-starter."

"How much was it?" said Laurie.

"Well, I guess it was around three thousand, but I don't know."

"We don't want an auto, do we, Florence?" said Laurie.

"What would we ever use it for?"

"To go on trips," said Clayton. "A lot of people buy cars and go visiting."

"Who would you ever want to visit, Florence?" said Laurie.

"Nobody that I know of," said Florence. "I have my aunt and uncle in Buffalo, New York, if it'd get that far."

"Supposed to be a very good car, one of the best. Rudy Schmidt says it compares with the Peerless. I don't know how the roads are between here and Buffalo, but it'll go that distance."

"Sounds to me like an awful lot of money," said Laurie.

"Don't worry about the money if you want one. If you two say we ought to buy a car, I'll put up the money. Otherwise, we can forget about the whole matter."

"Don't buy one on my account," said Florence.

"Do we have that much, that we can put that much money in an auto?"

"Was I ever the kind of a fellow that bought a Haynes car to drive to the poorhouse?" He laughed. "Yes, we could buy two and it wouldn't break us."

"Two cars, huh. Lantenengo Street," said Laurie.

"I was sorry when my father sold the horses, but I never wanted an auto," said Florence.

"Want me to buy you a team?" said Clayton. "Doc English is getting rid of his team of sorrels. He's in the market for an auto. Took a demonstration in the Haynes, George said."

"No thanks," said Florence.

"I'm afraid to death of horses," said Laurie. "But worse of autos."

"All right, then we won't say no more about it. Subject is closed. Meeting adjourned. Pass me the paper, Florence. See what's going on in the world." He took the paper, folded it several times down to one-column width and handed it back to Florence. "I take notice you didn't read the paper."

"Laurie, lend me your glasses," said Florence. She then read: "Clayton Bunter to bank board. Clayton Bunter, well known real estate man, of town, was elected to membership on the board of the Citizens Bank & Trust Co., South Main St., at the recent meeting. Mr. Bunter, who resides at 752 W. Market St., is a native of town. He was graduated from Gibbsville H. S., then entering the real estate business. He is married to the former Miss Florence Cutshall—*my name in the paper!*—daughter of Mr. and Mrs.

Percy D. Cutshall, also of town. Poppa will kill them for saying Percy. Mr. Bunter is a member of Trinity Lutheran Church. He is the son of the late Mr. and Mrs. Daniel C. Bunter, the former a well known carpenter and builder of town. I didn't know your father was a builder."

"Every carpenter is a builder, according to the *Standard*. They always have to fancy it up," said Clayton.

"Well. Bank director," said Florence.

"Do you get paid for that?" said Laurie.

"Get a two-and-a-half gold piece every meeting I go to."

"How often is that?" said Florence.

"Once a week. Monday."

"Ten dollars a month, a hundred and twenty a year," said Laurie. "I don't see why that's worth bragging about."

"All right, then I won't give you any of the gold pieces. I was going to give them half to Florence and half to you."

"Oh, come on, Clay-ton. I didn't mean anything by it," said Laurie.

"Then hereafter you'll know better."

"It's a big honor, Laurie," said Florence. "But I'll make him give you half of the gold pieces."

"I wouldn't take them if he didn't give them to me of his own free will," said Laurie.

But she did, and saved them, two dozen of them a year until she had an accumulation of more than two hundred gold pieces. Once a year she would take them out of their woollen sack and wash them with soap and water, dry them, and arrange them in stacks of ten. They were pretty little coins, and though she knew that sometimes there was a nickel premium on them at the banks, she never regarded them as money to spend. They were playthings. After she had the stacks lined up on her bedroom table, as a boy would do with lead soldiers, she would mow them down with a sweep of her hand and push them into a glittering pile, and lift handfuls of them and pour them back onto the pile. Although this was a game she played only about once a year, it always happened on nights when Clayton had said to Florence, "Let's turn in." It was well understood by all three that when Clayton said that to

Florence, Laurie was not to attempt to prolong the conversation. She was, in fact, being told to go to her room on the third floor and to stay off the second floor until morning.

There were, of course, many nights when she was given the signal to retire to her room, and she had other quiet pastimes to occupy her until she was ready to turn out the Welsbach and go to bed. She was not much for reading, and in any case she kept the Welsbach burning low so as not to waste gas. Crocheting was too fine to be done in that light, but knitting was all right; she could practically do that with her eyes closed. She could have darned Clayton's socks or patched his shirts, but Florence had assigned that chore to herself, and Laurie would not have liked to work on her brother's clothes at such times, when she was trying not to think of Clayton or of Florence. It was bad enough to be made to feel out of it without having a basketful of her brother's socks to remind her of him and Florence in that terribly still house. And so she would knit something for the church bazaars, or work on her rag rugs for the house, and some nights she would turn off the gas and sit at the window.

That was one of the best ways to get your mind off things. The Market Street trolley, going west or coming east, went by every fifteen minutes; the Collieryville trolley, to or from town, passed the house at half-hour intervals until the last one from Colliery-ville, which passed 752 West Market Street at a quarter to mid-night, headed for the carbarn. After nine o'clock the trolleys bound for the western end of town or for Collieryville would be half filled with young couples and a few married ones on their way home from the moving pictures. Later on Laurie would see the single young men, riding in the trolleys or walking to save a dime after their dates were over. From her window it was impossi-ble to get a very good look at the passengers, except those who were seated next to the window on the Collieryville trolleys. The Collieryville trolleys were twice as big as the Market Street trolleys, which were known as dinkies and were operated by one-man crews. The conductors and motormen were trying to organize a union to fight the one-man trolleys, but the Irish were afraid that the Pennsylvania Dutchmen would run the union, and the Pennsylvania Dutchmen were afraid that the Irish would get everybody fired from their jobs. Clayton said that the Company couldn't put an Irish motorman on the same car with a Dutch conductor or vicey versa. The conductor would get out to throw a switch, and the motorman would leave him a hundred yards behind and make him walk in the rain and snow. Such foolishness made the trolleys go off their schedules, but Clayton said that as long as the crews were fighting among themselves the Company didn't have to worry about any union. The Irish were the real troublemakers, but they were that way about everything, Clayton said. The only tenant who had ever actually hit Clayton was an Irishman he had dispossessed. Walked right up to him on Main Street and gave him a bloody nose. Clayton must have bled a lot, too, from the condition of his shirt and underwear and his handkerchief. A terrible thing to have happen to your own brother, in broad daylight and right on the main street of town. Ripper Hennessey, the man's name was. He got thirty days in jail for it. People were always picking on Clayton, because he was that much smarter than they were. His own father had picked on him, but which one was the director of a bank, and which one could talk about buying two Haynes automobiles? Sometimes even Florence didn't seem to fully appreciate Clayton, but Laurie would never say anything in criticism of Florence. Never. Florence was the best thing that ever happened to Clayton, and even if she didn't seem to fully appreciate Clayton, she never complained. Some women complained about their husbands when it came to certain things, but not Florence. When Clayton said, "Let's turn in," Florence would get up and have a last look at the kitchen range and see if the back door was locked and say goodnight to Laurie and then go upstairs and wait for Clayton, and you would not know from anything she said or did, not even from the expression on her face, that there was anything different about that particular night from any other night. If you knew what kind of a woman Florence really was, you'd know that she was keeping up her end of the bargain without so much as one word of complaint. And in the morning she would have the coffee on at seven o'clock and everything just the same as every other morning. It was Laurie who was inclined to be a little grouchy on those mornings, and the last thing in the world she would blame it on was not having slept very well.

THE CLEAR TRACK

Mr. Loxley hung his dinner jacket on the valet stand, undid his tie, took off his shirt and began to remove the studs and links. His wife, already in her bed, was lying with her head propped up, partly by her hand, partly by pillows. "I'm not a bit tired, and I thought I would be," said Nan Loxley.

"Then get dressed again and we'll go to El Morocco," said Joe Loxley.

"Are you out of your mind? El Morocco?" she said.

"Are *you* out of *your* mind? I was kidding. Nothing could make me leave this house."

"But it wasn't a bad party," said Nan. "I can't get over how well Amy looks. The operation slowed her down and made her take it easy. Which she wouldn't have done otherwise."

"Yes, but she's building up a full head of steam."

"Well, more power to her. Think of what it must be like to go on living with George Brown."

"We don't know anything about that. Personally, I don't imagine living with Amy would be any great treat." He tossed his shirt in the laundry hamper.

"Probably not, but she saved that marriage."

"I suppose she did. But then George was there to help her through the operation."

"Yes. But when it comes his turn, she'll be there, too. He looks seventy."

"Oh, the hell he does."

"He looks sixty-five," she said.

"Well, he damn near is. Three classes ahead of me," he said. "But he doesn't look seventy."

"I hope all our friends stay married, the rest of their lives. There isn't anything worth getting a divorce over, at our time of life."

"Unless two people hate each other," he said.

"No, not even that. Two years ago George and Amy hated each other. George and his damn little movie actress."

"And Amy," he said.

"And Amy, with her ambassador. But she was the one that made sense, and now I think they'll stick it out together. I hope so. They were very nice to each other tonight."

"You didn't expect them to be at each other's throats, did you?"

"No, but a couple of times I thought I detected real tenderness. They look after each other now, and they never used to."

"Don't count on it," he said. "You were in the other room, so you didn't see what I saw."

"What?"

"Amy and that guy Harrington."

"You have a blind spot where he's concerned. I don't think we ought to have him any more. He always rubs you the wrong way, and I don't understand why."

"He sure does."

"He didn't use to. You used to say how much you admired him."

"Not any more," he said. "Are you through in the bathroom?"

"Yes," she said.

When he came out of the bathroom she was lying in the same position. "You'll get a crick in your neck," he said.

"I was thinking," she said. She turned off the light above her bed. "Goodnight."

"Goodnight," he said. "I'll only read for a few minutes."

"That's all right," she said.

He opened a copy of a business magazine. "There's an article in here that mentions Harrington. Somebody told me about it tonight." He read in silence, then tossed the magazine into a chair and turned out his light.

"What did it say?" she said.

"Oh, you still awake? It didn't say very much about Harrington. Just mentioned him among a list of others. Pretty fast company for him to be in, but I suppose he belongs there. A bunch of Americans that are trying to do something about Canada."

"To do what about Canada?"

"Oh—to try to straighten things out between them and us."

"We having trouble with *them,* too? I thought they were our friends," she said.

"That's just what they don't like. Americans taking them for granted."

"Well, Ben Harrington doesn't seem to be worried about it. At least he never mentioned it this evening," she said.

"Oh, it isn't a crisis. It's a long, drawn-out affair. Been going on since the war."

"I remember when Ben used to go skiing up there. Tremblant. Fishing, too. And in fact I think he has relatives in Canada. Maybe that's why they picked him."

"They must have had some reason. I can't stand the fellow."

"Why not? What did he ever do to you?"

"Nothing. On the contrary, he's always so damn polite. Complimentary. Always dropping me little notes. Not lately, though. I stopped answering his notes, and I guess he finally got the hint."

"Bad manners are a pretty strong hint. I'm surprised he came tonight."

"He wants something," said Loxley.

"So must you, or you wouldn't have let me ask him."

"Me? What can he do for me? What has he got that I want?" said Loxley.

"I don't know. Maybe I could find out what he wants from you," she said.

"Oh, go to hell."

"*You* go to hell," she said.

He wanted to be gone before she sent for her breakfast, but she was awake before he was. "You're up early," he said.

"I have to be. I have some ladies coming for breakfast."

"Ladies coming for breakfast?"

"At ten o'clock. A committee meeting, and it was the only time we could all agree on. Will you have some of my coffee?"

"Is there anything in it—like arsenic?"

"I'd have put some in last night, willingly," she said.

"And as Churchill said to Lady Astor, I'd have drunk it." He poured coffee in her cup and drank it. "I take it you're putting off your breakfast till your ladies arrive?"

"Yes."

"Well, don't forget to have some," he said. "You don't eat enough. Let yourself get fat. After all, who cares?"

"I do."

"I don't mean that you have to get like Sophie Tucker. But you could eat a lot more, and you should. You could put on ten more pounds and it wouldn't do you a bit of harm."

"That isn't the same as getting fat," she said.

"I'm going to take off about ten pounds, then I'll be just about right."

"Yes, you can afford to lose ten pounds," she said.

He slapped his belly. "I'm going to cut out thick soups and dessert. That way I can lose ten pounds in a month."

"That's two and a half pounds a week. I don't think it will be that easy," she said. "It's much easier to put on ten pounds than it is to lose it."

"In other words, we should both stay just the way we are?" he said.

"I didn't say that," she said. "No, you *should* lose ten or even fifteen pounds if you can do it slowly. I'll see that you're not tempted with thick soups and desserts, but that doesn't mean you're going to lose ten pounds in a month. After all, you're never home for lunch, and we go out a lot. We have dinner at home—what? Average twice a week. Next week we're out for dinner every night except Monday."

"We are? I hadn't realized that," he said.

"Well, *you* are. You have two dinners that I'm not going to."

"I know that. But what are the others?"

"Except for one, they're invitations we accepted long ago. The one exception is I told Ben Harrington we'd go to his dinner a week from Friday."

"I wish—"

"I know what you're going to say. You wish I wouldn't accept that kind of invitation without consulting you. But I did accept it, and I hope you're not going to ask me to get you out of it."

"But that's what I *am* going to ask you. You have an easy out. Tell him you forgot we were going away that weekend."

"He knows we're *not* going away that weekend. His dinner is before Amy's dance, and he knows we're going to that. You wouldn't let me go to Amy's dinner, and I mentioned to Ben that we weren't going. So he invited us to his dinner and I accepted."

"I'd much rather have gone to Amy's dinner than to any dinner Ben Harrington's giving. Haven't I made it clear that I don't like the son of a bitch?"

"You made it clear enough last night, but by that time I'd already accepted," she said.

"Well, get me out of it," he said.

"No."

"Of course you will," he said. "Do it politely, if you like, but I'm not going. I'm just not going to his house, and you can count me out right now."

"But I'd like to go. I've never seen his new house, and I want to see what he's done with it."

"You mean what some decorator's done with it," he said.

"All right, what some decorator's done with it. Stanley Kurtz, as a matter of fact. I almost got Kurtz to do this house three years ago, and I hear he's done a wonderful job with Ben's. If we like it, we might consider him for Montego Bay."

"*I* won't consider him for Montego Bay. I can't imagine liking the same things that Ben Harrington likes. However, that's not the point right now. The point now is that you got us into the Harrington dinner, and you can get us out of it. I—am not going. If you're so dying to see the house, you can go without me."

"And meet you at Amy's dance? You want to be that pointedly rude?"

"I didn't get us into this."

"All right," she said.

"All right what?"

"I'll meet you at Amy's dance," she said.

"And go to Ben Harrington's without me?"

"Yes."

"Why don't you make a really big evening of it? I'll stay away from the dance, too."

"If that's what you want to do, all right," she said.

"How to start the day wrong," he said.

"Yes. And it's settled then, that I'm to get you out of Ben's dinner party."

"I was never really in it," he said. "I would like to know one thing. I know you never mentioned Ben Harrington as an old beau of yours, but was he, ever? Briefly?"

"Never. Not even briefly."

"Is that the trouble? That he wasn't and you wish he had been?"

"He was never *that* hard to get," she said. "Don't be any more unbearable than you have to be, Joe."

"Big word, unbearable," he said.

They carried on the numerous small transactions that are the formalities of a marriage during trying times, and though they avoided the topic of the coming Harrington dinner, it could not remain avoidable forever. On the morning of the dinner Joe Loxley said to his wife, "I'm leaving right after lunch. Henry Pope and I are playing golf this afternoon, and I'm spending the night at his house."

"Will you be back tomorrow?"

"Late tomorrow afternoon, unless I call you," he said. "Arnold Palmer's playing in an exhibition somewhere in the neighborhood, and we may go see him. That's Sunday."

"In that case you'd stay at Henry's both nights?" she said. "And maybe even Sunday night."

"Yes."

"Did you forget that we were going to the Carters' tomorrow night?"

"I did. I forgot all about it," he said.

"I told you last week that we were busy every night this week," she said. "That means I'll have to get you out of the Carters' too. It's their anniversary, and they're *your* friends. Weren't you an usher at their wedding?"

"I was. And Dan was an usher for me when I married Louise."

"Well, are you still going to spend tomorrow night at Henry's?" she said.

He hesitated, then said, "Yes."

"It's their fortieth anniversary."

"I know that," he said.

"And you're going to pass up their party so that you can watch Arnold Palmer play golf. I'm not going to tell them *that*."

"Listen, I went to their first anniversary party. Their fifth. Their tenth. Their twentieth. Their twenty-fifth. Their thirtieth. And some in between."

"They're not going to have any more till their fiftieth," she said. "You grew up with Dan Carter. Your oldest friend. I don't see how you can do this to him, but apparently you can. I think it's disgusting."

"Say what you mean. You think *I'm* disgusting."

"Very well, I think you're disgusting. All because of a fit of pique over Ben Harrington's dinner party. I don't mind so much your ruining my evening, tonight. But if you do this to Dan Carter —I really don't know what I'll do."

"Why are you making such a big thing about the Carters?"

"I'll tell you why," she said. "Because when you were separated from Louise, and I was still married to Harry, who were the only people we could trust? They didn't do that for me. They did it for you. But I seem to be the one that remembers it, the times we used their house."

"When it comes to favors, believe me I don't owe Dan Carter a thing. Not a thing. Favors that you never heard about, and you can be damned sure Elsie Carter never heard about."

"I see. You keep a score of favors. Bookkeeping. And Dan

Carter has run out of credit. Maybe I ought to do that, keep books on small favors, given and received. I wonder what our score would be."

"I'd be heavily in your debt, no doubt about it."

"That's nice to know, because I may start drawing on my debits, or credits, whichever it is. However, that doesn't help Dan Carter now."

"I have no doubt he'll survive."

"Till his fiftieth anniversary?" she said.

"Look, Nan, don't keep trying to make me a heavy. I'm not a heavy. Most of the time I'm a pretty nice guy, and you know it. But lately everything I do gets twisted, turned around, till I find myself on the defensive about everything. And I don't think it started with that night we had Ben Harrington to dinner. It goes back farther than that."

"Maybe it does. Maybe it goes back thirty years."

"That's possible. You were married before, and so was I. Maybe we should have stayed married to the other people. You said to me a couple of weeks ago, something to the effect that at our time of life people ought to stay married. Maybe everybody ought to stay married, no matter how bad it is."

"With some exceptions."

"With no exceptions," he said.

"Oh, come on. You know plenty of cases where there would have been actual murder if there hadn't been a divorce."

"No I don't, and neither do you. We say we do, we think we do, but the only actual murder we know about, the two people were supposed to be very much in love."

"That is utter nonsense. When young people make a mistake, they ought to rectify it as soon as they can and get started again. You made a mistake, and so did I."

"And look at us now. Be truthful," he said. "The way we feel about each other now, I ought to walk out of here and never come back. There isn't an ounce of love in this room. I wonder how long it's been that way. What keeps us together?"

"Love and patience. I don't like you very much, but I don't love anyone else but you. And you take me for granted. I'm useful to you. I make you comfortable. I run your house for you and I like being good at it. And I don't believe in divorce for people our age."

"I'm beginning to not believe in it at all, for people any age, for any excuse at all."

"You wish you were still married to Louise? I'm glad I'm not still married to Harry."

"I think—and you don't have to take this personally, although you probably will. But I think I should have stayed married to Louise, and you should have stayed married to Harry."

"They had something to say about that, don't forget. After Harry found out about you he never came near me again."

"I know, and you got a divorce. But if you couldn't have got a divorce, if we were living in some Catholic country, you would have made the best of it, and so would I."

"Do you know who you sound just like?"

"Who?"

"Ben Harrington. Don't forget, he's a Catholic."

"Yes, and do you know what Catholics call people like him? They call them deathbed Catholics. Chases around all his life, mixed up in one nasty thing after another. Doesn't go to church, doesn't confess. But when they're dying they send for their priest. That's one of the *many* things I don't like about him. And how did he happen to be preaching to you? Have you discussed divorce with him?"

"Yes. Several times."

"Oh. Does he want to marry you?"

"No."

"Is he in love with you?"

"He was. I guess he still is. But he doesn't approve of divorce."

"Then you lied to me. He was a beau of yours."

"Not exactly, Joe. I told you about my beaux before we were married. Ben was later, much later."

"You mean now?"

"Oh, no. Back in the Forties. After the war. When you were still not sure you wanted to break it off with Amy. Every time I see Ray Bolger I think of you. What did you expect me to do? It wouldn't have been half as easy to take you back if I hadn't had one fling of my own. And it was with Ben."

"You and Ben Harrington," he said.

"Yes," she said.

"Where did you go? Where did you meet?"

"Why, at his apartment, of course."

"And how long did it last?" he said.

"Very soon after I heard about you and Amy. Almost right away, in fact. That was when it started. It ended when Amy went back to George. What else would you like to know?"

"I would like to know if it ever really ended," he said.

"Yes, it ended."

"Automatically, when you were convinced that Amy and I were quits?"

"Not quite automatically," she said. "He ended it. He sent me home, back to you."

"This noble man, that I hate more than ever but now at least I know why. Did he tell you that you were really in love with me, and that you were only using him?"

"That's exactly what he told me. And one thing more."

"What?"

"That he was in love with me, and always would be. And he does. He loves me."

"You ought to have a very interesting evening, going to his house for dinner tonight. Sore at me. Convinced that I'm a heavy."

"If you think a moment, you'll realize that you arranged the evening."

"So I did, didn't I? In fact, I arranged the whole weekend."

"You may have arranged more than that," she said. "Rearranged, is probably the better word."

"Well, you've made it impossible for me to change my mind about the Carters', you understand that, don't you? I have to give you a clear track."

"Yes, I suppose you do," she said. "You also give yourself a clear track. I know you only planned to watch Arnold Palmer, but you have this afternoon, tonight, all day tomorrow, and all day

Sunday free. I'm sure you'll run into someone you used to know. Or maybe someone new."

"It would have to be someone new," he said.

"Why would it? You seem to think I'm rushing back to Ben. But he's not someone new."

"Right," he said. "But I'm not likely to run into someone that's been in love with me for twenty years. There isn't any such person."

"Except me," she said.

"Well, if you say so," he said. "I think I'll drive in with Henry on Monday morning. If you want me for anything I'll be at his house or The Links."

"All right," she said. "Remember me to Henry."

"Yes, I will," he said. He turned and left the room.

THE GUN

Herbert Roff was a most unusual man to be the owner of a pistol —more accurately, a .32 caliber revolver. Upon his retirement at fifty-two or so, a decision made possible by a large legacy which he had counted on throughout most of his life, he bought a Dutch colonial house in Litchfield County and announced to his friends that the city would see him no more. No one was surprised. In the city he had lived alone, never remarrying after the death of his wife twenty years earlier. His apartment consisted of a livingroom, bedroom, bath, and kitchen on the ground floor of one of the last brownstones on Murray Hill. He lived well within his salary in the accounting department of a real estate firm. He had breakfast at a drug store on his way to work, he lunched every day at the Princeton Club. A woman came in to clean the apartment three times a week; he made his own bed every morning. He dined out a good deal, thanks to his proficiency at the game of contract bridge, from which he also profited to the extent of about a thousand undeclared dollars a year. He carefully rotated his three Brooks suits, never wearing a suit or a pair of shoes two days running, never in the evening wearing the suit he had worn to the office. Once in the autumn and once in the spring he would give a buffet supper to men and women with whom he played bridge, and it was always very nicely done, on a Sunday evening. On these occasions he would gather together some men and women who never saw each other except at his parties.

At the last of these parties he made his announcement. Just before the cherries Jubilee he rose and tapped on his wine glass.

"Dear friends, I have some news for you that I trust won't be too distressing," he said. He smiled at one and all to reassure them. "I don't think many of you know, although some do, that thanks to a rich uncle, *I* have just become a rich uncle. In other words, they've finally settled my uncle's estate, and I'm retiring from my job and from New York, and—this is the only sad part—from our meetings at the bridge table."

He waited out the murmurs, then continued. "I've bought a house in Connecticut, which all of you will see at various times, and I shall go there next week to live out the rest of my days as a gentleman of leisure."

"The county squire!" a man called out.

"Anything but," said Herbert. "Can anyone imagine me in that role? Shooting birds and hooking fishes?"

"Probably join the Fairfield Hunt," the man said.

"Now I know you're kidding, Charley. Anyway, it's not that part of Connecticut," said Herbert. "The house isn't on a main road, and in fact I've had little maps made so you'll be able to find it. It has a small pond that I *don't* intend to stock with trout."

"You'll go crazy up there after living in town so long," said Harry.

"On the contrary, I expect to regain my sanity. On a serious note, and because I know you all so well, I feel relaxed for the first time in many, many years. I've always known that Uncle Ben, my mother's brother, intended to leave me the money he would have left my mother. He told me so. But the dear old thing certainly did hang on, and I could never be positively sure that he wouldn't fall for some chippie and I'd be out in the cold. It's been known to happen. So I've had to go on being a wage slave at McLoughlin & McLoughlin—and *McLoughlin* and *McLoughlin* and *McLoughlin*. And if I have any sanity left, it's thanks to you dear friends. That's why you're getting champagne tonight, and I hope you'll all get *plastered* in it." He sat down, and someone started the applause and someone else started the little speeches.

During the first summer and autumn his friends came for weekends, to some extent out of curiosity, but in the succeeding years they came because the house was attractive and comfortable, and Herbert was a good host. At no time were all the bedrooms occupied, and a man and wife who were accustomed to separate rooms were not compelled to double up. The house was not yet fifty years old; electricity and modern plumbing had been laid on from the beginning. "Do you remember J. Brigham Stanley, the playwright? He had one hit after another, although I never saw a one of them. Anyway, he built the house, and his widow and children used to lease it to people they knew. The children only put it up for sale about the time I came into my money. The widow and children didn't want to live in the house because it was too gloomy. That I got, of course, after I bought it. The property is twenty acres, and as you see, most of it heavily wooded. They all wanted to be at the seashore. Anyway, it's perfect for me." Herbert's pleasure with the property and his new life was self-evident. He was even putting on a little weight. "I don't let the servants go to the mailbox. If they did I'd never get any exercise, after all those years of apartment to office to club to office to apartment. I've been thinking of taking up tennis. The court's in good condition. But I don't want to get that chummy with my neighbors. Besides, I'm not very popular with some of them. My land is posted, and I don't make any exceptions. Nobody hunts on my land, at least not with my permission, and as soon as I hear shots I call the game warden."

In answer to a question frequently asked during his first years he would say, *"Do?* What did I *ever* do? In New York I didn't really *do* anything. I was like an automaton. Do you realize that I only ever had two jobs in my life? When I got out of N.Y.U. my father got me a job in one real estate office, and I left there to take a job in another real estate office. The only difference was that one job paid more than the other. The work was the same, the people might as well have been the same. My wife died in childbirth when I was thirty-two years old, and I suppose that made me more of an automaton than ever." Few of his more recent, bridge-playing friends knew much about his wife; none of them had ever seen her; one or two were not aware that he had been married at all. It was remarkable how little they knew about Herbert that was not related to his pleasant company at the bridge table. He was a member of the Princeton Club and had taken accounting at N.Y.U. He had inherited a considerable fortune from an uncle, and as host for a weekend of bridge in the country he left nothing to be desired.

"Is he a Jew? I'm not even sure if he's a Jew," said one friend.

"I don't know," said a second friend. "I've always thought he was half."

"Well tell me this, do you think he's a fairy?"

"There again, I have to give you the same answer. I think he's probably half."

"Listen, if you're *half,* you *are,* in that department."

It would have been simple enough to obtain biographical material out of Herbert's yearbook at Princeton, but none of his friends went to the trouble of doing so. The lack of enterprise precisely matched the lack of curiosity, and soon Herbert's friends were thinking of him less as a person than as an annual event. In groups of three, always three, they would drive up to Litchfield County, for weekends of bridge, good food, fine wine, overwhelming quiet, and undemanding conversation; and they would drive away on Monday morning with no deeper understanding of Herbert and indeed with no actively continuing interest. As one friend said, leaving Herbert's house after a weekend was like leaving a ship after a pleasant crossing; you never gave another thought to the captain; next year you would go again, and the year after that and the year after that.

Apart from Christmas cards, no correspondence was maintained by Herbert and his friends from one annual invitation to the next. There was one exception to this custom, and it occurred last fall. Leonard Mackenzie, a Yale man, invited himself and his wife Rhoda to spend the weekend of the Yale-Princeton game with Herbert—conditional, of course, on its being convenient for Herbert. Perhaps Herbert, an old Princetonian, could even be persuaded to go to the game with the Mackenzies?

Two weeks passed, and no reply had come from Herbert. "It isn't like him, not to answer," said Leonard.

"He may be abroad," said Rhoda. "Or he may be dead. We wouldn't know unless we saw it in the paper."

"I hate to call him up on the telephone—"

"Well, you're damn well *not* going to call him on the telephone," said Rhoda. "Just start making other plans. Try the Lords, in Stamford."

"Oh, we'll hear from him," said Leonard.

A note arrived the next day: the Mackenzies would be more than welcome to spend the coming Friday and Saturday nights at Herbert's house; he would not, of course, go to the game; if he happened to be out when they arrived, Ralph, the butler, would take care of them.

"Let's get out of it," said Rhoda. "There's not a word in there about not answering your letter, and if you want to know what I think, he doesn't want us."

"We can't do that now, Rhoda. And anyway it's only for a weekend, and most of the time we'll be in New Haven."

The butler came to help them with their bags. "Good afternoon, sir. Ma'am."

"Good afternoon, Ralph," said Leonard.

"Good afternoon," said Rhoda.

"Mr. Roff will be back shortly. He asked me to show you to your rooms. The same rooms you always have. Would you care for tea, ma'am?"

"What time is dinner?" said Rhoda.

"Dinner is at nine, ma'am."

"Nine? Is there anyone else coming?" said Rhoda.

"Oh, *no* ma'am."

"Then I would like some tea."

"For you, sir?"

"I'd like a cup of tea," said Leonard.

"In your rooms, sir? Ma'am? I don't think Mr. Roff will be joining you for tea. In fact, I know he won't. I rather think he's expecting to have cocktails with you whenever you come down for dinner. A quarter to nine? In that neighborhood?"

The Mackenzies had their tea in the bedroom assigned to Rhoda. "Tea really does something for the inner man," said Leonard. "In college we drank it all the time."

"Not *all* the time," said Rhoda. She was in her underclothes and a dressing-gown; smoking a cigarette, her legs crossed, her foot swinging, her body bent forward, all in an attitude indicative of abstraction.

"What's on your mind?" said Leonard.

"I wish we hadn't come here," she said. "For two pins I'd get dressed and go."

"And where would you go?"

"To a motel. Anywhere."

"Have you got a feeling of impending doom?"

"Yes, smarty, I have," she said. "And so have you. I can tell. We've practically been told to stay in our rooms till a quarter of nine. Then we can have a cocktail with the squire, sit down to a dinner à trois, and then what? Do you realize that we've never been with Herbert when we didn't play bridge. And don't say we often had supper with him. That was we and a dozen others. We just don't know this man, Leonard, and we're just beginning to find it out."

"Well, he's not going to *do* anything to us. You talk as if we were going to be cut up into little pieces and our remains put in the incinerator." They heard a car in the driveway, and he went to the window. "It's him."

"Don't let him see you," she said.

"I won't. He looked up, but he didn't see me. He put the car in the garage and came in by the kitchen door."

They maintained complete silence. They heard footsteps on the stairs, which continued audibly but softly on the hall carpet until they heard a bedroom door being closed. "In his room," said Leonard. They remained silent until they heard the surge of water running through the pipes. "Taking a tub," said Leonard.

She sighed. "Well, he knows we're here, and he's made no effort to greet us. Probably getting undressed. Definitely we needn't expect to see him before cocktails, two hours away. Shall I ring for the maid and have her take the tea things?"

"No, let's play it his way. We'll isolate too."

"Don't isolate too much. Leave your door open."

"Rhoda, what *are* you afraid of?"

"I don't know. The unknown. He's always been a good host, almost too good. So good that he was all host and no person. But this time he really didn't want us to come, and he's doing absolutely

nothing to be hospitable. That's the unknown. Him. He's the unknown, because we've never really known him."

"You remind me of a story by Henry James."

"What story by Henry James?"

"I don't know. I never read Henry James, but isn't that the
kind of thing he wrote?"

"Water stopped running," said Rhoda. "Now he's getting in the
tub. Bath salts, I'm sure. I'll bet he's hairy. I'll bet he has a thick
mat across his chest and shoulders."

"We can ask him at dinner."

"The kind of bald he is, they often have thick black hair all
over their bodies."

"We can ask him."

"The Italian ones, they go in for religious medals on gold
chains. The boys' version of the Bikini, but always those religious
medals. Ah, the water was too hot or too cold. Running some more.
Just a little, it's stopped."

"This ought to take quite a while," said Leonard.

"Why?"

"To wash off the blood from his latest murder. All the perfumes
of Arabia. And if you look out the window, Birnam wood has come
to Dunsinane. Murder most foul. Fair is foul, foul is fair."

"You're horrible, you're making it worse for me," she said.
"Leonard, tonight I want you to tell him that we've had a change
in plans, and we're not coming back here after the game."

"Well, all right. Cook up a story. Where are we going?"

"We don't have to tell him. Just say we're driving back to New
York when the game is over."

"And that's what we'll be doing, too. Because there won't be
a bed within fifty miles of New Haven."

"I don't care. We can go to the Fence Club after the game, or
the Lawn Club, or some place, and then take our own good time
getting back to town. But I will not stay in this house another
night."

"Oh, all right. And now I think I'll have a hot bath and I suggest you have one too, to relax you."

"Leave your door open," she said.

"You've gotten yourself into a real state, I must say," said Leonard.

He fell asleep after his bath and when she came in to call him she was all dressed. "Did you get a nap?" he said.

"You snored. It's twenty of nine. You were *so* deep in sleep, I didn't have the heart. Splash some cold water on your face and get dressed quickly. He went down an hour ago."

They went downstairs together, and Herbert, in a blue velvet smoking jacket, white shirt, black tie and trousers and embroidered velveteen slippers, kissed Rhoda's hand. He had never done that before. "I'm so happy you could come," he said. "Football games you can have, but weren't you nice to remember me? I never would have thought of Yale and football games. What will you drink? People are getting afraid of martinis, but that's what I'm having."

"I'm afraid of them. I'll have a bourbon on the rocks," said Leonard.

"Yes, I think a bourbon, too," said Rhoda.

"You two have never been here in the fall," said Herbert, from the bar. "I adore it. So spooky."

"Well, I had altogether ten years of New England in the fall. Six in school, four in college. It is the best time. Something sad about it, but nice."

"I went to school in Virginia, but of course being married to Leonard I've been coming to games for—oh, almost forty years, I guess. Just about forty."

"Thirty-eight, with me. Forty all told," said Leonard.

"Do you know that I haven't been to a football game since I left Princeton? For a fact. Now I understand the professional games are the thing to see."

"No doubt about its being better football, and I watch it on TV, but it hasn't got the same spirit." Leonard accepted his drink and sat down.

"Do you understand the game, Rhoda?" said Herbert.

"Oh, yes. Actually when we were younger and living on the North Shore, we used to play touch on Sunday afternoons."

"That's gotten *very* popular, of course."

"Yeah," said Leonard. "You'd think they discovered it. We were playing touch before Brother Bobby was born. *God!*"

"I tried to get a friend of mine to come over for bridge to-night, but to no avail. However, tomorrow night we can have a real orgy. Two tables of duplicate. Four people coming from Waterbury, and my friend that couldn't come tonight. I thought you'd rather have a good rest tonight, to be ready for the trip down to New Haven, and then tomorrow night you'll enjoy Mr. and Mrs. Harris from Waterbury. I consider her one of the finest players I ever knew, and he's good too. The others are a Mr. and Mrs. Coleman and they're good but not in the same caliber as the Harrises. And my friend Tommy Chandler, he could be very good."

"Oh, I used to know Tommy Chandler, if it's the same one," said Leonard.

"He *said,*" said Herbert. "As soon as I mentioned your names. Tommy lives only about six and a half miles from here. He just moved here recently. He and his mother, Mrs. Chandler."

"Is she still alive? My goodness."

"Eighty-nine years of age," said Herbert. "And he's devoted to her. Devoted. *She* plays. She's terribly slow, but it's interesting to watch her mental processes. I don't mind playing with her, not a bit. You can almost see the wheels go around. And of course a slow player has a certain kind of an advantage, in that, in that, when they hesitate it doesn't give them away. And she knows that, the old darling. Well, let's to dinner, shall we?"

Since it was now impossible to trump up an excuse to leave early, Leonard and Rhoda tacitly agreed to make the best of it. After dinner—filet mignon with pâté de foie gras—they listened to some Brahms and Beethoven on Herbert's hi-fi, and retired at half past eleven.

"Well, do you feel safer?" said Leonard, in Rhoda's room.

"I guess so. Lulled by a false sense of security—and Mr. Beethoven's Ninth."

"And that food and that wine. My God. No wonder he's put on weight, if he eats that way all the time."

"What about Tommy Chandler?"

"He's an old maid that I've been seeing around the Yale Club for the last three hundred and seventy-five years. Quite a good figure skater at one time."

"But didn't play hockey."

"Not ice hockey," said Leonard. "I imagine he and Herbert ought to get along very well together. I used to have a drink with him once in a while, before I gave up the Yale Club. He was always around there somewhere. Do you want me to sleep in here tonight?"

"No, I'll be all right. You get a good night's rest. I ordered breakfast at half past eight. In bed. Goodnight, dear."

"Goodnight, old spunky," he said.

They got under way shortly after ten the next morning. "Why so taciturn? Didn't you sleep well?" said Leonard.

"No, I didn't. As a matter of fact, I had the prowls. I got up at about three o'clock and went downstairs and had a glass of milk."

"I didn't hear you," he said.

"I know you didn't."

"How long did you stay up?"

"Oh—over an hour. I was wide awake. I even wrote a letter."

"Who to, at that hour?" he asked.

"Nancy," she said. Nancy was their daughter, who lived in New York, nine blocks away from them. "A very sentimental letter. Told her a lot of things that we'd like to tell each other but never do. How pleased with her we were. What a good life she has made for herself, she and Joe. How worried we used to be, but that you'd always insisted she'd turn out all right."

"Well, she'll be pleased. But what prompted you to write that kind of a letter all of a sudden?"

"I didn't stop to think of why I was writing it. I just wrote it," said Rhoda. "And that was how I found the gun. Looking for stamps."

"What gun?"

"Herbert has a gun. Actually it's not a gun. It's a .32 caliber Smith and Wesson revolver. And it's loaded. He keeps it in a desk drawer."

"Well, why shouldn't he have a gun? I have one."

"You have two. You have the automatic in town and the revolver in the country, and you've only got a license for one."

"I know, I've got to get a license for the revolver. But don't start imagining things because Herbert has one. It's a lonely place up here in the country."

"That isn't the point, Leonard," she said. "You could have a whole arsenal—and you *have,* if you count rifles and shotguns. But that's *you.* You've had guns all your life. You shoot, I shoot, Nancy learned to shoot when she was ten years old. Herbert Roff isn't at all the gun type. Remember how he protested when he first moved up here, how he hated shooting and fishing and all the rest of that? But right now, sitting in his desk drawer, he keeps a loaded revolver."

"Rhoda, you seem almost determined to have a bad time this weekend. I hope the game cheers you up."

"That's not fair. I am never determined to have a bad time. This whole thing started because *you* wanted your own bathroom and bedroom, and all the luxuries. There were a dozen places we could have stayed, but you didn't want to put up with any inconvenience."

"Not if I could help it. I'm much too old to get any enjoyment out of noisy, drunken cocktail parties, and shaving in cold water. If I want to rough it I'll rough it in a duck blind, dressed for the occasion. For some reason or other Herbert didn't want us this weekend, but why didn't he say so? Now that we're here, he's making the best of it. Tonight we'll play bridge, and we can leave any time tomorrow morning. And we'll never come back, invited or not. Does that suit you?"

"Suits me fine," she said. She changed her position in the car seat, and he could tell that for the rest of the day she would try to enjoy herself.

They lunched according to plan with friends whose station wagon was parked near the Bowl; they sat with friends at the game; saw more friends between the halves. It was one of their most successful trips to New Haven—except for Leonard's certain belief that the evening to come was hanging over Rhoda's enjoyment of

the day. Two Darien friends urged them to come and spend the
night, and Leonard did not dare look at Rhoda. It had become important to make her endure the remaining time at Herbert's house;
it was unwise to let her alarm herself over nothing, and it was surely
inadvisable to yield to her capricious hostility to a man who had
always behaved well toward her and him. "The traffic is hell," he
said to her. "I think we pass up the Fence Club and go back to
Herbert's."

"Very well," she said. She was too readily acquiescent.

"No use beating our brains out going into New Haven and—"

"I *said* all right," she said.

"You actually said 'very well,' " he said. "Now let's not make
a big thing of this, Rhoda. You found a revolver in Herbert's desk.
I promise you that if he points it at you, I'll take it away from him.
Naturally I hope that if he points it at me, you'll take it away from
him."

"You're terribly funny, dear. You have been, all afternoon."

"Got a few laughs," he said.

"Well, maybe you'd better save a few for tonight. I have a
feeling we're going to need them."

They did not speak again until they reached Herbert's house.
Herbert was not in, and the butler informed them that the dinner
guests would arrive at eight-thirty. "I'd like to write a note to Mr.
Roff," said Leonard.

"Yes sir, you'll find paper and all in the desk. You wish me
to give it to him, the note?"

"No, I'll just leave it on the hall table, thanks," said Leonard.
"We'll have tea in Mrs. Mackenzie's room, Ralph."

Ten minutes later he went to Rhoda's room. "Well, did you
find it?" she said.

"Yes, it's there," he said. "I assume you're speaking of Herbert's revolver."

"And what did you say in your note?"

"I didn't write one. Told Ralph I changed my mind," he said.
"It's a Smith and Wesson .32. You were quite right. And it's loaded.
But it's loaded with blanks. Five blank cartridges."

"You're joking," she said.

"Give me credit for knowing the difference. I examined all five, and they are blanks."

"On your word of honor?" she said.

"On my solemn word of honor. If they'd been anything else I was going to remove them and put them where he couldn't get at them right away."

"When did you decide to do all that?"

"Driving back from the game, of course. You were so God damn unpleasant I knew I had to do something."

She bowed. "You know, Leonard, sometimes you're really a very wonderful man."

"You're God damn right I am."

"But why would Herbert Roff want to keep a revolver loaded with blanks in his desk?"

"Oh, for God's sake, Rhoda," said Leonard.

THE HARDWARE MAN

Lou Mauser had not always had money, and yet it would be hard to imagine him without it. He had owned the store—with, of course, some help from the bank—since he was in his middle twenties, and that was twenty years ago as of 1928. Twenty years is a pretty long time for a man to go without a notable financial failure, but Lou Mauser had done it, and when it has been that long, a man's worst enemies cannot say that it was all luck. They said it about Lou, but they said it in such a way as to make it sound disparaging to him while not making themselves appear foolish. It would have been very foolish to deny that Lou had worked hard or that he had been a clever business man. "You can't say it was all luck," said Tom Esterly, who was a competitor of Lou's. "You might just as well say he sold his soul to the devil. Not that he wouldn't have, mind you. But he didn't have to. Lou always seemed to be there with the cash at the right moment, and that's one of the great secrets of success. Be there with the cash when the right proposition comes along."

Lou had the cash, or got hold of it—which is the same thing —when Ada Bowler wanted to sell her late husband's hardware store. Lou was in his middle twenties then, and he had already been working in the store at least ten years, starting as a stock boy at five dollars a week. By the time he was eighteen he was a walking inventory of Bowler's stock; he knew where everything was, everything, and he knew how much everything was worth; wholesale, retail, special prices to certain contractors, the different mark-ups for different customers. A farmer came in to buy a harness snap, charge him a dime; but if another farmer, one who bought his barn paint at Bowler's, wanted a harness snap, you let him have it for a nickel. You didn't have to tell Sam Bowler what you were doing. Sam Bowler relied on your good sense to do things like that. If a boy was buying a catcher's mitt, you threw in a nickel Rocket, and sure as hell when that boy was ready to buy an Iver Johnson bicycle he would come to Bowler's instead of sending away to a mail-order house. And Lou Mauser at eighteen had discovered something that had never occurred to Sam Bowler: the rich people who lived on Lantenengo Street were even more appreciative when you gave them a little something for nothing—an oil can for a kid's bike, an ice pick for the kitchen—than people who had to think twice about spending a quarter. Well, maybe they weren't *more* appreciative, but they had the money to show their appreciation. Give a Lantenengo Street boy a nickel Rocket, and his father or his uncle would buy him a dollar-and-a-quarter ball. Give a rich woman an ice pick and you'd sell her fifty foot of garden hose and a sprinkler and a lawn mower. It was all a question of knowing which ones to give things to, and Lou knew so well that when he needed the cash to buy out Sam Bowler's widow, he actually had two banks to choose from instead of just having to accept one bank's terms.

Practically overnight he became the employer of men twice his age, and he knew which ones to keep and which to fire. As soon as the papers were signed that made him the owner, he went to the store and summoned Dora Minzer, the bookkeeper, and Arthur Davis, the warehouse man. He closed his office door so that no one outside could hear what he had to say, although the other employees could see through the glass partitions.

"Give me your keys, Arthur," said Lou.

"My keys? Sure," said Arthur.

"Dora, you give me your keys, too," said Lou.

"They're in my desk drawer," said Dora Minzer.

"Get them."

Dora left the office.

"I don't understand this, Lou," said Arthur.

"If you don't, you will, as soon as Dora's back."

Dora returned and laid her keys on Lou's desk. "There," she said.

"Arthur says he doesn't understand why I want your keys. You do, don't you, Dora?"

"Well—maybe I do, maybe I don't." She shrugged.

"You two are the only ones that I'm asking for their keys," said Lou.

Arthur took a quick look at Dora Minzer, who did not look at him. "Yeah, what's the meaning of it, Lou?"

"The meaning of it is, you both put on your coat and hat and get out."

"Fired?" said Arthur.

"Fired is right," said Lou.

"No notice? I been here twenty-two years. Dora was here pretty near that long."

"Uh-huh. And I been here ten. Five of those ten the two of you been robbing Sam Bowler that I know of. That I know of. I'm pretty sure you didn't only start robbing him five years ago."

"I'll sue you for slander," said Arthur.

"Go ahead," said Lou.

"Oh, shut up, Arthur," said Dora. "He knows. I told you he was too smart."

"He'd have a hard time proving anything," said Arthur.

"Yeah, but when I did you know where you'd be. You and Dora, and two purchasing agents, and two building contractors. All in it together. Maybe there's more than them, but those I could prove. The contractors, I'm licked. The purchasing agents, I want their companies' business, so all I'm doing there is get them fired. What are you gonna tell them in Sunday School next Sunday, Arthur?"

"*She* thought of it," said Arthur Davis, looking at Dora Minzer.

"That I don't doubt. It took brains to fool Sam Bowler all those years. What'd you do with your share, Dora?"

"My nephew. I educated him and started him up in business. He owns a drug store in Elmira, New York."

"Then he ought to take care of you. Where did yours go, Arthur?"

"Huh. With five kids on my salary, putting them through High, clothes and doctor bills, the wife and her doctor bills. Music lessons. A piano. Jesus Christ, I wonder Sam didn't catch on. How did *you* catch on?"

"You just answered that yourself. I used to see all those kids of yours, going to Sunday School, all dolled up."

"Well, they're all married or got jobs," said Arthur Davis. "I guess I'll find something. Who are you gonna tell about this? If I say I quit."

"What the hell do you expect me to do? You're a couple of thieves, both of you. Sam Bowler treated everybody right. There's eight other people working here that raised families and didn't steal. I don't feel any pity for you. As soon as you get caught you try to blame it all on Dora. And don't forget this, Arthur." He leaned forward. *"You were gonna steal from me.* The two of you. This morning a shipment came in. Two hundred rolls of tarpaper. An hour later, fifty rolls went out on the wagon, but show me where we got any record of that sale of fifty rolls. That was this morning, Arthur. You didn't even wait one day, you or Dora."

"That was him, did that," said Dora. "I told him to wait. Stupid."

"They're all looking at us, out on the floor," said Arthur.

"Yes, and probably guessing," said Lou. "I got no more to say to either one of you. Just get out."

They rose, and Dora went to the outer office and put on her coat and hat and walked to the street door without speaking to anyone. Arthur went to the back stairs that led to the warehouse. There he unpacked a crate of brand-new Smith & Wesson revolvers and broke open a case of ammunition. He then put a bullet through his skull, and Lou Mauser entered a new phase of his business career.

He had a rather slow first year. People thought of him as a cold-blooded young man who had driven a Sunday School superintendent to suicide. But as the scandal was absorbed into local history, the unfavorable judgment was gradually amended until it more closely conformed with the early opinion of the business men, which was sympathetic to Lou. Dora Minzer, after all, had gone away, presumably to Elmira, New York; and though there were rumors about the purchasing agents of two independent mining companies, Lou did not publicly implicate them. The adjusted public opinion of Lou Mauser had it that he had behaved very well indeed, and that he had proven himself to be a better business man than Sam Bowler. Only a few people chose to keep alive the story of the Arthur Davis suicide, and those few probably would have found some other reason to be critical of Lou if Arthur had lived.

Lou, of course, did not blame himself, and during the first year of his ownership of the store, while he was under attack, he allowed his resentment to harden him until he became in fact the ruthless creature they said he was. He engaged in price-cutting against the other hardware stores, and one of the newer stores was driven out of business because of its inability to compete with Lou Mauser and Tom Esterly.

"All right, Mr. Esterly," said Lou. "There's one less of us. Do you want to call it quits?"

"You started it, young fellow," said Tom Esterly. "And I can last as long as you can and maybe a *little* bit longer. If you want to start making a profit again, that's up to you. But I don't intend to enter into any agreement with you, now or any other time."

"You cut your prices when I did," said Lou.

"You bet I did."

"Then you're just as much to blame as I am, for what happened to McDonald. You helped put him out of business, and you'll get your share of what's left."

"Yes, and maybe I'll get your share, too," said Tom Esterly. "The Esterlys were in business before the Civil War."

"I know that. I would have bought your store if I could have. Maybe I will yet."

"Don't bank on it, young fellow. Don't bank on it. Let's see how good your credit is when you need it. Let's see how long the jobbers and the manufacturers will carry you. I *know* how far they'll carry Esterly Brothers. We gave some of those manufacturers their first orders, thirty, forty years ago. My father was dealing with some of them when Sam Bowler was in diapers. Mauser, you have a lot to learn."

"Esterly and Mauser. That's the sign I'd like to put up some day."

"It'll be over my dead body. I'd go out of business first. Put up the shutters."

"Oh, I didn't want you as a partner. I'd just continue the name."

"Will you please get out of my store?"

Tom Esterly was a gentleman, a graduate of Gibbsville High and Gettysburg College, prominent in Masonic circles, and on the boards of the older charities. The word upstart was not in his working vocabulary and he had no epithet for Lou Mauser, but he disliked the fellow so thoroughly that he issued one of his rare executive orders to his clerks: hereafter, when Esterly Brothers were out of an article, whether it was a five-cent article or a fifty-dollar one, the clerks were not to suggest that the customer try Bowler's. For Tom Esterly this was a serious change of policy, and represented an attitude that refused to admit the existence of Mauser's competition. On the street he inclined his head when Mauser spoke to him, but he did not actually speak to Mauser.

Lou Mauser's next offense was to advertise. Sam Bowler had never advertised, and Esterly Brothers' advertising consisted solely of complimentary cards in the high school annual and the program of the yearly concert of the Lutheran church choir. These cards read, "Esterly Bros., Est. 1859, 211 N. Main St.," and that was all. No mention of the hardware business. Tom Esterly was shocked and repelled to see a full-page ad in each of the town newspapers, announcing a giant spring sale at Bowler's Hardware Store, Lou Mauser, Owner & Proprietor. It was the first hardware store ad in Gibbsville history and, worse, it was the first time Mauser had put his name on Sam Bowler's store. Tom Esterly went and had a look, and, yes, Mauser not only had put his name in the ad; he had his name painted on the store windows in lettering almost as large as Bowler's. The sale was, of course, a revival of Mauser's price-cutting tactic, even though it was advertised to last only three days. And Mauser offered legitimate bargains; some items, Tom knew, were going at cost. While the sale was on there were almost no customers in Esterly Brothers. "They're all down at Mauser's," said Jake Potts, Tom's head clerk.

"You mean Bowler's," said Tom.

"Well, yes, but I bet you he takes Sam's name off inside of another year," said Jake.

"Where is he getting the money, Jake?"

"Volume. What they call volume. He got two fellows with horse and buggy calling on the farmers."

"Salesmen?"

"Two of them. They talk Pennsylvania Dutch and they go around to the farms. Give the woman a little present the first time, and they drive their buggies right up in the field and talk to the farmers. Give the farmers a pack of chewing tobacco and maybe a tie-strap for the team. My brother-in-law down the Valley told me. They don't try to sell nothing the first visit, but the farmer remembers that chewing tobacco. Next time the farmer comes to market, if he needs anything he goes to Bowler's."

"Well, farmers are slow pay. We never catered much to farmers."

"All the same, Tom, it takes a lot of paint to cover a barn, and they're buying their paint off of Mauser. My brother-in-law told me Mauser's allowing credit all over the place. Any farmer with a cow and a mule can get credit."

"There'll be a day of reckoning, with that kind of foolishness. And it's wrong, *wrong,* to get those farmers in debt. You know how they are, some of them. They come in here to buy one thing, and before they know it they run up a bill for things they don't need."

"Yes, I know it. So does Mauser. But he's getting the volume, Tom. Small profit, big volume."

"Wait till he has to send a bill collector around to the farmers. His chewing tobacco won't do him any good then," said Tom Esterly.

"No, I guess not," said Jake Potts.

"The cash. I still don't see where he gets his cash. You say volume, but volume on credit sales won't supply him with cash."

"Well, I guess if you show the bank a lot of accounts receivable. And he has a lot of them, Tom. A lot. You get everybody owing you money, most of them are going to pay you some day. Most people around here pay their bills."

"You criticizing our policy, Jake?"

"Well, times change, Tom, and you gotta fight fire with fire."

"Would you want to work for a man like Mauser?"

"No, and I told him so," said Jake Potts.

"He wanted to hire you away from me?"

"A couple months ago, but I said no. I been here too long, and I might as well stay till I retire. But look down there, Tom. Down there between the counters. One lady customer. All the others are at Mauser's sale."

"He tried to steal you away from me. That's going too far," said Tom Esterly. "Would you mind telling me what he offered you?"

"Thirty a week and a percentage on new business."

"Thinking you'd get our customers to follow you there. Well, I guess I have to raise you to thirty. But the way it looks now, I can't offer you a percentage on new business. It's all going in the opposite direction."

"I didn't ask for no raise, Tom."

"You get it anyway, starting this week. If you quit, I'd just about have to go out of business. I don't have anybody to take your place. And I keep putting off the decision, who'll be head clerk when you retire. Paul Schlitzer's next in line, but he's getting forgetful. I guess it'll be Norman Johnson. Younger."

"Don't count on Norm, Tom."

"Mauser been making him offers?"

"I don't know for sure, but that's my guess. When a fellow starts acting independent, he has some good reason behind it. Norm's been getting in late in the morning and when ha' past five comes he don't wait for me to tell him to pull down the shades."

"Have you said anything to him?"

"Not so far. But we better start looking for somebody else. It don't have to be a hardware man. Any bright young fellow with experience working behind a counter. I can show him the ropes, before I retire."

"All right, I'll leave that up to you," said Tom Esterly. On his next encounter with Lou Mauser he stopped him.

"Like to talk to you a minute," said Tom Esterly.

"Fine and dandy," said Mauser. "Let's move over to the curb, out of people's way."

"I don't have much to say," said Tom Esterly. "I just want to tell you you're going too far, trying to hire my people away from me."

"It's a free country, Mr. Esterly. If a man wants to better himself. And I guess Jake Potts bettered himself. Did you meet my offer?"

"Jake Potts wouldn't have worked for you, offer or no offer."

"But he's better off now than he was before. He ought to be thankful to me. Mister, I'll make an offer to anybody I want to hire, in your store or anybody else's. I don't have to ask your permission. Any more than I asked your permission to run a big sale. I had new customers in my store that I never saw before, even when Sam Bowler was the owner. I made *you* an offer, so why shouldn't I make an offer to fellows that work for you?"

"Good day, sir," said Tom Esterly.

"Good day to you," said Lou Mauser.

Tom Esterly was prepared for the loss of Norman Johnson, but when Johnson revealed a hidden talent for window decorating, he felt cheated. The window that attracted so much attention that it was written up in both newspapers was an autumnal camping scene that occupied all the space in Mauser's window. Two dummies, dressed in gunning costume, were seated at a campfire outside a tent. An incandescent lamp simulated the glow of the fire, and real pine and spruce branches and fake grass were used to provide a woodland effect. Every kind of weapon, from shotgun to automatic pistol, was on display, leaning against logs or lying on the fake grass. There were hunting knives and compasses, Marble match cases and canteens, cots and blankets, shell boxes of canvas and leather, fireless cookers, fishing tackle, carbide and kerosene lamps, an Old Towne canoe, gun cases and revolver holsters, duck calls and decoys and flasks and first-aid kits. Wherever there was space between the merchandise items, Norman Johnson had put stuffed chipmunk and quail, and peering out from the pine and spruce were the mounted heads of a cinnamon bear, a moose, an elk, a deer, and high above it all was a stuffed wildcat, permanently snarling.

All day long men would stop and stare, and after school small boys would shout and point and argue and wish. There had never been anything like it in Bowler's or Esterly Brothers' windows, and when the display was removed at Thanksgiving time there were expressions of regret. The small boys had to find some place else to go. But Norman Johnson's hunting-camp window became an annual event, a highly profitable one for Lou Mauser.

"Maybe we should never of let Norm go," said Jake Potts.

"He's right where he belongs," said Tom Esterly. "Right exactly where he belongs. That's the way those medicine shows do business. Honest value, good merchandise, that's what we were founded on and no tricks."

"We only sold two shotguns and not any rifles this season, Tom. The next thing we know we'll lose the rifle franchise."

"Well, we never did sell many rifles. This is mostly shotgun country."

"I don't know," said Jake. "We used to do a nice business in .22's. We must of sold pretty close to three hundred of the .22 pump gun, and there's a nice steady profit in the cartridges."

"I'll grant you we used to sell the .22 rifle, other years. But they're talking about a law prohibiting them in the borough limits. Ever since the Leeds boy put the Kerry boy's eye out."

"Tom, you won't face facts," said Jake. "We're losing business to this fellow, and it ain't only in the sporting goods line or any one line. It's every which way. Kitchen utensils. Household tools. Paints and varnishes. There's never the people in the store there used to be. When you's first in charge, after your Pa passed on, just about the only thing we didn't sell was something to eat. If you can eat it, we don't sell it, was our motto."

"That was never our motto. That was just a funny saying," said Tom Esterly.

"Well, yes. But we used to have funny sayings like that. My clerks used to all have their regular customers. Man'd come in and buy everything from the same clerk. Had to be waited on by the same clerk no matter what they come in to buy. Why, I can remember old Mrs. Stokes one day she come in to borrow my umbrella, and I was off that day and she wouldn't take anybody else's umbrella. That's the kind of customers we used to have. But where are those people today? They're down at Lou Mauser's. Why? Because for instance when school opened in September every boy and girl in the public and the Catholic school got a foot-rule from Lou Mauser. They maybe cost him a half a cent apiece, and say there's a thousand children in school. Five dollars."

"Jake, you're always telling me those kind of things. You make me wonder if you wouldn't rather be working for Mauser."

"I'll tell you anything if it's for your own good. You don't have your Pa or your Uncle Ed to tell you no more. It's for my own good too, I'll admit. I retire next year, and I won't get my fifty a month if you have to close down."

"Close down? You mean run out of business by Mauser?"

"Unless you do something to meet the competition. Once before you said Mauser would have trouble with the jobbers and the manufacturers. Instead of which the shoe is on the other foot now. Don't fool yourself, Tom. Those manufacturers go by the orders we send in, and some articles we're overstocked from last year."

"I'll tell you this. I'd sooner go out of business than do things his way. Don't worry. You'll get your pension. I have other sources of income besides the store."

"If you have to close the store I'll go without my pension. I won't take charity. I'll get other work."

"With Mauser."

"No, I won't work for Mauser. That's one thing I never will do. He as good as put the gun to Arthur Davis's head, and Arthur was a friend of mine, crook or no crook. I don't know what Mauser said to Arthur that day, but whatever it was, Arthur didn't see no

other way out. That kind of a man I wouldn't work for. He has
blood on his hands, to my way of thinking. When I meet Arthur
Davis in the after life I don't want him looking at me and saying I
wasn't a true friend."

"Arthur would never say that about you, Jake."

"He might. You didn't know Arthur Davis as good as I did.
There was a man that was all worries. I used to walk home from
work with him sometimes. First it was worr'ing because Minnie
wasn't sure she was gonna marry him. Then all them children, and
Minnie sick half the time, but the children had to look just so. Music lessons. A little money to get them started when they got married. They say it was Dora Minzer showed him how they could
knock down off of Sam Bowler, and I believe that. But I didn't believe what they said about something going on between him and
Dora. No. Them two, they both had a weakness for money and
that was all there was between them. How much they stole off of
Sam Bowler we'll never know, but Arthur's share was put to good
use, and Sam never missed it. Neither did Ada Bowler. Arthur
wouldn't of stole that money if Sam and Ada had children."

"Now you're going too far. You don't know that, and I don't
believe it. Arthur did what Dora told him to. And what about the
disgrace? Wouldn't Arthur's children rather be brought up poor than
have their father die a thief?"

"I don't know," said Jake. "Some of it was honest money.
Nobody knows how much was stolen money. The children didn't
know any of it was stolen money till the end. By that time they
all had a good bringing-up. All a credit to their parents and their
church and the town. A nicer family you couldn't hope to see. And
they were brought up honest. Decent respectable youngsters, all
of them. You can't blame them if they didn't ask their father where
the money was coming from. Sam Bowler didn't get suspicious,
did he? The only one got suspicious was Lou Mauser. And they say
he kept his mouth shut for six or seven years, so he was kind of in
on it. If I ever saw one of our fellows look like he was knocking
down off of you, I'd report it. But Lou Mauser never let a peep out
of him till he was the owner. I sometimes wonder maybe he was

hoping they'd steal so much they'd bankrupt Sam, and then he could buy the store cheaper."

"Well, now that's interesting," said Tom Esterly. "I wouldn't put it past him for a minute."

"I don't say it's true, but it'd be like him," said Jake. "No, I'd never go to work for that fellow. Even at my age I'd rather dig ditches."

"You'll never have to dig ditches as long as I'm alive, and don't say you won't take charity. You'll take your pension from Esterly Brothers regardless of whether we're still in business or not. So don't let me hear any more of that kind of talk. In fact, go on back to work. There's a customer down there."

"Wants the loan of my umbrella, most likely," said Jake. "Raining, out."

Esterly Brothers lasted longer than Jake Potts expected, and longer than Jake Potts himself. There were some bad years, easy to explain, but there were years in which the store showed a profit, and it was difficult to explain that. Lou Mauser expanded; he bought the store property adjoining his. He opened branch stores in two other towns in the county. He dropped the Bowler name completely. Esterly Brothers stayed put and as is, the middle of the store as dark as usual, so that the electric lights had to burn all day. The heavy hardware store fragrance—something between the pungency of a blacksmith's shop and the sweetness of the apothecary's —was missing from Lou Mauser's well-ventilated buildings, and he staffed his business with young go-getters. But some of the old Esterly Brothers customers returned after temporarily defecting to Mauser's, and at Esterly's they found two or three of the aging clerks whom they had last seen at Mauser's, veterans of the Bowler days. Although he kept it to himself, Tom Esterly had obviously decided to meet the go-getter's competition with an atmosphere that was twenty years behind the times. Cash customers had to wait while their money was sent to the back of the store on an overhead trolley, change made, and the change returned in the wooden cup that was screwed to the trolley wire. Tom never did put in an electric cash register, and the only special sale he held was when he

offered a fifty percent reduction on his entire stock on the occasion
of his going out of business. Three successive bad years, the only
time it had happened since the founding of the store, were unargu-
able, and he put an ad in both papers to announce his decision. His
announcement was simple:

50% Off
Entire Stock
Going Out of Business
Sale Commences Aug. 1, 1922
ESTERLY BROTHERS
Est. 1859
Open 8 A.M.—9 P.M. During Sale
All Sales Cash Only—All Sales Final

On the morning after the advertisements appeared, Tom Esterly
went to his office and found, not to his surprise, Lou Mauser await-
ing his appearance.

"Well, what can I do for *you?*" said Tom.

"I saw your ad. I didn't know it was that bad," said Lou.
"I'm honestly sorry."

"I don't see why," said Tom. "It's what you've been aiming
at. Why did you come here? If you want to buy anything, my clerks
will wait on you."

"I'll buy your entire stock, twenty cents on the dollar."

"I think I'll do better this way, selling to the public."

"There'll be a lot left over."

"I'll give that away," said Tom Esterly.

"Twenty cents on the dollar, Mr. Esterly, and you won't have
to give none of it away."

"You'd want me to throw in the good will and fixtures," said
Esterly.

"Well, yes."

"I might be tempted to sell to you. The stock and the fixtures.
But the good will would have to be separate."

"How much for the good will?" said Lou Mauser.

"A million dollars cash. Oh, I know it isn't worth it, Mauser, but I wouldn't sell it to you for any less. In other words, it isn't for sale to you. A week from Saturday night at nine o'clock, this store goes out of business forever. But no part of it belongs to you."

"The last couple years you been running this store like a hobby. You lost money hand over fist."

"I had it to lose, and those three years gave me more pleasure than all the rest put together. When this store closes a lot of people are going to miss it. Not because it was a store. *You* have a *store*. But we had something better. We never had to give away foot-rules to schoolchildren, or undercut our competitors. We never did any of those things, and before we *would* do them we decided to close up shop. But first we gave some of the people something to remember. Our kind of store, not yours, Mauser."

"Are you one of those that held it against me because of Arthur Davis?"

"No."

"Then what did you hold against me?"

"Sam Bowler gave you your first job, promoted you regularly, gave you raises, encouraged you. How did you repay him? By looking the other way all the time that you knew Arthur Davis and Dora Minzer were robbing him. Some say you did it because you hoped Sam would go bankrupt and you could buy the business cheap. Maybe yes, maybe no. That part isn't what I hold against you. It was you looking the other way, never telling Sam what they were doing to him. *That* was when you killed Arthur Davis, Mauser. Sam Bowler was the kind of man that if you'd told him about Arthur and Dora, he would have kept it quiet and given them both another chance. You never gave them another chance. You didn't even give them the chance to make restitution. I don't know about Dora Minzer, but Arthur Davis had a conscience, and a man that has a conscience is entitled to put it to work. Arthur Davis would have spent the rest of his life trying to pay Sam back, and he'd be alive today, still paying Ada Bowler, no doubt. Having a hard time, no doubt. But alive and with his conscience satisfied. You didn't kill Arthur by firing him that day. You killed him a long time before that by looking the other way. And I'm sure you don't understand a word I'm saying."

"No wonder you're going out of business. You should of been a preacher."

"I thought about it," said Tom Esterly. "But I didn't have the call."

HIS EXCELLENCY

Miss Tasmer obviously had something on her mind. She had made two unnecessary trips to the office in less than an hour, and now here she was again.

Norman White looked up from his desk. "What is it, Tazzie?"

"Oh, just this," she said. She placed a letter in front of him. "It's from Miller and Ralston. They want to know if you're planning to go ahead with the black-top."

"Oh, hell, I'm not going to worry about that now," said Norman White.

"A lot of work piled up while you were away," she said.

"It certainly did, but that was to be expected."

"The first week back, there's such a pile of it it hardly seems worthwhile taking a vacation."

"Well, it was worthwhile to me. I'll tell you what we can do, though. Things like this Miller and Ralston letter, and the one from Chalmers, don't give them to me one at a time. They can all wait till the end of the week anyway, and I can take care of them then."

"Notice it says in the Miller and Ralston letter, if they don't get an answer by the fifteenth, they're going to have to go ahead with another job."

"Then let them. I'm not that anxious to spend twenty-two hundred dollars. Not as anxious as they are to get me to spend it. The same way with Chalmers. I know what he wants to see me about. So do you, for that matter. These guys aren't busy just now, but I am. This week let's concentrate our efforts on making a buck instead of spending it, huh?"

"Well, I just thought, Miller and Ralston said the price will go up after the first of the month," she said.

"I know. And if the price goes up they don't get the job. I can put the whole thing off for another year. So if they're pressuring *you,* Tazzie, you just tell them that."

"Oh, they're not pressuring me," she said.

"Then what's on your mind? I can always tell when you have something bugging you. You haven't gotten pregnant again, have you?"

"Mister White! That's uncalled for. I don't think that was called for at all."

"Well, is your mother lushing it up again?"

"That either. Now you just stop *saying* those kind of things."

"I don't know, Tazzie. You have these problems all the time, and I can usually—"

"What if there was somebody listening? Salesmen come in and sit out there, or one of the men. The salesmen I don't care, but if one of the men heard you talk that way, the story'd be all over town. It's bad enough as it is."

"What is?" he said. "Now we're getting somewhere."

"Well, I'm not a tattletale, but the new man, that Heckman, he talks worse than you do. It's got so I just dread going out in the shop, the things he says."

"Heckman? What kind of things?"

"Fresh things. And right in front of the other men. I told him to stop or I'd report him to you, but he just goes right ahead."

"What kind of things?"

"About *me,"* she said.

"You mean about—your *person?"*

"Yes, my person. He says things about my person. And not only about my person."

"Well, you know he's only kidding you. It's a sign he likes you. But if you want me to, I'll give him a bawling-out. What would you like me to say to him? You could have complained to George Skillman. After all, he's the foreman, and he could—"

"That's just the trouble. George Skillman laughs, and that only encourages Heckman. You'd think George Skillman, married to my cousin, it was up to George to put a stop to it, but instead of that he laughs. I almost quit while you were away."

"Oh, come on, Tazzie. These guys are—they're just kidding you. Putting you on. You're the only woman among six men, and—"

"They never used to do it before Heckman started working here."

"The others do it, too?"

"No, but they laugh," she said.

"Well, I hope you don't want me to fire Heckman. He's a good mechanic."

"I didn't say anything about his work, and I don't want to cost anybody their job. But it upsets me whenever I have to go out in the shop."

"Listen, Tazzie, we're all out here on the edge of town, and you're the only female surrounded by six men. If they didn't take some notice of you, that wouldn't be much of a compliment either."

"I have no illusions about that, Mr. White. If I were some glamor girl, some Bridget Bardot or one of those. But I'm practically the same age as George Skillman and not a glamor girl. If I was a glamor girl I would of been married long since and not working for a living."

"They work. I understand they work very hard, at certain things."

"You think this is something to laugh at, make a joke of, but if I can't go out in the shop without this Heckman and George Skillman making their insulting remarks. They should have more respect."

"All right, Tazzie. I'll speak to both of them."

"Don't say anything to George. Don't do that. But I don't care what you say to Heckman."

"Okay," said Norman White. "The only thing is, Tazzie, Heckman is going to know you complained. He's never said anything out of the way while I've been in the shop. Therefore, he'll know you complained to me. Wouldn't it really be better if I got George to speak to him? Just dropped a hint to George to tell Heckman to cut it out?"

"No, no. I don't want George brought into it," she said.

"But a minute ago you were just as mad at George."

"I'm mad at him, but I don't want him brought into it," she said.

"He'll be brought into it, one way or another, the minute I say anything to Heckman. He'll tell George I bawled him out. He may even quit. Good mechanics are pretty darn independent these days. So why don't you let me have a quiet word with George and let him handle it? Frankly, I don't like to bypass George. He's been my foreman since I started this business, and I just don't like to bypass him. He'll be sore if I do, I know he will."

"Mr. White, I'd rather you didn't say anything to anybody if you're going to drag George into it," she said.

"*Drag* him into it? Come on, now, Tazzie. *I* never dragged him into it."

"Oh?" The sound she made was a moan of bewilderment.

"You know what could happen, don't you?" he said. "I could give Heckman a bawling-out. He could tell me to go to hell. George would get sore, and he could quit. Or if they didn't quit, they would start kidding you again because you reported them. Then you'd quit, and I don't want that."

"Well what shall I *do?* I have to go in the shop, in and out of there fifty times a day, and I'm a nervous wreck. I really am. All the time you were away that Heckman was saying things, and George would laugh every time. How can I go in the shop?"

"It's a real crisis," said Norman White.

"I can't tell whether you're serious or not, but it is for me."

"Sit down a minute, Tazzie. Sit down and tell me what kind of things Heckman says."

"I did tell you. Things about my person," she said.

"You didn't say that. I did. I put the words in your mouth. Suppose you tell me in your own words. Or Heckman's own words."

"I wouldn't repeat what he says."

"You're making it tough for me," he said.

"Tough for *you?* How about for me?" she said. "I've been here over twelve years and always behaved like a lady. Never gave anybody any cause to make personal remarks, and nobody *did,* till you hired Heckman. Even when you had that Rodriguez. He used to look at me, but he never said anything."

"Rodriguez? I don't remember any—oh, Rodriguez. Yeah. He was only here a few weeks. God, that was a good five years ago. George fired him. Was that because of the way he looked at you?"

"No, of course not. George fired him for coming in late. He never knew anything about how Rodriguez looked at me."

"Looked at you. Is that all?"

"No, it's not all. He made gestures, too."

"What they call lewd gestures?"

"Lewd? Yes. Lewd. Personal."

"Well, now, Tazzie, I know how old you are. To the day. All this red tape we have, I have to know. Right?"

"Oh, sure."

"So I happen to know you're forty-one years of age. I also happen to have a good pair of eyes. Right?"

"Reading glasses, that's all. Yes, you have good eyesight," she said.

"What I'm getting at is, I've known you just about all your life and it just doesn't seem possible to me that the only time you ever had any comments on your shape were right here. In the shop."

"I can't help it if I'm over-developed, in certain ways."

"You don't want to help it, do you? After all, look at all these Italian movie actresses. Sophia Whatever the Hell Her Name is, and the other one? Gilda Brigitola. I never get time for the movies any more, but I see their pictures in the *Life* magazine. What have they got that our own Irma Tasmer hasn't got just as good?"

"I'm not pretty, and I can't act."

"Well, the point is, Tazzie, you're not much different now than when you used to be the cheerleader at the basketball games. I remember you then. I'm surprised you didn't get married."

"I could have."

"I'm sure you could have. Still could. Forty-one is nothing."

"I had other offers, too, but they all treated me like I was some kind of a freak. I'd rather be an old maid than just because I— well, I'd rather stay single."

"Uh-huh," he said. "What I'm trying to get at is, do these personal remarks bother you more because we're out here on the outskirts of town and you're outnumbered six to one? You're not afraid, are you?"

"Afraid? Afraid of what? I could hit that Heckman one on the head and knock him down."

"Maybe that's what you ought to do—when I'm not around," he said. "Although I'd hate to miss that."

"Honestly, Mr. White, you're trying to make a joke of the whole thing and it's no joke. Not to me it isn't."

"Not making a joke of it, Tazzie, but I honestly don't see why you have to get so upset over a thing like this. I remember the first week you were here. Several truckdrivers whistling at you, and you telling me you just laughed it off."

"That wasn't the same thing. Truckdrivers. I'm used to that. But this Heckman, he whistles at me and makes personal remarks in front of George Skillman and all George does is laugh. I'm just not going to put up with it any more."

"I don't like the sound of that. It sounds as if you were thinking of quitting your job, and we'd practically have to close down if you did that. My goodness. You're not thinking of quitting, are you?"

"I'd give you time to break in a new girl, but yes, I've thought of going some place else."

"You just now said Heckman makes these remarks in front of George. Is that what embarrasses you the most, because it's George? Was George an old sweetheart of yours, Tazzie?"

"George Skillman? An old sweetheart of mine? Huh."

"Well, was he?"

"George Skillman. Where'd you ever get that idea?"

"From you," he said. "I may be wrong, but it kind of seems to me that you don't mind Heckman as much as you do George laughing."

"Well, he's married to my cousin."

"I know that, and you still haven't answered my question."

"All right if you must know. I dated George a few times before he married Geraldine Singmaster. A few times, after he got out of the army."

"You see, Tazzie, I didn't want to pry into your personal affairs, but now I know how to handle the thing."

"But don't you say anything to George."

"One more question. Has Heckman ever asked you for a date?"

"I suppose you could call it asking for a date. But I'd never go out with anybody that asked me the way he did."

"Now there's where I think you're making a *big* mistake," he said.

"Go out with somebody that says, 'Wuddia say, babe?'?"

"Never mind about how he asks you. The point is, he has asked you. Just think it over a minute, Tazzie. You have nothing to be afraid of. As you said a minute ago, you could clout him over the head the minute he got fresh."

"I sure could," she said. "And would, gladly."

"All right. Now suppose you go out with him, have a date with him. Just shut up till I finish. The next day, you come to work, the two of you. You know as well as I do that he's not going to make any personal remarks if you go out with him. Why not? Because either you get along fine, and maybe agree to have other dates with him. Or else you don't get along at all. But either way he won't make any more personal remarks."

"If we didn't get along he'd make worse ones," she said.

"No he wouldn't, and even if he did you could laugh at him. You could tell the other men that Heckman went out with you and got nowhere. But he'd know that himself. He wouldn't want to look like a bad loser, if you know what I mean."

"Yes. Yes," she said.

"And our friend George—well, the only person he could laugh at would be Heckman. Not you. The question is, does Heckman still try to date you?"

"Only every day is all."

"There's your problem, all settled. Go on out in the shop, now, and if Heckman says anything about a date, you just fool hell out of him. You say something like, 'All right, if you think you're man enough to go out with a real woman.' "

"You mean right now?"

"There's no time like the present, Tazzie."

"I don't have any excuse to go out there now," she said.

"Here," said White. He picked up a piece of yellow paper. "Here's his timesheet on the Gruber job. Tell him I wanted to be sure it's okay. That's a good enough excuse. Just walk straight to him with the timesheet in your hand and tell him the boss wanted to check this. If it doesn't work this time, we'll think of something else."

"You know, Mr. White, you should have been some kind of an ambassador."

"Oh, that takes money, Tazzie. But I used to think about it when I was younger. That was one thing I always wanted to be."

"An ambassador. Well, you'd have made a good one," she said.

"Maybe," he said. He took off his glasses and chewed the sidebar. "His Excellency, Norman J. White."

THE HOUSE
ON THE CORNER

It went all the way back to a day when George Wentz came home from shoveling the snow off the neighbors' sidewalks. "How much did you make?" said his father.

"Ninety cents," said George.

"For how many sidewalks?"

"Oh, gee, I don't know."

"Well—was it two? Four? Six? Eight?" said his father.

"It sure wasn't two, and it sure wasn't four. At least six. Do you want me to count up?"

"Wouldn't that be a good idea? You made ninety cents, and that could be a lot of money if you got it for one sidewalk. But if you did six, that's fifteen cents a sidewalk. And if you did nine, that's a dime apiece. Count up and see."

"Well-ll, starting with our house, Mama gave me a dime. That's one."

"One sidewalk, one dime," said his father. "Then who?"

"Mrs. Williams, fifteen. Mrs. Chester, ten. She didn't want the whole thing shoveled, just a path. It sure looked funny, just a path, and all the others swept clean. Let me see now. After Mrs. Chester, Mrs. O'Brien, fifteen. Next to them is the Reveres."

"And they have Jake Loomis to shovel theirs," said his father.

"No, I did it," said George.

"Where was old Jake? That's supposed to be part of his work."

"I don't know, but when Mrs. Revere saw me cleaning Mrs. O'Brien's she called to me and said would I clean hers."

"A man-sized job, all the way around the corner," said his father.

"And the driveway."

"And the driveway? How much did you get for that?" said his father.

"Twenty-five cents."

"A quarter? For the whole thing? The front sidewalk, and around the corner, and the driveway? A quarter for that? Is that all?"

"That was the most I got from anybody, a quarter."

"But the work. How long were you at it?"

"That took me the longest."

"Who paid you? Mrs. Revere herself?"

"No. Mr. Revere."

"Oh, *Mister* Revere. He came out and graciously bestowed upon you the enormous sum of twenty-five cents. What did you say to him?"

"What did I say? Oh, you mean did I say thanks? Yes."

"Tugging at your forelock," said his father.

"What?"

"Just an expression," said his father.

Amy Wentz called from the diningroom. "Supper's ready, you two."

"Be there in a minute," said the elder Wentz.

"No, now," said his wife. "It's on the table."

When they were seated George Wentz's father said to his wife, "Well, did you hear what Franklin Revere paid George for clearing his sidewalk and his driveway?"

"Twenty-five cents," said Amy Wentz.

"I have a good notion to go up there and tell him what I think. The boy should have got at least a dollar for that work. Twenty-five cents. Old Jake Loomis is no fool. He's not going to break his back on a day like this. I'll bet you Jake had a look out the window and went right back to bed—with a bottle of hooch, most likely."

"I wouldn't put it past him," said Amy. "But you're not going to say anything to Franklin Revere, do you hear? We're in no position to go around making enemies of people like the Reveres."

"Why not? They don't own us," said Wentz.

"I didn't say they did," said Amy. "But they come closer to owning us than we are to owning them."

"Nobody owns anybody in this country," said Wentz.

"No, but some people own their own houses and some people are paying rent."

"And others are mortgaged," said Wentz. "To the hilt. But the Reveres don't happen to hold our mortgages, and they don't have any financial control over us whatsoever."

"Ethel Revere was a Stokes, and who do you have to go to when you need money? Her brother, at the bank. So let's not start something because they underpaid George seventy-five cents."

"All right, all right," said Wentz. "But the boy's never going to do any more work for them, shoveling snow or anything else."

"I doubt if the opportunity will come up again," said Amy.

But it did. A few days later there was another heavy fall of snow, and the last thing Ben Wentz said to his wife before leaving for work was that under no circumstances was George to clear the Reveres' sidewalk. Shortly after ten o'clock the Wentz telephone rang, and it was Ethel Revere. "Amy, this is Ethel Revere. I was wondering, when George gets home from school this afternoon, could he come and clear our sidewalk? He did such a good job the other day, and Jake Loomis is staying home."

"I'm sorry, Ethel, but George won't be able to," said Amy.

"Oh, dear. I was really counting on him. He more or less promised. Franklin was so pleased the other day, and he told George he could have the job any time Jake didn't show up."

"You mean the job of shoveling snow?"

"Yes. Of course I didn't mean Jake's other work. Jake *is* a good gardener, and of course George has to stay in school."

"And George isn't going to be a gardener," said Amy. "He's going to study architecture."

"Oh, good for him," said Ethel Revere. "Well, you don't know any other boys in the neighborhood that I could ask?"

"I don't think you'll get anybody to do it for twenty-five cents," said Amy.

"Oh, *that's* why we can't have George," said Ethel. "Well, we could make it fifty."

"That's not enough, either."

"Then what do you think would be a fair price?"

"A dollar seventy-five," said Amy.

"A dollar seventy-five?"

"A dollar for today, and seventy-five additional payment for Tuesday," said Amy.

"*I* see. Holding us up, eh?"

"No, not holding you up at all, Ethel. Only getting a fair price. You won't get a man to clean your sidewalks and driveway for under a dollar. If you think you can, you're free to try. But we didn't call up and ask you to hire George. You called us."

"Very well, Amy. I'm sorry to've troubled you. Goodbye."

All day the Reveres' sidewalk and driveway was covered with snow, until late in the afternoon when Amy saw two colored men with shovels and ice-choppers on the job. She recognized one of the men, Peter Lejohn, who was a porter at the bank, and the other man might easily have been Peter's brother. Whoever they were, they were grown men and Amy guessed that each of them was getting at least two dollars for his work . . .

That was the start of it. Thereafter, whenever Ethel and Franklin Revere had to pass the Wentz residence on foot, they would nod and utter the greeting appropriate to the time of day, but without adding any names. This would occur three or four times a year, but the years multiplied the number of times and the combination of times and years hardened, solidified, the relationship between the Wentz family and the Reveres. There was nothing as dramatic as a feud between them, and nothing approaching cordiality. George Wentz came home from his last year at Princeton, having lived twenty-three years on the same block as the Reveres, and had never been inside their house. He brought with him a friend.

"Who lives in the big house on the corner?" said Adam Sturgis.

"People named Revere. Mr. and Mrs. Franklin Revere."

"Mr. and Mrs. Gotrocks?" said Adam.

"Not *the* Mr. and Mrs. Gotrocks, but they're well fixed. She has the money. He comes from Maryland somewhere."

"It's a nice house," said Adam.

"Yes it is," said George. "At one time it and one other house were the only houses on the block. The houses in between—our house, for instance—were built on ground that used to be a grove of trees. That was before I was born, but my father remembers it. He used to play there. They used to come and have picnics under the trees. It was almost like a public park, but then I guess the land got too valuable and the trees were cut down and they put up sixteen or eighteen small houses. Income producers. Although we never paid rent. My father bought our house when he and my mother got married. Subject to mortgages, of course, but he finally paid them off. I guess that's why we never had a car. My father and mother gave up a lot to own their own home. There were two things they were determined on. To own their own home, and send me to college."

"Well, you helped there. It didn't cost them much to send you to college."

"No, but they were ready, in case I didn't get any scholarships. In a way, I suppose the help I got at Princeton paid off the last mortgage, indirectly. And my father had the satisfaction of owning his own house the last year of his life."

"And knowing you were all set. Phi Bete junior year, he didn't have to worry about you," said Adam.

"He worried enough. I'm sure he never made more than three hundred a month, and he had to keep up appearances."

"Is that all? He owned a jewelry store," said Adam.

"It's Wentz's jewelry store, but my father didn't own it. It was owned by his older brother and my grandmother. My father was never anything more than a clerk. A combination clerk and book-keeper. He had to wait on customers and keep the books. If they had a good year, the extra profit was cut up between my uncle and my grandmother, and maybe a small Christmas present for my father, but it was never much. My uncle liked the dames and the booze. Oh, the store made good money. Uncle Lou had a wife that knew how to spend it, too. But my father saw very little of it. He handled it, and that was about all. Handled it, is right. A clerk in a jewelry store has to have his hands clean and his fingernails just right. I remember every Sunday evening, my mother used to give my father a manicure. Every Sunday evening. My uncle had his manicured at the ladies' beauty parlor. The barbershops in town didn't have manicurists then. But my mother was my father's manicurist. As a matter of fact, she got good enough to give manicures to some of her friends. She never said so, but I'm sure she picked up a few dollars that way. Just from friends. They did a lot of things like that. My father kept the books for a couple of little stores. He'd bring their books home, or rather they'd bring them to our house. My uncle never knew my father did that. Little stores like Miss Jenny Albright's. She had a store in the front room of her house. Sold yarn and things like that. Linen and handkerchiefs. My father kept her books for her. A hundred and twenty dollars a year. And Joe Orsino, had a shoe repair shop on Second Street. My father charged him more, twenty-five a month. Three hundred a year. And he got something for being financial secretary of his lodge. He never told me how much that was, because everything about the lodge was secret. But it was probably two or three hundred a year."

"But you were never actually poor," said Adam.

"Compared to some, no. Compared to others, we were worse than poor. There was never a time when we didn't have enough to eat in the house, that's true. The cheaper cuts, but unskimmed milk. My mother used to want to deal at the Bell Store. It was a cash-and-carry chain store. But we had customers among the grocers and butchers, and believe me they put the pressure on people that bought at the Bell. And they were right. Why should they buy an engagement ring from us if we were spending our money at a store that was slowly putting them out of business? An early lesson in economics for me, when my father told my mother we had to stop buying at the Bell. One of the few times I ever heard them fight. 'Let Lou Wentz make up the difference,' she said. Money was the enemy in this house."

"It must have been," said Adam.

"But there's nothing like a common enemy for keeping people together. We missed a lot. Do you know that in four years at Princeton I've yet to see New Haven? My father used to say, 'All your friends are going up to Yale. It won't break me to treat you to one game there.' But I'd think of the train fare, and the tickets to the game, and meals for a girl and me, and it would just about amount up to a suit of clothes. My suits, Adam. Not yours. And I'd refuse. Then in junior year he sent me a check and said this was the last time I'd be able to see Princeton beat Yale on their own home ground, the Yale Bowl, and he insisted I go."

"But you didn't go. I remember. They beat the hell out of us, too," said Adam.

"No, I didn't go, but I didn't tell him. I wrote him a letter of thanks, faking it as if I'd gone. And I kept the money, fifty bucks, and that year I gave them both pretty decent Christmas presents. As it happened, that turned out to be my father's last Christmas alive. My mother asked me how I could afford such nice presents, and I told her I'd saved up my winnings at bridge. She gave me a look and she didn't say anything, but *she* knew I'd never gone near New Haven. That little gold bar pin. I got it wholesale through the store. She wears it all the time."

"What did you buy your father?"

"A cashmere sweater. He was wearing it when he died. He was down-cellar, tinkering with the oil burner, and he started up the stairs and got about halfway. Heart attack."

"You know, George, I have a confession to make," said Adam.

"Go ahead," said George.

"Ever since we've been friends, a little over three years, the one thing I had reservations about was your being a student of the dollar. I knew you weren't Rockefeller, but you used to get these letters from Wentz's jewelry store. Wentz's. Jewelers and Silversmiths, Established 18-something. And I used to think, well he doesn't have to play it *that* close to the vest. It was very hard to pull you loose from a buck. And then I thought, well, the Pennsylvania Dutch. Not notoriously spendthrift. So when you invited me here, frankly I came out of curiosity as much as anything else, and I fully expected to be met with a 1915 Pierce-Arrow. And when I saw that house on the corner, I thought it was going to be yours."

"Well, I guess I was stingy," said George. He laughed.

"You were never stingy in your life, you dumb bastard."

"Pretty stingy. There were times when I could have spent more than I did. But I'm not going to change right away, Adam. I'm pretty sure of getting the Prix de Rome, and I've had offers of jobs. By the time I'm thirty I should be making pretty good money, and then maybe I'll be able to do what I want to do. What I really want to do."

"Which is?"

"Give my mother the keys to that house on the corner."

"Why?"

"Because those bastards, they used to go by this house and they'd just barely speak to my father and mother. Just barely speak to them. And for no reason at all."

I CAN'T
THANK YOU ENOUGH

Arthur Felzer stopped at the desk, and allowed the woman behind him to get ahead of him. She said whatever she had to say to the clerk and moved on.

"Yes, Mr. Felzer?" said the clerk.

"I'm gonna be checking out of 1214 and will you have my bill ready?" said Felzer.

"We'll send it to you, as usual," said the clerk.

"No, no. This one I want to pay cash," said Felzer.

"Cash? Well, I guess we're always glad to accept cash," said the clerk. "Your bill'll be ready whenever you come down. You have no extra charges since breakfast, Mr. Felzer?"

"No, I don't think so. Since breakfast. Maybe some phone calls. I tell you, Ray. Let me pay the bill now, and I'll give you a few bucks in case there was any charges since breakfast."

"You don't have to do that, Mr. Felzer. We'll bill you or carry it over, whatever you like."

"No, let's do it my way, Ray. I don't want this bill sent to my office. I'll give you, oh, say twenty dollars and you take care of any phone calls or anything since breakfast. What's left over, you can have that for yourself. Buy yourself a couple neckties, maybe. I don't want to have to stop here on my way out."

"I see," said the clerk. "Will I have them bring your car around?"

"Yeah, would you do that, Ray?" said Felzer. "And have the boy take the luggage out to the car."

"I'll send one right up. You be ready to go in about how long?"

"Oh, a half an hour, maybe less. How much do I owe you?"

The clerk stepped to the cashier's cage and asked her for the total charges on Room 1214. "Ninety-four sixty-two," she said.

"Ninety-four sixty-two, Mr. Felzer."

"Ninety-four sixty-two. Well, all right, here's a hundred and twenty, Ray. You take care of everything for me?"

"Yes indeed, and thank you very much, Mr. Felzer. Hurry back, as they say down South."

"Right," said Felzer. "Oh, I'll leave the key with the bellboy."

He went to his room and let himself in. She was sitting in the easy chair, reading a newspaper. She had on a skirt and shirtwaist, and the jacket that matched the skirt was hanging on the desk chair. "Hello," she said.

"Good, you're all ready," he said.

"Oh, sure. I've been ready for about a half an hour or so."

"I'm a little later than I said I'd be, but I got tied up," he said.

"That's perfectly all right," she said. "Gave me a chance to read the paper. I don't often read the paper at breakfast except on Sundays."

"No, I guess not. What time do you have to be at work?"

"Well, that depends. School starts at nine and we're supposed to be there at eight-thirty. But we take turns getting there at eight."

"Eight A.M., I guess that's pretty rough, eh?" he said.

"Yes, but fortunately it's only every ninth week. Did you get everything accomplished?"

"Yes, more or less."

"I was still asleep when you left. That's very unusual for me, to sleep past eight o'clock, even on Sunday. You must have had breakfast downstairs."

"A cup of coffee around the corner. I don't ordinarily eat a very big breakfast."

"Neither do I, but I did this morning. I had everything. A *big* glass of orange juice. Two poached eggs. Toast. Marmalade. And two cups of coffee. And I haven't got a hangover. I thought I might have one, but I didn't. Did you?"

"Well, maybe a little one. Nowadays when I get up in the

morning I often have a hangover and I didn't do any drinking the night before. Are you all packed?"

"Just to put a few things in, hairbrush and things. I notice your bag is ready. I'll be ready in less than a minute. I won't hold you up."

"That's all right," he said.

She went to the bathroom and closed the door, and came out presently with a plastic toilet kit in her hand. She put the kit in her suitcase and closed it, and her fingers lingered on the bag.

"Trying to remember if you forgot something?" he said.

"No. Just thinking," she said.

"What?"

"Oh, I don't know," she said.

"Sure you do," he said.

"Yes. I was thinking as I closed the bag, I was closing a chapter in my life."

"Oh," he said.

"Wasn't a very long chapter, was it?" she said.

"Well, who said it was over?"

"Who had to? We both know it," she said. "Well, I'm ready whenever you are."

"Boy'll be here any minute."

"I guess we just have to wait for him," she said. She sat down and lit a cigarette. "I was wondering, Arthur. Don't you think it'd be better if I met you somewhere outside? I really don't want to stand in the lobby while you're paying the bill."

"That's all taken care of," he said. "I paid the bill on my way up, and we don't have to hang around. The car'll be waiting outside. Do you want to go down and wait in the car? I'll take care of the bags."

"Would you mind if I did that?"

"Hell, no. You know the car."

"You're very considerate. I can't thank you enough."

"You didn't expect it from Arthur Felzer, did you?"

"It isn't you, it's anybody. I don't think men *are* very considerate as a rule."

"Well, I don't know. Some are, and some aren't."

"Well, you happen to be one of those that are," she said.

"And you're surprised. You forget, Jane. I had a lot of experiences since I used to work for your father. Two years in college, an officer in the war. *I* stayed in some of the finest homes in England. And I made a bundle of dough."

"Papa said you would, too," she said.

"Well, he was all right, Mr. Campion. He sent me a copy of the letters he wrote when I used him for a reference. College *and* the Air Force. Maybe I wasn't as honest as he said I was, but I was neat and orderly. What else did he say I was? Energetic. *Diligent!* That's the word I was trying to think of. You know, some son of a bitch when we were in England, if you left anything lying around they'd go through your private papers. Letters and all. And some bastard came across the copy of the letter your father wrote, so for a while there the guys called me the diligent bombardier. The diligent bombardier. But that nickname didn't last very long. They didn't either, the guys that called me that. You know I was tempted to send your father my first Air Medal, but my mother would have killed me."

"Oh, he would have been so pleased," she said.

"Well, I figured the old lady was entitled to it. Then when we got the D.F.C. I *couldn't* send *that* to your father. That *had* to be for my old man. So I guess I never showed your father any appreciation."

"That's not why he helped you. He didn't expect anything in return."

"He sure as hell wouldn't think *this* was showing any appreciation," he said.

"Taking his innocent daughter to a hotel in Philadelphia? I don't think he had any illusions about me. I often caught him looking at me, trying to puzzle me out. He—"

"That's the boy for the bags," said Felzer. "You go on down and get in the car. I'll stall this guy."

She was sitting in the car when he showed up with the luggage. He tipped the doorman and they drove away. "We had a narrow escape," she said.

"How do you mean?" he said.

"I'd just got in the car and was lighting a cigarette when who do you suppose came out of the hotel and *stood* there, waiting for a taxi? Albert Stout."

"Yeah, he always stays there. Did he recognize you?"

"No, fortunately. I sat with my cigarette in my hand, over my face."

"Well, that'd be all over town by tomorrow night, if he recognized you."

"Do you think he could have seen us last night?"

"Not Albert," said Felzer. "He doesn't hit the hot spots. He wouldn't spend a nickel if he could help it. Were you scared?"

"Well, startled," she said. "What would your wife do?"

"My wife? You know what she'd probably do? She'd probably go somewhere and buy herself a new fur coat."

"Oh. What if she knew it was me?" she said.

He smiled. "If she knew it was you? If she knew it was you I guess maybe she'd buy two fur coats. I don't know."

"And that's all? She wouldn't go see a lawyer?"

"No. I got her old man working for me, and her brother. She's got her own car, a nice home. She isn't giving all that up because I took a girl to Philly."

"A girl," she said. "You know how old I am, Arthur. But thanks for the compliment."

"Well, a woman. Any female."

They were silent until he got out of the midtown traffic.

"If you turned left up here," she said, "I could show you where I went to school."

"You want to do that?" he said.

"Oh, no. I was just thinking how this city's changed. All these new highways and boulevards. I just happened to recognize that bridge. I was there for four years, and I've never gone back."

"Do you want to have a look at it? We have plenty of time. I was thinking we'd get out of town and then stop some place for lunch."

"No, I have no feelings about the school. That's all past history, all of that."

"Yeah, I guess it is or you wouldn't be sitting here. You

know, Jane, I got a confession to make. You know when I asked you if you'd go with me, on this trip, I didn't expect you to say yes."

"Well, I was a little surprised to hear myself saying yes, but I popped right out with it, didn't I?"

"Yes. Right away I thought, Jesus, I should have asked her ten-fifteen years ago, or more. Except then I guess you would have said no."

"Then I would have said no. I had someone else I was in love with."

"A married man?"

"Well, he *got* married. I guess he must have found out about my father's financial condition. That's a nasty thing to say, but I'm afraid it's true. A lot of things changed for us then. I certainly never thought I'd become an old-maid schoolteacher. I only took that job for a year, so I wouldn't have to take any money from my mother. And now I've been at it, this is my twenty-third year."

"And my kid went there. Boy, I was surprised when they let her in."

"You needn't have been. She was a perfectly nice little girl, and you have all that money."

"There's some things we're kept out of," he said.

"Well, maybe they're not worth getting into, Arthur. I hope you don't fret over them."

"I don't, but Leonia does."

"You're speaking of the Tuesday Club?" she said.

"Yeah, she never even heard about it till we joined the country club. Then she said well if we were good enough to join the country club, why didn't we get invited to the Tuesday? I said what did she want to get invited to the Tuesday Club for?"

"Actually, you know there is no such thing as the Tuesday Club any more. They stopped being a club a long time ago. It's just a group of people that have dinner together."

"Sure, but always the same people."

"Well, yes, but as long as they don't call themselves a club she doesn't have to feel that she's being kept out of anything."

"Who are you kidding? That makes it so much worse, for her."

"Well, *that's* too bad, because that's one group that will never change. They'll die off, maybe, but you have to be at least a cousin to get invited now."

"She hates them. I said to her, what did she want to have dinner with a lot of people she hated."

"And now she'd hate one of them more than ever, if she knew."

"Yes, she would."

"Did you ever hate us, Arthur?" she said.

"Did I ever hate you? Candidly, not till the first Christmas I came home from State. They had some dance and I got an invitation, but I didn't get invited any place for dinner. And I figured out I was one of the suckers. They invited us to pay ten dollars a head for the dance, so they could hire a name band. But all they cared about was our ten bucks. Glen Gray, or somebody, they got. But they didn't get me again. You were at that dance, Jane."

"Was I? I suppose I was. At the hotel?"

"At the hotel. I went over and cut in on you, and the guy you were dancing with said no cutting in. A God damn lie. Everybody was cutting in. But I was a meatball. No meatballs cutting in on your crowd. Ed Stokes, Junior. That was who was dancing with you. Was that who didn't marry you when your father went bust?"

"Yes," she said.

"Kind of figured it was," he said. "Well, the poor son of a bitch, I guess when you have one of those dinners you have to serve him milk."

"Yes, when he comes at all. They took out part of his stomach, you know."

"Yeah, I heard. The son of a bitch. No stomach, married the wrong girl, lost over eighty-five thousand dollars on that motel he put up. I said to him at the time, I said 'Ed, for Christ's sake, take a look around at some of the other motels.' I said you drive around at night and all you see is the neon signs, vacancy, vacancy, vacancy. So he blew over eighty-five thousand dollars. How I happen to know that, they asked me to come in for a one-quarter piece, the same as Ed. I said, 'Gentlemen, I'll wait two years and pick up the whole thing for eighty-five.' Oh, Christ, were they sore at me. But I got news for you. I could get it for sixty, and I don't want it. Fifty is all I'd give them. It's worth it to me. Not for the motel. Oh, no. But they got the land, all graded and all, and the water lines are in. Electricity. Black-top parking space. Filling station. I'll give them fifty, and then I'll go to town, with a supermarket *and* a bowling alley. That's why I was in Philly this time. Lining up some of the concessions for the supermarket. The fellow I talked to this morning, you think the women go to the supermarket to buy meat and vegetables. Canned goods. Well, sure they do. But this morning I was talking to the fellow that wants the drug and cosmetics concession. Once I got him signed, I'm going after some of the smaller ones. Like I got a guy, he won't use much more space than the front seat of this car, but I'm gonna sign him for the watch repair concession. Not big, you know, but it all adds up. When I was out in Vegas a couple years ago, you know if I could put in just penny and nickel slot machines I'd coin money, but I can't do that here. They got the slot machines next to the cashier's counter, and all the small change goes into the one-armed bandits. It breaks your heart to think how much money I have to pass up."

"How do you make your money now, Arthur? I know it's something to do with real estate."

"Jane, I got so many irons in the fire. Real estate, yes. But I don't limit myself to real estate. How much do you know about depreciation, tax-wise?"

"Nothing."

"Then I'd have a hard time explaining it to you. What it amounts to, I can own a property and over twenty years the depreciation works out so I can sell the property and it's all gravy. I'm not going to try to explain it to you."

"No, don't. It's too depressing."

"Yeah, but not to me. I own a record shop, where the beatniks buy rock-and-roll. I got an interest in a drive-yourself car rental. This car we're in now, the registration isn't in my name. If Leonia wants to get even with me and hit me with two fur coats, I don't get them wholesale. I do better than that, or the furrier has to pay his rent on time. And they don't, you know. They're seasonal. The bill I just paid at the hotel, that's the first time I paid cash at a hotel since I was incorporated. They don't know what cash is at hotels any more. I got Leonia down for manager of the record shop and she never goes near the place. She took a trip to New York to hear those Beatles. Why not? She's in the record business. Rented one of my cars and drove to New York."

"I don't want to hear any more, Arthur. But thanks for paying cash for our bill."

"Oh, well."

"How much was it, may I ask? Do you mind telling me?"

"Ninety-four sixty-two."

"Good Lord! Where did it all go?"

"Well, the room was thirty-five. There's seventy right off. The rest was breakfast, around eight or nine dollars."

"But why did they charge you for two nights? We were only there one."

"I reserved the room for two, in case you could get away the night before last."

"And they made you pay?"

"I didn't make any fuss," he said.

"And it wasn't worth it," she said.

"Well, what the hell, Jane? Yes, it was worth it. Certain things, certain people. If it was just you and me maybe it would have been all right. But we had too many other people in that room with us. Your father. Your mother. I guess probably Ed Stokes."

"No, not Ed Stokes, Arthur."

"Well, I'm glad of that, anyway," he said. "Listen, you don't hear any beef out of me. Maybe if we would of stayed another night it would of been all right. I don't know, Jane. We're not kids."

"I know we're not, and that's what makes it a little worse. I behaved like one. How can a middle-aged spinster behave like a teenager?"

He smiled. "That's not what I hear about teenagers."

"I guess not," she said. "Something you said a minute ago, about depreciation."

He shook his head. "No, you have to own the property twenty years."

"Well, I'll tell you this, Arthur. You own me now more than any man I've ever known."

"No, you don't have to say that, Jane," he said. "Candidly, I'd just as soon we didn't talk about it any more."

"But I would, Arthur," she said. "Don't you see that—do you remember what I said about closing a chapter? In the room?"

"Oh, yes. I remember."

"What I'm afraid of is closing the whole book."

"Yeah, yeah. I see. You don't have to think of it that way."

"But I do. Couldn't we go away again sometime?"

"I'll tell you, Jane," he said. "It's kind of hard for you to get away. The school and your mother and all like that. And I got a kind of a you might call it a commitment. A girl, a young woman lives in Reading. I usually take her on trips once in a while. You know?"

"I know I don't believe you," she said. "I can always tell when my pupils aren't telling the truth, and you're making this up."

"Well, I could tell you her name, but you wouldn't know her."

"Ruth Miller," said Jane.

"I don't know any Ruth Miller."

"Neither do I, but I'm sure there are a lot of Ruth Millers in Reading. Probably a lot of them in Allentown. Lebanon. You've given up on me, haven't you, Arthur? There is no girl in Reading."

"No, there's no girl in Reading. I play the field."

"You don't know what my life is like, do you? You don't know what it is to have been attractive, to have had love affairs. Real love affairs. And then to have it all stop completely, while you teach first and second grade nine months of the year, and take care of a mother that's half dotty. And be a lady, and watch every penny while the Leonia Felzers drive around in fur coats and Cadillacs. Now do you know why I said yes when you asked me to go away with you? No one else had asked me in so long that I had no other answer. And now what? You'll drop me at home, and if anybody shows the slightest interest I can tell them that you gave me a lift from Philadelphia. And they'll believe me. That's all anyone cares. No one would think for a minute that I went away with you or anyone else. Jane Campion, the spinster schoolteacher. Didn't you *want* me to go with you, Arthur?"

"Sure. I asked you, didn't I?"

"Then ask me again," she said.

"No, I don't want to do that."

"All right," she said.

"Wuddia say, shall we see what's on the radio?" he said.

"Yes."

"Any particular station you like?" he said.

"No, I don't hear the radio very often. Mother likes the TV," she said. "And at this time of the day I'm usually in school."

"Is that window too much for you?"

"Not now, but it may be later on," she said. They would be stopping for lunch soon, and she could roll up the window then.

IN THE MIST

Rex Sinclair eased the Sixty Special into the garage, put on the brakes, switched off the engine. "Well, you see we made it," he said.

"Yeah, I never thought we would," said Buddy Longden. "For a while there I wished I had my rosary beads."

"You a Catholic?" said Rex Sinclair.

"I used to be, but now I'm nothing."

"I wouldn't say you were nothing," said Rex. "Anybody that can play your kind of piano. I'd rather be able to do that than anything I can think of."

"I'll trade you," said Buddy.

They got out of the car and stood in the driveway. "Ordinarily this is one of the best views around," said Rex. "You can look down that way and you get the famous Los Angeles at night. The magic carpet of lights and so forth. Then over there all the little houses on the mountain. That's a view I like. The lights in the little houses."

"I have to take your word for it tonight," said Buddy.

"Yeah, well you get a fog like this and personally it gives me a wonderful feeling. It gives you a feeling of accomplishment, to be able to do something that there aren't many people can do."

"You mean driving your car home?" said Buddy.

"Don't make it sound like nothing. I'll bet you a thousand dollars to ten that you couldn't take my car and make it back to Hollywood the first try. I'll bet you five hundred to ten you couldn't make it the first try *in daylight*. Don't bet me. I had taxi drivers can't find this place even when they have directions. There's two or three places if you don't make the proper turn, you find yourself back on Franklin. Another place, if you don't make the right turn you find yourself in a dead end and if you're making any kind of speed, you could easily go through the fence and that'd be bye-bye."

"You like that, living so isolated," said Buddy.

"It's not isolated for me. I can be from here to Paramount in under fifteen minutes. I've done it. I can be at Columbia in twelve. I'm not isolated. Christ, I could live in Beverly if I wanted to, but this is what I like. What do you think is on top of that garage?"

"You got me."

"A tennis court. In Beverly if I had a tennis court I'd have to use up land that the taxes are murder. Here I have as big a garage as anybody in Beverly *and* a tennis court, and I'm paying taxes on the same amount of land. Two for the price of one, you might say. We do have one problem here."

"What's that?"

"Rattlesnakes. These mountains are full of them. So here, take a flashlight. I never saw one at night, the nine years I've been living here, but I don't take any chances."

"Jesus, you make me wish I didn't come."

"Don't worry. I always have this, too, and I know how to use it." Rex showed Buddy Longden a .38 caliber Banker's Special.

"How about if we go inside and get a drink?" said Buddy.

"Certainly. I'll lead the way," said Rex.

"You're damn right you will," said Buddy.

The livingroom was large and comfortably furnished. Before the fireplace were two low, deeply upholstered davenports facing each other and a circular table between them. At one end of the room was a card table, with decks of cards and bridge score pads and pencils on it. At the other end was a bar, professionally equipped. The floor was polished hardwood and on it lay rugs of varying dimensions as well as the skins of a white bear and a leopard. In all there were probably two dozen chairs scattered about. The walls were covered with pictures, running largely to blown-up photographs of movie actors and actresses, interspersed with seascapes and detailed paintings of sailboats. An oil portrait of Sinclair in the costume of a captain in the Army-in-India was the only picture with its own illumination. One corner of the room contained a Steinway concert grand, a studio piano, and a set of drums and traps which included a hi-hat and two bongo drums.

"Quite a layout," said Buddy.

"Yeah, when I got rid of Marcy I made this room into a place where I could sit down and relax. She had it all gussied up in case Noel Coward ever came here. But he didn't. She wouldn't have known what the hell to say to him if he had, but that was my life for six years. Waiting for Hollywood society to take us up. Big star, I ought to be in society. She could never understand that. She used to wonder why the hell Cesar Romero got invited to places and I didn't. I never had the answer for that. Pour yourself a drink, have a cigarette, and sit down and play me 'Washboard Blues.' "

"God, I don't know if I know it any more, it's so long since I got a request for it," said Buddy.

"You'll remember it. It'll come back. I heard you play it two years ago at a party at Hank Fonda's. Hell, play anything you like. If you want any help with the lyrics of 'Washboard,' I'm word-perfect in it. Then I'd like you to play 'Blue Lou.' Then 'Stop, Look and Listen.' Then I'll try you on some real oldies."

"That depends on how far back you go," said Buddy.

" 'Helen Gone.' You remember that? 'She could dance all night until the dawn? I said dawn.' "

"Fletcher Henderson?"

"I'm not sure," said Rex Sinclair.

"You want to sing, that's it," said Buddy.

"I want to sing, I want to hear you play the piano. Mostly I want to hear you play the piano," said Rex. "Will it bother you if I go along on drums? Just the brushes."

"That depends."

"Oh, don't worry about the beat. I have a solid beat. I come home from the studio some days, have a snort, put on some records, and I can sit here for two hours, just beating it out with the brushes."

"Did you ever do it for a living?"

"High school, I used to play in a little band we had in high school. No union. Two, three dollars a night. Snare, bass, two cymbals, wood block, cowbell. Sixty dollars for the whole set. Ludwig. Maybe it wasn't even sixty dollars. My aunt gave it to me and my old lady wanted to have her put in the insane asylum. But oh, boy, when I got paid real money, two dollars, three dollars. Then the old lady changed her mind."

"With me it was just the opposite. My old lady had me taking lessons from the time I was six years of age," said Buddy. He went to the piano and played a few chords. "After what I'm used to, the action on this is a little stiff."

"But there's nothing the matter with the tone," said Rex.

"No, there sure as hell's nothing wrong with the tone," said Buddy. Out of nowhere he began to play, four repeated chords, some right hand, followed by four repeated chords higher on the scale.

"God damn it, man! I know what that is," said Rex. He sprang to the drums. "It's the verse, the *verse* of 'Stairway to Paradise.' "

Buddy nodded and smiled and went on playing. They played steadily for half an hour, mostly Gershwin, some Porter, some Berlin, some Kern, some Henderson, some Ellington. Rex would suspend the beat of the brushes between pieces until Buddy got into the next tune, then he would pick up the beat and they did not need to speak. At the end of a half hour Buddy lit a cigarette and opened and closed his fists.

"Not used to a good piano," he said.

"Take five, and I'll get you a drink. Take ten," said Rex. "As we used to say, I never had so much fun with clothes on." He poured drinks for Buddy and himself. "Where else have you been since I saw you at Fonda's?"

"Oh, I don't know. Ratting around."

"You don't want to talk?"

"I don't mind talking, but what the hell? I had a couple of club jobs. CBS for a while. Made a few cuts."

"What's that, cuts?"

"Recording dates."

"What's your trouble? The booze?"

"I guess that's what some people would say," said Buddy.

"The broads? *A* broad?"

"Now look, Mr. Sinclair, you promised me a hundred bucks to play piano for three hours, right?"

"In other words, don't get too inquisitive. All right. You ready to play again?"

Buddy took a long sip of his drink and a long drag of his cigarette and turned back to the keyboard. "I remembered 'Washboard,' but let me do it without the brushes, huh?"

"Sure," said Rex.

"I'll do it the way Hoagy did it, but he had a band behind him. I think Beiderbecke was in that band if I'm not mistaken. Then I'll do 'In a Mist' for you. That's kind of logical, isn't it?"

"You're the maestro," said Rex.

Buddy did a faithful rendition of "Washboard Blues" and when he had finished the playing and singing he stopped.

"Now 'In a Mist,' " said Rex.

"No more. That's it," said Buddy. "You owe me thirty-three dollars."

"What's the matter, Buddy?"

"I don't know."

"Some kind of a sentimental association?"

"Christ, no. You mean on account of Beiderbecke? The great Bix? I never went for that stuff. That's for guys like you, Mr. Sinclair. Amateur trap drummers. How's for calling me a cab? I'll give you the concert for free."

"You get your hundred," said Rex. "But the cab is another story. Till the fog lifts, you're stuck. Call the taxi company and see what they tell you. I know from experience."

"I'd walk if I wasn't afraid of snakes. Will you lend me your gun?"

"No. You can have a flashlight and I'll give you a cane."

"Like a God damn blind man," said Buddy.

"You want to spend the night in the guest room? There's everything there. Pajamas. New toothbrush. You might as well."

"What are you gonna do? Play records?"

"Well, I was just thinking. I know somebody that can get here in the fog, if she isn't busy."

"Maybe she has a friend," said Buddy.

"Maybe she has, if you want me to ask her."

"How much would this set me back? I'll go for the hundred, but not any more."

"I'll take care of that," said Rex.

"You don't have to do that."

"I don't have to do anything, but I wanted company, so I guess I'm going to have company." Rex went to the telephone, dialed a Crestview number, and waited. "Sandra? Rex. Oh, come on, it isn't all that late. Well, how about getting into your car and— oh, listen, I have a friend of mine here spending the night. Can you persuade a friend of yours to make it a foursome? No, he's not in pictures. I doubt if you'd know him. I'd say he was in his middle thirties. He's a business man. In the piano business. Very important guy in the piano business. Well, if you must know, I met him several years ago at a party at Hank Fonda's. Why all the questions? Well, if she's a new girl she wants to meet all the right people, doesn't she? All right. But you'll have to bring her in your car. The fog is terrific. That's a good girl, Sandra. I'll remember you in my prayers." He hung up. "She has a friend, and they'll be here in about a half an hour. How about a sandwich or something?"

"Who's Sandra?"

"Well, I guess you could gather from the conversation, she's a high-class hooker. She makes more that way than she did in pictures, so that's how she makes it. And it has to be cash with Sandra. No cheques. She doesn't believe in the income tax, and I'm right with her there."

"Who's she getting for me?"

"Some new girl. Lives in the same building as Sandra. That's as much as I can tell you now. You afraid she's going to turn out to be your ex-wife or something?"

"I never said I had an ex-wife," said Buddy.

"No, but you figured to," said Rex.

"You're right. Not one, but two," said Buddy. "But I don't have to worry about them turning up as call girls. One's dead, and the other's married to a trombone player, NBC house band back in New York."

"Which one does 'Washboard' remind you of?"

"The dead one. She liked 'Lazybones,' and there's a part there in 'Washboard' that I'm positive Hoagy took out of 'Washboard' and made into part of the melody of 'Lazybones.'"

"Show me," said Rex.

Buddy looked at him. "You want to get me back to the piano. All right." He sat down and demonstrated his theory of the source of a segment of the "Lazybones" melody. "What else do you want me to play?"

"Nothing, if you don't feel like it."

Buddy turned around on the tufted stool. "You know, this is the first time I was ever in a movie star's home that there wasn't a party going on. I worked for Henry Fonda and Jimmy Stewart and some others, but there was always a lot of people. It's altogether different."

"How do you mean?"

"Well, you. You come into a joint and right away the boss comes over and says it's Rex Sinclair, as if we didn't know. And he says to play show tunes, that you always like show tunes. Figures you to be good for a hundred bucks or so if you stay a while. So I play some show tunes and you come over and bring your drink over and you *know* it's a lousy piano, so you offer me a hundred bucks and I come up here. Just you and me. You, one of the biggest stars in the movie business. Me, a club piano player."

"Not one of the biggest stars. Not as big as Fonda or Stewart. But steadily employed. I'll work in pictures they wouldn't spit on."

"Well, I don't know about that part of it, but I consider you a big star. And then when I get here we have a session, me on piano and you on drums. Nice. You could never work in a good band, but in about a third-rate band you could get a job. Can you read?"

"Yes, I used to be able to read."

"Your kind of drumming you'd be better off if you couldn't read. Forget about your drum lessons and just fake. You'll loosen up. Get more enjoyment out of it."

"All right. So you were saying how different it is than you expected."

"Well, I wouldn't want to be you. I thought I might be willing to trade places, but you got damn near nothing. This house, and a tennis court on your garage, and three cars inside the garage. But you got damn near nothing. At ha' past four in the morning, you have to call a hooker."

"That's right. That's the story. Half past four in the morning I have to call a hooker."

"So where are you better off than I am?"

"Well, I guess except for the fact that *I* can pay *you* a hundred dollars to play piano for *me,* and another hundred dollars for a hooker, I guess I'm no better off. Does that make you feel better?"

"It sure does. Temporarily," said Buddy. "I got one room down on Melrose. A Chevy coop. At the end of the week I got my bar bill to take out of my pay, so I'm lucky to go home with fifty or sixty dollars. But I don't have to dress up or any of that, and once you're asleep the cotton sheets are just as good as silk."

"Keep talking, if it makes you feel any better. Have a drink," said Rex.

Buddy looked at him with a dead resentment. He suddenly swung around and played four bars of the fast instrumental part of "Washboard," then abruptly stopped. *"You* can't do that."

"No, and you didn't do it so good then, either," said Rex. "You hit a couple of clinkers. Have a drink, Buddy, and quit trying to make me feel sorry for myself. I'm going out and make a sandwich. You want a sandwich? Come on out and help yourself."

"I'll drink my sandwich," said Buddy.

"You do that," said Rex. He went to the kitchen and made himself a cold roast beef sandwich on rye bread. He sat eating it in the breakfast nook, washing it down with a glass of Dutch beer, and had been gone about ten minutes when the quiet and the calm, a quiet and a calm which seemed to *come from* the livingroom, to emanate from the livingroom, made him wonder what his guest was doing. On a strong impulse he got up, half a sandwich in one hand, beer shell in the other, and went back to the livingroom, making as little sound as possible.

Buddy was standing in front of the portrait, the illuminated one of Rex in a turban and gauntlets and tunic and breeches. Buddy had in his right hand a large pair of library shears.

"What the hell would you want to do that for?" said Rex.

"I don't know. I was just debating whether I ought to," said Buddy. He put the shears back on a table.

"It cost me twenty-five hundred dollars, that picture," said Rex.

"That didn't worry me," said Buddy. He returned to the tufted stool, the only place where he had actually sat since coming to the house.

"It's supposed to be a pretty good portrait. I don't mean of me. But it was a good artist. He died last year up in Carmel. He was supposed to be pretty good. He didn't usually paint portraits of people."

"So you gave him a hundred dollars to play the piano for you," said Buddy.

"I see what you mean," said Rex. "Yes, as a matter of fact. It was something like that. I heard he was on his duff, financially, so I gave him the job. Commissioned him. And I paid for it myself. The studio didn't pay for it. And it's supposed to be pretty good, according to some people in art. But you weren't going to cut it up because you didn't think it was artistic. You wanted to cut *me* up. Why?"

"Because you're a phony. Having your picture painted in that uniform."

"I was pretty good in that picture. That's the closest I ever came to an Academy nomination. The picture got nominated. If it'd been directed by John Ford it probably would have got the Oscar."

"The hell with that. You just wanted to have your portrait painted in that uniform," said Buddy.

"Partly that. But I only got the idea through meeting Ben Leisenring, the artist that painted it."

"You took pity on him," said Buddy.

"Partly that, too. But when he started coming here to do the actual painting, I didn't pity him any more. He was as good in his line as you are in yours. Better, in fact. And he wasn't a sorehead cry-baby. Also he could drink better. He put away a bottle of Martel's every time he came here, and he always left sober. And he knew he was dying. He was here five days a week for almost two months."

"I suppose you gave him two bottles of Martel's for the other two days," said Buddy.

"I guess it amounted to that. I sent him a case of it."

"Another whore. Just like me, or the two broads you got coming tonight."

"Don't put yourself in the same class with Ben Leisenring."

"As a whore, you mean?" said Buddy.

"As a man, as an artist."

"Where would *you* put me? About the same class as you?"

Rex smiled. "Yeah, just about. You're far from a Joe Sullivan, Buddy. And I think I know why you didn't want to play 'In a Mist.' Bix didn't only play it. He *wrote* it. Did you ever hear of Charley Dawes?"

"Yes. He was with Whiteman. He played tenor saxophone."

"Now who's the phony? He was the vice-president of the United States."

"I'm thinking of somebody else. Charley Somebody."

"You had to pretend you knew. You were faking. Charles G. Dawes, vice-president of the United States. Do you recognize this?" Rex went to the piano and with one finger played thirteen notes.

" 'All in the Game,' Tommy Dorsey made a cut of it," said Buddy.

"Yes he did. But the melody was written by Charles G. Dawes, vice-president of the United States."

"Well good for him, and so what? To me it sounds like Rube Bloom. *You* heard of Rube Bloom."

"The way you say it, you expect me to say no. Well, if you're talking about the Rube Bloom that wrote 'Sapphire' and 'Soliloquy,' yes, I heard of him. Buddy, you're just an argumentative, disagreeable sorehead."

"I know I am, and I was supposed to be here as an entertainer. You sure made a bad deal tonight."

"Oh, I don't know. I had about a half an hour's pleasure that first set."

" 'That first set.' Greetings, Gate, let's syncopate. You like to talk musician talk. You're hep to the jive, man. Yeah, man. Hep to the jive."

"I'm going to put the lights on for the girls. And you better start getting into a better mood," said Rex. He went to the front hall and switched on the driveway floodlights. "It doesn't help much, but it helps some."

"What's the name of this dame you got for me?"

"I have no idea."

"What if I don't like her?"

"Then you can play gin rummy with her."

"What if I don't like her but I do like this Sandra?"

"Then you can still play gin with the other one. You don't get Sandra. Sandra's a money proposition but I also happen to like her."

"Now I understand you, Mr. Sinclair. If you can buy it, it's fine. A hooker, an oil painter, or a musician."

"No, Buddy, it just happens to work out that way," said Rex. "You're close, but that's not the whole story. *There,* that's Sandra's horn." Rex picked up a flashlight and went out to greet the girls.

He came back with his arms around both girls' shoulders. "Ladies, this is my friend Mr. Longden, very big in the piano business. This is Sandra, and this young lady is Karen."

"Do you manufacture them, or sell them?" said Sandra.

"I'm in the sales end," said Buddy.

"That makes you a piano salesman. Well, I know a joke about a piano salesman, but maybe I better not tell it," said Sandra.

"Save it for later," said Rex. "Ladies, how about a little libation. Sandra, I know what you want. Karen?"

"Never touch it," said Karen.

"Are you serious?" said Rex.

"She's leveling, she doesn't drink," said Sandra.

"I could tell that right away," said Buddy.

"You could? How?" said Sandra.

"Karen knows I could tell it," said Buddy.

"Did you know each other before?" said Rex.

"I never saw her before in my life, did I, Karen?"

"No," said Karen.

"Can you always tell if a person doesn't drink?" said Sandra.

"No, but I could tell with Karen, couldn't I, Karen?"

"Oh, shut up," said Karen.

"Well, now that the ice is broken," said Rex. "Sandra, brandy and ginger ale, the Sandra special."

"He likes people that drink brandy, I notice," said Buddy.

"Who else? Nobody else is drinking brandy that I see," said Sandra.

"Oil painters, hookers."

"Watch it, Buddy," said Sandra. "You're just liable to get a bottle of it cracked right over your skull. And by me, if you want to know who by."

"You wouldn't want a thing like that to get in the papers," said Buddy. "Drunken brawl at home of big movie star. And Karen wouldn't like to be locked up overnight."

"Give me your keys, Sandra. I want to get away from this fellow."

"Don't be afraid of him, he's just a jerk," said Sandra.

"She's not afraid of me," said Buddy. "She just doesn't want to be locked up. She has claustrophobia. Claustrophobia of the needle."

"Oh," said Sandra. "Is that what he meant, Karen?"

"Yes."

"Oh," said Sandra. "You didn't tell me that."

"I don't go around bragging about it."

"How did *he* know?" said Rex.

"He knew," said Karen. "He looks like he was a user, too, but I wasn't sure. Kicked it, maybe. But he pegged me, and I knew he did. There's a certain look. This guy is trouble and I want out. Give me your keys, Sandra."

"You'd have a hell of a time in this fog," said Rex.

"It's murder, and *I* know the way, Karen," said Sandra.

"That's right," said Rex. "So Buddy, I guess you're elected."

"To what?" said Buddy.

"To take a walk in the fog."

"Not me, I won't go out there with them snakes."

"Oh, they wouldn't hurt *you*. They'd know you were one of the gang," said Rex. "I'll let you have a flashlight."

"You can't make me go," said Buddy.

"Oh, but that's where you're so wrong."

"You mean you got a gun," said Buddy.

"No, I didn't mean that. Do you want me to throw you out? If you make me do that, I won't give you the flashlight. Then you *could* be in trouble. Take the flashlight and start walking. Make plenty of noise and keep walking, and maybe in an hour or two the fog'll clear. Then you can ask the milkman for directions. About an hour they start delivering. So which is it? I throw you out on your can, or be a nice boy and I let you have the flashlight?"

"Throw him out," said Sandra.

"No, I invited him here. He's my guest. But now I'm asking him to leave. Oh, forgetting something." Rex reached in his pocket and took two fifty-dollar bills out of his money clip. He tossed the money on the bar.

Buddy picked up the money. "Gimme the flashlight," he said.

"First I'll go with you to the end of my driveway. *Then* I'll give you the flashlight. I want to be sure you left. Not that I don't trust you, Buddy. I'll be back in a minute, girls."

Rex followed Buddy to the front door, opened it, and told Buddy to go out. "The floodlights are on, as you see," said Rex. "But once you're on your way I'm turning them off. And I want to tell you something, Buddy boy. Don't come back. Honestly, don't come back, because then you won't be invited."

"What'll you do? Shoot me?"

"No, I'll just call the cops. If they want to shoot you, that's their business. But if I were you, on a night like this, I'd take my chances with the snakes. You know, the cops get irritable, and you're kind of an unpredictable son of a bitch. I'll give you a tip. Not that you deserved it, but take the first two turns to your right, and the next left, and stay on that till you get to Vista del Monte. From there on it's downhill all the way."

"How can I trust you?"

"That's the funny part of it. You can't," said Rex. "But you'll have plenty of time to figure that out. *I* don't trust *you,* so I'll put the flashlight on the ground and you can pick it up yourself. I want both hands free in case you try to slug me."

"Cheap actor," said Buddy.

"All right, but you learn these things playing cops and robbers," said Rex.

Buddy picked up the flashlight and started walking. "First two turns to your right, next left, and stay on that road till Vista del Monte," Rex called to him. Then he ran to the house and switched off the floodlights.

"What happened?" said Sandra.

"Nothing, so far. But a lot could, to a guy that's afraid of snakes and has enough imagination," said Rex. "You know what he almost did? You see those big scissors?"

I SPEND MY DAYS
IN LONGING

It was bad enough to feel lousy when you knew what was wrong with you, knew that something was wrong with you, but none of the doctors he had seen could find anything wrong—organically, at least. The lungs, okay; the ticker, okay. Go easy on the cigarettes and coffee, they said. Be better if he did not drink so much brandy. But they were just whistling "Dixie," and they knew it and he knew it. He was a transient patient, a one-shot visitor to the offices of hotel doctors, mostly, from Boston to San Francisco. He would get an appointment, usually through the desk clerk, and half the time he would be the only patient in the reception room, the only *person* in the reception room, because hotel doctors did not have much of a setup. Two little rooms on the mezzanine, nobody in the reception room, a sign that said to push the button and be seated. The doc would open the door of his private office, come out and hand him a form to fill out which would provide his name and occupation, age, health record, married or single, by whom recommended. "I'll be with you in just a moment," the doc would say, and go back to his private office while Jimmy filled out the form. The form was all part of the act, like the doctor's pretending to be busy. You got inside the private office and the doc would give you a hard look. It was, it had become, a recognizable look, from coast to coast. As soon as they saw that his occupation was musician they would try to anticipate his request for heroin. Some of them were very quick about it. "Musician, eh? With a jazz band? Well, if you're sick, that's one thing, but if you came here hoping to get some dope you came to the wrong man." By the time they got through examining him they would know he was not a drug addict, but they were not all convinced that he had not been sent to get some dope for a friend. But they found nothing wrong with him, and they did not try to understand why a fairly healthy young man should want to spend ten dollars because he felt low all the time. "What you probably need more than anything I can prescribe is a night in bed with a woman," some of them had said. "How long since you've been laid?"

In reply he had once lied to the doc. "I guess it's close on to three years, Doctor."

"Three years? Why? Did you get burned?"

"No, I guess I just didn't find the right girl," Jimmy said.

"Listen, the right girl for you is the one that will get in bed with you. You're a good-looking young fellow, shouldn't have any trouble. Did you happen to notice the girl behind the cigar counter downstairs?"

"No."

"Well, instead of giving me ten dollars you should have given it to her. She'd be good for what ails you. If you want me to I'll give her a ring right now and introduce you to her over the phone. From then on it's up to you, but that's my advice. Take her out to dinner, get a few drinks in her. Straight gin is what she likes. And for the price of a good meal, a young fellow like you she'd most likely take you back to her apartment and she'd forget about the money."

"I have to work tonight. We're playing at some park and we have to be there at ha' past eight."

"Oh, all right. If you're afraid of women," said the doc.

"Yeah, I guess that's it, Doctor. But thanks anyway."

"You *have* had intercourse, haven't you?"

"Oh, sure. I was married four times. But that's all they want, women. They want to go to bed all the time, and it's all they ever talk about."

"Well, what do *you* want to talk about?"

"My hobby."

"What's your hobby?"

"Crocheting. I do beautiful work."

"Oh, you think you're funny. Well, let me tell you something, young fellow, you may not be as funny as you think."

"I am so, you old doctor you. So long, pal."

His musician friends blamed his depressions on his choice of instrument. A bass player, unless he happened to be a Steve Brown, never got any recognition outside the business. There were jokes about oboe players, that the instrument made them screwy. But the musicians had a theory that a man had to have a few screws missing to take up the bass fiddle in the first place. Steve Brown had recently gone from Goldkette to Whiteman, not only because he was a good musician but because he was a showman. The people who went to hear orchestras as much as to dance to them had begun to catch on to Steve Brown, and college boys were buying bull fiddles and imitating Steve's slap. But until Steve's new popularity a bass player might as well have been playing for his own amusement. He lugged that cumbersome instrument around and he and it were the butt of jokes about the doghouse. The more reliable he was, the less likely it would be that anyone but a musician would appreciate how good he was. The sound was there, the *music* was there, but if it was not unobtrusive it was disturbing. The arrangers for the big bands had got away from the Sousaphone and the tuba and were writing parts for the bass fiddle, but the bass player got no solo. "You're like a left fielder against a ball club that's all lefties," said Jimmy's friend Percy Ballard, the trumpet player. "You're just standing there, and nobody paying a God damn bit of attention. You used to play a little tenor sax, around the edges. Why don't you give up the box and take up the saxophone again? There's worse tenor players than you making a living."

"You don't understand, Percy," said Jimmy. "I don't like the tenor sax. I don't like what comes out of it. Anyway, not when I play it. And I do like the bass viol. I like what comes out of it. Voom. Voom-voom-voom. No noodling. I hate noodling. I'd sooner work in the post office than play saxophone. I'd sooner get a job with the National Biscuit Company."

"What doing?"

"At the National Biscuit Company? I don't know. Whatever they had for me."

"No, you don't wanta go there, Jim. You wouldn't be able to stand it for long. That would tell on you in no time. My brother had a job like that one time."

"What was he doing?"

"I don't know, but boy, he hated it. But you're down there all the time with the bass. You know? You don't get up."

"I get up as high as I want to. That's as high up as I want to get. You know who I don't like? I never knew her personally, but Lily Pons."

"Oh, yes."

"Or Harry Goldfield. Or Busse."

"What about me, Jim? I get up there."

"Well, what the hell? You're a friend of mine."

"Armstrong?"

"Singing. On the vocal I like him, but when he gets up there I want to go away."

"He's good, Jim. Honest he is."

"All right, but I don't like it when you guys get up there. Why do you have to? You know, they got a dog whistle that you and I can't hear. Only dogs can hear it."

"I heard about it. I was thinking of buying one."

"Yeah, but what if you learned to play it? Busse couldn't hear you. Goldfield couldn't hear you. I can tune my bass a little lower and play the bottom string open and that'd be the same idea as you playing that dog whistle, but you could *hear* me."

"Not if you tune it too low. The string'll be too loose, you won't get any sound."

"I could make the box bigger. I'd get a sound."

"Well, there's no use talking to you, Jim. Down there is where you like it."

"But I don't like to *be* there all the time," said Jimmy.

"Why don't you buy yourself a little tin flute at the dime store? Then when you're in the dumps maybe you could play yourself out of it on the flute?"

"Why don't I buy myself a kazoo and go to work with the Mound City Blue Blowers? I go around and see all these doctors and they all tell me there's nothing wrong with me. I guess I'm intended to be this way, but that don't say I have to like it."

"The broads go for it, I'll say that much," said Percy.

"That isn't much of a compliment, when you look at some of the guys broads go for. Who's the ugliest man you can think of, quick?"

"No doubt about it, Ernie Mundy."

"That's who I was thinking of. Who's the handsomest?"

"The handsomest? Hard to say. Smith Ballew. Or maybe a young guy from Yale, plays saxophone."

"You mean Vallee?"

"No, this is another fellow. I don't remember his name."

"Well, I'll bet he can't compare with Ernie Mundy when it comes to the broads."

"Nobody compares with Ernie. And a drummer, at that," said Percy.

"That's what I mean. He's ugly, and he isn't even a musician. But wherever he goes they line up for him. They follow him. There was two of them followed him from Mahanoy City, P A, to Cincinnati in a car. A red Jordan Playboy. He couldn't get rid of them. Or was it Dayton? No, Cincinnati."

"I remember one that followed you, Jim," said Percy.

"Yeah, but that was one. Two followed Ernie, both in the same car. You'd think they'd fight over him. Jealous. But they were the best of friends. Broads go for ugly trap drummers, they go for leaders that can't read a note. They go for singers that sit there with a prop guitar. And they go for me."

"Well, is that bad?"

"It's not bad. But it isn't good. I used to think when I was a young kid around sixteen, my idea of heaven would be a job with a name band and a Marmon, and a different broad every night."

"I remember that Marmon you had."

"I bought it for eighteen hundred dollars, a place up near Columbus Circle. It had a crack in the engine block, but I sold it to a fellow played trombone with Fletch. I got what I paid for it."

"It was a beautiful car. You had it that summer you were in Atlantic City."

"I had to put in four quarts of oil every time I took it out, but

in those days I used to think you had to do that with every big car.
I soon found out."

"It was a yellow roadster. I envied you that car. Do you remember that yellow Rolls-Royce George Mingo had in L.A.?"

"No."

"It belonged to some movie star, formerly. George paid six
thousand for it."

"George Mingo never had six thousand dollars."

"Yes he did. He won it in a crap game—and he lost it in a
crap game."

"How much was he shooting for?"

"I wasn't there, but I know that's how he lost it. He was
cleaned, and the guy with the dice said, 'So much open,' and
George threw in the keys of his Rolls-Royce. 'You're faded,' he
said, and the guy rolled a natural."

"I wish I would of been there. George Mingo was the worst
guy to work for I ever saw. The union should have took away his
card. He owed everybody. I was working for scale, but he still held
out on me. The hell with George Mingo. I hope he croaks."

"He did."

"What? Croak?"

"Sure. Didn't you hear about George?"

"No."

"Do you want to hear about him?"

"If it's bad, I do," said Jimmy.

"Well, I guess it was bad enough," said Percy. "They operated on him for a brain tumor, and he never came to."

"Maybe that's what I have. How do they know if you have a
brain tumor?"

"You got me. I guess you get dizzy or something."

"He was plenty dizzy all right."

"Compared to some we know he wasn't so dizzy."

"When did he check out?"

"You're asking me when he checked out, but I couldn't tell
you that, Jim. I'm no good on dates. Last year, I guess it was. He
had a band was playing in some hotel in Chicago."

"We're in Chicago," said Jimmy. "That's where we are now."

"You're right," said Percy. "When I get talking to you I always think we're back in New York."

"No. Chicago. You're at the Edgewater Beach, and I'm at the Drake."

"Oh, I know, once we get it straightened out that we're in Chicago I know where I'm working. Anyway, they operated on him and he never came to."

"Well then I guess I'll wait till we go to Kansas City. It'd be just my luck to draw the same doctor that operated on George."

"You don't have no brain tumor, Jimmy."

"How can you say that when I don't even know it myself?" He smoothed down the hair on the top of his head.

"What are you, feeling for a lump? It's inside. I know that much. It don't show up in a lump."

"Where's Janet living now?"

"George's wife? As far as I know she was in Chicago the last I heard, but that was last year sometime. The union would probably know. Or look up some of the band bookers if you want to get in touch with her. Al Rosen was booking George the last heard."

"Did he book him into the hospital? I know Al. He probably took his end off the doctor. Fifteen percent of what the doc charged for the operation."

"I wouldn't put it past him. He sure as hell didn't get any money when George checked out. George was in him for plenty."

"That's the best news I heard all day. Six for five."

"Huh?"

"Al. You could always put the arm on Al as long as you paid him his rate. Six dollars a week for five he loaned you. And you paid up or you got a broken arm. You think he had George insured?"

"How would I know that? I wouldn't want to know it. This is a town where I don't want to know anything. In New York the hoods don't bother us much, but here they're there to meet you when you get off the bus. Protection. Not only us. The big stars from show business, right down the line."

"Yeah, well that's why I always ask for more money when I'm booked into Chicago."

"Right down the line and every whichway. Even Al has to pay protection, or that's what I was told. Dog eat dog, here, boy."

"Did Janet get fat? She had a tendency to get fat. If she wasn't working she'd sit around all night, putting away the grog. A lot of those girls, they sing it off. As long as they're working they can keep the weight down, but as soon as they lay off they sit around all night, drinking drink for drink with the guys, and then they have a hard time getting rid of the lard. It affected her disposition, too. The fatter she got the worse dispositioned she was. As long as she could get up there and sing, she was all right. But when she married Mingo he made her quit her job, and I didn't want to be around her then."

"Mingo didn't want you around her, maybe."

"That's for sure."

"She oughtn't to married George. If she was gonna marry anybody she oughta married you, Jim."

"Why do you say that?"

"That's what everybody said."

"How could I marry Janet when I had a wife in New York?"

"Only you didn't have a wife in New York," said Percy.

"Well, she wasn't my wife but I was paying her alimony—when I paid it. That's why I had to stay out of New York nearly two years. Sophie wanted to put me in jail for back alimony."

"They always want to put you in jail. How can you make any money in jail? I had the same trouble."

"That's right. They always want to put you in jail."

"Getting even with you. Revenge," said Percy.

"Yeah, but not the money angle. They want to put you away where you can't get in the hay with another woman. It isn't the money angle, Percy. Sophie had plenty of money. Her first husband left her a bundle."

"I didn't know that."

"A bundle," said Jimmy. "You never knew Sophie. She was ten years older than me."

"I knew she was older. I didn't know that much."

"Ten years. And she watched me like a hawk. She wasn't so old. Thirty-four when I was twenty-four, but she was ten years older. If I wanted to step out I had to plan it like I was gonna hold up a bank. Then half the time she outsmarted me. She used to belt me all over the place."

"A big broad?"

"Not so big, but I was never a fighter. I never heard anybody say anything to me that made me want to fight them. If I got sore at somebody I'd hit him with a music stand, maybe, but you'd never catch me in any fist fight. Supposing I hit a guy with my left hand and broke a finger? Where would I be for the coffee and cakes? Up the creek is where I'd be. Sophie used to belt me around all over the place, and I always used to put my left hand under my right arm."

"Didn't you ever hit her back?"

"No. I'd just wait till she got tired. I will say this for her. Every time she gave me a thumping, the next day she'd go down to Cartier's and buy me some present."

"To remember it by?"

"Right. If I would have been a little smarter I would of cheated more and got caught, because she'd give me a beating and the next day buy me a present. You know when I finally powdered out on her I had a boxful of stuff. I had one set of studs and cuff links I got eight hundred dollars for, which'll give you an idea how much they cost her new."

"Three or four gees, I imagine."

"Easily," said Jimmy. "It's all gone now, though. I don't have any of it left. Now I understand the shoe is on the other foot. She gets thumped around. She married her brother-in-law, the brother of her first husband. He married her to get hold of the stock in the family business. You wouldn't think a dame as smart as that would be so stupid, but she was. She thought she was gonna take him, but he took her, and when he don't like something he works her over. She called me up one night in St. Paul and talked long distance for three hours. She wanted me to take her back. She said she was all covered with bruises. What the hell would I want with a broad that was all covered with bruises. That used to work me over and tried to get me put in jail? You know what?"

"What?"

"She said she knew I really loved her, because she found out she really loved me."

"What did you tell her?"

"I said I'd be in New York on the next train. Not the next train, but to meet the Broadway Limited two days later. For all I know she's still waiting."

"You never heard from her again?"

"No, but she'll show up someplace. I hope I see her first."

"Maybe she's why you got the miseries all the time."

"No, I had them before I ever knew her."

"When did you start getting them? When did you begin to notice it first?"

"I don't know. They came on me gradually. You know there's not many arrangements I have to read. Give me the key and I don't care if it's a tune I never heard before, I can fake, because what I fake is probably what they got written down anyway. But when I was with Charley Van he had a piano player named Augie Gunsel or something like that—"

"Augie Gundle. I know the guy. A bald-headed queen."

"That's the guy. Fancied himself as an arranger, and he wrote an arrangement of 'Body and Soul' that Johnny Green would have shot him dead. You know the release in 'Body and Soul,' ya da da dada, da dada, da dada, da dada, da da da da—"

"Ya da da dada, da *dada,* da dada, da dada, da dada, da da da da da. I know it, sure," said Percy. "Great."

"Yeah, but pretty tough. I mean, it's not 'Always,' or 'My Blue Heaven.' But to make it tougher, this Augie has a key change in the middle of the release."

"No! But yeah, I could see where he'd put it."

"Sure you can. But I'd always forget it, so the second part of the release I was playing one clinker after another. I stayed with the same key, and the guys in the brass section would hunch up their shoulders as if I was sticking pins in them. And I don't blame them. It sounded just as bad to me."

"But you had the miseries before that, Jim."

"Right, I did. But that was the first time I began to think I was slipping. I couldn't even play that arrangement if I had it in front of me. We got a lot of requests for the number, it was brand-new, but I told Charley, I said if he didn't want me to louse it up I had to be tacit. So you know Charley, good-natured and kind of sloppy, he said all right, I didn't have to play it. With four in the brass, four in the reeds, piano, guitar, and drums, he had enough volume. It was a small room, too. Maybe the size of the Roosevelt Grill."

"And that's when you began to think you were slipping?"

"As best I can remember. Oh, I was going to doctors before that, shelling out a sawbuck to be told there was nothing wrong with me. But I got plenty wrong with me, Perce. I got no life in me any more. I'm thirty-one years of age and I'm like I was eighty."

"You never tried muggles, or sniffed?"

"I'd be afraid to. I smoked a couple reefers when I was first getting started, but they scared me and I only got sick. I guess what scared me was seeing guys that had to have a drag after every set. Brandy don't seem to have much effect on me, but a couple of guys tell me that's when I better watch out. Maybe they're right. I don't know. You notice I never get stewed, but I wouldn't want to go to bed at night if I didn't have, oh, five or six of these."

"How about in the mornings, when you wake up?"

"One is enough. I only need the one, then I can go all day without it. I don't miss it till I'm through work."

"It's supposed to be very bad for the ticker, brandy," said Percy.

"No, the only time I notice it is if I'm somewhere and I have to go to bed without it. Boy, then the ticker is thumping away and I get these nightmares."

"Did you ever mention that to any of these doctors?"

"Why the hell should I? They'd only tell me to lay off the brandy, and what the hell do they care if I wake up with the sheet wrapped around my neck? You know, I made pretty good money since I was eighteen years of age. I been all over this country three or four times, and to Europe twice. Broads, I had the best in the world. All kinds, shapes, and colors. And the kind of work I like to do, the only kind of work I could do. Could you see me opening up a store every morning at eight A.M., and going around with a feather duster? My parents owned a shoe store, and that's what I was supposed to do, run a shoe store in North Philly, only I had an aunt that paid for my music lessons. Violin and piano. I took both."

"I didn't know you played piano."

"Well, if you heard me you wouldn't feel sorry for Phil Ohman or any of those, but I can play everything but trum*bone*. My arms aren't long enough for trum*bone*. I can play your instrument, Percy. You never knew that, either."

"No, I never knew that."

"I don't have a lip any more, but I played cornet in high school. Hated it."

"You play guitar?"

"Guitar, tenor banjo. Dick McDonough recommended me for a job one time."

"And you stupid bastard, you end up a bass player."

"No, that's not how I end up. I end up playing nothing, not even the kazoo. One of these days I'm just gonna walk out after a set, and I'm not coming back. I give myself till about the sixteenth of August, 1935."

"And what'll you do then?"

"That'll be my thirty-fifth birthday. Number thirty-five in the old book."

"What are you going to do?"

"Well, I'll tell you, because you wouldn't try to stop me. I'm going to hire a rowboat and go out as far as I can and jump in. I can't swim."

"You figure thirty-five is all you ever want to be?"

"Thirty-one is all I want to be, but I'll give it four more years."

"Well, I don't know, Jim," said his friend. "I thought of it sometimes, too."

"Yeah, whenever you think about playing Mahanoy City again."

"Mealey's, in Allentown."

"Bach's, in Reading."

"That one I never played. Reading, I remember a park on top of a mountain. Revere Beach, in Boston."

"That island, in Harrisburg. Maybe I'll be playing Harrisburg. It would save me a lot of trouble. What the hell is that river? The Susquehanna."

"Thirty-five, eh? I'll be that before you will. I'm thirty-three right now. Am I supposed to forget this conversation, Jim?"

"No, if you want to remember it there's nothing wrong with that. But keep it to yourself."

"I won't blab," said Percy.

"I know you won't. And don't even talk about it to me. I'll be seeing you here, and probably New York. Nobody else knows about my intentions, and I don't know why I told you tonight, but somehow we got to talking."

"Yeah, I had a good time tonight," said Percy. "This town gets me down."

"You ever been down to the Stockyards, Perce?"

"No."

"Go down there sometime if you ever want to hear the high note."

"Oh, you mean the pigs?" said Percy.

"I sure as hell mean the pigs."

"My high note don't sound like that."

"All high notes sound like that to me."

"Well, that thing you play sounds like a grunt."

"To you I guess it does. Speaking of grunts, here comes the grunt." A waiter laid their bill on the table. "Let me get this, in honor of the occasion."

"All right, it's yours," said Percy.

They met again, several times in Chicago, frequently in musicians' hangouts in New York and Los Angeles, but they had had their final conversation and they knew it. Percy was therefore solemnly proud on the morning of August 17, 1935, when a telegram was delivered to him, which read, "Thanks for not blabbing." It was signed Jimmy, and it was sent from Cincinnati. Cincinnati, of course, is on the Ohio River.

THE JET SET

At parties sometimes Lawrence Graybill would sit at a table, drinking slowly one of the long rye and ginger ales that he never seemed to be without. His face would be expressionless, his eyes telling nothing. He would sit that way sometimes for as long as half an hour, getting up when the nearby women got up to dance or when a woman who was not a member of his party would join his table temporarily. The same people did not always sit at his table, but those who did were always drawn from the same group of twenty men and women, the same crowd who did things together and who, when the term was new, were called the Jet Set. Lawrence Graybill would have these half-hour spells of silent inactivity, but the members of his crowd were not deceived. They had never put the thought into words, but they knew him so well that they could be certain that he was contemplating some new horror, turning over in his mind some strategy of conversation that would be an attempt to shock the women, infuriate the men, and humiliate his wife. Through the years he had lost most of his power to shock the women. He had said so many awful things to them that he had come to occupy a special category of ineffectuality. They were no longer insulted by his most grievous remarks about their appearance, their morals, their intelligence. The men could still be made angry, but Lawrence Graybill knew exactly how far he dared go with those of the men who might take violent action, and the others would exchange insult for insult. Only Ann Graybill continued to respond according to his intention. At some point during every party she would suffer from his humiliating com-

ments to the precise degree that his comments called for, and she
was as vulnerable after twenty years as she had been on their
wedding trip. She could still cry.

The group as now constituted was different from its original
membership, as two couples had taken the places of those who
had dropped out. Whatever they may have been in their relations
with people outside the group, the regulars when together took
pride in their toughness, and the habit of putting up with Lawrence Graybill was a continual test. There were other standards of
toughness that had to do with sports, the summer games and
skiing in the winter; with drinking and the demands of sleepless-
ness over weekends; with, in several cases, the threat of financial
difficulty. The women competed in matters of wardrobe, the men
in nearly everything. Lawrence Graybill was in no sense a leader
of the group, and yet he was unique in that he contributed a stimulation that was not to be found in mere competition. His rudeness
was tolerable only in a group that was brought together by a passion for competitiveness and held together by the habit of toughness.

The Jet Sets of other towns had their heroes and their clowns.
In one town it might be an eccentric millionaire, as was the case in
one Illinois town where a third-generation brewery owner maintained a coach-and-four that he trotted out for the county fair and
for weddings in the families of friends. He did no harm. In another
town, in Central Ohio, the standout member of the local Jet Set
was a scratch golfer, who could beat everyone for miles around
but had never got within five strokes of winning a major national
tournament. The Jet Set of a small city in North Carolina had an
unpredictable member who entertained his group at dinner parties
at which he acted as hostess, dressed expensively in women's
clothes and playing his role as straight as his guests would permit.
His house guest was always some man of prominence from a dis-
tant point, and an element of surprise lay in the fact that the visitor
was often an individual who had achieved no notoriety as a homo-
sexual. The Jet Set in every town could have been transferred intact
to any other town, but in each group there was a hero, a clown,
or a special personality such as Lawrence Graybill, the bully.

Whatever he was, the special personality at least kept his own group from being a complete duplication of all the other Jet Sets, and for that reason he was encouraged or tolerated. Attention was focused on him, and he thus diverted the members' attention from a prolonged look at themselves. Lawrence Graybill would not have been readily acceptable to the Illinois group, who had become accustomed to the harmless joviality of the brewery owner; but Lawrence Graybill's group would not have been entertained by a coach-and-four. Once upon a time, at the very beginning, the Graybill group could have been a coach-and-four group, but that time was long past, although neither group was aware of the permanent effect its Graybill or its brewer had achieved.

The High Ridge Country Club is fairly old as such establishments go. If its history is dated from its organization as a tennis club, it goes back to the earliest years of the century. The first nine holes of the golf course were playable in 1920, and the second nine was added in 1928. Some of the family names that were on the original tennis club roster appear now on the lists of governors and committees. The Graybill name was not on the pre-golf membership, but Oscar D. Graybill joined the club during the changeover, and his name is down on the list of the first governors of the country club. He was a well-to-do hardware merchant and bank director in High Ridge, a good Mason, a former captain of the High Ridge High School football team, and it would have been meaningless to attempt to form a golf club without inviting him to take part. He had the money, which was highly important, but equally important was to have Oscar Graybill among the sponsors in order to show what kind of club it was going to be. He was, for instance, a good shot, but he had always refused to join the gun club because there was too much beer drinking and too little trapshooting. It was a moderately courageous stand for him to have taken, since the gun club men bought their ammunition and bluerocks at his store, but when the clubhouse was destroyed by fire, it was never rebuilt. Oscar Graybill admitted that he had known all along that the gun club had been used for immoral purposes—women from Trenton. Such a man in the new country club would dispel the rumors that there would be drinking and all sorts of carrying-on. Oscar put in a line of golfing equipment in his sporting goods department, and the stuff just lay there because the club was rather prejudiced in favor of the members' giving their patronage to the pro, but Oscar took his loss good-naturedly as an error in judgment. The club itself was a good customer in many other lines. He hoped that at least they would not mind if he used up the balls out of his own stock.

Oscar's son Lawrence went to Blair and Princeton for a total of seven years without coming to a decision as to what he wanted to do. He was sure he did not want to go in the hardware business, and his mother backed him up. The pungent odors of the warehouse, particularly the smell of linseed oil, made his eyes water and shortened his breath. He was quite delicate for such a husky boy, and by the time he was eligible for the draft, the medical profession had given universal recognition to the existence of allergies. (Oscar himself learned that he was "allergic" to cats.) Lawrence was deferred from the draft for his allergies and for being overweight, and he spent the war years in an advertising agency in Philadelphia, where he displayed some ability as a writer of institutional copy for one of the big aviation companies. He married Ann Wentworth, a High Ridge girl, but because of the shortage of apartments in Philadelphia, she remained in High Ridge with the two children until the war was ended. It was an awkward arrangement. Lawrence insisted upon her living with his parents, but she went home to her own family every day. Relations with Lawrence's mother were especially difficult after the first and then the second child were born. The elder Mrs. Graybill was a great one for supervising the care and feeding of the children, but was somewhat less eager to baby-sit when Ann wanted to spend an evening with friends. Ann's mother was willing to baby-sit, but not at the Graybill house. No satisfactory compromise was ever worked out, and when the war ended and with it Lawrence's job, Ann Graybill was fed up with her mother and her mother-in-law equally. "I don't care where we go, just so we get out of High Ridge," she told Lawrence.

"All right with me, only what are we going to use for money?" said Lawrence Graybill. "All these guys coming back from the service, I don't know when I'll get a decent job."

"You're certainly not going to get one sitting in High Ridge, and playing golf with your father every day."

"Oh, shut up."

"No, *you* shut up."

The Graybill and Wentworth families each put up half the money to buy Lawrence and Ann a house that was larger than their needs but that was available and in a nice part of town. Lawrence took a job in the office of the water company, which paid him a hundred dollars a week and did not greatly interfere with his golf game with his father. "Now we'll *never* leave High Ridge," said Ann.

"No, we probably won't," said Lawrence. "And you just show me where else we'd have it so good. Who's paying most of our bills right now? My father. How did I get the lousy job at the water company? Because my father is a director. What do we get from your family? A stinking hundred dollars apiece at Christmastime."

"Would you like my family to support us?"

"I'd love it, but fat chance of that."

"And you're not even thirty years old. You have about as much ambition as I don't know what."

"My ambition is to get out of this house in the morning, where I can't hear you yakking at me. If you wanted to marry a go-getter why didn't you take on Charley Johnson? Or maybe you do take him on, I don't know. And care less." Lawrence Graybill knew that there was not and never had been anything between his wife and Charley Johnson, but he also knew (as did all his High Ridge contemporaries) that every mother and father of a nubile daughter had once regarded Charley Johnson as the most eligible boy in town. Charley was also so regarded by his own parents, who did nothing to encourage his interest in the local girls, and Charley married an out-of-town girl, Maisie Johnstone, from Roanoke, Virginia. It was very easy for Lawrence Graybill to get a rise out of the young wives in High Ridge, simply by recalling their, or their parents', designation of Charley Johnson as the answer to a maiden's prayer. It was effective, too, as a way of needling the young husbands. In the group that later came to be known as the Jet Set, all the husbands had had to recognize the fact that Charley Johnson had once come first in the eyes of High Ridge parents, and a few of the young men went through life unconvinced that their wives would not have married Charley if he'd asked them. By thus bringing it out in the open, Lawrence Graybill made it possible for the young couples to repeat at parties some of the discussions they had had at home, and Charley Johnson in something like five years was metamorphosed from most desirable prospective husband to a combination of traitor, hypocrite, and stuffed shirt. Charley had not done much to deserve his place in either of the four categories. The High Ridge parents had made him their candidate for son-in-law; the disappointed girls, with the help of Lawrence Graybill, had done the rest. As far as Charley Johnson was aware, he had not changed nor had he been anything to change from. He was rich, well brought up, intelligent, and self-confident. He knew he was good-looking; voted the handsomest in his prep school class and runner-up for handsomest in his class at Princeton; but he had lost out to homely men or plain ones in minor amatory contests often enough to have a sense of proportion about that. "Don't you-all think my Charley is the handsomest boy y'ever did see?" Maisie Johnson would say, and Lawrence Graybill would say, "He don't pretty much, honey. He doesn't compare with George Bender," and all the others would laugh because they knew, as Maisie then did not, that George Bender was a High Ridge town character with a record of molesting children and petty theft. As boys the young husbands had thrown stones and snowballs at George Bender. Charley Johnson had thrown stones and snowballs at George Bender.

In the years immediately following the ending of World War II Lawrence Graybill took the offensive against those of his now forming group who had been in the armed services. "There wasn't a one of you in favor of this war," he said. "Every single damn one of you hated F.D.R.'s guts. You could have been shot for treason, the things you said about him. Not that I didn't agree with you wholeheartedly, but you can't say I was a hypocrite about it." The

member of the group best qualified to reply to Lawrence Graybill
was so bitter that he offered no comment. Dave Rodney had the
Silver Star and the Purple Heart and had been given a field promotion to major before being badly wounded at Anzio, but he would
sit and listen to Lawrence Graybill's attacks on his war record and
grin approvingly. Without his leadership a counterattack was bound
to be weak, and when one was attempted, Lawrence Graybill was
ready for it. Joe Ripple, who had been a navigator in daylight
bombings of Germany, said with heavy sarcasm that it was too
bad Lawrence Graybill had not been running the show, instead of
writing advertising in Philadelphia. "I'd have done much better.
Ask Dave," said Lawrence Graybill.

"Much better," said Dave Rodney. As a combat infantry-
man he refused his support to anyone who had been a fly-boy. But
he was also the first to drop out of the group before it became
the High Ridge Jet Set. One night in 1952 he went home from a
dance at the country club, so drunk on leaving that his wife would
not ride with him. She was taken home by Joe and Doris Ripple,
who noticed that Dave had managed to put his car in the garage
and that the upstairs lights were on. The Ripples said goodnight
to Lila Rodney, and no one has ever known what happened from
then on. The Rodneys left High Ridge the next day and stayed
away for three months, and when they returned Dave Rodney did
not seek out any of the group, Lila did not let anyone know they
were back in town. They declined all invitations, and issued none
of their own. Twice a week they were seen at the movies together,
and it was reported that they had become regular attendants
at the Episcopal church. They obviously had made some kind of
agreement to cut themselves off from the group, and the group, individually and collectively, were frustrated in their efforts to penetrate the mystery of that night of the dance. "Knowing Dave. I'd
say he probably tried to kill her," said Doris Ripple.

"Knowing Dave, I'd say if he tried, he'd succeed," said her
husband.

"Well, maybe. But it was something like that," said Doris
Ripple. "You just don't get religion overnight like that."

"There I'll agree," said Joe Ripple. "But I'll bet you a case of bourbon to a bottle of beer that we never find out."

"What's the time limit, on the bet?"

"One year," said Joe Ripple. "Why? Do you think you have ways?"

"I have one way."

"What's that?"

"I'll put Lawrence on the trail," said Doris Ripple. "He and Dave were always the closest."

"I can start drinking that beer right now," said Joe Ripple.

But Lawrence Graybill accepted the assignment. "I may get a punch in the nose for trying, but I'll ask him," he said. "He comes in the office once in a while."

The next time Dave Rodney visited the water company Lawrence Graybill said, "Hey, Dave, I'm just going out for a cup of coffee. You join me?"

"I guess so. All right," said Dave Rodney.

They walked to the diner together. "Let's not sit at the counter," said Lawrence Graybill. "I like to stretch my legs."

"Sure," said Dave Rodney.

"Piece of pie or something?"

"Just coffee. Sugar, but no cream," said Dave.

"Reducing, eh? I ought to, but everything's stacked against me. Namely, I like rich food and I've never been able to discover any booze I didn't like. And golf doesn't take it off you. The old man and I play at least three times a week from about the middle of March till late November."

"How is your father?"

"Oh, he's one of those people that never change. Speaking of *which,* Dave. How about *you?*"

"Yeah, how about me? I was wondering how you'd get around to it."

"Well, what the hell? They couldn't have been more surprised if *I* suddenly mended my ways."

"Yes, but you never will. Underneath it all you always were a jerk."

"But you weren't? Basically, fundamentally you're a good Christian?"

"I think so," said Dave Rodney.

"That's funny, because the story around town was that you came close to murdering Lila."

"Is that what the story around town was? The only one I heard was that I tried to commit suicide."

"That was one version, but most people were inclined to believe the other one. All right, level with me. Which was it?"

"You couldn't possibly believe that I just got fed up, that Lila and I both got fed up?"

"Nope. That doesn't happen in real life, not to guys like you. Or, if you don't mind my saying so, to gals like Lila."

"Well then I tell you what to do, Lawrence. You and the others go right on believing your favorite versions. If you knew how little we cared, Lila and I. This much I'll admit. Something did happen that night, but it was between Lila and I and that's the way it's going to stay. Here's two bits. I don't want you to be out the price of my cup of coffee."

"You know, pal, you're more of a stuffed shirt than Joe Ripple ever thought of being."

"You mean Charley Johnson."

"No, I mean Joe Ripple. Charley looks the part, but Joe is the real genuine article."

"Then there's some hope for Joe, if he can shake free of you."

"Don't count on it. Joe's a hypocrite, too. A phony. And he's got himself in too deep with—never mind. You're not entitled to our little secrets any more."

"You don't have any secrets. That's why you'll never know about Lila and I."

"That should be Lila and me, not Lila and I."

"I know, but I was never an advertising writer. Winston tastes good like a cigarette should. So long, boy."

Lawrence Graybill's failure to get anything out of his conversation with Dave Rodney was a greater disappointment than he had been prepared for, since he had always considered himself the intellectual superior of Dave. Nothing in their lifelong friendship had indicated that in a match of wits Dave would be a formidable opponent, and during the succeeding days he avoided Doris Ripple and her inevitable questions; but on the Saturday night of the next dance he knew what was coming. He nursed his highball in solitary silence as long as he could, then Doris took the vacant chair beside him.

"All right, Lawrie, you've stalled me off long enough. Ann told me you had a talk with Dave Rodney. Give."

"Your dress is cut too low. This is a family club, not El Morocco."

"My dress isn't cut any lower than Ann's, and don't try to change the subject."

"I never notice how low Ann's dress is cut. If she wants to give the boys a cheap thrill, that's up to her. But I was under the impression you saved everything for Charley."

"In other words, you didn't find out a damn thing. So I owe Joe a bottle of beer."

"Pay him. But I didn't say I didn't find out anything."

"You're faking. You can't stand to admit defeat."

"No, I can't, and that's a fact. Whatever it was that happened that night, it must have been so scary, or disgusting, that we're better off not knowing."

"That from you?"

"Yes, from me. It might put ideas in my head, or Joe's, or Charley's, or anybody's. I don't mean that we'd reform. I just mean the thing that would make us reform. I have it all figured out except the actual thing Dave did. I don't think he tried suicide. I've ruled that out. But he sure as hell did something to Lila that was so awful that it frightened him."

"We all guessed that much," said Doris Ripple.

"I'm not guessing. I know. I just don't know what it was, exactly."

"Do you think anybody will ever know?"

"I doubt it. Dave doesn't want to tell it, and it was so awful that neither does Lila. What could Joe do to you that would be so awful that you'd be ashamed to tattle on him?"

She was silent.

"Ah! What *has* he done, I wonder?" said Lawrence Graybill.

"I wonder which of us wives hasn't got some secret she'd be ashamed to tell about her husband. Ann must have a trunkful."

"No doubt she has, but not many that wouldn't involve her, at least as much as they involve me. What's the worst thing you ever did in your life? The absolute worst. Tell Uncle Lawrence."

"That *I* ever did? I thought we were talking about husbands."

"That *you* ever did. Do you know?"

"Yes, I know. But you'd be the last person I'd ever tell. The very last. I wouldn't tell you, Lawrence Graybill, if your head was lying on the block and the guillotine ready to drop."

"That's pretty final, isn't it?"

"Yes."

"You realize that the rest of my life I'm going to try to find out what it is."

"Won't do you any good. I'll say this much. It hasn't got anything to do with sex."

"Oh, you wouldn't be that ashamed of anything to do with sex, Doris. Not you. When you make the load, the really good, five-A.M. load, and especially if Joe's been over-attentive to some other dame—the things that come out of those ruby-red lips are really something. The things you've told me, right in this very room."

"You trying to scare me?"

"No, trying to make you realize that I can keep secrets."

"I don't believe you," she said.

"All right. Let me think. I will mention one name, and one name only. Someone you told me about at least three years ago, and you told me everything. As soon as I mention the name you'll know you told me everything."

"Just give me initials."

"H.C."

"Not enough. There are lots of H.C.'s. Give me the name of a location, a place."

"Hell, I might as well say the name, but all right. A location? Westhampton, Long Island."

She nodded. "I told you that, did I? You know, Lawrie, for

the first time in our lives I know something nice about you. You didn't even tell Ann?"

"If I had told Ann—"

"I know. Well, thanks for not telling *everything* you know, but I'm sorry I can't tell you the worst thing I ever did. That's a secret that if I told it, if I ever tell it, I'll fall completely apart. Don't ever try to get it out of me at five o'clock in the morning, when I have what you call a good load. Drunk or sober, if I ever tell anyone, I'll know it the minute I've told it, and I'll go out and jump off some tall building. I mean that, Lawrie. I have no great desire to sleep with you, but if you're going to take advantage of me when I'm tight, please make it sex and not this other thing. Will you promise? Please?"

"What makes you think I'd keep my promise?"

"Because I don't think, heel though you may be, that you'd want to be responsible for a suicide."

"Well, Doris, when five o'clock comes, five A.M., I'm usually pretty well along myself. I'm just going good by five. So I can't tell what I'm liable to do after you've all spent the evening trying to hurt my feelings."

"*We* trying to hurt *your* feelings?" said Doris. This was at a time when Lawrence Graybill's use of the insult technique was still something of a novelty. Nevertheless he kept his unspoken promise to Doris Ripple, even after several years had dulled the novelty and he seemed to be completely uninhibited in his search for points of vulnerability among his group. The years, the vicissitudes, provided him with new points of attack, but the toughening process of the years made the group less vulnerable, until almost nothing he could say was provocative. He could be funny but not dangerous, and Ann Graybill was the last member of the group to suffer any humiliation from his taunts. Privately the others were disposed to agree that Ann got a masochistic pleasure out of being such a reliable victim. "He says much worse things to the rest of us," said Maisie Johnson. "But he could never make me cry. I'd like to kill him sometimes, but give him the satisfaction of makin' me cry? Not little old yours respectfully. The way it appears to me, Ann would rather be insulted than ignored, you know what I mean?

When I's first married to Charley and came here to live, I was shocked beyond belief when I heard Lawrence talk that way and not one of the boys fetched him a right smart blow in his big mouth. Kind of men were they? First time he made his cutting remarks to me I told Charley Johnson I's gonna lock my door and keep it locked till he made Lawrence apologize. But I weakened, and the next time it was someone else's turn and you know something? I found out he was so outrageous to everybody that there's nothing personal in what he says. I mean it's personal, but *im*-personal, you know what I mean? And oftentimes there's some truth to what he says, like calling Ann the large economy-size Shirley Temple. It wasn't a nice thing to say about your own wife, but it sure fits Ann. Shirley Temple's married and all, now, but I knew exactly what Lawrence meant. That trying-to-please, make-everybody-happy routine, that Shirley could get away with but not Ann. She doesn't even look like Shirley Temple, but that's why it was such a clever remark to make. Everybody got it right the minute he said it, and silly Ann, dashing out to the ladies' room in floods of tears. Where's her womanhood?"

Oscar Graybill died in 1957, seventy-two years old and active in business and on the golf course right up to the end. If he felt any disappointment over his son's undistinguished career, he kept it well hidden. Actually, practically, Lawrence was a good son; he was his father's companion, always available for golf and for the annual trips to the World Series and Palmer Stadium. The mortality among Oscar Graybill's contemporaries would have left him pretty much at loose ends if he had not had Lawrence to depend upon. His wife was and always had been an unstimulating woman, who ran an orderly household and never gave Oscar a minute's trouble; but she did not enjoy travel, her conversation dealt only with the people and things that directly concerned her, and she could sit silent for hours at a time, crossing one leg and then the other, her jaw resting in the palm of her hand as though she had a toothache. When she broke the silence it would be to announce that she had decided to move a floor lamp from one room to another, to bake two small cakes instead of one large one for the church sale. She hated the Wentworths, but as it was wrong to hate she seldom expressed her intense disapproval of her daughter-in-law and her parents. "Well, I see Adam and Marie Wentworth are off on another trip," she would say. "Seems to me they only just got back from some place or other. What's the good of having a house if you don't live in it?"

She now had a house all to herself. She had, in an only slightly different sense, the world all to herself. She had expected that Oscar would will everything to her, in trust, and that the principal would then pass on to Lawrence, but leaving her meanwhile in control of the purse-strings so that he would have to be nice to her as long as she lived. But Oscar must have changed his will; the estate was divided in half, Lawrence to get his share immediately, and her half to be held in trust and handed on to him. There were other provisions to take care of the distribution in the event that Lawrence died first; but the big feature of the will was that she had the income from approximately $300,000 instead of $600,000, and Lawrence got his free and clear and right away. The money was enough for her needs, more than enough, but now she could not compel Lawrence to move into the house and be dominated, and Lawrence did not even have to come to the house to ask for money. "My devoted son," Oscar had called him in the will, and Roberta Graybill thereupon resented the reference to her as a devoted wife. The only devotion Lawrence had ever displayed was a willingness to play golf and go on trips with his father—all paid for by Oscar—and his refusal to knuckle under to Ann and her desire to leave High Ridge.

"Be glad to have the children any time you want to go away. Plenty of room," said Roberta Graybill.

"Yes," said Ann Graybill later in her own house. "She'd love to have them, now that they don't cry at night or want their diapers changed. She forgets, but I don't."

"Oh, well, she's all by herself and she's getting on. Don't slam the door on her offer," said Lawrence Graybill. "They may have a better time at your mother's, but she and your old man are never here."

Lawrence Graybill got a good deal of his inheritance in the form of water company stock, and it was enough to give him a lot to say in company affairs. The day he became a director, the manager resigned without being told to, and Lawrence Graybill succeeded him. "There isn't a hell of a lot to running a water company," said Lawrence Graybill. "So why should that son of a bitch have the job when I can handle it just as well? We have Laubenstein, a good engineer, and Murphy, a good foreman. The company doesn't need me, it more or less runs itself, but I own that stock and I want the job." It was characteristically perverse of Lawrence Graybill to be over-modest; to ward off boredom in the office he had learned everything there was to know about the High Ridge Water Company, from the rate schedules to the pressure controls. The most satisfactory part of being manager was to be able to say to Ann Graybill, "So I missed a few putts and threw a few close matches to the old man. But I'm not quite forty and pulling down fifteen thousand dollars pay and another twelve gees or more income. I'm not kidding myself that I'd be doing as well if we'd moved away when you wanted us to. One of these days I'll come into that bank stock the old boy left Mother, and then I'll be really sitting pretty. And so will you, I might add."

"If somebody doesn't smash a bottle over your head," said Ann Graybill.

"Who would do a thing like that, to good-natured affable Lawrie Graybill?"

"Bad-tempered Ann Wentworth Graybill, for one."

"That's the least of my worries," he said. "The *least* of my worries."

"What's the greatest, may I ask?"

"The greatest of my worries? Well, I ought to have a quick answer for that, but I haven't. The greatest of my worries. That I have to have a tooth pulled this week. But you want something better than that. All right. That your old man won't be as generous to you as mine was to me. And he won't be if your old lady doesn't stop reading those travel folders. One of these days your old man is going to cool in some God-forsaken place like Madagascar, and the old girl's going to find she hasn't got enough dough to bring the stiff home."

"You know that's not true, and anyway, it's their money."

"I don't look at it that way. What about their grandchildren? I expect your old man to put Larry through Andover and Yale. He has the kid all sold on both places, so let him foot the bills."

"He wouldn't deprive you of that pleasure."

"It'll be no pleasure to see a son of mine at Yale," said Lawrence Graybill. "The way he's going now, even Yale wouldn't take him, but maybe your old man has some influence there. I'm sure he's always paid his alumni dues, and he bought those Whiffenpoof records year after year."

"Oh, dear. The Princeton inferiority complex, all over again," she said.

"Notta tall. It's just that I don't want to see my son scarred for life."

"Well, *your* father wasn't scarred by *any* place, was he?"

"No. And you never heard him sing 'Bow wow wow' in the locker-room, either. Your old man with a towel around his middle, singing 'Bingo that's the lingo.' That's one of the great treats of the Twentieth Century. That's one of the really powerful arguments for a college education."

"I hope they have towels big enough to go around your middle."

"You make cracks about my anatomy and one of these nights I'll bring a towel in from the locker-room and cover your anatomy. I'm surprised the house committee hasn't done that very thing."

On the night of the next club dance she remembered to wear a dress with a high neckline. From experience she had learned that he could reach back into any earlier conversation for a topic with which to taunt her, and in this instance she read his disappointment when he saw the black austerity of her dress. "My little Annie is on a modesty kick tonight, I want you all to notice," he announced as they joined their table. "She got a whole raft of anonymous letters after last week."

"I don't believe it," someone said.

"Gospel truth. And mysterious phone calls. I listened in on one and it sounded to me like old George Bender—"

"Old George Bender! Now I *know* you're keeding," said Maisie Johnson.

"Why? Do you think you're the only one gets calls from George?" said Lawrence Graybill.

"Oh, you curl up and die, you Lawrie. I declare, why do we have to submit to this man's everlasting, week-after-week attamps to be humorous? Let's just nobody say a word to him all evening long. You-all game?"

"I'm game," said Lawrence Graybill.

"You're gamy, is more like it," said Maisie.

"I thought you were going to stop talking to me, Magnolia."

"Who wants what to drink?" said Charley Johnson. "While the waiter is here, come on, everybody."

The evening proceeded, not remarkably different from a hundred other evenings, until about one-thirty, when Lawrence Graybill came out of one of his long silences. There were six out of the ten members of the party at the table.

"Maisie, come and dance with me," said Lawrence Graybill.

"Dance? Dance with *you*? Makes you think I want to do the Turkey Trot? You haven't been on the dance floor since I don't *know* when. Thanks, but no thanks."

"Doris, how about you?" said Lawrence Graybill.

"I'd really rather not, if you don't mind," said Doris Ripple.

"Well, I *do* mind," he said. "I feel like dancing, and you're elected."

"No, Lawrie. Ask someone else."

Lawrence Graybill got up and stood behind Doris Ripple's chair. He bent down and whispered in her ear, the single word "Westhampton," which no one else could hear. She looked at the others, who were looking at her, expecting her to refuse. "Oh, all right," she said, and rose.

"I want to know what he said," said Maisie Johnson. "Lawrie Graybill, what'd you say to Doris that made her change her mind? It wouldn't work with me."

"No, it wouldn't work with you," said Lawrence Graybill. He led Doris to the dance floor.

They were gone only long enough to make one circuit of the dance floor, but the others watched them throughout their

dance, and no one spoke until Doris, with a forced smile, and Lawrence Graybill, triumphant, came back to the table. Among the
group, during the years that they had been a group, they had developed a hardness, a toughness, that made them immune to the
vexations of Lawrence Graybill's taunts. But he had never compelled anyone to *do* anything. He had never tried. Heavy teasing,
rough kidding, brutal frankness was as far as he went. This was
new, and they were not ready for it.

The music stopped, the bar closed, and the party was over.
The Graybills invited the others to their house for a nightcap, but
no one accepted. There had been no chance for collusion, but the
Johnsons and the Lewises wanted to be together without the Graybills and the Ripples. There was a lot to talk about, and the Lewises
followed the Johnsons home.

"Couldn't have been more than one or two words he said to
her," said Maisie Johnson. "Betty, could you hear?"

"I didn't have a chance," said Betty Lewis. "He made sure
Doris heard him, but no one else."

"It wasn't something dirty. At least I don't think it was. Doris
can be a pretty dirty talker, and she doesn't shock easily," said
Maisie Johnson. "And you know, as long as I've been living here,
which is since the end of the war, I never knew Lawrie to make a
pass at anybody. Not at any of us. What he does elsewhere, I
don't know, but here in High Ridge I never heard of him being a
pass-maker. So what has he got on Doris that he can order her
around like that?"

"Not exactly order her around, Maisie," said Johnny Lewis.

"She was afraid to say no. She said no, but he changed her
mind for her p.d.q.," said Maisie.

"What is p.d.q.?" said Betty Lewis.

"Oh, you're such a child, Betty. That's old-time slang for
pretty damn quick. My daddy was always saying p.d.q. Anyway,
Doris was scared to say no. Terrified. Downright terrified. And it
only took one or two words."

"Joe Ripple was dancing with Ann," said Betty Lewis.

"Yes, more's the pity," said Maisie.

"Well, the only way you're going to find out what the magic words were is by asking Doris and Lawrie. And I have a hunch neither one of them will tell you," said Charley Johnson.

"That's my hunch, too," said Johnny Lewis.

"You don't think *you* could find out, if you said pretty-please?" said Maisie to her husband.

"Not even if I said pretty-pretty-please. What makes you think I could?" said Charley Johnson.

"Well, now I just thought possibly you could," said Maisie. "From Doris, I'm speaking of, of course."

"I guessed that. I'd hardly be saying pretty-please to Lawrie."

The mystery of Lawrence Graybill's power over Doris Ripple might have ceased to be entertaining if it had not been for Lawrence Graybill. At the next dance, and at all the dances of that winter season, he would wait until the final half hour, and then he and Doris would go once around the floor. He continued to dance with no one else, to sit silent for longish periods, to pass out his little insults. But as the group became accustomed to his weekly dance with Doris they noticed that he no longer had to say the magic words, or word. He would nod to Doris, she would get up, they would dance. He would merely nod; all he had to do to make her dance, once around the floor with him. The mystery of his power changed to the mystery of why he should want to have that brief dance with her. The others tried to treat it as a joke, and they made some jokes about it; but a strange and disquieting thing was growing up for them all to see, and these toughened people could not satisfy themselves with the easy explanations that came readily to mind. They were made alert from week to week, ready for any sign that would confirm one of the easy explanations. But they were unrewarded for their vigilance: if Doris Ripple and Lawrence Graybill were having an affair, they must be meeting at hours when they could escape observation, and there were no such hours, not under the conditions existing while their friends' curiosity was so active. The town was too small, the opportunities too few.

Then it was spring, and the winter dance series was at an end. There would be a dance on Memorial Day eve and on the eve of the Fourth of July, but the regular weekly dances would not be

resumed until Hallowe'en. The gatherings of the Jet Set were frequent, but they were not taking place where there would be
dancing, and Lawrence Graybill and Doris Ripple were not always
at the same parties. When they were, Lawrence Graybill would
sometimes take a seat near Doris, but without the excuse of dancing they could never be quite so sure of five or ten minutes alone.
Ann Graybill made it difficult, Joe Ripple made it difficult; one or
the other was always close at hand, and there was no orchestra to
drown out the conversation between Lawrence Graybill and Doris.
Shortly after the Memorial Day dance, at which Lawrence Graybill had danced with Doris Ripple, the members of the group
were shocked and saddened to learn, first over the radio and then
by newspaper and word of mouth, that Doris had fallen or leapt
from a room on the twelfth floor of a New York hotel. The police
called it suicide. She was registered at the hotel under her right
name, and her room was on a floor to which unaccompanied women
were usually assigned. She had stayed there many times before, and
was fairly well known to members of the hotel staff. She had neither said nor written anything to confirm the theory of suicide, but
the police put together enough circumstantial evidence to substanti-
ate their theory, and the most telling detail was that when Joe Ripple was reached by telephone and the police asked him if his wife
was in New York, he replied that he was sure that at that very moment she was at home in High Ridge. She had, in fact, driven him
to the station that morning. Had she seemed cheerful? Well, nobody's overly cheerful at that hour of the morning. Had she been
depressed lately? Well, yes. She was always a little depressed
around Memorial Day, because she would visit the grave of a
younger brother who had been killed in a training accident at Pen-
sacola during the war. A detective was on his way to accompany
Mr. Ripple uptown to identify the body. Later the police wanted
to know if Mr. Ripple knew a man named Howard L. Candry, who
lived in Westhampton, out on Long Island. No, he had never heard
the name before. Why? Well, Mrs. Ripple had put in a telephone
call to Candry shortly after checking in at the hotel. It was a
person-to-person call, and when the number did not answer Mrs.
Ripple asked the operator to try again in fifteen minutes. The op-

erator did so, twice in the next half hour, and when the number still did not answer, Mrs. Ripple cancelled the call, approximately two minutes before her body landed in the hotel courtyard. No, Howard L. Candry was not a name Mr. Ripple had ever heard of, and as far as he knew, his wife had never been in Westhampton. As a boy he had spent several summers at Quogue, the next town to Westhampton, but that was fifteen years before he married Mrs. Ripple. In recent years they had spent their summers at Mantoloking. Just who was Howard L. Candry? Did the police know? Well, yes, he was a middle-aged man. Unmarried. An architect. Owned a cottage on the beach that he kept open the year round, but was at present traveling in Europe. He was a partner in the firm of Chisholm, Candry & de la Verne, whose offices were on Rockefeller Plaza. Other than that the police had no information to give Mr. Ripple. Did that mean they had information that they were not giving? They were sorry, but that was all the information they had at this time. Would that mean that Candry's name would not be mentioned in the newspaper accounts? Well, the police had not mentioned the telephone calls, so it did not seem likely that Candry's name would appear in the papers, unless something further developed. So far the reporters had not shown any indication of wanting to make a big story of Mrs. Ripple's death.

The police were tactful. All of the accounts in the daily papers did not come to a total of two columns. The coverage lasted twenty-four hours, and it was of a routine character: Broker's Wife in 12-Story Plunge. One of the papers dug up the fact that Doris had once reached the semi-finals in a tennis tournament at East Hampton, but the others confined themselves to the briefest possible account of her death and biographical items. No paper ran her picture.

In High Ridge there was sadness. They knew her there, remembering her in pigtails (which she had never worn) and as a promising tennis player who did not quite have the makings of a national singles star, but had won every mixed doubles she and her younger brother had played at the High Ridge Country Club. Some of her fellow-townsmen now recalled her disappointment at making a mediocre showing at East Hampton. She had entered the

tournament with such high hopes that when she got no further than
the semi-finals, she was ashamed to come home. She hung around
East Hampton for almost a week, until her family sent her brother
to bring her back, and he had some difficulty finding her. After that
she stopped playing tournament tennis, and abandoned the strict
training regimen. With her brother she could still beat the club
mixed doubles champions, but when the war came and Tommy
Berry went to Navy pre-flight, Doris gave up tennis altogether. She
worked hard at the Red Cross blood bank and wherever else she
was needed, which did not entirely divert the gossip that her family were disturbed by her unexplained absences from High Ridge
and one rumor in particular that she was having an affair with a
married man in New York. She had been seen with a much older
man at "21" and El Morocco, presumably the same one whose appearance in her life was distressing to her parents. Her marriage to
Joe Ripple was a surprise to everyone, but it put an end to the gossip about the older man. It was believed that she had the inside of
the track, if any High Ridge girl had, where Charley Johnson was
concerned. He had shown more attention to her than to any other
girl in town; but his interest was concurrent with the rumors about
the married man, and there was even one absolutely incredible
story that she was using Charley Johnson as a cover-up for the
really serious affair. Most people said there was not a grain of
truth in that; that any girl in High Ridge would jump at the chance
to latch on to Charley Johnson. Moreover, the position of Charley's
parents was only too well known, and if they had withdrawn their
opposition to his marrying a High Ridge girl, it would not have
been in favor of Doris Berry. Ann Wentworth would have been
their only possible choice, and she was positively mesmerized by
Lawrence Graybill; the only girl in town who so completely committed herself to one boy that she did not leave the latchstring out in
case Charley Johnson turned up.

A memorial service was held for Doris, the remains having
been cremated in New York. Considerately, it was scheduled for
late in the afternoon so that the men who commuted to New York,
Philadelphia, Newark and Trenton would not have to give up a
whole day's work. As a consequence the church was well filled,

and no one was absent who should have been there. Joe Ripple
and his two teenage daughters occupied the first pew; his and
Doris's parents occupied the second pew; then, in the only remaining reserved pews were the members of the High Ridge Jet Set,
and the two former members, Dave and Lila Rodney. Their presence was somehow reassuring to the Jet Set, as though Dave and
Lila, having achieved salvation, were proof that all the others
could do so as well whenever the time came. The service, even
with three hymns, took less than half an hour, and most of those
present had been invited back to Joe Ripple's house, but because
of the time of day—just before the dinner hour—and the fact
that Joe's and Doris's friends had already paid sympathy calls, the
invitations were declined. As the congregation was filing out of
the church Doris Ripple was already a member of the dead, and
the living were hungrily lighting their cigarettes and meeting the
problem of unparking their cars. It was not yet time to say so, but
Doris was the Jet Set's first casualty.

The next gathering of the group was at the Fourth of July
dance, and the members were determined to make it a special occasion. No one person, but all of the group, decided that
Doris would not be mentioned, and she was not mentioned. A
full attendance was aimed for, a busy schedule was arranged.
A swimming party at one house, a cocktail party, nine o'clock dinner at the club, breakfast and another swim at another house. "If
we all get through this alive—" said Charley Johnson, leaving the
thought unfinished.

"Isn't that the whole point?" said Maisie Johnson. "If we survive this, we can survive anything."

"You know, Maisie, you say things sometimes that amaze me."

"I know. You don't give me credit for having a brain in my
head," she said.

"No, that's not what it is."

"Yes, that's just what it is. Exactly. Our little groupee, nobody
saying anything about Doris, but everybody knows she like to dis-
organize us permanently. We go all out for this party or else we give
up the ghost. We're all scared of Doris and middle age, and there
isn't a one of us isn't."

"I don't mind middle age," said Charley Johnson.

"Then quit having those scalp treatments. You mind it as bad as anyone I know."

For twelve hours, beginning with the swimming party, the group, eighteen in number, never let up, never let down. For some the drinking had begun at lunchtime, so that when the Lewis's poolside gathering got under way, the guests who had an early start were competing at the diving board, and every woman at the party had a brand-new bathing suit. "Anybody doesn't show up in a bikini is chicken," said Maisie Johnson. "And you just wait till four o'clock tomorrow morning. Anybody *does* show up in a bikini will be chicken. Oh, honey, they're gonna swing tonight, I just know it so sure."

Henry and Googie Peterson had to leave the dinner table to rescue their sixteen-year-old who was in the clutches of the High Ridge police. Something to do with illegal firecrackers. Dick and Kay Falls went home at one A.M. because they were driving to Saunderstown, R. I., in the morning, and wanted to get four or five hours' sleep. And just before three o'clock Lawrence Graybill disappeared. He had been extraordinarily subdued all evening, and at just about the time that everyone expected him to recharge the party, he was nowhere to be found.

"Don't worry about him, Ann," said Maisie Johnson. "I'll just bet you forty-five dollars he's at our pool."

"What makes you think I was worried about him?" said Ann Graybill.

"Because you were, that's why," said Maisie. "You kept looking for him to come back."

"That doesn't say I was worried," said Ann Graybill.

"Well, no, I reckon it doesn't. My error."

The group, now thirteen in number, moved from the clubhouse to the Johnsons' pool. "Who'll be the first skinny-dipper I wonder," said Maisie.

"Well, it's usually Betty," said Charley Johnson.

"Uh-oh. Not this time. It's gonna be our little Ann. The cat's away, the mouse will play. Taking her good time about getting into the water, too, if you ask me. There she goes. Ah, there's Madam

Lewis now. And the first man? Lew. *Spa-lash!* What a terrible dive. Well, I guess as a good hostess I have to drink outa my saucer, too. Here goes. You coming in?"

"What?" said her husband.

"Which is it? Ann, or Betty? Must be Ann's got you bug-eyed."

"Well, yes," he said.

"A new face, huh?" said Maisie.

"You go in and tell me how the water is."

"Yes, I'll do that," said Maisie. "You just wait here till I make a full report. Is there anything else I can do for you?"

"Huh?"

"Never mind." She got out of the towel bathrobe and lowered herself into the water from the side of the pool. But the water was too cold, and no one stayed in. "When it's too cold for Lew, it's no fun."

"I was enjoying it," said Charley Johnson, still in his dinner jacket.

"Well, enjoy it some more," said Maisie, and pushed him into the water. "That's about the right score. Five without any clothes, one with all his clothes."

"You bitch," said her soaking husband.

The coldness of the water had a sobering effect on the skinny-dippers, the briefness of the exhibition had made a failure of the nude show. Even the novelty of Ann Graybill in the nude was not allowed to develop into a sensation or a crisis. For the record she had taken off her clothes and exposed herself to the group, and the fact would be remembered, but it was not the defiant gesture it would have been if Lawrence Graybill had been there. The bathers dressed and rejoined the others who were now cooking breakfast at an electric stove.

"You were a sensation, honey," said Maisie.

"Was I?" said Ann.

"You sure were."

"Now I feel like a fool."

"Why should you? I don't," said Maisie.

"It's different with you. Charley doesn't mind when you

skinny-dip, but I never would have had the nerve if Lawrie'd been here. And everybody knows that. So all I did was make a fool of myself. My shape isn't all that good any more."

"There's nothing wrong with it. You have a good shape," said Maisie. "We've all seen your *shape* before."

"Oh, you know what I mean, Maisie. I wanted to do something against Lawrie, but it doesn't count for much if he's not here."

"He'll hear about it," said Maisie. "Have you any idea where he is?"

"No, not the slightest."

"Do you want to call home and see if he's there?" said Maisie. "Do you want me to?"

"That's one place I'm sure he's not. Two places I'm sure he's not. Our house, and his mother's."

"Ann, is there trouble? I mean that I can help," said Maisie. "I know there is, or you wouldn't have gone skinny-dipping. You weren't just having a swim without any clothes on. You were advertising yourself, and advertising 'man wanted,' both at once."

"Yes, I was. I still am. Tonight I'd go home with anybody."

"I'm going to keep an *eye* on *you*," said Maisie.

"Yes, even Charley."

"I didn't mean only that."

"I know you didn't, Maisie, but I'm telling you. Charley, or anybody. I don't care. I'm as low tonight as I've ever been in my whole life, and I don't know why. Lawrie walking out like that was only the final thing, the last straw. I've been hating this party since we started talking about it."

"I want you to stay here till the last person leaves."

"It's too late for that kind of protection. I have to do something awful tonight."

"It'll be daylight soon," said Maisie.

"Then I have to work pretty fast, don't I?"

"I'm not going to give you the chance to. Who'd you come here with?"

"Betty and Jack."

"That's who you go home with, or I'll take you home myself," said Maisie.

"Look," said Ann.

Coming through the gate of the tall fence that surrounded the pool was Lawrence Graybill. He was completely sober, but he was obviously worn out. He made his way directly to Ann and Maisie. He ignored the greetings of the others. "Hello, Maisie. Ann, you ready to go home?"

"No, I'm not ready to go home, and who do you think you are, arriving when it suits you, and ordering me home. I got here without you, and I'll go home when I'm good and ready."

"I'll keep out of this," said Maisie, and left them.

"I would *like* you to come *home*," said Lawrence Graybill.

"From now on what you'd like isn't going to bother me one bit," said Ann Graybill.

"Suit yourself," he said, and started to turn away.

"Where have you been?"

"I've been to Joe Ripple's."

"Joe Ripple's? All this time? What were you doing there?"

"I'll tell you tomorrow."

"Why did you go to Joe's at three o'clock in the morning? I consider that about as cruel a thing as anything I ever heard of."

"It was, but I went," he said.

She hesitated. "Wait till I say goodnight to the others."

"I'll be in the car," he said.

He waited for her, and when she got in the car he said, "Your hair is wet. You been swimming?"

"I have."

"You didn't bring a suit."

"I didn't wear a suit," she said.

"Well, now. That must have been quite a treat."

"I'm told it was," she said.

"What's the matter, was the water too cold? I expected to find a pool full of beautiful female bodies, disporting themselves."

"The water was very cold. What were you doing at Joe Ripple's at this hour of the morning?"

"This was the night for the Graybills to expose themselves. You did, in your way, and I did in mine. Let's wait till we get home."

"Very well," she said.

He left the car in their driveway. She was undressed and in bed when he came upstairs. "Have you always wanted to go swimming in the nude? I seem to remember that you disapproved of it. Thought it was kind of childish."

"Never mind about me, please."

"Just had an uncontrollable desire to take your clothes off in front of a lot of people."

"If you must know, that's it exactly."

"You haven't had time to wonder why, I suppose."

"I didn't need much time," she said. "I know why."

"Yes, I guess I do too. You wanted to thumb your nose at me, and at the same time let it be known that you were ready to receive any offers. Get any offers? I wouldn't think so, judging by the fact that you were so deep in conversation with Maisie."

"Lawrie, you might as well give up. You're never going to be able to bully me again."

"Just because you walked around naked in front of a bunch of drunks? That's nothing very startling or unusual."

"It was when I did it."

"A point. You have a point. Therefore you've asserted your independence and let the world know that I'm not your lord and master from here on out."

"I have."

"Don't overestimate the value of one gesture. You're still Ann Wentworth plus Graybill. You don't change that much simply by taking off your clothes at a party."

"I did."

"Not really. You've been half taking them off for years, cutting your evening dresses a little lower."

"Tonight was different."

"No. The difference will be when you take your clothes off for some particular man, and *then* tell me. That time may come—"

"I was about to say," she said.

"But it's not here yet."

"Why did you go to Joe Ripple's?"

"All right," he said. He sat on the edge of his bed, and waited a moment before beginning. "I wanted to tell Joe that I was responsible for the death of his wife. I am."

"Apparently he doesn't think so, or you wouldn't be here."

"He believes me. I told him the truth. One night when she was stewed, Doris gave me a long story about the time she was playing in the tennis tournament on Long Island and they couldn't find her. She was put out of the tournament, but they finally had to send her brother Tom to bring her home. The reason was that she met a weird character named Candry. Howard Candry. Older. An architect. He had a place in Westhampton and she went and stayed with him and some of his weird friends. Apparently she was so let down after the tennis disappointment that she didn't care what happened to her. It was a real orgy, lasted three or four days. But it was what she wanted. I mean, there was something in Doris that every once in a while wouldn't be satisfied with anything less. Once or twice a year she had to let go completely. She'd get in touch with Candry, and he was only too glad to make the necessary arrangements. This has been going on since the first time she met Candry. The day she committed suicide she phoned him twice from her hotel room. She'd gone to New York without telling Joe she was going, and when she phoned Candry and didn't get him, she must have gone completely out of her mind. Maybe it was disgust with herself, or frustration, or whatever. But that's what she was in New York for, to have Candry make the arrangements."

"Where do you come in?"

"A kind of blackmail. Doris also told me—I asked her one time what was the worst thing she ever did. She wouldn't tell me. She would only say it had nothing to do with sex. And I didn't believe her. With Doris everything had to do with sex. And I kept pestering her to tell me. You know when I used to make her dance with me?"

"What did you say to her to make her dance with you?"

"Just one word. Westhampton. We'd get up and dance, and at first she'd always deny that her big secret had anything to do with sex. But at the Memorial Day dance she broke down and admitted it *was* sex."

"What was it?"

"It went all the way back to that tennis tournament. The time her brother was sent to get her."

"Yes."

"Do you remember Tommy?"

"Of course."

"The only person in the world Doris ever cared about. He tracked her down to Candry's house, and she let Candry seduce him. We never knew it in town, but Tommy was a fairy. And she started him. Until then he'd been an absolute virgin, but when he showed up at Candry's house she wanted Tommy to be just as bad as she was. Or, if not as bad, the same. Once or twice a year they'd go to Candry's parties together, till Tommy was killed in the war. But Tommy didn't only go to those parties with her. He went on his own. After Candry got through corrupting him, he was a full-fledged homo, but she'd started him. She'd handed him over to Candry."

"And never forgave herself."

"And never forgave herself—except maybe those two or three times a year when she had to see Candry herself. Then she was out of her mind. And knew it."

"But why were you responsible for her death?"

"Because I made her tell me about Tommy. She'd warned me, if she ever admitted what the worst thing she ever did was, she'd commit suicide. Jump out of a window, she said. Which is what she did."

"Yes. And now, what earthly good did you accomplish by telling all this to Joe Ripple?"

"What good? You fool. Joe Ripple is still alive, with two young daughters to bring up. I had to tell him about Doris, because he's been blaming himself for her suicide, but without knowing why. Now he knows that it wasn't his fault. That Doris was no good. Or, if you want to be kind about it, that she was nuts. But at least Joe Ripple won't go through the rest of his life blaming himself, and maybe he can be a better father to those girls."

"Maybe," said Ann. "What did he say when you told him this lovely story?"

"He told me to get the hell out of his house. I didn't expect him to thank me. His daughters won't, either."

"No," said Ann Graybill. She lowered herself into the bedclothes and covered her shoulders. "Goodnight," she said.

THE LAWBREAKER

Morton Whitehill is the man who used to appear in his speedboat and circle around the steamers that plied between Nantucket, Martha's Vineyard, and Woods Hole. Out of nowhere he would appear in the *Nancy II,* a craft that looked dark and dirty and longer than its thirty-eight-foot hull. The *Nancy* was actually a two-step hydroplane, but on first seeing it a steamer passenger might be inclined to dismiss it as just another motorboat, and on its last legs at that. Then he might get a closer look at Morton Whitehill and form an opinion of him that more or less matched his opinion of the *Nancy:* a nondescript man in a nondescript boat. But if the passenger happened to be on the right side of the steamer when the *Nancy* pulled away, he would be astonished at the sudden display of power as the *Nancy*'s Wright Typhoons began to roar. The engines seemed to rebuke anyone who thought less than highly of the *Nancy,* and when the craft got up on the second step, a few seconds and a hundred yards away, our passenger would forget all about his first impressions of the *Nancy* and the man at the wheel. Now, watching the boat half out of the water and sprouting wings of spray, the man on the steamer deck would almost certainly say, "I'll bet that's a rum-runner."

It was a long time ago that Morton Whitehill had the *Nancy II* and he and his boat were suspect. He was a young man then, just past twenty-five but already known to his parents' friends as a bad lot. It was said of him, for instance, that he had driven his parents off the Island. His mother and father had been coming to Vineyard Haven since early in the century, even before their marriage. But in 1925, after Morton's long history of boyhood pranks and adolescent mischief and youthful scrapes, Mr. and Mrs. Whitehill sold their cottage and became summer residents of Lake Placid, New York. Rather lamely they offered the explanation that the Lake Placid region was better for Mr. Whitehill's hay fever, although their Vineyard Haven friends could not recall his having suffered from hay fever. Someone else offered the explanation that it was not so much hay fever as the fumes from Morton's high-powered speedboat, and this explanation was accompanied by a knowing look. It was that summer, 1925, that Morton had acquired the *Nancy II*.

The departure of the elder Whitehills made it easier for their friends to drop Morton, and they did so immediately, with an eagerness that indicated how long they had been postponing their decision. In some cases the postponement went back to Morton's misconduct at seventeen, when he was accused of casting off the moorings of a dozen sailboats at the Edgartown Yacht Club. There was no proof of his guilt but there was an overwhelming unanimity to the belief that no one else would have done such an outrageous thing. At eighteen Morton was given his first taste of social ostracism as a result of the scandal he got into over a Portuguese fisherman's daughter. Again, no proof, but the girl's brothers gave him a terrible beating and were not prosecuted, which seemed proof enough that Morton was not innocent. He did not get invited to any more parties that summer. During the next summer he was in the Navy, a seaman first class in the destroyer squadron at Cobh, Ireland, and out of harm's way so far as the Vineyard people were concerned. But he came back after the war with what seemed to be a determination to make up for lost time; in the Navy his frame had filled out and a chief petty officer had taught him to box. He sought out individually the Portuguese boys who had given him a beating, and he gave each of them a beating to even the score. When someone suggested that Portuguese boys carry knives, he replied that they were not the only ones, and patted his pants pocket.

In the winter Morton's father commuted from East Orange, New Jersey, to his office and warehouse in downtown New York. Mr. Whitehill was the third generation of his family to engage in

the business of tea, coffee, and spices, but he made no strong effort
to persuade Morton to join him. Mr. Whitehill knew things about
his son that he kept to himself, especially where money was involved. Mrs. Whitehill likewise had secrets from her husband and
she did not try to induce him to admit her boy to Whitehill
Brothers. Their caution was wasted; Morton had no intention of
going into tea, coffee, and spices. At the end of his first civilian
summer Morton shipped out as deckhand and able-bodied seaman
on a succession of ships that kept him at sea until the next summer,
and he repeated this routine for the next two years. Then, in 1924,
he informed his parents that he planned to spend the winter in
Florida. A Navy friend, he said, had offered him a good job as mate
on a charter fishing boat. Mrs. Whitehill was pleased; Mr. Whitehill
offered no comment then or ten months later when Morton returned
to the Vineyard in a red Jordan Playboy and a wardrobe of summer suits bearing the labels of shops in various British colonial is-
lands. He had a present for his mother: a diamond wristwatch
from Asprey's, London; and for his father, who did not smoke, a
gold cigarette case. "When you retire from tea-tasting you'll probably start smoking," said Morton. "Anyway, if you don't want to
keep it you can give it to somebody that does smoke."

A week later Morton took his father to Oak Bluffs to show him
his new boat. "Where did you get this?" said Mr. Whitehill.

"Oh, bought it from a fellow over in Woods Hole," said Morton. "Want to go for a ride?"

"Sure," said Mr. Whitehill. He had little more to say as they
proceeded to the channel.

"Now I'm going to let her out," said Morton. His father was
nearly thrown back on the deck as the *Nancy* went up on the second
step. The engines made conversation impossible until after ten
minutes the boat slowed down.

"How fast were we going back there?" said Mr. Whitehill.

"About forty-eight."

"Knots?"

"No. Miles per hour. But she'll go forty-eight knots."

"You don't need all that power for fishing."

"Who said anything about fishing? This is a pleasure boat, Pop."

"I see. Not exactly luxurious, though," said Mr. Whitehill. He looked about him at the bareness of the cabin. "All that empty space, not even benches to sit on. How many does it sleep?"

"She's not a cruiser, Pop."

"No, I can see that," said Mr. Whitehill.

"Would you like to take the wheel?"

"No thank you," said Mr. Whitehill. "I think I'd like to go home now."

That evening, after a conversation with his wife, Mr. Whitehill telephoned a friend in the real estate business and put his cottage on the market. Much later that evening, when Morton came home, Mr. Whitehill handed him the diamond wristwatch and the gold cigarette case. "We don't want these, Morton," he said.

"Why not? The first good presents I ever gave you."

"There's nothing good about these presents."

"O.K. I'll give them to somebody'll appreciate them," said Morton.

"You do that."

"Those questions you kept asking me about my boat," said Morton.

"I don't have to tell you that the Coast Guard have machine guns," said Mr. Whitehill.

"Oh, they have bigger than machine guns. One-pounders. Three-pounders."

"I'm selling the cottage. That *is* something you didn't know," said Mr. Whitehill.

"You mean giving up the Vineyard?"

"Exactly," said Mr. Whitehill.

"Not me. I'm staying."

"I was sure of that," said Mr. Whitehill.

"How much are you asking for the cottage?"

"Whatever I'm asking, I wouldn't sell it to you. I'd rather set fire to it and burn it to the ground. This is the last straw, Morton. All the rest was understandable. A bad boy. A nasty bad boy. But you're not a boy any more. You're a mature criminal."

"You know I ought to clip you one for that."

"I was taking that chance when I said it. Maybe if I'd clipped *you* oftener when you were younger—but what's the use? Get your things and go."

"Tonight?"

"Tonight. Now. You can sleep on your damn rum-runner."

"I don't have to sleep there. There's other places I can sleep. But I want to say goodbye to Mother."

"No. I've given her a triple bromide and she won't wake up till morning. She doesn't want to see you."

"You talked her into that."

"It wasn't hard," said Mr. Whitehill. "She told me a few things I never knew till tonight."

"The two of you must have had a great old time."

"Yes, you can imagine. A great old time. No, you *can't* imagine."

"It's a small place, the Vineyard."

"Yes, and a good place, we thought. That's why we're leaving it."

"What are you going to tell your friends?"

"We're not going to be here. Your mother and I are going abroad for the rest of the summer, and next year we're going some place else. You have it all to yourself. For as long as you get away with it. Now please get your things and get out of here."

"Pop, is it true your grandfather imported slaves before he imported tea?"

"Yes. Is that your excuse, Morton?" said Mr. Whitehill.

"Well, if I needed one," said Morton.

The departure of Mr. and Mrs. Whitehill and the vendetta with the Portuguese family left Morton without many friends; he had been rejected by the summer people and by the fishermen, and as an off-Islander he had never become acquainted with the Yankee natives. But he had money to spend, time on his hands, a snappy little automobile, and youth. He rented a room in a house in Oak Bluffs that provided lodgings for seasonal workers, the men who had jobs as waiters, short-order cooks, garage mechanics, and the like. The room was a place to hang his hat and hardly more than that for him and the other lodgers. He sometimes would be gone for days at a time, and when he returned he would sleep around the clock.

It was taken for granted that he was engaged in rum-running. Although it was not considered tactful, or safe, to discuss the matter with him, one night a man named Ruggles had enough liquor in him to bring the subject out in the open. "Whitehill, you ought to have a helper," said Ruggles.

"Doing what? Stirring my coffee?" said Morton.

"Quit your kidding. You know what," said Ruggles.

"All I'm doing is stirring my coffee, and I don't need any help with that."

There were other men at the table, and they sensed a promise of excitement. It was late at night in the diner near the pier. "Cut the comedy, Whitehill, there's no federal men here," said Ruggles. "I'm looking for a soft job that pays good."

"You had one. Didn't you work on the concessions on the boats?"

"I got fired."

"Well, the season's almost over," said Morton.

"Not for you," said Ruggles. "The way I got it figured, White-hill. You take that boat of yours and you go out and get a load of case goods, and you got enough speed so the Coast Guard could never catch up with you."

"Is that what I do, Ruggles?"

"Sure. But I never figured out where you land the stuff. It ain't here. That would be foolish. I been figgrin it out, and the best way I can figure it, you *don't* land it. It goes from you to another boat, a couple boats. Smaller boats. Then they bring it in and un-load it."

"You're nuts, but suppose you were right. Where would you fit in?"

"As your helper. I had experience with all kinds of boats. And if worst comes to worst, I got marksman, sharpshooter and expert rifleman badges. I done a hitch in the Marines."

"How are you with a bayonet?" said Morton.

"A bayonet? I don't know. I done drill with a bayonet, but I never got overseas. You mean would I be any good with one? I guess I would."

"Then why don't you cut your tongue out? You talk too damn much," said Morton. The other men laughed. "A lot of people talk too damn much."

Ruggles had stumbled on the exact procedure followed by Morton Whitehill and the other units of the rum-running fleet, and while the methods were no secret from the Coast Guard, the New York people who operated the fleet considered such information no business of the public's. Morton's boat was only one of many of equal speed and power in the rum fleet on the Eastern seaboard, and such boats were expensive. One of them cost as much as three or four smaller boats, or five or six. Now and then a small boat was seized by the Coast Guard, but the expense to the rum-runners was minimized by having the cheaper boats closer inshore.

"He as good as told you to cut your tongue out, Ruggles," said one of the group. "You gonna take that?"

"He's going to take it, and so are you," said Morton. He got up and hit the speaker with a left hook to the right eye. No one else made a move. It was a situation that needed one fighting man to begin mixing it with Morton Whitehill, whereupon the others would have joined in. But in this gathering there was not that one man who would stand up to Morton, and in the minds of some there may have been recollection of the rumor that he carried a knife.

"If you wanta fight, fight outside," said the owner, who was behind the counter. "Or I'll send for the police."

"There won't be any more fighting, Tony," said Morton. He laid a dollar bill on the counter and went out.

Reports of the scene were exaggerated in the next few days, until the accepted version depicted Morton Whitehill as a hero in a bloody brawl when set upon by four bruisers who tried to rob him of his bankroll. Since none of the actual participants in the scene wished to boast of his part in it, the new legend had it that the attackers were members of a rival rum-running gang. Morton, by denying everything, became not only a hero but a modest hero, and only a few cranky individuals among the summer people continued to call him a hoodlum and a disgrace to his family.

THE HORSE KNOWS THE WAY   (248)

Thus on the strength of his two fights with the Portuguese brothers and one left hook to a man's right eye, Morton Whitehill had established a reputation as an invincible man with his fists. He was invited to appear in the local weekly boxing matches, but he declined. "You don't pay enough, and anyway I don't fight Marquis of Queensberry rules," he said.

Twice or three times a week he would fill the *Nancy*'s gas tanks and, just before dark, put out to sea. He would pick up a couple of hands from one of the smaller boats, then proceed to the ship that lay never less than fifteen miles out. The extra men would load the *Nancy* with whiskey and brandy in cases, and Morton would get his orders from the syndicate representative on the ship, a Bermudian who was no stranger to these waters. Morton's responsibility ended when he had delivered the case goods to the smaller boats, and he would then move out of the immediate vicinity, cruising without lights in the dark in an effort to deceive any Coast Guard cutters that might be listening for the sound of his engines. At first light he would head for home, his night's work accomplished, and with the knowledge that in a day or so a deposit would be made to an account he kept in a Boston bank. At the end of his first summer he had, in the name of Martin White, $6,000 in the account. It was more than he would have earned in coffee, tea, and spices, and he would double the amount before the Atlantic weather forced him to suspend activity and put the *Nancy* up for the winter.

In his previous winter in Florida he had made enough money to buy the *Nancy* (at City Island, New York, and not at Woods Hole, Massachusetts). He now planned to buy out his Florida partner, a married man with a timorous wife. It could be done if he cut down on various extravagances. He got along very well with the English members of the Florida syndicate; he knew about boats, which was more than could be said for the American members of the syndicate, who cared about nothing but money. The Englishmen were not a bit concerned with the illegal aspects of their trade; the laws they violated were American laws and ridiculous, and young Whitehill was a gentleman, which was also more than could be said for his compatriots in the syndicate. Rather wild, he was, or adventurous, to say the least, but a gentleman. They recognized him as an American copy of the English prototype of the younger son, a recognition that came easily since they had among them a couple of the prototypes. The recognition was mutual, and Morton was counting on the Englishmen for future financial backing when he would need cash to add more boats to his personal fleet. He failed to recognize this as American optimism.

At the end of October he pulled the *Nancy* out of the water and took off in the Jordan for Miami Beach, stopping over in New York to pick up Rosalie Jerriman, his best-kept secret of the summer season. Rosalie was at the most thirty-five, but for three years she had been making a success of Jerriman's Inn, a summer hotel in East Chop that she inherited from her husband. Those in the know were aware that Rosalie had been the real manager of the Inn for more than the three years of her ownership. Tom Jerriman, who had inherited the Inn from his father, could never have held on to the business without Rosalie. He had come out of the army at thirty-one, legal owner of the Inn but with no talent for hotelkeeping and no interest in it except the interest he had always had in the waitresses and chambermaids. Rosalie, the daughter of a Yankee father and an Irish mother, was the most beautiful waitress Tom had ever laid hands on, but she resisted him until after the quiet but nevertheless binding marriage ceremony. Then he found that she was too much for him. His casual little affairs in the past had not prepared him for the demands of this healthy young woman who had been a virgin for twenty-seven years. She said she wanted a child—children—but in her efforts to become pregnant she gave him literally no rest, and though Tom's death certificate gave pneumonia as the cause, he died of a complication of love and shame. He could not admit to anyone—certainly not to his mother—that Rosalie did all the work in the daytime, and still had too much energy at night. And so he died, and his wife and his mother mourned his gentle soul and became close friends. The elder Mrs. Jerriman had always wanted a daughter, and now she had one who was a real comfort to her. The Inn was making more money than ever in its history, and the old lady would never have to worry about a place to live. The Vineyard in summer, and Rosalie's little hotel in Fort Lauderdale in the winter.

Not a soul had ever seen Rosalie and Morton together, even so much as chatting together. Their affair began, appropriately enough, with the approaching visit of a girl whom Morton had known in Florida. At his urging she agreed to spend a week at the Vineyard, but she insisted on stopping at some respectable hotel. Morton accordingly went to Jerriman's Inn to make the reservation, but when he told the clerk that the reservation was for a single young lady the clerk was not sure. He hemmed and hawed until Morton asked to see the manager. The clerk retreated to the manager's office and came out a minute later. The manager would see Mr. Whitehill.

"Good morning, Mr. Whitehill," said Rosalie.

"Good morning. I want to see the manager."

"You're looking at her," said Rosalie.

"You're the manager? Since when? Where's Tom Jerriman?"

"You're behind the times. Tom passed on a couple or more years ago. I'm his widow. The manager and the owner. What's your trouble?"

"I want to reserve a room for a young lady, the first week in August. That pansy at the desk was no help at all."

"He was using his head. You're familiar with Jerriman's Inn. A very respectable place for over forty years. We're very careful who we let in. Your own mother and father had people stay here."

"I know they did. Now what about this reservation?"

"No," said Rosalie.

"No?"

"Not a chance. If your parents asked, that'd be a different story, but I hear they're leaving the Vineyard for good. In fact, I hear a lot of things."

"About me, you mean?"

"Uh-huh," said Rosalie. "Why don't you get your friend a room at Mrs. de Paulo's?"

"Because I want to get her a room at this dump."

"Well, this dump, as you call it, has no room for her. If she gets in Mrs. de Paulo's she'll be lucky, with your reputation."

"She'd take one look at Mrs. de Paulo's and take the next boat out."

"I can't help that," said Rosalie.

"Yes you can. Come on, be a sport. This girl is no tramp, and it's only for a week anyhow."

"Do you want to know why I really won't give her a room, Whitehill? Because I can't afford to have *you* hanging around here. The young lady may be as pure as the driven snow, although I doubt that, but my regulars know you since you were a young kid, and they'd complain. You'd give my place a bad name. You're starting to give the Vineyard a bad name. If my mother-in-law came in and saw you here she'd faint dead away."

"I noticed *you* didn't, though."

"Not me. I'm not afraid of you. I think you're just a show-off kid that never grew up. Where I come from I saw a lot of bad little boys."

"Were you a bad little girl?"

"No, not that it's any of your business."

"What's your name?"

"My name? Rosalie Jerriman. Mrs. Thomas P. Jerriman, owner and proprietor of Jerriman's Inn."

"Rosalie, huh? Well, Rosalie, just from standing here and listening to your blabbing about respectability, I found out one thing."

"You did, did you?"

"Yeah," he said. "You can be had."

"Perhaps. But not by you."

"By me," said Morton. "Nine o'clock tonight I'll be in a red Jordan roadster outside your garage. Is it a date?"

She laughed. "Go on, peddle your papers."

"Nine o'clock," he said.

She was there, as there was never any doubt in the mind of either that she would be there. She was wearing a blue linen dress and had a scarf on her head that also served to hide her face. "Where are we going?" she said.

"Oh, I know a place."

"I'll bet you do, but where?"

"You'll see, " he said. He reached behind him and handed her a pint-size silver flask. "Have a snort?"

"Fresh off the boat? No thanks, I don't drink."

"It's real cognac. You'd pay twenty dollars a bottle for that in Boston."

"I wouldn't pay twenty cents for it unless I could sell it."

"Why, you have the heart of a bootlegger," he said.

"No, but that kind of a profit," she said. "I wish I would of thought to bring my bathing suit."

"Don't let that stop you," he said.

"No, I would of had to bring towels and all. I don't want to get my hair wet anyway. We have to be back by eleven. That's final."

"On a night like this?"

"Listen, you, if I'm not back by eleven this is the last time you'll ever see me."

"I like the sound of that," he said.

"Then it's understood?"

"All right," he said.

"Then I can relax," she said, and slunk down in her seat and closer to him. "You're about what? Twenty-five?"

"Correct."

"Kind of robbing the cradle, but you seem a lot older," she said. "If I didn't know I would of said you were around thirty-one or -two."

"You get a lot of wrinkles around the eyes when you've been to sea as much as I have."

"The wind does it as much as the sun, I guess," she said.

"Yeah, it does. Dries up the skin, too."

"You're darker than most of the Portuguese."

"Well, I was in Florida all last winter, you know."

"Bootlegging?"

"Charter boat. Fishing."

"In other words, bootlegging," she said. "What happens if they catch you?"

"First they have to catch me," he said. "Then they have to prove I was breaking the law. And that goes for you, too, Rosalie. Stop asking those questions."

"Well, one of these days I suppose I'll be reading in the paper how Morton Whitehill got shot by the Coast Guard. It'll break your mother and father's heart. Why do you do it? Your parents have plenty."

"Why do we do a lot of things? Why did you come along tonight? You can't explain it. How did I know you would? I can't explain that, either."

"Oh, I can explain about myself. You talk to nothing but old ladies and dried-up old men all day long. When you came in my office this morning it was like a breath of spring. Honestly. I don't mean to just flatter you personally. It was anybody young. Once in a while we get a young honeymoon couple, but it's mostly people over fifty. They don't give me any trouble and they pay their bills right on the dot, but I sure as hell welcome a young person."

"You didn't welcome *me*. Or the dame I wanted to get the reservation for," he said.

"The dame, huh? Then I was right, if you call her a dame. Is she a prostitute?"

"No, you wouldn't call her that. She's a cabaret singer. She isn't famous, but she makes good money and she could pass for a —well, not a schoolteacher. But not a prostitute. She's better than that."

"How long have you known her?"

"Oh—maybe six months. Since last winter."

"Were you living with her?"

"Listen, I don't live with anybody. Male or female. I have to stay independent. Anyway, she has a husband somewhere. He was working in Palm Beach last winter and I think he goes to Saratoga around this time of the year. But the hell with her, what about you? Who have you got?"

She did not answer.

"Huh? I said who have you got?"

"I heard you," she said. "I was just thinking. Who *have* I got?"

"Well, temporarily—me." He looked at her and smiled.

She smiled back. "Mm-hmm."

He got her back to the Inn well before eleven. "The bridge games will be just breaking up," she said, as he stopped the car. "Will you phone me tomorrow?"

"Not till the day after tomorrow," he said.

"Oh. You're going out with your boat, huh?"

"Well—I won't be near a phone," he said. "But I'll phone you day after tomorrow."

"Say you're Mr. White, if anybody wants to know. Mr. White from the supply company. That sounds harmless enough. But I won't say much to you. That pansy listens in on the switchboard, and I'll call you back from my room. I have a separate phone that doesn't go through the switchboard." She smiled. "I had it put in when I didn't trust my mother-in-law. She used to listen in on the switchboard."

"Busybody," he said.

"I had a lovely evening, Morton."

"So did I."

"I don't feel a bit sleepy, but I have to go now. Goodnight, honey. Till we meet again."

If they saw each other on the street they did not speak, and when his name came up in porch conversations she showed no interest. They met at irregular intervals, some as much as a week long. He put off the girl from Florida by telling her he could not get her a suitable room, and it was the last he heard from her. He had other women besides Rosalie, but it amused him to provide each girl with a cheap scarf for her hair to confuse anyone who saw him with Rosalie. As the season was coming to an end he thought of Rosalie and of the *Nancy II* in the same terms—putting them up for the winter. But he discovered that Rosalie could be and had been as reticent as he: throughout their affair she had not mentioned to him that she and her mother-in-law had leased, with an option to buy, a hotel in Fort Lauderdale.

"I'm going down there right after Labor Day," said Rosalie.

"That's early for Fort Lauderdale," he said.

"Oh, then I'm coming back up North. I'll be in New York for

a couple weeks. We won't open the Lauderdale Jerriman's till November sometime."

"You're a smooth one, all right. Never said a word," he said.

"Listen to who's talking," she said.

"Where are you getting all this money?" he said.

"I didn't have any trouble. *I* have a *good* reputation, honey. The bank in Fall River for some of the money, and some of my own, some of the old lady's, and the rest from my summer people. I could have got it all from one old man, summer people. But that's not good business. This way I have five couples and three others, all thirteen of them stockholders in my company, and all wanting to stay at the Lauderdale Jerriman's. But it's my company, honey. They can't sell their stock to anybody else but me. And you know why it was so easy to get the money? Because I was always nice to the old lady. Those other old people, they appreciated that as much as if I was doing it for them. But thank God for you, honey."

"Why me?"

"I had to have somebody young to be with. You'll never know what you did for me this past summer. Wait till you're thirty-five. You won't think it's so old."

"I never did think it was old."

"It's ten years more than you are. If it was only five I'd make you marry me, but twice five is too big a difference."

"You couldn't *make* me marry you, Rosalie."

"Couldn't I? I think I could. You're in love with me but you don't know it."

"Sure I know it," he said. "I've told you I am."

"Oh, I never went by what you told me. For a long time you weren't. But now you are, as much as I am with you but in a different way. If I went to California, you'd follow me out there."

"You're pretty sure."

"Oh, if you went there I'd follow you, too."

"Make me marry you," he said.

"You mean you dare me to? I could. But I won't, and why? Because it wouldn't last. This isn't going to last, but when we break up it's just a fellow and a girl. Not a married couple. Nobody even knows you and I were anything to one another, let alone married. I'm that good-looking young widow that runs a hotel for a lot of old people. I wish one thing. I wish you and I could have a child. That's my only regret. The mortal sins? Well, maybe I'll go to hell if there is a hell. But I do regret it that I couldn't have your child. I wasn't thinking about you being much of a father, but you're strong and healthy. A man."

"I'm not a show-off kid any more?"

"No, you're not."

"Who changed, Rosalie? Me, or you?"

"You. You love me like a man now. The first night you loved me like a show-off kid. You tried to hurt me the first night, but not lately. Now you can love me like a real man loves a woman. I'll bet you never loved another woman the way you loved me lately."

"No? Well, maybe I didn't."

"Every woman you ever love from now on, they can be thankful to me," she said.

"You keep talking as if we were bidding a fond adieu."

"Well, not tonight, but soon," she said. "You're going to Miami Beach and Bimini and all those places. And I'll be in Fort Lauderdale. I might as well be in Bangor, Maine, and you in South America. If you don't get shot *before* then."

"You mean by the federal men?"

"Them, or stabbed by one of those hoodlums in Oak Bluffs. You have a lot of enemies."

"I'll be able to see you in Fort Lauderdale."

"I doubt it."

"What's so different about there from here?"

"Me," she said.

"You? How?"

"A new place. A whole new business. I won't be able to sneak away there, the way I can here."

"Are you giving me the air?"

"I'm just telling you what I know it's going to be like. Here I know where everybody is at such and such a time. But down there it'll be all different, and I won't be able to take chances. The old lady and all my stockholders, I'm going to be like in a convent.

Twenty-eight rooms there, all in the one building. Here I have forty
rooms in the main building and the two cottages to wander around
in."

"Well, I guess you call this breaking it gently," he said.

"I told you more than I started out to," she said. "But now I'm
glad I did."

"You just got finished telling me you love me, and in the same
sentence you start giving me the air."

"That's something about me, Morton. I was a decent girl till I
got married. Twenty-six years of age, and fellows after me from the
time I was sixteen. And I was pretty, too."

"You're still pretty, what are you talking about?"

"I just want to tell you about myself. Old and young were
after me, married and single, but I stayed decent. Tom Jerriman
didn't want to marry me, a waitress, but it was that or nothing, so
he did."

"But you didn't love Tom Jerriman, you can't tell me that."

"No, I didn't. But I didn't love anybody else, either, so why
not marry a fellow that owned a hotel and didn't have any brothers
and sisters, only a mother in her sixties. Believe me, I saved the Inn
from going bankrupt, so I'm entitled to it. The old lady'd be in the
poorhouse if it wasn't for me."

"I thought you told me she's your partner. Where did she get
the money to do that?"

"One thousand dollars. That's all she has in it. I put her on
the payroll when I inherited the Inn."

"What do I care how much Mrs. Jerriman has in your hotel?"

"Just listen a minute, will you?" said Rosalie. "I feel an
obligation to take care of the old lady as long as she stays alive. I
like her now, and she brings me luck. Not only luck. She's a front.
With her around you know it's a respectable place. I get fresh guys,
salesmen and guys like that, they come in my office and start
getting personal, and I tell them just a minute, I want to get my
partner to hear what they have to say, and I bring in the old lady
and from then on they stick to business. Another thing, maybe
I'll need more cash next season, and I'll be able to get it from those
old people."

"Back again to where we were," said Morton.

"No, I'm getting there. All this is why I am giving you the air, only I'm not giving you the air. I'm giving you up because I have to think of my future. I'm not going to die poor, like my father and mother."

"One of these days you'll hook on to some rich guy, one of your summer people."

"I want to have my own, then I won't have to marry a man because he's rich. Unfortunately I don't see any rich guy my own age wanting to marry me now."

"You know, Rosalie, you're a cold-blooded proposition."

"Where I have to be," she said.

"With me you don't have to be," he said.

"Ho-ho! If I didn't watch out you could ruin the whole thing for me. You even cheated on me this summer. If I didn't see you one night over in Menemsha, with some girl in the car, I would of come pretty close to losing my head over you."

"What were you doing in Menemsha?"

"Taking the old lady to a friend of hers. It scared me, you know, to think how close I came to falling for you. I mean really falling. That was an act of Providence, seeing you that night."

"Well, we never made any promises to each other," he said.

"I know. In some ways I guess we have a lot in common," she said. "How old was she, that girl?"

"I don't know. Eighteen or nineteen, I guess."

"Yeah, I couldn't tell with that scarf on," said Rosalie. "Eighteen or nineteen. Young enough to be my daughter if I matured a little earlier. So you see? I don't have all the time in the world, even if I am only thirty-five years of age. And that's what makes the difference between you and I, and why I have to be cold-blooded, you call it."

"Who will you get in Fort Lauderdale?"

"Who will I get? For loving, you mean?"

"Yes."

"I don't think of that. It'll be all I can do to keep from getting in the car and driving down to Miami Beach. I'm not looking forward to that part of it. You know what I'm like."

"Oh, some guy'll come in some day and want to reserve a room for his girl friend—"

She slapped his face. "That never happened with anybody else, and it never will again. Take me home, you bastard."

He saw her once again before meeting her in New York, and they had four lovely days together on the southward journey. At Jacksonville he put her on the train so that she could arrive in Fort Lauderdale by rail. "A farewell present," he said, and handed her the diamond wristwatch his mother had spurned.

"Oh, honey, and I never got you anything," she said.

"That's all right," he said. "Maybe you'll bring me something to Miami Beach."

"Ah, I wish I could, honey. I wish I could," she said.

He had a profitable winter, but in terms of his larger schemes the season was a failure. It became apparent in January, for instance, that his partner, Red Williams, had resisted the pleadings of his wife and was not of a mind to be bought out. "I told her, I said I'd sell at the end of the year, next December or November if you still want to buy," said Williams. "By then I'd have enough to go back up North and open a garage. She wants to be with her folks in West Virginia. What for, I don't know. Her old lady wants to live down here and she might as well, she's here enough."

"I thought we kind of shook hands on this deal, Red. That I was to buy your share and you'd have so much a month for two years, a steady income."

"You don't call it a steady income when the money's owed to you on the instalment plan," said Red.

"No, that's true, but you did say you'd sell."

"Mort, when you got a wife pestering you to sell, but she don't have the least idea how long it takes to start a new business, and two kids and a mother-in-law—as far as that goes, *I* could buy *you* out and you go partners with another guy. Do you want to sell?"

"No, I want to buy."

"There you are, so I guess we put it off till December," said Red. "I got another thing I want to talk about, Mort. You only come down here from November to June."

"Correct."

"I know you got your boat up there on the Martha's Vineyard. But I'm honestly gonna need help this coming summer. I don't mean somebody to load. I want to have a fellow I can trust with the boat. Last summer I made every trip myself, and look at me. My face, my arms. That's from too much sun. I cover up with cold cream but it don't do much good. The cold cream clogs up my pores and I get one infection after the other. She says I look like I had leprosy."

"Maybe you have," said Morton.

"Huh?"

"I was kidding."

"Listen, it ain't a kidding matter, a wife afraid she'll catch something from her husband."

"Lulu exaggerates it because she wants you to quit."

"She ain't that smart," said Red. "Anyway, Mort, what if I found a guy that could take half of the trips? Would you be willing to sell your share then?"

"Why should I?"

"Only one reason. Money. We're in this on the basis of nine months of the year we split even, but three months of the year you don't get anything."

"Correct," said Morton.

"Well, say toward the end of May a guy came along and offered you three thousand dollars for doing nothing all summer, would you be willing to sell your share of the boat?"

"For how much?"

"Twenty thousand," said Red.

"I'll let you know in April," said Morton.

"Think it over, Mort. It's a fair and honest proposition. We're going to need new engines this year, I'm almost positive. Maybe even a new boat. You know what a pounding the *Lulu* takes."

"I'll tell you in April," said Morton. "Who's the fellow you've been talking to?"

"Well, there was a couple different parties innarested," said Red.

On his next trip to Bimini Morton had the first of several conversations with the Englishmen. Only after the fourth conversation did he fully comprehend what should have been obvious in the first, that the Englishmen thought him a good fellow and a fine seaman but were not going to lend him one red cent. Moreover, they reported the conversations to the American member of the syndicate, and he was summoned to headquarters in a large, no longer first-class hotel. It was a suite of rooms, with some of the hotel furniture moved out to make way for the business-office equipment. Behind the steel desk in the inner office was a man named Terry Cassidy, and seated at his right in a Louis Quinze chair was Jack Elias. Elias was smoking a cigar and he nodded but did not speak when Morton entered the room. The meeting was to be conducted by Cassidy, with Elias there as an observer. As to their respective standings in the syndicate Morton was not certain, but they were not the top command, although they were so much higher than the men Morton had worked with that this was only his second meeting with Cassidy and his first with Elias.

Cassidy was a fortyish man with an abundance of white hair brushed back in a pompadour. He was wearing a striped silk shirt with sleeve garters and a white soft collar with a loud, heavy silk tie. Elias was wearing a black mohair suit but with a tie as bad as Cassidy's. "Hello, there, Whitehill," said Cassidy. "Sit down. Care for a cigar? Oh, shake hands with Jack Elias."

Elias nodded and extended a limp hand, and Morton took a seat across the desk from Cassidy. "Let's get down to business," said Cassidy, and his momentary affability vanished. "Why did you want to go to those other fellows when you wanted money, White-hill? Why didn't you come to us first?"

"I thought I knew them better."

"We're Americans, they're English. Wouldn't it look funny to you?"

"Maybe it does to you, but it didn't to me. They seemed more like friends of mine. And it's all the same syndicate. There was nothing secretive about it."

"Four times? Pretty secretive, I call it. You could of tried us once."

"I thought I was making progress with them. It turns out I was wrong."

"You were wrong from the start, Whitehill. We want to find out how wrong you were."

"Ask them. All I wanted was enough money to go in business for myself. Williams won't sell out to me, and lately he's been talking about buying my share."

"We know all about that," said Cassidy.

"Look, Mr. Cassidy, all I did was try to get backing from some members of the syndicate. I don't see anything wrong about that. Are you trying to make me look bad?"

Elias spoke. "Ask him which Englishman he knew best," he said.

"Yeah, which one did you know best?" said Cassidy.

"I didn't know any of them very well," said Morton. "But I guess you'd say I knew John Haydock a little better than the others. He and I used to talk about sailing."

"Sailing? Where were you going to sail to?" said Cassidy.

"We weren't going to sail to anywhere. We talked about the sport of sailing. Yachting. The way you might talk about horse-racing. Haydock used to sail in England and Norway, and I used to sail around Massachusetts and the State of Maine. Don't try to make anything out of that, Mr. Cassidy. It won't get you anywhere."

"Keep your shirt on, young fellow."

"I will. I like *my* shirt," said Morton.

"Wuddia mean by that, may I ask?" said Cassidy.

"He means he don't like your shirt," said Elias.

"Yeah, well I got two dozen and they cost fourteen dollars apiece. The one he got on you can get for a deuce," said Cassidy. "What else did you know about Haydock?"

"Not much. I never even went to his house. I only mention him because he and I had that one thing in common. Boats."

"Well, it's too bad he didn't know more about them," said Cassidy.

"Terry!" said Elias.

"Hell, he'll find out the next trip to B," said Cassidy. "Your pal got drownded."

"Haydock? Not in these waters. He sailed boats in the English Channel."

"I don't know about that, but he went out in his little sail-boat the day before yesterday. They found the boat but they didn't find him. So he must be feeding the fishes."

"He was a damn nice guy," said Morton.

"Nobody said he wasn't," said Cassidy. "For an Englishman, I thought he was a *pretty* nice guy."

"I guess there's no use asking whether he was in trouble with the syndicate?"

"In trouble? How would he be? He was a *member* of the syndicate. We're taking excellent care of his wife and kids. Excellent."

"Excellent," said Elias. "A good thing he *didn't* loan you any money, Whitehill. The wife would most likely want it back now. You wouldn't of had the use of it very long."

"I'm sorry to hear about Haydock. He was a real gent," said Morton.

"Well, they're having a service for him the day after tomorrow. You could go over to B for that. Pay your last respects. We'll pay for the gas. Williams is over there today, isn't he?"

"Correct," said Morton. "But I'll pay for my own gas, this trip, and come back empty."

"Suit yourself, Whitehill," said Cassidy. "We made the offer. One more thing. Did you hear from New York lately?"

"No."

"As far as you know, you're going back to Martha's Vineyard this summer?"

"Correct. Why wouldn't I?"

"Just checking up on your plans," said Cassidy.

"Go ahead and tell him," said Elias.

"Well, there's some talk that New York is pulling out of your section. Concentrating on Long Island and New Jersey. You didn't hear anything to that effect?"

"No."

"Maybe just a rumor."

"They wouldn't tell me anything important," said Morton. "I just run a boat."

"But you have ambitions to run more than one boat," said Cassidy.

"You can't shoot a man for trying," said Morton.

Cassidy chuckled. "No, I guess not," he said.

"Or maybe I said the wrong thing," said Morton.

"No, no," said Cassidy. "Well, Jack, do we have any more questions to ask Whitehill?"

"No. But if he hears anything from New York we'd appreciate him passing the information along to us," said Elias.

"Yes," said Cassidy. "We'd appreciate that, Whitehill."

Morton was dismissed, and he wandered around Miami and Miami Beach that night, having drinks with acquaintances but reluctant to remain long in one place or with any of his friends, male or female. The murder of John Haydock—and he was convinced it was nothing else—had a more depressing effect on him than the rubbing-out, as they called it, of two other men he had known better than he knew the Englishman. The British were more thorough and relentless about murder than the Americans, even when the victim was a member of a gang. The syndicate must have had their own extremely good reasons to defy the British. Morton doubted that he would ever know their reason, and he doubted that Haydock's body would ever turn up. In all probability he had been shot first, or, better yet, killed with a knife so that his body would not fail to attract the sharks. Morton recalled that he had never seen Haydock on American soil, although all the other non-Americans frequently came to Miami on business and pleasure trips. Thus the only way to execute Haydock would be to go to Bimini and do the job there. It seemed likely that Haydock knew what he was doing when he stayed away from Florida. Incidental comments during their conversations had revealed Haydock as a man who liked women and parties, and the syndicate parties were notorious. No one as far down as Morton in the syndicate operations ever got invited to the parties, but they were worth the trip to important gangsters from St. Louis, Chicago, Detroit, Jersey City, New York, and Boston. Morton's sources of information were girls who had attended the parties and who were perfectly willing to supply details that concerned everyone but themselves. Thus he had known, while sitting in Cassidy's office, that Cassidy had certain peculiarities and Elias certain others, and the knowledge had made him more flippant than he had intended to be. He wondered whether he had been too flippant, but flippancy alone was not in the catalog of offenses that called for capital punishment, and he was not alarmed. The only grounds for fear were Cassidy's remark about ambitions and the fact that early in the conversation Cassidy seemed to be trying to make something of Morton's attempts to borrow money from the English members of the syndicate, with special reference to Haydock.

As he went from one joint to another, drinking ale and staying sober, Morton realized that Haydock was undoubtedly the man who had reported his attempts to get backing from the Englishmen. But he did not feel that Haydock had in any sense betrayed him. It was the proper, so typically British proper, thing for Haydock to have done. It was one thing for Haydock to have committed some act of treachery that would cost him his life, but something else again to let their harmless conversations go unreported. Haydock was a man of great charm, the pleasantest of company while inspiring instinctive distrust. Conversationally he was armed with the English public school clichés that make it possible to be reticent without being rude. He contradicted you not with a flat statement but with a question. ("Oh, do you really think you could pay it back inside a year?" instead of "You couldn't pay it back in a year.") Haydock was a thin man with a large long nose and a very long neck. The first upper molar was missing from the right side of his mouth, and his lower teeth popped up haphazardly in his gums, but he talked so rapidly and well of many things that you listened rather than looked. *He* didn't care about his bad teeth, and they might not have been so bad if he had ever gone to a dentist. But he could not have had much time for dentists while living the life that had provided him with so many odd bits of information. "It isn't much of a plane, you know," he once said of an airplane settling down in the bay. "It handles very badly on takeoff. Needs every bit of its power to lift itself out of the water."

"Can you fly?"

"Oh, I have. There's nothing to it. I could teach you in two hours," said Haydock.

"Did you fly in the war?"

"Heavens, no. Wish I had. I was cooped up in a dreadnought most of the time. Got in too early for the R.F.C. Wish I'd waited and had some fun."

He spoke a great deal of fun in relation to women, liquor, sailing, shooting, flying, and gambling, but in doing so he maintained an unsmiling expression, as though fun were a synonym for activity that gave him pleasure without cause for laughter. And always, even when he was at his most entertaining, he seemed to be preoccupied with some unfinished task that would take him away; literally, away from the table, or figuratively back to some moment in the past. Curiously it had not occurred to Morton that Haydock's preoccupation might be caused by any of the activities of the syndicate, or anything to do with his wife and children, whom Morton had not seen. Haydock's wife and children were a fact of his life; he went home to them. But they were kept out of his conversation, as was much of his personal history. "Are you an old Etonian?" Morton once asked him.

"Hardly that, my dear chap. Eton—a bit rich for our blood. My school has never had a prime minister, not in two hundred years. No chance I'll be the first, do you think?" He spoke without personal bitterness but rather with pity, as though it would be nice to supply his old school with some distinction. That was a thing he had; the surprise in store not only *when* you least expected it, but of a nature you did not expect. In this case it was a softness toward his old school that was conventional enough in an Englishman but not in this Englishman, who had probably not had a school record that he or the school would boast of. In age he was somewhere past thirty, hard of muscle and large of feet and hands, surprisingly so for a man who was so slender. Morton had seen him squeeze bottle caps with thumb and forefinger, casually, without making a feat of it. In a small boat he would not have been easy to kill with a knife, and Morton now theorized that Haydock had been shot first with a rifle bullet. It made no great difference how he had been killed, except that Morton wanted to know and could only guess.

On the day of the services for Haydock, Morton took the *Lulu* to Nassau, but his plan to go alone was altered by Red Williams's insistence on going along. "I liked old Haydock," said Red. "And anyway that's too long a trip for you to make by yourself."

"Afraid I wouldn't get her back alone?" said Morton.

"Not that exactly, but it is too much of a trip for one man, I think," said Red.

Haydock had a cottage on the outskirts of Nassau, and when Morton and Red found it they were given another of Haydock's surprises. The cottage was on less than a half acre of hilly ground, surrounded by a wire fence, with a small stable back of the cottage. A family of goats wandered about. The cottage itself was in poor condition, with signs of neglect everywhere. The two men knocked on the front door and a stout woman appeared. She had a cigarette in her mouth and she breathed smoke while resting a baby on her hip bone.

"Could you tell us where we'll find Mrs. John Haydock, please?" said Morton.

"I'm Mrs. John Haydock. May I ask who you are?" The woman was of mixed white and Negro blood.

"We're friends of his that came over for the services. Americans," said Morton.

"No services," said the woman. "I dispensed with them. You wish to come in and rest a bit?"

"Don't want to bother you," said Red Williams.

"My husband may not be daid, though they did find the boat. Gentlemen care for a bottle of beer? Come on in, please, and I get you a bottle of beer off the ice. Not very fond of warm beer myself."

The two men went inside, took chairs while Mrs. Haydock went to get the beer.

"One thing, sure," said Red Williams. "Haydock didn't squander his money on this joint."

"No," said Morton. "It makes me wonder what he did with it. What would you say she was?"

"She don't talk like Florida. Jamaica, maybe. Pretty, once upon a time, you can see that."

"Beautiful when she was sixteen, probably. But there's too much of her now."

Still with the cigarette burning in her mouth and the baby on her hip, Mrs. Haydock returned with three bottles of beer which she held by the necks. She set the beer on a table beside a portable phonograph. "Get you some glasses," she said. "Tastes better coming out of a glass." She got two shell glasses and a water tumbler and a bottle-opener.

"Help yourselves, gentlemen," she said. "What do the gentlemen think of this thing? Is it your opinion John is alive, or dead?"

"Well, there's always hope," said Red Williams.

"Mr. Harry Carstairs—you gentlemen acquainted with him? My husband's business associate? He don't hold out any hope, and I fear he's right. Nevertheless I don't like to give up entirely. My husband was so proficient sailing boats, I continue to expect him to walk in that door. But I may be hoping forlornly. The beer the right temperature?"

"Fine. Just right," said Morton.

She looked at him. "I guess you gentlemen were with him in business, too?"

"Yes," said Morton.

"I deduced that. My husband wasn't acquainted with very many American gentlemen. Or any others, truth to tell. English, you know. Not one for social mingling. Reading was his pastime. Reading books and sailing his boats. I never went over to Bimini, but I know that boat was smaller than the one he had here. Not being a very proficient swimmer I never went sailing with him, he wouldn't let me. Well, he prophesied right. He said if one of us got drowned, there'd still be the one to take care of these children. My other child is at school, but this one it'll be a few years before he starts his education. Isn't that right, little fellow? You keep me company a few more years, little fellow?"

"Well, we hope everything turns out for the best, Mrs. Haydock," said Red Williams, rising.

"We mustn't keep you," said Morton.

"I do thank you kindly for wishing to pay your respects. Thank you very much, gentlemen."

They had kept their taxi waiting. "Now what do we do?" said Morton. "Go see Carstairs? Maybe we should have done that first."

"We should have, but we didn't know any better," said Red. "Yeah, we better go see Carstairs. Driver?"

"Yes sir, I take you to see Mr. Harry Carstairs," said the driver.

Carstairs's office was called the Inter-American Export Co., Ltd. "Too bad you gentlemen had to come all this way. I could have cabled you if I'd known. I take it you did meet, the uh, Mrs. Haydock? Bit of a shock if you're not prepared for it, but I must say she was a beauty and not too long since. Must go fifteen stone now, but when I first saw her she was no more than a man's woman, if you know what I mean. Something there to take hold of, don't you know. Yes. Mm. I believe she might have some legal difficulties lying ahead. Appears old Haydock had a wife in England who never divorced him or he her. A bimbo, as you chaps would say, but with a perfectly legal claim to her share of Haydock's estate. If and when, that is. Presumed dead isn't quite the same thing as declared dead, is it? We'll do the right thing by the lady you met today, at least for the time being. But now, gentlemen, what about you two? Have you come to a decision, or in other words is one of you going to sell out to the other? No immediate problem, but we don't like to have these things hanging in the air."

"We'll know in April," said Red Williams.

"April. Well—all right, then," said Carstairs. "And now is there anything I can do for you while you're in Nassau? Cash a cheque, or uh, female companionship? I know where you could spend a very pleasant evening or afternoon, for that matter. These are two young women who aren't exactly professionals, but I assure you they're not amateurs either. Five quid is what you're expected to leave on the way out, so you see they're not common tarts."

"I'm a married man," said Red Williams.

Carstairs chuckled. "Yes, but you see these are married women, and being a bachelor I'm inclined to be cynical about the vows."

"Twenty-five bucks," said Morton. "I'm game."

"You'll save a little if you use English money, Whitehill," said Carstairs. "And we don't want to spoil them do we? Williams? Are you unshakable?"

"Aw, what the hell, I'm game if Whitehill is."

They spent the next two nights in Nassau, and now Morton had something on Williams. It was not much, but it was enough to improve his position, as Red Williams inadvertently revealed on the homeward journey. They were out in open water, Williams at the wheel, before Red displayed his troubled conscience. "I swarr, I wish I woulda never listened to that Carstairs," he said. "Lulu ain't gonna believe a thing I tell her—unless I was to tell her the truth. She'd believe that soon enough, because that's what she's thinking anyhow."

"Well, you enjoyed yourself for two days."

"I guess maybe I did, what I can remember of it," said Red. "I never knew a woman like that Vickie. Some woman! Burn my clothes!"

"She liked you, too," said Morton.

"Seemed to, but that didn't keep her from taking me for two hundred dollars. Two hundred dollars for what started out to be twenty-five. Pig-drunk. Hung over. Out two hundred. And the worst is yet to come."

"Blame it on me," said Morton.

"How so?"

"I mean, tell Lulu I got into some kind of trouble and you had to stay and bail me out."

"I could do that, providing you fix up a good story. My mind ain't working so good. This'll be one time I won't stick up for you."

"Oh, I know what Lulu thinks of me," said Morton.

"You sure you don't mind?" said Red.

"I've got nothing to lose," said Morton. "You tell Lulu I got into a fight. We don't have to say anything about women or getting drunk. If you say anything about getting drunk, she'll put two and two together and start asking you questions. Just say—just say I caught a fellow on board the *Lulu*. Some stranger. Looked as if he was going to steal something. I hit him, and he had me arrested."

"Where was I at the time?"

"Talking to Carstairs, in Carstairs's office," said Morton. "The first you heard of it was when the police asked Carstairs if you knew me. They wouldn't let you go my bail. They kept me in the can because I was a foreigner, an American. Then they gave me a hearing and fined me two hundred dollars. No, that's stretching it. Keep it simpler than that. Just tell her you waited over till they gave me a hearing."

"Where did I stay those nights?"

"On the *Lulu,* of course."

"That's good. I like that," said Red. "If I get away with this story I'm your friend for life." He glanced at Morton. "And I guess I better be, huh?"

"Hell, I wouldn't want to see you in any trouble, Red."

"I love Lulu," said Red. "I never play around much. She don't give me much chance to, but I wouldn't anyhow. She don't, so I don't. I know *she* don't, because her old lady's with us half the time and she's more scared of her old lady than she ever was of me. So am I, to tell you the truth. I couldn't get away with this story to the old lady. I'm just gonna tell Lulu and make out like it's a secret. She'll right away go and tell the old lady, but that'll be all right."

They ran into a squall that made the sea choppy enough to discourage casual conversation during the next two hours, and when the weather was calm Red went below to take a nap. He slept until the different sound and vibrations of the *Lulu* in the bay awakened him. He came up and stood beside Morton.

"You look better," said Morton. "The sleep did you good."

"I feel better," said Red. "Maybe I won't have to tell her any story."

"Just have it ready," said Morton. "But if you don't think you're going to need me to back you up, I won't go out to your house with you."

"Maybe it'd be better if you didn't come," said Red.

"Suits me all right," said Morton. "I can use some sleep myself."

"Thanks anyway, Mort," said Red.

He was so transparent. A few hours' sleep had restored his physical well-being, and now he wished to be free of obligation to Morton.

"Got the old self-confidence back, eh?" said Morton.

"How do you mean, Mort?"

"Just that. You think you can handle her now," said Morton.

"Lulu? Yeah. I was shaky back there, but a little shut-eye, you know?"

"Sure, Red," said Morton. "Sure."

"Now not that I don't appreciate," said Red.

"Listen, I get it. You don't want to owe me any more favors than you have to," said Morton. "Well, I'd be the same way in your position."

"I don't mind owing you a favor," said Red. "We're pardners."

"All the more reason why you don't want to owe me anything," said Morton. He eased the boat into the berth and Red, agile again, leapt to the dock and tied up.

"Can I give you a ride anywhere?" said Red.

"Got my car up at the garage. Having a valve job done," said Morton.

"You're always spending your dough on that car," said Red.

"Well, why not? Some day I may want to get away fast," said Morton.

"Who from?"

"I don't know yet," said Morton. "Maybe some jealous husband."

"Oh."

"Why? Who did you think, Red?"

"Nobody in particular," said Red.

"I don't think a fast car would have saved Haydock," said Morton.

"Nothing would of saved Haydock. He double-crossed everybody."

"You must know something I don't know," said Morton.

"No, but I can guess. So can you. That's all we better do, is guess. But a double-crosser gets it sooner or later."

"Let's sit in your car a minute, Red," said Morton. "I want to talk a little."

"Okay, if it don't take too long," said Red.

"Only a minute or two," said Morton.

Red had a Buick Master 6 sedan. "You've got room in the back here for a dozen cases," said Morton.

"Never used this car to haul with," said Red. "Car belongs to Lulu." He sat behind the wheel and Morton got in beside him.

"You're anxious to buy me out," said Morton. "I thought by this time I'd be able to buy *you* out, but what's your offer?"

"Why do you want to sell all of a sudden?"

"Come on, Red, what's your best offer?"

"Well, I have to think," said Red. "I'll give you five thousand for your interest in the boat, and five thousand for you to quit the partnership."

"I said an offer, not an insult," said Morton.

"I heard what you said," said Red. "You didn't answer me, though. Why do you want to sell, all of a sudden?"

"Give me forty thousand dollars cash, and I'll shake on it," said Morton. "I'll get out of town, leave Florida the same day."

"Nope. Ten thousand dollars."

"We're two guys that ten thousand dollars isn't a lot of money to," said Morton. "But one of us seems to have some information that's worth about thirty thousand."

"How do you mean, Mort?"

"I wish I knew what you know," said Morton. "Have you been talking to Cassidy? Elias, maybe?"

"No more than usual," said Red.

"Maybe no more than usual, but I wish I knew what they said. What *did* they say?"

"I offered you ten thousand, Mort. If I's you I'd take that," said Red.

"My guess is, Elias and Cassidy think I was mixed up with Haydock, but they're not sure. Whatever the hell Haydock was doing, I don't know that either. But it sure looks as if I made one hell of a big mistake trying to get Haydock to back me."

"That may be, Mort. That may be," said Red.

"And so, Elias and Cassidy have hinted to you to get a new partner," said Morton. "They'd save you the trouble if they were sure I was in with Haydock, but they're giving me a break."

Red reached in the glove compartment and took out a couple of foil-wrapped cigars. "Have one?"

"No thanks. Cigarettes for me," said Morton.

Red unwrapped his cigar and made an ugly ceremony of biting off the end and spitting it out, spitting even after the last tiny leaf was gone from his lip. He lit a kitchen match with his thumbnail and slowly revolved the cigar between his lips to get an even light. Then he drew a deep breath and sat forward with his hands on the top of the steering wheel. "We been friends and pardners near two years, Mort. Liked you from the start. You done more than your share of the work, and you took your share of the chances. I got no complaints personally. Personally I just as soon we keep on being pardners. That's personally."

"*But,*" said Morton.

"Well, yes. *But.* I ain't saying you guessed right or you guessed wrong. I ain't saying you was in with Haydock or in with anybody. I ain't saying *Haydock* was in with anybody. I don't know what happened to Haydock no more than you do, Mort. I'll say this much, if that little fat woman ever sees him again I'll be surprised. Or anybody else. You cut open some shark's belly and you'll most likely come across that big round wristwatch and that gold ring he used to wear. You remember that gold ring. You got one like it."

"Something like it," said Morton.

"That's where it is now, in some shark's belly—is my guess."

"Mine, too," said Morton.

"Oh, sure. We know that, even if we can't swear to it," said Red. "Mort, I'll give you fifteen thousand, and that's the most I'll say."

"The hell with that, Red. You were just getting started on telling me something. There's no dictograph in this car."

"Ain't worried about no dictograph," said Red.

"Then what *are* you worried about?"

"Talking too much," said Red. "I hinted too much already."

"All you hinted was that I may have guessed that Elias and Cassidy think I was in with Haydock. But that was my guess. You didn't tell me that."

Red put the cigar in his mouth and puffed on it a little. He looked at it. "Good cigar," he said. "All right, Mort. I'll give it to you straight. They're almost *sure,* they're almost *positive,* you was in with Haydock. If you wouldn't of gone over to Nassau with me, that would of convinced them you's afraid to go. And if you's afraid to go, *why* was you afraid to go? Because you and Haydock were in cahoots. You's in the same double-cross Haydock was in—and I don't know what that was."

"And you were keeping an eye on me for them?" said Morton.

"Yep. Wherever you went, I went. Including them two hookers. Whoever you saw, I saw. That was my orders, Mort. I don't expect you to thank me, but I'll tell you this much, Mort. You's better off with me keeping an eye on you than if you's by yourself."

"I came that close, eh?"

"Very close," said Red. "So if I's you, Mort, the best thing you can do is take my offer. The fifteen offer. Because I know these fellows, Mort. Once they get suspicious of a guy, I don't care if they got no reason, they never get over it. The next time they don't like something, you're the fall guy. The Coast Guard knocks off a boat in Lake Erie, for God's sake—they'll blame you. They gotta blame somebody. They gotta take it out on somebody else beside themselves. Haydock knew he was gonna get it, and he was pretty high up. But this past year he was walking around in a cloud. You know why? He knew. Before you's in the business the federal men knocked off a big truckload on the way North."

"Why blame Haydock for that?"

"The only time Haydock was in Florida for over a year."

"But he wouldn't tip off the federal men," said Morton.

"No. But he was in Florida, and he could of said something to some dame."

"Doesn't make sense," said Morton.

"Sense? Does any of it make sense?" said Red.

"Yes," said Morton. "Your offer does. I'll take it."

"You know what it means, Mort? You get out of the business and stay out. You *know* that?"

"Up North, too?" said Morton.

"I would, if I's you. But you sure as hell gotta get out of Florida."

Morton smiled. "Do I have to drive fast?"

"Well, maybe not as fast as that Jordan'll go," said Red.

"I want to make one stop, in Lauderdale," said Morton.

"Take my advice and keep going. Lauderdale is too near."

"When will you have the money—and how do I know I won't be knocked off when I get it?"

"I'll send the money to that bank in Boston. If it ain't there when you get there, you can come back and knock *me* off."

Morton smiled again. "And I would, you know."

"Oh, I know you would," said Red. "I'd do the same."

"Have you ever?"

"Knocked anybody off? Mort, that's a question you got no business asking."

"But I got my answer."

"Then why did you ask it? Cassidy didn't have to ask it. Elias didn't have to. You know why they didn't? Because for the same reason I know you never *did*. But you would. You'd knock me off if I double-crossed you. Then you'd be one of the boys, Mort. You and Cassidy and Elias and me and Haydock."

"Haydock?"

"Are you kidding? It wouldn't no more bother Haydock than squeezing one of them bottle caps. You ever take notice to him doing that?"

"Often," said Morton. "I guess I never knew much about Haydock."

"What was there to know? A skinny English double-crosser that got what was coming to him. And I wonder what he done with the money?"

"I thought you liked him," said Morton.

"Well, now liking a fellow—I like you, Mort, but I'll be sure and put that money in the Boston bank. Because you'd come back and knock me off."

"Yes, I would."

"With Haydock, for instance. With him there had to be a first time, and I bet it was something like that. Had a grudge against somebody, went gunning for him and got him. You're ready to do the same thing, and I don't want it to be me. So don't worry about your money, Mort. It'll be there. And if I don't see you again, good luck."

"We saying goodbye?"

"I guess we might as well, as good as any time," said Red. "Go on, have a cigar."

"I'll take one, Red," said Morton.

They shook hands and Morton got out of the car. "Luck, kid," said Red.

"Thanks, Red. Same to you." He watched Red pulling away in the motherly Buick. As the car came to the first intersection there was something excruciatingly funny about Red slowing down and putting his hand out to signal that he was making a turn.

THE MADELINE
WHERRY CASE

Mrs. Wherry got off the train and waited on the platform until the train went on its way. There were offers of a lift, which she declined. "Thank you," she said. "I have my car. Just waiting in case Bud was on this train." She became the last person to leave the platform, and she made her way slowly to her sedan, parked on the outermost edge of the lot. She had to pass her husband's VW, which was much nearer to the platform, and if she could have remembered where he hid the key she would have taken his car and left him hers. Her feet hurt.

She got in her sedan and kicked off her shoes and put on a pair of loafers that lay on the floor. She took off her hat and ruffled her hair and lowered the windows in the front doors. She lit a cigarette and had a few long drags on it before tossing it away. Now she started the car and headed for home.

The cool draft she had created by opening the car windows mussed her hair, but she no longer cared. There was a smudge on the fingers of her white glove, where she had grasped the handrail in getting off the train. That didn't matter. She caught a glimpse of her face in the too honest rear-view mirror, and she saw individual grains of face powder and little splits in the texture of her lip rouge that looked like a row of wrinkles. She saw the real wrinkles and the crow's-feet, and she wondered how much worse they would be if she had not always, all her life, been so religious about her cold cream and her facials. "Never soap," her mother had told her. "Not even the mildest soap on your face. I haven't used soap on my face since I was sixteen years old, and if I'm proud of one thing I'm proud of my skin." That was when she was fourteen and leaving for boarding-school, and her mother was giving her parting instructions. That was more than thirty years ago. Thirty-three, to be exact. Thirty-*four*. That whole conversation came back to her now, and she recalled her confusion when she tried to pay attention to her mother's advice. Some of the advice was obvious stuff, but some of it had given her a new look at her mother. How had her conventional, rather prim mother acquired the information to give? "Make it a rule never to lend things," her mother had said. "Things, or money. If the other girls find they can take advantage of you, they will, so you start right out by making it a *rule*. They'll respect you more in the long run." Her mother had not been to a boarding-school; how did she know all that? What's more, her mother was a generous woman, with a reputation for large and small kindnesses. Madeline Wherry wondered now what else her mother could have told her. "You'll let boys kiss you—if you haven't already," she had said. "But you mustn't believe a word they say when they're kissing you. It isn't that they're lying to you. They believe what they say at such times. But how is a young boy to know anything? How are *you* to know anything unless I tell you? And don't trust your instincts, Madeline. They'll play you false."

That was the one she should have remembered.

She put her car in the garage and lowered the door. With her town shoes in one hand she entered the house at the back porch. Theodora was sitting at the kitchen table, doing a crossword puzzle, the radio going full blast. "Oh, you're home early," said Theodora.

"No. This is the train I said I'd be on. Would you mind turning that down just a little?"

Theodora got up and lowered the volume of the radio. "Mrs. Farr called. Mrs. Eubank. Mrs. Farr said she'd call again this evening, nothing important. Mrs. Eubank wanted me to make sure and tell you about the change in plans. You and Mister were supposed to go there at seven o'clock, but now she don't want you till ha' past. You were supposed to have dinner at her house, but their cook's mother took sick and she had to leave hurriedly for Wilmington, so you're all having dinner out. Was a person-to-person call for you, but the party didn't leave no name. I told them you were expected about now. You know it rained here around lunchtime? Did it rain in New York?"

"No. It looked as though it might, but it didn't.."

"Rained steady for about a half an hour. You just can't go by the radio. They said fair, partly cloudy toward evening. I was giving some of those blankets an airing and they got soaked. Me too, I got soaked bringing them in. The shower came so quick I wasn't ready for it. I was busy on the phone talking to my sister and I didn't notice when it started to come down. You'd think they'd know on the radio. Don't they get those reports from the government?"

"I imagine so. What station are you listening to?"

"That? Ain't that Trenton?"

"I don't know. I thought *you'd* know."

"Oh, I don't always keep track of what station."

"Well, I'm going to have a bath, if anyone should call. Tell them to call again in an hour."

"What about your person-to-person?"

"I'm still going to have my bath."

"Uh-huh."

"Did you hang the wet blankets in the cellar?"

"Yes ma'am, I did."

"Good. They should dry out there overnight, and we can hang them outdoors again in the morning."

"There! It *was* Trenton. He just gave the station identification. I can usually tell if it's Trenton. You get to know their voices. There's one I always get mixed up with—"

"Is the mail on the hall table?"

"The mail? Oh, a letter from your daughter. The rest is all ads. It's in there on the hall table, you'll see it."

"Yes."

"Can I have the stamp off of your daughter's letter? I got my nephew is starting a stamp collection. I don't know whether he got an Italy one or not."

"Of course," said Madeline Wherry.

She was half out of her clothes when the telephone rang. It was the person-to-person call. "I'll take it, Theodora. You can hang up, please," said Madeline. "Hello?"

"Are you all right?" he said.

There was no need for him to identify himself. "What a strange question," she said. "Why yes, I'm all right. Why?"

"I was wondering. Have you had your talk with Bud?"

"He's not home yet. But I'll be all right. And please don't call me again, will you? Please?"

"All right, I won't," he said.

"Then why did you call now? You're not making it any easier for anybody. For me or for you. Now don't call again, please. It's over and settled and done with."

"I know that, but I had to call you this once."

"No you didn't. There won't be any trouble with Bud, and even if there was I wouldn't tell you about it. He's got what he wanted, and he can't make any trouble."

"Yes, he's got what he wanted, all right," he said. "Well, I'm sorry to've bothered you."

"We've said it all, including goodbye," she said.

"Right," he said, and hung up.

His anticlimactic call was a minor annoyance, and she tried to think of T. S. Eliot's line about ending in a whimper. The call was almost a whimper. Two hours ago, less than two hours ago, there had been pain, tears, strong feeling. He should have left it at that. Strong feeling had given her strength; now all she wanted to do was sink into her tub, to complete the lethargy that the call had produced.

She was still in the tub when she heard the VW in the driveway, and the routine sounds of her husband's return from his day in town that could not have been a routine day. Then, "Are you taking a bath?"

"Yes," she said.

"Do you want a drink?"

"No, I don't want a drink," she said.

"Well, did you *see* him?" he said.

"Yes, I saw him. I'll be out in a minute. Get yourself a drink if you want one."

"I have one," he said.

She dried herself and ran a comb through her hair and put on her dressing-gown. He was sitting uncomfortably on her daybed, highball glass in hand, smoking a cigarette.

"I saw you in Penn Station," he said.

"Oh, you did?"

"Yes. *I* was in time for the five-eleven, too. I was having a drink and I saw you waiting for the gate to open."

"But you didn't take the five-eleven."

"No, I certainly didn't," he said. "I didn't feel like discussing what we had to discuss on a railroad train."

"Probably very wise," she said. "Well, we're here, and here we can discuss anything."

"All right. You start."

"Well, I telephoned him around ten o'clock and asked him to meet me for lunch."

"Where?"

"Georgetti's. It's on Lexington Avenue, near Thirty-eighth Street."

"Is that where you usually met him?"

"Yes."

"From the beginning?"

"Almost. At first we never went to the same place twice, but then he discovered Georgetti's. Out of the way, off the beaten path, but actually quite convenient, especially for me. Only three blocks from Fifth Avenue, the stores."

"And not too bad for him, either," said her husband.

"No. He could walk from his office."

"Did he have any inkling of what you wanted to see him about? Or did he think you just wanted to have a cozy afternoon?"

"The latter, I think," she said. "He was totally unprepared for what I had to say."

"Too damn bad. What *did* you say?"

"What you told me to say. That I had to stop seeing him.

That I was never to see him again. That you've known about it now for three or four months."

"Oh, come on. You didn't hit him one-two-three with three sentences. What did you say?"

"If you think I'm going to try to repeat the whole conversation word for word, you're wrong. I refuse to."

"Did you tell him that you love me?"

"Yes. I told him that you had been unfaithful to me, and that was why you were willing to forgive me. *If* I stopped seeing him."

"What did he say to that?"

"I won't tell you. I'm not going to tell you any of what he said. That was said to me, not to you. Maybe you're entitled to know what I said to him, but not what he said to me."

"You must have told him that you loved him. Didn't you?"

"I have."

"Did you today?"

She hesitated. "No," she said.

"You're lying to me, Madeline. You told him that you'd always love him."

"No, I didn't."

"Didn't he ask you?"

"Yes."

"Oh, I see. He asked you, but you refused to say yes or no. It was going to be all over between you, so you were starting by refusing to say you did or didn't love him. Am I right?"

"Yes," she said.

"Now, the big question. Does he think you do love him?"

"It's such a big question that I'm not going to answer it," she said.

"I'm not getting much out of you, am I?"

"You got what you wanted. I told him I'm not going to see him any more, and he knows I mean that."

"And where did you go from this Georgetti's?"

"Nowhere. We were there till it was time for me to catch my train."

"Do you swear to that?"

"I won't swear to anything. I said what you wanted me to say, and he knows I'm never going to see him again."

"Why are you so sure that he knows it?"

"Because I convinced him of it. And *I* know I'm not going to see him again."

"No, you and I aren't the kind of people that are very good at that." He stood up. "I'm glad it's over, aren't you?"

"What do you expect me to say?"

"That you're glad it's over—if you are."

"I am, only I wish I had made the decision, not you."

"I didn't hold a gun at your head."

"No, not a gun," she said. "Oh, it wouldn't have lasted much longer. Only last week he said he was getting tired of Georgetti's. The food, the menu, the waiters."

"Where did you usually go after Georgetti's?"

She shook her head. "No, Bud. If you want it to be over, it has to be over for you, too. I didn't put *you* through a cross-examination, and I didn't make you stop seeing Marcia Eubank."

"I've told you a hundred times. Marcia and I were never a real affair. She means absolutely nothing to me, and never did mean very much."

"No, but she meant something to me. And so did you. My best friend and my husband."

"It's this damn life we lead," he said. "But maybe some good'll come of it. If I didn't believe we love each other, you and I, I wouldn't have been so tough."

"I know," she said.

"Theodora said you had a letter from Nan."

"Yes, I haven't read it."

"Do you mind if I take it with me? I'll bring it down to dinner."

"All right," she said.

With his empty glass in one hand, and the letter in the other he went out, leaving her with nothing. The telephone was there, and that man could be summoned back into her life, but so easily that he was useless to her. The scene at Georgetti's had been confusing. For her it had begun with the moment in the morning when she decided that this was the day she would obey Bud's order. This was the day she would give up her lover, and she knew that there would be tears, but she had not expected the tears to be his. Angry protest, angry refusal, yes, but not tears. He was not a man who was given to any such emotional display. He was not a man whom anyone would pick out as any woman's lover. She, yes, she might be picked out as a woman who might be some man's mistress. She spent money on her clothes, she prided herself on her *chic,* she took care of her hair and her skin, she kept up with things to talk about, she made the effort to be pleasing to men and women. And then when she was at last ready to take a lover —partly out of pique, partly out of fear, partly out of boredom— the man she chose was Morton DeKalb. Morton DeKalb, whose work she never quite understood. "No, I'm not a draughtsman," he had said on their first meeting.

"But I understood you to say you were," she said.

"No. I said I was working on some blueprints. That's where you got that impression. I'm an industrial engineer." It turned out that he was over-modest; that he had quite a good job, made between twenty-five and thirty thousand a year, but on their first meeting she was ready to picture him as a man who worked over a draughting board, with his shirt sleeves rolled up and a pencil in his mouth like a horse's bit. The occasion was a Sigma Chi cocktail party at the University Club. Her husband was somewhere around, and her meeting with Morton DeKalb was prolonged only because Bud Wherry was on the cocktail party committee. "I never met your husband," said DeKalb. "But I know him by name. He's a Dartmouth man."

"Yes."

"I'm from Penn State," said DeKalb. "I don't get to many of these things. They usually want to put the chew on you for something. But I more or less had to come to this one. The guest of honor is a member of my chapter, although considerably after my time. Even so he's pretty old to be a major, considering how important he is to the Air Force. I guess they don't hand out those stars the way they used to."

Their conversation was as impersonal as that, and it terminated when Bud beckoned to her to join him. She excused herself, and forgot all about Morton DeKalb, from Penn State. One week later she was sitting next to him in a restaurant, only vaguely conscious of him as a man who kept trying to compel her to recognize him, leaning forward and looking into her face. Finally he spoke. "Been trying to get you to say hello," he said. "I'm Morton De-Kalb. I met you at the Sigma Chi party."

"Oh, yes, I'm sorry," she said. "This is Mr. DeKalb, Mrs. Durbin."

"This is Mr. Overton, Mrs. Wherry, and Mrs. Durber," said Morton DeKalb. "Overton's a Sigma Chi."

"So is *my* husband," said Margaret Durbin.

"Oh, where from?" said DeKalb.

"Oh, all the way from Southern California. S. C. Sigma Chi, Southern Cal."

"Perhaps you ladies would like to have a drink on that," said Overton.

Madeline Wherry saw that Overton was ready to move in, and she thought she sensed some annoyance on the part of DeKalb. She was right. "No, I heard the ladies say they didn't want a cocktail," said DeKalb. "Nice to've seen you again, Mrs. Wherry. Nice to've met you, Mrs. Durber." He was obviously in a position to make decisions for Overton that Overton would have to accept, and he saw to it that Overton's threat to become a nuisance was averted. Luncheon proceeded with no further communication between the two tables, and Madeline Wherry heard DeKalb say, "Well, you go downtown and talk to McCann and tell him what I said. I'll be at the office till six o'clock, or even later. I'll wait there for you." Overton left, and DeKalb ordered a demitasse, lit a cigarette, and stared straight ahead.

"Have your coffee with us," said Madeline Wherry.

"Well, I was hoping you'd ask me," said DeKalb.

"Not me, Maddie. I have to run," said Margaret Durbin. "Goodness! Five of two."

"Run, Margaret. It's my turn to pay," said Madeline Wherry.

Now they were alone, he at his table, she at hers. "Shall we join forces?" he said.

"It can't be for long. I have to go, too. But yes, you sit here, or I'll sit there. You slide over," said Madeline Wherry.

"Funny I never saw you before, and then we meet twice in the same week," said DeKalb. "I guess that's not a very original thing to say. But it's true. You don't come here often."

"No, my friend does, but I have another place I usually go to when I'm in New York."

"You don't live in the city?"

"High Ridge, New Jersey," said Madeline Wherry.

"Oh, yes, I know where it is. We looked at a house there several years ago, but my kids like sailing, so we bought in Rye."

"They decide everything for us, don't they?"

"I guess they do, more or less. What have you got?"

"One, a daughter. Just got married and she's gone to live abroad. Her husband has a Fulbright, and she just graduated from Wellesley. I don't suppose they'll ever come home, they both love Europe so."

"Make it kind of lonely for you, won't it?"

"At first, I guess. But I'll have to get used to it. How many have you got?"

"We have three boys. Two at Deerfield and one a freshman at Wesleyan."

"Then they're all away, too."

"Yes, for most of the year. House is really quiet now, with all three of them away. But they make up for it in the summer. They all have their own friends, and they call our place the DeKalb Yacht Club. We never know how many will show up for break-fast."

"That must be fun."

"It has its disadvantages, but for the most part it's enjoyable."

"I was an only child and my daughter's an only child. I always envied those that had a large family."

"Well, there again," he said. "I had two brothers and two sisters. My father was a schoolteacher, and he educated us all on what it costs me to send one boy to Deerfield. I don't suppose he could have managed *that* if my grandfather hadn't left my mother some money. Student loans got me through State, and one of my sisters came down with polio. We never seemed to be able to get ahead, always scratching for a dollar. But I guess we turned out all right, considering. Both of my brothers went into teaching and they're full professors, one at Cornell, the other at Pitt. And the sister that didn't get polio married a classmate of mine that's doing very well in Pittsburgh Plate Glass. One of their coming men. So between us we've been able to take care of our parents in their senior-citizen years. At least moneywise."

"What happened to the other sister?"

"Oh, she died. That was long before any vaccines like the Salk vaccine."

"I'm still terrified of polio," said Madeline Wherry. "Especially with my daughter planning to live abroad. What would I do? I'd have nobody."

"You'd have your husband," he said.

"Yes, of course." She looked at him quickly, and saw that he was really looking at her for the first time. "I didn't mean that the way it may have sounded. I mean that *we'd* have nobody, if anything happened to her. Don't look at me that way, Mr. DeKalb."

"What way? I was just surprised at the way you suddenly sounded—at the way you *sounded*. Afraid. Or desperate. You mustn't worry about your daughter. They get shots for this and shots for that. It isn't like the old days."

"That had nothing to do with the way you were looking at me," she said.

"All right, it didn't," he said.

"Then would you mind telling me *why* you thought I was desperate, or what I was afraid of?"

"Well, you'll probably walk out on me, but I'd say that all was not well between you and Mr. Wherry. That remark of yours just slipped out, but you think you *would* have nobody if something happened to your daughter. You're wrong, though. You'd have yourself, and a woman like you, it wouldn't be long before you'd have someone else."

"I've never had anyone else," she said.

"No, but you could have. I imagine that's been proven a hundred times. A woman like you, you didn't have to wait around for a guy like me to tell you you're attractive. Look around this room. Who was the most attractive woman here today? I considered myself lucky just to get the seat next to yours."

"You're very nice to give me this build-up. I need it."

"I know you do, and it's a pleasure to be able to give it. I never expected anything as good as this to come out of a lunch date with Charley Overton. Jesus! But I hope you noticed, Overton's a guy that gets around, and he spotted you right away."

"And you protected me."

"Oh, you caught that? Yes. I was to get Mrs. Durber, and he was to get you. You didn't overhear that part of the conversation, I hope."

"No, but I knew something was going on in his mind."

"In his mind that's the kind of thing that's going on all the time. It's amazing how many women there are that fall for it."

"Did he think I was in a receptive mood? You can be honest."

"Well, yes, I guess he did, more or less."

"But I've never been in a less receptive mood," she said. "So there he's wrong."

"Can I still be honest?"

"Yes, why?"

"Because I think you *are* in a receptive mood, but you don't like to admit it, even to yourself. Especially to yourself."

"Well now, what about you, Mr. DeKalb? You've never so much as mentioned your wife. Your boys, your father and mother, sisters and brothers, and various in-laws. But not a word about Mrs. DeKalb. I assume there is one, and that she's home in Rye, in that quiet house."

"Yes, and she's the quietest thing in it."

"Maybe that's because she's used to being a lone woman in an all-male household."

"Yes, and maybe it's because we have nothing more to say to each other. I don't know."

"How old is she?"

"Forty-six. I guess that has something to do with it," he said. "She won't talk about it, but I guess that's what it is. I was never very smart when it came to women."

"Men that *think* they are, are usually anything but," she said.

"Listen, can I talk to you again? I have to get back to my office. There's a man waiting for me that came all the way from South America. But I can talk to you, I know I can. Will you do that, as a Christian act of kindness?"

"Do you mean, meet you for lunch?"

"Anything you say. Lunch. Cocktails. Anything."

"Give me your phone number, and the next time I'm coming to town I'll call you."

"Would you do that? I'm not a pass-maker, Mrs. Wherry. But I am a guy in a hell of a lot of trouble and with nobody to talk to about it. And I wouldn't be the only one you'd be helping, although you don't owe her a damn thing or me either, for that matter."

She smiled. "You gave me a little build-up. That can be very important at the right time."

"I have to fly out to Seattle the week after next. You couldn't make it next week sometime?"

"I probably can," she said.

She went home that day with a new sense of being not entirely defenseless against Marcia Eubank. If Bud was being no more to Marcia than any of the other men who liked to have her put her hand on their shoulders when she talked to them, he was making an ass of himself. If he was more than that, Madeline Wherry was defenseless—short of an accusation that might be unsupportable. There was no question in her own mind that she would see Mr. DeKalb. At certain moments, when he was intense with his thoughts of the people he loved, he had a habit of clenching his fist that she found very attractive. She always noticed men's hands, when the men themselves were worth noticing.

In the next four years it was usually she who did the telephoning. Theodora, and Theodora's predecessors, were not to be trusted. In a situation like this, no one was to be trusted. But there was more to her precautions than that: always, between one meeting and the next, there was her shameful, disloyal fear that someone like Marcia Eubank would discover that her lover was a man like Morton DeKalb. Her lover should have been someone irresistible to all women, the kind of man who had a terrible reputation, who married women for their money and went through life undismayed by his unpopularity with other men. Once or twice a year Madeline Wherry would buy a hat at a Fifty-seventh Street shop which was patronized by a woman who had been victimized by two such cads. Madeline Wherry would study this woman, watch her trying on hats, eavesdrop on her conversations with the manager and the saleswoman. Josephine Carling, heiress to an automobile fortune. Ex-wife of a Georgian prince and a South American. Some of the indignities Josephine Carling had endured had appeared in the newspapers. Locked out of her own house in Palm Beach without a stitch of clothes on (the Georgian prince). Punched in the face at El Morocco (the South American). No one envied Josephine Carling her sordid notoriety. And yet when Madeline Wherry would see her at the hat store Josephine Carling was always cheerful, profanely witty, quite genuinely liked by the people who waited on her, and unmistakably enjoying life. Madeline Wherry was never introduced to Josephine Carling, but one day when Madeline was sitting at the triple mirrors, hesitating about a hat, Josephine Carling called to her, "Take it! It's perfect for you. I wish I could wear it." Madeline bought the hat and wore it that day to her rendezvous with Morton DeKalb. "Do you know who almost bought this hat?" she said. "Josephine Carling."

"Don't tell me she's a pal of yours," said Morton DeKalb. "Her old man was a production genius, T. T. Carling, and when you think of where all that money's gone to. Her kind will bring on communism quicker than anything I can think of." He could spoil a hat for her. What kind of a lover was it that could spoil the fun of a hat? The answer was, a safe lover, who would return her to her husband unbruised and unsuspected.

But lover he was, with love to give that he gave without stint. His wife had been the only other woman he had been to bed with, and Madeline fell heir to the passion and fidelity that he had bestowed on her. "Where I would be without you," he said to Madeline, "I hate to think. Beth and I came from the same kind of people. Her father owned a drug store, but the big thing in his life aside from his family was church work. I guess he had the record for being reelected president of the inter-church council. Something like fourteen years, I think it was. If he was alive today I know he'd be trying to get one of my boys to enter the ministry. Sure of it. He wouldn't have a prayer, but all the same our boys had a religious upbringing."

"It's a good thing they don't know about me."

"I don't know, Madeline. They are a little young to know about us, and they never will. And yet when you think of how I might have gone haywire. And I could have. I'm just the kind of a guy that does go haywire when he gets to be around my age, and the wife is having her own problems in that department. One of our best men, Stu Knapp, in charge of our Atlanta office, we had to give him a six months' leave of absence. Ill health, we announced it as, but the fact of the matter was it all stemmed from his wife. Same problem as Beth, and Stu got himself involved with a girl that used to be a stenographer in the Atlanta office. She came back to help out during the summer vacations, and the first thing you know she and Stu are going off on trips together and her husband came in one day waving a revolver at everybody, demanding to know where Stu was. We only have sixteen people in our Atlanta office, and of course everybody knew what was going on. But the point is, Stu Knapp was one of the last fellows you'd ever think of as liable to go haywire. Phi Beta Kappa from the University of Georgia, man that never smoked or drank in all the years I've known him."

"Well, my husband isn't likely to come into your office waving a pistol. There's a man in High Ridge that could wave one at him."

"Yes, you told me. That hurts, doesn't it?"

"It did. It doesn't so much any more, except when they think they're pulling the wool over everyone's eyes."

"I don't know what a fellow like Bud Wherry wants to fool around for, when he had someone like you. I guess the same thing could be said about me, but it's a different situation. But then I guess every situation is different. No two alike."

"No."

"For me you're perfect," he said. "You're beautiful, and you're the type woman that I guess every dull bastard like me wants secretly. Only we know we're dull bastards, so we don't make a try for a woman like you. Then something happens, like we run into each other twice in the same week, and out of niceness you listen to my troubles, and then there we are. How I ever got the nerve to come out and say it, 'Will you go to the hotel with me?' God knows I was thinking it, morning, noon and night."

"I must have been, too."

"Just don't ever be sorry, Madeline. I'd kill myself before I ever gave you any cause to be sorry. I'd hate to do anything to disgrace the boys, and Beth. But you come first, now. I can tell you something now that I couldn't have told you three years ago."

"What's that?"

"At first, you know, I didn't love you. I was—dizzy, you might say. Thinking, Good Lord, me in bed with her? I couldn't believe it. And I thought what the hell have I got that she wants? Suspicious. Unsure of myself, was the reason. But you see you didn't make it very difficult—"

"I didn't make it difficult at all," she said. "I just went."

"Yes, that's what I mean. But why me? All right, I'm clean, and I always kept myself in good physical condition. But my own mother wouldn't call me handsome or even good-looking. I'm not rich. I don't get around in café society circles, and outside of a few people in my own profession nobody ever heard of me. I guess love is like lightning. You don't know where it's going to hit, and when it hits it hits quick." At his most profound he was never hard to follow, and since the making of love was a part of their every meeting—lunch, the hotel room that his company kept on a yearly basis, the taxi ride to the Penn Station—the little time before and after their lovemaking partook of the excitement and relaxation of the act itself, and his utterances on the subject of love were not isolated from passion. In four years he had almost no chance to prove that he was the dull bastard he said he was, and she did not want to risk giving him the chance. She was not even very apprehensive about being come upon accidentally in Georgetti's by a woman like Marcia Eubank. The wrong clothes that he constantly wore, his plain and uninteresting face, and the things he would say if he had to be introduced to a Marcia Eubank would convince a Marcia Eubank that he was a nothing. That would be how Marcia would express it, too: a nothing. Marcia Eubank might even suspect that Morton DeKalb was a cover-up for the real lover, a man at least as interesting as Bud Wherry. Madeline could practically hear Marcia Eubank: "Yes, Madeline Wherry, having lunch with a man at some little hole-in-the-wall on Lexington Avenue. The man was a nothing, strictly Dullsville, but I'll just bet you our little Madeline has *some*body. She doesn't waste all that haute couture on High Ridge, New Jersey." Madeline never did run into Marcia Eubank, but it was odd how often it was Marcia, even more so than Bud, whom she saw in her imagined encounters at Georgetti's, in the hotel lobby, in a taxi with Morton DeKalb during a traffic delay.

One dreadful morning she inexplicably had a need of Morton that transcended any she had ever had before. She sat near her telephone, touching it, taking her hand away from it, then lifting the phone from its cradle and spinning the dial as fast as she could. The voice at the other end of the line said only, "Hello," but Madeline instantly hung up. Accidentally she had dialed Marcia's number.

That was the most terrible day of her life. Without letting Morton know she was coming—she could not touch her telephone again—she drove to New York because there would be an hour's wait before the next train. A policeman stopped her on the Turnpike, and though he let her off with a warning, she was angry with herself for the kittenish coquetry she used to talk him out of giving her a ticket. His look as much as told her to act her age. In New York the garage she and Bud patronized was full up, and she was forced to drive from avenue to avenue, street to street, before she found a parking lot that had room for her car. When she finally got to a pay telephone Morton was in a conference and could not be disturbed until half past twelve. "Then please tell him to meet his cousin at Georgetti's at one o'clock," she said to the switchboard operator.

"I put two and two together," Morton said. "I don't have any

cousins, at least none I ever see, but Georgetti's was the tipoff. Is
something wrong?"

"I had to see you. Let's get out of here."

"We can't have the room," said Morton. "It's being used by
the manager of our Omaha branch. That's who I was in conference with, and was *supposed* to have lunch with."

"Can't you get another room?"

"I don't know if that's such a good idea, dear," said Morton.
"McGaffney may want to go there and wash up, change his shirt
or something."

"Try another hotel."

"I could do that, I guess. Excuse me," he said, and went to
Georgetti's telephone booth. He came back in a few minutes. "All
set. But I'll have to go in first and register and you come up later."

"What hotel is it?"

"It's the Kingston," he said. "It's a kind of a small place on
East Forty-eighth Street. The company has an account there but
we don't use it very often."

"I never heard of it," she said.

"Well, it isn't the best, but it isn't the worst," he said.

She had to wait in a drug store to give him time to register
and get to his room. She telephoned Morton and learned the room
number. The lobby was small and nearly deserted, and her un-
familiarity with the layout caused her to go to the right while the
elevators were to the left.

"I feel like one of those call girls," she said.

"I'm worried about you," said Morton. "Tell me what's the
matter?"

"I wish I knew myself," she said. "I think I must be going
off my rocker. I got *that* expression from *you*."

He was in his shirt sleeves. He put his arms around her and
held her to him. "You'll be all right. Smoke a cigarette."

"No. I think I got you here under false pretenses," she said.
"I'm sorry."

"Oh," he said. "Well, *I'll* smoke a cigarette."

She began to cry. "I don't know what's the *matter* with me.
Maybe I *am* going off my rocker."

"Listen, we all get funny moods. We wouldn't be human if we didn't."

"Oh, God, Morton, you only make it worse feeling sorry for me."

"I'll tell you what," he said. "I really have to get back to the office. I'm up to here in work, conferences and all. You take a bath and lie down a while. Maybe get a nap. Then when you're ready to leave, give me a ring. I'll leave word that I'm expecting a call. This morning the boss told everybody that nobody was to be interrupted by outside calls, that's how that happened. But you get a little rest and phone me."

"No. I'll leave now and I'll call you tomorrow. You're very sweet, and I'm sorry. I *am* sorry, but I'll make it up to you." She squeezed his hand and rubbed her cheek against his, and left.

She took a taxi to Penn Station and caught a local train. Not until she got off the train at High Ridge did she remember that she had left her car in New York.

It was easy enough to cook up a story for Bud, and she had a plausible one ready when he got home. She did not need it. He came into the sitting-room, tossed his newspaper and hat on a chair and stood and stared at her with his hands folded behind his back. "What the hell were you doing at the Kingston Hotel? And don't try to lie out of it. You didn't have a room there, because I called up and asked."

"What makes you think I *was* at the Kingston Hotel?"

"Because I saw you coming out. Who's the guy, Madeline?"

"Why does it have to be a guy?"

"Because the reputation the Kingston has, I doubt if you know many of the women that live there. Hundred-dollar girls and kept women."

"It sounds like a good place for Marcia to stay."

"You can talk your silly head off, but I'm going to find out who the guy was. If I don't find out one way, I'll find out another. If I have to beat it out of you, I will. And if that fails, I'll get a copy of the register. You can't win, so you might as well tell me."

"Keep your voice down, and close the door," she said. "If

you ever hit me, I'd kill you. I've taken quite enough from you the last few years, making a fool of me with Marcia Eubank. Stupid, both of you. You haven't fooled anyone, not a soul. Yes, I met somebody at the Kingston."

"Who?"

"A man named Morton DeKalb."

"Who?"

"Morton DeKalb."

"Who's he? I know that name. Morton Cobb. They always give his middle initial. Morton D. Cobb. Who the hell is Morton D. Cobb?"

"DeKalb. He's a fraternity brother of yours, and that's how I met him."

"That's the son of a bitch. Now I know who he is. He's with some engineering company. And that's who you're having an affair with. Well, I'll be a son of a bitch. When did this start?"

"A few months ago. When I was sure about you and Marcia. I always suspected you and Marcia, but I was never sure till a few months ago."

"What made you so sure?"

"You and Marcia. What's the use of talking about it? I wouldn't believe anything you told me, and I don't really care."

"What do you mean, you don't care? You cared enough to have an affair with this DeKalb. Well, I'll have a little talk with him tomorrow."

"You do, and I'll divorce you and name Marcia. If you make the slightest effort to embarrass him in any way, by phone or letter or any other way, or go to see him, I'll make it so unpleasant for you and Marcia that you'll both have to move out of High Ridge. You're the only one knows anything about Morton DeKalb, but everybody's seen you and Marcia jitterbugging and twisting and going off by yourselves. People will be on my side, Bud."

"Not when I get through with you," he said.

"You are through with me. Or I'm through with you, either one, it doesn't matter."

"No, it doesn't matter a damn bit."

"I'll tell you what does matter, and that was your threatening to beat it out of me. You remember what happened the time you did slap me."

"That was twenty years ago. One slap."

"And one dead baby."

"The doctor said the slap had nothing to do with the dead baby."

"The baby was inside of me, not inside of the doctor."

"Madeline, we don't have to go through all that again. And don't trot out that old argument that the doctor lied to save my self-respect. Medically, two doctors, not one, said that one slap in the face wasn't responsible. I know, I made sure. And *you* believed them at the time, but the older you get, the easier it is for you to forget what the doctors said, and blame me. I never blamed you, but I could have. You weren't taking proper care of yourself. Oh, God, I know every word you can say and I go on repeating the same words myself. And any time it suits you, you blame me for that. Jesus Christ! Don't you think I wish my son'd been born alive?"

They fell silent, he busy with his resentment, she with hers, until the silence became a sizable thing that they could not ignore. Ceasing to ignore the silence, they could no longer ignore each other, but they had exhausted themselves.

"Well, who's going to do what?" said Bud Wherry.

"I don't know," she said.

"You have to stop seeing this fellow," he said.

"Why?"

"*Why?* All right, you don't. Go on seeing him, but move out of here."

"Tonight?"

"Preferably. If not tonight, if you have no place to go, find some place. But don't be here tomorrow night. I don't want you here, and I don't see why you'd want to be here."

"You could stay in New York. You're there every day," she said. "Oh, yes, but Marcia's here. I didn't think of that."

"Marcia is nothing to me, and I'm nothing to her," he said. "There was never a time when it couldn't have stopped, and it did stop."

"And started again when it was convenient for her."

"Yes."

"And that's the way it will be, all over again. Whenever it's convenient for her. All right, it'll take me a few days to find some-place in New York. I'll have to look for a furnished apartment, temporarily."

"That means, of course, that you're going on seeing this DeKalb fellow."

"Is there any reason why not?"

"Are you planning to marry him?"

"I don't know. Are you planning to marry Marcia?"

"Certainly not."

"Don't say certainly not. You may have to. This may be a pretty big house, but High Ridge isn't very big. Marcia always liked this house. Or what I did with it. Copied my clothes, copied my house, the way I brought up my daughter. No wonder she appropriated my husband. Well, you have her, or she has you. And she can have the house. It's too bad I was never interested in her husband, then we could have arranged one of those swaps. I just read about another one the other day."

"Stop talking like that. We were never those kind of people."

"We are now. Or would be if I liked Greg Eubank. Maybe you'd like Mrs. DeKalb. I can't help you on that, because I've never seen her. But she has sons, three of them. That didn't keep her husband from falling in love with me, but she has them. Three of them."

"I only wanted our son," he said.

"Yes," she said. "Well, the facts of everyday living. Do you want your dinner at the usual time? Theodora goes home at half past eight no matter whether you and I are separating or not. What do you want me to tell her?"

"About dinner?"

"About dinner. The future plans, arrangements, you'll have to make them yourself. You can't expect me to ask Theodora and Emily to stand by while you and Marcia work things out."

"Suddenly this is all so ridiculous."

"Well, laugh then."

"I didn't say it was funny. I said ridiculous."

"So you did. But you still haven't told me what to tell Theodora, and any minute now she's going to come in and ask."

"Tell her to go home. I don't want any dinner."

"You can have it alone. I'm not going to have any."

"No, if I want anything later I'll go over to the diner. I'm not hungry now."

"You could take potluck at Marcia's," said Madeline. "You might as well start having your serious talks with her."

"Just tell Theodora to go home, will you please?"

"Very well." She went to the kitchen. "Mr. Wherry and I won't be ready for dinner till nine o'clock, so you might as well go home, Theodora," she said. When she returned to the sitting-room Bud was fixing a drink.

"I think she'd like to stay around a while for the fireworks," said Madeline. "At least I got the impression that she knew something was up. However, there goes the back door. She's having a little trouble at home, too. Oddly enough, her husband is carrying on with a neighbor's wife."

"Is she carrying on to get even?"

"Oh, Theodora would never tell me a thing like that."

"Do you want a drink?"

"No."

"Do you mind if I have one?"

"Heavens, why should I? You put it off as long as you could. I never knew you to postpone it this long. This is really an important occasion."

"Yes it is, Madeline," he said. "At least it is to me. From your attitude anybody'd think it was some minor Mister-and-Missus over what TV program to watch."

"Oh, that can be terribly important. Didn't I read about a wife shooting her husband on account of that? Something like that. He wanted to watch one thing, and—"

"Cut it out, will you? Let's see if we can make some sense out of this."

"I thought everything was settled. None of the details, but the major decision. I'm to leave, and you're to stay. The rest will take time, but let's do it through the lawyers. That's what they're paid for."

"If you agree not to see DeKalb again, I say let's give it a six-months' try, or three months, or whatever. A cooling-off period."

"Why?"

"Well, I just got finished doing that with a strike at the factory. I don't know if it's going to work out there, but if we can do it with a labor union, it ought to be worth a try for you and me. Unless you're determined to marry DeKalb. Then, of course—"

"I'm not determined to marry DeKalb."

"Do you love him?"

"Oh—I can't answer that, because I don't know. I can't say I *don't* love him."

"He loves you?"

"Yes, I'm sure of that. Right now it's the only thing in the world I am sure of."

"That may pass away, Madeline. You haven't given it much time."

She refused to correct her earlier lie, to yield her ethical advantage. "I've given it time enough," she said.

"You see, in my case, this thing with Marcia's been going on long enough for both of us to know that it isn't love. And it was never as much as you may have imagined. I swear that to you. There was a time there that for two years I didn't even kiss her. You hate Marcia, but if she was all you say, she could have wrecked our marriage. I admit it. Three years ago, the time you went to Italy, I was with her every night for almost a month. Greg was away, too, if you remember."

"In this house?"

"No."

"You're lying to me."

"All right, twice in this house."

"In my room?"

"Not in your room."

"In yours?"

"Yes, in mine. But that's not the point. The point is, when you came back from Italy that time, it was all over between Marcia and I, and it stayed that way for just about two years. Since then —well, it couldn't have been more casual. A couple of times in New York, twice or maybe three times here."

"She simply had to come to this house, didn't she? Once I thought Marcia Eubank was my best friend. I used to feel flattered when she imitated me, copied everything of mine. 'Oh, Madeline, you have such *chic!*' And where did I get this, where did I get that? I don't see how *you* could do it, though—bring her to this house. Wouldn't it remind you too much of me? I don't see how the two of you could keep from talking about me—but then I suppose you did."

"Madeline, I'm not responsible for her being jealous of you. She is, and she admits it. But that goes way back to when you were young girls, long before I came into the picture. Maybe that's how I got into the picture. Probably was. But only once was she ever any threat to our marriage, and that was when you visited Nan in Italy. I'm sorry for what I did, but I can honestly promise you that I'll never be alone with her again if you give me your word that you'll put an end to it with DeKalb. Now."

"What do you mean by now?"

"Well, tomorrow. Or the next few days. You can't put it off too long. Sometime in the next few days you write him a letter—"

"No, no letter."

"Well, see him, if you have to. But make it final. I don't want him to have any doubt in his mind. None whatsoever. I don't know him, not sure I'd know him if I saw him, but from what I know *of* him, he doesn't sound to me like the kind of a guy that would like all this kind of thing. I know the firm he's with, and they're a very serious-minded outfit. This isn't one of your Madison Avenue advertising huckster setups. Troutman, Von Hurzburg and Muldowney. They made it big during the war, and they've expanded since. We thought of them for the San Diego plant, when we were having that trouble with Campellini and Johnson. I had several talks with Karl Troutman, and he's just not the kind of a man that would tolerate hanky-panky in his organization, believe me. He's the old-time high laced boots and Stetson hat type of engineer."

"If you're trying to show me that you're on good terms with Morton DeKalb's boss, all right. You've shown me," she said. "Another way of saying I didn't make a very good choice."

"I thought we were past that. I thought we were talking a cooling-off period, giving our marriage a second chance. Do you want to give it a second chance? If you don't, say so. If you do, I've told you how."

"I don't know what I want."

"I wish your mother were still alive. I could make better sense with her than I seem to be making with you."

"You always think Mother would have been on your side. She wouldn't have been, you know."

"Not a question of being on my side, Madeline. Just a matter of making *sense,* making the best of a bad situation, saving the pieces and maybe putting them together again."

"I've decided," she said.

"You have? What?"

"I'm not going to see Morton any more. That is, I'll see him once more and tell him it's the last time. What you and I do after that will have to be a separate decision."

"When will you tell him?"

"Soon. A few days, a week."

"All right," he said.

It took three days and nights for her to make up her mind to telephone Morton, and when she called him he was gentle and reassuring, painfully so in his belief that she was ready to make amends for her frenetic behavior at their last meeting, more painfully so in his ignorance of the purpose of her call. "We don't have to go to Georgetti's," he said. "Let's have a change of scenery? Name some snappy restaurant and I'll take you there."

"No, I'd rather go to Georgetti's," she said.

"Are you sure?"

"Yes, I'm sure," she said.

He was at their usual table when she got there. "You look as if you'd just stepped out of a bandbox," he said.

"Do I? I've often wondered how anybody'd look that just stepped out of a bandbox. Rather crumpled, I should think. I'd like a vodka martini."

He picked up her hand and looked at her. "I missed you," he said. "I almost made some excuse to drive down to High Ridge to see you."

"It's a good thing you didn't."

"Well, I knew that when you were ready to see me, you'd phone."

The waiter served their drinks and went away. She had a long sip of hers and lit a cigarette. "I don't know where to start," she said.

"Yes, there's something on your mind. That I can tell," he said. "But if it has anything to do with our visit to the Kingston, that was my fault. I realized later that I didn't want to make love that day either. We ought to see each other oftener when we aren't going to make love."

"Strange you should say that. Because that's the way it's going to be, that's why I wanted to see you today."

"Oh, don't take me too seriously on that. I'm not suggesting that we turn Platonic."

"Oh, Morton. It isn't even going to be that. It isn't going to be anything. This is the last time I'm ever going to see you, at all."

"Bud?"

"Yes. He saw me coming out of the Kingston. He knew there was something wrong anyway. Oh, God, that whole day was so awful. I could have faked some lie about the Kingston, but I was all the way back to High Ridge before I remembered that I'd driven in and left the car in New York. You'll never know what I went through that day. I started the day with such a surge for you that I had to see you. Then they wouldn't let me talk to you, and I came here not knowing whether you'd got my message, or would understand it. And, oh, everything. So that when Bud got home and accused me of meeting someone, it was anticlimactic. Then the long scene with him."

"Does he know it was me?"

"Yes. I told him. But you're not going to be dragged into it. I don't know why I say dragged in. There isn't going to be a divorce, or at least I don't think so. But you have nothing to worry about. I told him I'd been having an affair with you for three months only."

"Nothing to worry about? How can you say that? I have you to worry about. Haven't I convinced you that I love you, that I've never loved anyone else? Madeline, I'm a man that never knew what love was till four years ago, and that's pretty late in life. Everything before that was—mechanical. Flavorless. I never had any beauty in my life before. I didn't know what it was. To find myself singing little songs when I thought of a person, you. Holy God, girl, this isn't going to stop because—whatever reason Bud Wherry wants it to stop."

"It isn't only Bud. I want it to stop, too."

"Why?"

"Because it has to. It always had to, sometime, and this is the time. I want another vodka martini."

"No. You're not used to them."

"Don't be ridiculous. I *want* another *drink.*"

"Well, we're not going to fight over that," he said, and pointed to her glass and nodded to the waiter. "What have I done, or not done, that you can just suddenly like this put me out of your life, and take yourself out of mine?"

"Nothing you've done, nothing I've done. Except every damn thing we ever did with other people before we fell in love. You married a girl called Beth, and I married a man called Bud. And you had three sons and I had a daughter and a son born dead."

"A son born dead? You never told me that."

"No, and you see, there are so many big and little things we kept from each other because we had to. There are some things I told you that I never told Bud, but there are some things he *knows* that I never told you. It's the same with you and Beth."

"Nonsense. I want to know why you decide all this now. You aren't afraid of Bud Wherry. You know I'd marry you if you'd say the word, you've always known that. We'd have financial problems, but the boys are all educated except the youngest, and I've had good offers that I turned down because they'd have meant moving away from New York. Why are you deciding to get rid of me?"

The waiter set her drink on the table.

"I don't know," she said.

"Yes you do," he said.

"Oh, all right, then I do! It's because I'm sick and tired of the whole thing."

"Of me?"

"Yes, of you as part of the whole thing. Of myself, too, don't forget. And of other people, too. Of Bud. Of Marcia Eubank. Of Greg Eubank. Of wanting to go to bed with you and coming to New York, but only seeing you when I had that need. Every time I saw you it was that. I didn't have to say it, but every time I telephoned you you thought it. She wants to go to bed with me, she wants me to make love to her. Four years of that doesn't make it any less humiliating."

"You knew I wanted you all the time."

"You didn't the last time, and neither did I. I thought I did, but as soon as I got here I wanted to leave, and the last straw was that awful hotel. The Kingston. Morton, I don't want to start hating you, but I will. I'll hate you just as I do all the others."

He did not speak. At first the silence was more noticeable in his eyes than in the absence of speech, and the normal plainness of his face was an appropriate setting for his unhappiness. He had spoken the truth, that all his life had been lacking in beauty as he had come to know it four years ago, and the eyes and the mouth were once again as she had first seen them. But there was nothing she would do to end the suffering that had begun for him, his contemplation of the bleak future and the old bleak past.

"*I'll* have a vodka martini," he said.

"Not on top of rye," she said.

"Oh, yes. I can handle rye." He gave the order and waited in silence until the waiter brought the drink. "My friend Charley Overton would know what to do in a situation like this," he said. "Do you remember Charley Overton?"

"Yes. What ever happened to him?"

"I told you. He got the sack, couple of years ago. His days were numbered from the start. The big boss was bound to find out about Charley sooner or later. Always more lenient about booze than about women. And all of a sudden I'm beginning to understand why."

"Why?"

"Well, because at this moment, having had only one drink since yesterday, I have no desire to go back to the office, or go home this afternoon. I've been put in charge of all the basic planning for a fully automated plant that's going to be built near Schenectady. The biggest thing they ever handed me. And I'll tell you something—I couldn't care less."

"And for that you blame me," she said.

"Yes, I guess I do. Inside myself I gave you the credit for the good work I've been doing the last three or four years."

"Be patient. In a little while you'll hate me."

"How can I? I never did as much for you as you did for me," he said.

He had much more to drink, and they went through two cycles of anger and pleading, anger and refusal, until it was time for her to catch her train. In the taxi he was quite drunk, and she had never seen him drunk. His attempts to kiss her were so clumsy that when she got out of the cab it was just like getting away from any pest. He did not leave her with much to weep over.

She was in her room, and she was not sure how long she had been there, sitting on the daybed, staring at her feet, not staring at her feet; hearing the downstairs sounds, not hearing the downstairs sounds. Then there was the undeniable sound of Bud's footsteps on the stairs, and the undeniable presence of Bud in her room. "Say, I was just talking to Theodora. She said we're going out for dinner. I thought it was tomorrow night," he said.

"Tonight," said Madeline Wherry.

"Are we supposed to dress?"

"Yes."

"Well, isn't it time you got a move on?" He took off his jacket and started undoing his necktie. "I'll take a quick shower, if you wouldn't mind putting the studs in my shirt. You know where they are."

"Yes."

"Now come on, Madeline. Don't be late just because it's Marcia. I'm going to prove to you that Marcia doesn't mean a God damn thing and I'm going to prove it tonight."

"Go take your shower," she said.

"Well, you start stirring your stumps, too," he said.

She waited until she heard the water running in his shower bath. She got up and went to his room and got an evening shirt out of his bureau and hung it over her arm. She opened the top drawer of the bureau, where he kept his studs. The little leather box was there, but she never saw it. All she saw, all she focused on, was his revolver, and she took it in her hand without hesitation. With his evening shirt still hanging over her arm she stood with her back to the bureau. The glass door of the shower bath swung open and he came out and reached for a towel.

" 'Dyou find the studs? Put that thing away, Madeline," he said.

"No, I won't," she said. She raised it and fired the first shot, which tore away part of his throat. The second shot broke the glass door of the shower bath, the third and fourth entered his chest, the fifth went into his belly, the sixth, which she aimed carefully, entered the region of his heart. He quivered a couple of times, then lay still, and she tossed the revolver on his bed.

She looked down at him once, then returned to her room and sat on the daybed. She looked at the shirt on her arm. "Now don't tell me you didn't deserve it, because you did," she said. "You know damn well you did, Bud Wherry." Then she put her hands to her face and sobbed. "You did, you did, you did, you did," she said.

MRS. ALLANSON

Mrs. Frank B. Allanson's great gift is her ability to impart impor-
tance to people and things because they are her people and things.
Back in the days when the motor car provided a precise and subtle
index of taste and financial circumstances, the Allansons owned a
series of Franklins. The late Frank Allanson had chosen the Franklin because it was an air-cooled car, and the cult of the Franklin
included three or four men with whom Allanson was congenial in
many matters. But Sara Allanson, although she did not drive, very
soon was proclaiming the Franklin to be the superior of the Pierces
and Packards, the Stearns-Knights and Peerlesses, the Hayneses
and Paiges and Chandlers that belonged to the families she knew
best. She was particularly hard on the Pierce-Arrow, since the
Pierce spoke for itself as an indication of money spent, while the
Franklin in its way spoke for itself as an example of money saved.
It would have entailed no financial hardship for the Allansons to
have bought a Pierce; Frank Allanson's firm was the local legal
representative for the Lehigh Valley Rail Road, the Prudential Insurance Company, and the Ingersoll-Rand people, as well as one
of the larger independent coal companies, a lumber company, a
department store, and the Keystone Bank & Trust. But as it happened, Robert B. Stokes, whose firm represented the Pennsylvania Railroad and the M. A. Hanna Company locally, owned a
Pierce-Arrow, and so did George W. Ingersoll, lawyer for the
Light, Heat & Power Company. Sara Allanson never missed an
opportunity to say something disparaging about Althea Stokes's
and Pansy Ingersoll's Pierces, always with the implication that

anyone who went higher than the Franklin price range was doing it for show. (It was a major-minor triumph for Sara when the Allansons' William learned that the Ingersolls' Pierce was technically a second-hand car, almost brand-new but purchased from the estate of a Chestnut Hill widow. "Frank and I would never own a second-hand car," Sara said. She did not specifically identify the Ingersolls' Pierce, but her friends could infer what they pleased about all Pierce-Arrows and Packard Twin Sixes.)

Frank Allanson died of pneumonia in 1927. He was given a nice, dignified send-off at the Second Presbyterian Church, and in a very short time Sara had so successfully adjusted herself to widowhood that most of her friends had a hard time believing that Frank's death had been so recent. George Ingersoll, who had a forked tongue, described her as a born widow. She was only in her late thirties, with a daughter in boarding-school, but it never occurred to anyone to suppose that Sara Allanson would ever marry again. She wore black for the full year's period of mourning, but as she went on wearing her Persian lamb after the year was up, there was an illusion that publicly the mourning period was being continued. This is not to say that she flaunted her grief. Not even her closest friends had been subjected to any teary outbursts, and when she spoke of her late husband it was with admiration and respect, but no one was permitted to be witness to a display of emotion. During his years on earth Frank Allanson had been so completely protected against invasions of his private life with Sara that she was not going to let down the bars now that he was dead. There had not been much curiosity about their intimate life, but there had been some. There is always some. But as George Ingersoll said, when a man like Frank marries a woman like Sara it's the wife that's in charge of such matters and the husband does exactly what he's told. If there was some truth to George Ingersoll's comment, it explains why it was so easy for Sara to achieve the transition from matrimony to widowhood. She had always wanted to be a widow, a single woman whose husband had been taken away from her in orderly circumstances.

At that time, early in her widowhood, Sara was somewhat inclined to be stout, with a tubular torso that was restrained by a

foundation garment. Her breasts were small and created no problem in corsetry. But she had never had a slim waist, and the most
she could hope for was a figure that would not be called fat. She
wore very high heels to give her legs a better line, and she watched
her weight. The overall effect was favorable. She dressed well, she
was tidy and clean, a member of the female sex, a widow. She was
not unpretty. Her nose was too large, long and hooked, and her
lips were so thin that without lipstick her mouth would have been
only a horizontal slit in her face. Nevertheless she had gone through
girlhood and young womanhood with her fair share of compliments
to her looks, and if the specific compliments invariably concerned
her blue-green-gray eyes, they were uniquely hers. She had often—
fairly often—sat amused at the bridge table while the other three
at the table discussed the true color of her eyes. "What are they,
really, Sara? What do *you* think they are?" someone would always
ask.

"Father always used to say they were blue, like Mama's, and
Mama said they were gray, like most of the Doerflingers'. Frank
thinks they're grayish green. I honestly don't know."

"Fascinating, really fascinating," someone would say. "Now
where do we go? Isn't that table finished *yet?* How many rubbers
are you *playing* over there?"

Sara's daughter Marjorie had not inherited the polychromatic
eyes of her mother, and in the field of feminine beauty she was
generally considered—as early as sixteen—a hopeless case. Her
misfortune began, ironically, with her eyes. She had had to wear
glasses since the age of five, and as frequently happens, the only
thing she liked to do was to read. She was not good at games; a ball
would come at her and she would not see it until too late for her
to raise her hands in self-protection. She would come home from
school, do her homework immediately, and resume her reading of
the multi-volume *Our Wonder World, Stoddards Lectures, The
Girls of Bradford Hall,* and the latest *St. Nicholas* magazine. Her
father worried that she was not getting enough fresh air, and her
mother would send her out to play, but Marjorie would go only as
far as a friend's house, where she would read whatever books were
available there. She was not a particularly unhappy child, nor an

especially brilliant one. She was, let it be noted again, her mother's daughter, and Sara Allanson saw to it that the other mothers ordered their sons to be at least polite to Marjorie at parties and dancing school. Marjorie was known as a duty-dance, but so were most of her contemporaries at that age. As for her intense reading, it supplied her with a large store of information without stimulating her to any creative effort of her own, but because she had always been a reader of books, she was not repelled by textbooks. Consequently she was regarded as a good student and was rewarded by her teachers with marks just below the top. It was nice for Sara Allanson to be able to say that Marjorie had never failed a subject during her entire school career, and it was quietly comforting to look back upon Marjorie's sixteen years and find nothing to be ashamed of. Being a plain child had some advantages, at least for the parents, and Marjorie had not been mentioned among the girls whose behavior was being criticized. Virginia Stokes, for example, was carried home from a picnic in a state of intoxication; Annabell Ingersoll was asked to leave Westover for the *announced* reason that she habitually violated the rule against smoking; and lower down the social scale was the scandal in the public high school involving four girls of Marjorie's age and several members of a visiting football team.

The high school mess was kept out of the papers, but it became a topic of discussion among Sara Allanson's friends. Sara, recently bereaved, was rather less concerned for her fatherless child than some of the mothers whose daughters were beginning to show signs of prettiness. "Thank heaven my Marjorie has always had a level head on her shoulders," said Sara. "Not that any of our girls would do that sort of thing. I actually heard that there were more than four boys involved, you know. Yes, there were four of the high school girls, but I've heard as many as ten boys. That sounds exactly like the Germans in Belgium, except that these girls were willing. Much too willing, from what I hear. It's going to be very difficult to know who to punish if any of those girls turn out to be pregnant. They wouldn't even know themselves who to blame, and you can't just put a whole football team in jail. Well, the whole unfortunate affair ought to make some of our friends stop and think, not mentioning any names."

With so many other things on her mind—what to do with Frank's law books and his clothing and personal effects; papers to sign; letters to write; accounts to be settled; furniture to be rearranged—Sara did not stop long to think about the high school scandal. If she had been able to look into the future and see what it held for Marjorie (and for her) she might have lingered over the high school situation to fortify herself with the knowledge to handle a somewhat similar situation. For in Marjorie's next to last year at boarding-school, with her marks holding up well and her deportment practically faultless, the girl became a problem. It was a rather nasty problem, and yet the absence of any dramatic episode to point it up was almost worse than the problem itself. The simple facts of the problem were that Marjorie had practically overnight developed a figure that was voluptuous enough to compensate for the beauty that Nature had withheld from her face, and that boys were hanging around the Allanson house.

Sara Allanson, being Sara, could quickly attribute this sudden popularity to a remarkable discovery of Marjorie's worthwhile qualities by boys who had been too immature to make the discovery earlier. "It's so nice to have the boys dropping in that way," said Sara. "Marjorie isn't what you'd call—well, you know how some girls are *forward* with boys. And boys do need a little urging at that age, fifteen or so. It wasn't till just recently that she showed the slightest interest. Gave them the least encouragement. But this summer, just since she got home from school, she seems to've suddenly realized that boys are just as interesting to talk to as girls. And the boys have been finding out that my Marjorie, the little girl that they used to tease about always having her nose in a book, she can talk on almost any subject. And I daresay hold her own in conversation with most of the boys."

The summer was well along before Sara noticed that the boys would come to call on Marjorie only in the afternoon; Marjorie and her caller would go off in the direction of the tennis club and be gone until suppertime. For the rest of the evening Marjorie was

alone, unless one of the girls in her crowd dropped in. Sara knew
that Marjorie was not one of the best dancers, but it seemed odd,
to say the least, that none of the boys had taken her to *any* of the
weekly club dances. Apparently the new popularity had its limits,
and Sara was not sure she liked that. Then along about the second
or third week in August the very disturbing incident of Herbie Ingersoll and Roger Bell occurred.

Roger was a new boy in town, the son of a construction engineer on the new dam, and he had lived in many places and undoubtedly was more sophisticated than the other boys his age. It
was common talk that all the young girls were crazy about him and
that the boys could not stand him. He played the ukulele-guitar
and sang songs in Hawaiian and Spanish, and he had just finished his
freshman year at Leland Stanford. He did not hesitate to ask any
girl for a date, even though he had been in town long enough to
have seen for himself that certain girls had understandings with
certain boys. They were all too young to be formally engaged, and
some mothers forbade their daughters to go so far as to accept the
boys' fraternity pins; but some of the understandings were well
rooted in time, and one of those was between Herbie Ingersoll and
Sue Lauderbach, the daughter of Jefferson Lauderbach, head chem-
ist at the steel mill. Herbie and Sue had been sweethearts for
five or six years, but that made no difference to Roger, nor did
the fact that Sue repeatedly refused to have a date with him. He
kept trying. He also appeared at the Allansons' at least one afternoon a week and would go for a walk with Marjorie.

Marjorie was out walking with Roger on the August day that
Herbie turned up. "Is Marjorie home, Mrs. Allanson?" he said.

"Why, no, Herbie. She and Roger are up at the tennis club.
Roger Bell. Why don't you go up there? I imagine they'll be on
the porch."

"She was supposed to go for a walk with me," said Herbie.

"Oh, was she? Are you sure? Because I know Roger called
up shortly after lunch."

"Will you tell her I'll be back around six, please?"

"Yes, I'll tell her that. But Herbie, does Sue like it when you
spend so much time with Marjorie? I know you're not engaged or

anything serious, but I understand that you object if Sue goes out with another boy, and I just wonder."

"Who told you that? Roger Bell?"

"No. Long before he ever came to town."

"Well, I have to go now, Mrs. Allanson. Will you give Marjorie my message, please?"

Herbie left quickly and thus put an end to further discussion, but he was back at six o'clock, waiting unannounced on the Allansons' porch, when Marjorie and Roger Bell returned from their walk. Sara Allanson, upstairs and getting ready for her bath, could not hear the conversation that was taking place on the porch, but presently Roger Bell left, and a few minutes later Marjorie and Herbie crossed the street and headed in the direction of the tennis club. It was seven o'clock before Marjorie came home, and she was alone.

"Marjorie, you *know* we have dinner at six-thirty this time of year. I think it was very inconsiderate of you to go off like that, and I don't want it to happen again. If you wanted to talk to Herbie you could have just as easily stayed on the porch."

"I'm very sorry, Mother."

"You look a sight, too," said Sara. "The least you can do when you come to the table is—go comb your hair, and honestly, Marjorie. Look at your dress. You look as though you'd been playing with mudpies, at your age. I'll wait dinner for ten minutes more while you make yourself presentable. I declare."

"You go ahead. Don't wait dinner for me."

"I'll do nothing of the kind, and then I want to talk to you about Herbie."

"No. I'm not going to talk about Herbie. Or anyone else."

"How *dare* you speak to me that way?"

"Mother, I'm not going to talk about Herbie Ingersoll and that's all there is to it, no matter what you say."

"Well, I'll say this. You're not going to *get* any dinner. If you want to behave like a naughty child, that's the way you'll be treated. Stay in your room without any supper, till you remember your manners."

"I don't want any supper."

"You can suit yourself about that, Miss Impudent. But we're going to have a talk about certain things, whether *that* suits you or not."

"No! I will not!" said Marjorie. She went upstairs and slammed her bedroom door.

All evening Sara waited, but the girl did not appear, and in the morning her room was empty, her bed not slept in. Sara was made dizzy in the rush of all the possibilities of disaster and disgrace, and by the realization that in this crisis she had no one to turn to. The fact lay bare that in the whole world, among all the women she counted as her friends and the men who had been friends of her husband, there was not one whom she loved enough to share her terror. Out in that bleak world, and now a member of it, was her child. *Her* child. But as a member of that world Marjorie could not love her, and she could not love Marjorie. She sat, for physical rest, in a Windsor chair at Marjorie's desk, and listened to this report from herself to herself, that testified to her loveless condition and her supreme remoteness from other flesh and blood. The ecstatic shudders of a kindly man, the water break, the cries in the night and the soiled diapers and the second teeth and the simulated pride and the secret appraisals were all lies, all equally spurious and unexperienced. There were some things to do, because out in that world was that world that must not be surrendered to, that billion of flesh and blood or chalk. Say nothing today, tomorrow call the police. No, next day call the police. No, never call the police. No, never say anything to anyone. Yes, call a detective agency. No, do it through Judge Eaton. Regret Althea Stokes's luncheon. Confide in Dr. English. At least have some coffee. A good strong cup of coffee. And think up a good story for the help.

"Mother?"

Sara Allanson did not turn. "Yes?"

"I'm sorry I was rude."

"Well, I should think you would be. Where did you sleep?"

"In the attic."

"In the *attic*?"

"In the old playroom."

"Why? What did you sleep *on?* There's no bed made up."

"I know. I'm stiff. I slept on the floor."

"Why? What made you do that?"

"I don't know. I just did."

"Well, you'd better get yourself a hot bath or you'll be stiff the rest of the day. I see you haven't changed your dress."

"I know."

"I was just going down to breakfast. What do you want? And rumple your bed. I don't want Agnes to think you stayed out all night."

"Mother, I don't *care* what Agnes thinks."

"I'm sure you don't, but I do."

"But I wish you didn't."

"You have to care what people think in this world."

"I don't."

"Well, you'd better start."

"It's too late for me to start."

"Oh, ridiculous. What shall I tell Bertha you want for break-fast?"

"Two soft-boiled eggs."

"And how soon will you be down?"

"Three quarters of an hour."

"Very well. One thing more. If Herbie wants to come calling this afternoon, I want you to tell him no. I think you're getting in too deep there, and I'd rather you didn't see him unless Sue comes along."

"Well, she won't come along."

"No, and I don't trust Herbie Ingersoll. Not that I trust Roger Bell, either, but *they're* only going to be here another year. Two soft-boiled eggs, you said. Three quarters of an hour."

"Mother?"

"Yes?"

"Nothing."

"Well, whatever is on your mind, Marjorie, I'll be home all day except for luncheon and bridge club at Mrs. Stokes's. I have a few things to say, too."

The things that were to be said were not said. The summer
vacation dragged and spurted along, and Marjorie went back to
school, the fall meetings of Sara's Tuesday bridge club were inau-
gurated, and Sue Lauderbach had a tiny diamond—embedded in
Herbie's fraternity pin. At Christmas, having made her reservation
in October, Sara took over the country club for a dinner dance for
Marjorie, which turned out to be as good a party as all the other
parties that it duplicated: same people, same orchestra, same food,
same place. But the occasion was ruined for Sara by an overheard
scrap of conversation between two young men. She did not know
either boy; they could have been out-of-town house guests, and
they could have been town boys who were not invited to parties
until they went away to college, whose parents were not members
of the club. Sara, on her way from a visit to the ladies' room,
halted in the vestibule behind the stag line, and over the heads of
the boys she saw Marjorie dance by.

"Marjorie Allanson," said the first boy.

"Yeah. Lots of lovin'," said the second boy.

"You said it," said the first boy.

"The hottest necking in town."

"I'll say."

Sara drew away unseen; there was more, but it was in slang
terms that she did not understand, and she had heard enough. She
was angered but not particularly shocked, not genuinely surprised.
It was her understanding that the word necking clearly implied in-
complete consummation; the word was not used in such cases as
the high school girls and the football players. From this Sara
drew some small but at least temporarily reassuring comfort. If the
boys had been able to say more, they would have said it.

The music stopped at four o'clock, and Sara went home with
Jim and Esther Truesdale, Frank Allanson's law partner and his
wife. She undressed and took a bath and got into bed. She could
not let herself go to sleep until Marjorie got home, but she was
not fully awake when she heard a car and voices and the storm
door and front door closing, then Marjorie's footsteps.

"I'm awake, Marjorie," she called.

Marjorie opened her door. "Thank you for a very nice party. It was really swell, Mother. Everybody had a good time."

"Yes, I thought it went very well. Who did you come home with?"

"Just now? That was Ralph Munson. I didn't come home with Bud Ogilvie because he got tight. We all went to the hamburger place."

"But you had scrambled eggs at three o'clock."

"Oh, we didn't go to the hamburger place just to eat, Mother. We go there to finish up the evening."

" 'We.' You make it sound as though you went to parties every night of your life. Well, it's over, and next year it'll be someone else's turn. Is Ralph Munson Dr. Munson's son from Mountain City?"

"No, he's no relation. As a matter of fact, Ralph Munson wasn't at our party. You don't know him."

"Well, explain that. How did you happen to come home with someone that wasn't even at the party?"

"Well, he works. He's the night manager at the Gibbsville Bakery, and he works every night from eight to four."

"How did you ever meet him? Have you ever seen him before tonight? No wonder I never heard of him. Is he married?"

"Separated. He came here from Allentown last year. Mother, can we talk about this tomorrow?"

"We'll talk about it now, whatever it is. Are you aware that your father helped to get the Gibbsville Bakery started? I have stock in it. Not enough to interest a fortune-hunter, I can assure you, but your father was one of those that put up the money for the bakery. How did you *meet* this Ralph Munson?"

"I don't know, I don't remember. But he isn't a fortune-hunter. He's nothing like that."

"He's a married man, and my guess is this isn't the first time you've seen him. A married man—"

Marjorie did not wait to hear any more, and the next day Sara did the only thing she could think of in the circumstances: she summoned Jim Truesdale.

"Yes, I know Ralph Munson," said Jim.

"Are you holding anything back from me, Jim? I have a feeling you are, and it's not fair to Frank."

"I guess I was Frank's best friend, but he never discussed family affairs with me. Or with anyone else, for that matter. I'll answer any questions you ask, Sara, but don't expect me to stand *in loco parentis*. In other words, I'm not going to take on the problem of Marjorie's love affairs. That's one thing I have no intention of doing."

"I only wanted to know about this Munson man."

"Well, they're pleased with him at the bakery. He makes about seventy-five dollars a week, somewhere in there. He isn't what you'd call a handsome fellow. Ordinarily you wouldn't give him a second look, and when I heard about him and Marjorie I was inclined to dismiss the whole thing as gossip. Exaggerated. I figured you must have known all about it and were letting it run its course, so to speak. I didn't like him being a married man, but it wasn't up to me to say anything. These girls, they seem to grow up overnight nowadays, and suddenly you hear all these stories. If you believed half the stories you hear, you'd wonder what's becoming of the young girls today."

"Now look here, Jim, don't start inferring that there were stories about Marjorie. That's just the kind of a remark that gets stories started, and coming from you I don't like it a bit. I could remind you that it was Frank Allanson that was responsible for getting all the best clients in the firm, not you. You never would have got very far without Frank, and it seems to me you're forgetting your obligations."

"Now, Sara, don't let's indulge in personalities. Frank and I were equal partners in every way, and I'm very sure that Frank never said anything to imply otherwise. If you wish to believe that Frank Allanson *carried* me, you're quite mistaken, but I won't go into that."

"Well, *I* will," she said. "You wouldn't have the Lehigh Valley for a client but for Frank, and as far as that goes Frank had all those big clients before you were made a partner."

"Sara, Sara, come on now. This is getting out of hand. You

put me on the defensive, and I don't like it. Let me say this much, to correct any wrong impressions you're harboring. The firm has all the clients it always had, plus certain ones that came to us *after* Frank passed on. *After.* Do I make myself clear?"

"You make it clear that you've taken clients that Frank probably didn't want to have anything to do with."

"Would you say Wadsworth & Valentine was one of those clients? One of the biggest construction companies in the United States? We handle all their legal business in this region now, but only in the past year, Sara. *Only* in the past year. You get some of that fee, but under the terms of the partnership, I didn't have to give you a nickel of it. So don't make such rash statements about our clients. I can understand your being upset about Marjorie, and all the talk. I don't think Marjorie is a *bad* girl. Small town, everything exaggerated out of proportion, and I don't know who's worse. The boys, or the mothers of the girls. If Frank were alive—"

"If Frank were alive he'd throw you out of this house, bodily," said Sara.

"Well, I doubt that, but that's my cue to leave."

"It certainly is. It most certainly is," she said.

Marjorie was still asleep after her party, and Sara sent Agnes to wake her. "Take her breakfast up to her, and tell her I wish to see her as soon as she's finished," said Sara. "I'll be in my room."

"Are you going to have it out with her?" said Agnes.

"Why? What do you mean?"

"Just so she don't think we tattled on her," said Agnes. "The lawyer here and all, I know you're getting ready, ma'am. But I wouldn't want her to think it was us, because it *wasn't* us. Not me or Bertha. We think we have a pretty good idea who you might say spilt the beans, but make sure the poor girl don't blame Bertha and I. It *was* William, wasn't it? *He* informed on her."

"I won't say," said Sara.

"It was him, all right. He was in the kitchen getting warm when the front doorbell rang and I went to answer it. He just come back from driving you to Mrs. Stokes's and was in the kitchen getting warm. I answered the door, and then I went back in the kitchen and William asked me who it was. I should of told him it was none of his business, but I didn't. That's how he found out. Worse than a woman for gossip. He hung around and hung around till it was time to go fetch you, and that's how he seen Munson. Munson went out the front door the very same minute William was driving away. But before you believe everything William told you, you gotta take this into account, that Munson fired William's elder boy from the bakery. I don't say Munson wasn't here. That he was, and I'm not denying that. But Munson did give William's boy the sack, and he has a grudge against Munson."

"Agnes, there were a lot of things you could have told me that you didn't, and you should have."

"Well, you were bound to find out sooner or later, and I don't think much of people that carry tales. I'd a cousin was murdered in the old country through a man carrying tales. Ambushed and shot down in cold blood. Left a wife and four small children. No, regardless of the provocation I'd still not inform on a person. I send a portion of my wages to help those children, the innocent victims of circumstances. It's only five dollars a month, but that's sixty dollars a year. Twelve pounds, in Ireland, you know."

"Well, I'm very glad you don't believe in carrying tales," said Sara. "There's altogether too much of it."

"Meaning would we say anything to outsiders? The answer is no. What goes on in this house is nobody's business outside, no matter how much they try to pump us. And they did, employers and servants alike, but got very little information for their trouble. As long as *I'm* living in this house, and the same for Bertha, they can pry around and snoop as much as they want to, but we're loyal. Loyal to the bone. A pity some women don't have something better to occupy their time. Naturally it's m'self they try to wheedle the information, Bertha being mostly in the kitchen and refusing to answer the telephone. But they don't get much out of me, you can be sure of that. There was one of them I'm ashamed to say give me a ride home from Sodality last Tuesday, and I was no sooner in her auto than she begun her cross-examination. And the two of us just come from Benediction, with the smell of the incense still in our nostrils."

"I can guess who that was. What did she want to know?"

"Well, what they're all asking these days. Last summer they'd be asking did young Ingersoll and that newcomer, Bell, did they come to blows? There was talk they'd a fist fight on the front porch. But now it's all Munson. Do you let him come to call, et cetera. I said to Miss R, I appreciated the ride home on a cold night, but if I had to pay me fare with bits of confidential information, then I'd sooner pay me dime and take the trolley. There the conductor'll take your ten-cent piece and worry about his own troubles."

"So true," said Sara Allanson.

"I'll be getting her breakfast, poor thing," said Agnes.

Sara Allanson, who had found no joy in the sexual act, was nevertheless a former participant in it, with a simple and straightforward definition of what constituted the act and what did not. She could no longer solace herself with that earlier use of the word necking and its implication of incompleteness: Marjorie had smuggled a married man into this house, and a married man did not go to all that trouble for anything less than completeness. Therefore Marjorie must be dealt with not as a girl but as a woman.

Sara did not have to wait long. She could read the household sounds, and obviously Marjorie was taking a cup of coffee and turning down the rest of her breakfast. Now, in her nightgown and bathrobe, wearing her glasses and with no sign of makeup, she was at her mother's bedroom door.

"Well, come in," said Sara.

Without a doubt the girl had been given some warning by Agnes. A defensive apprehension was in her manner. "What is it?" she said.

"Do you know what happens to girls like you if they're poor? They get sent away to the Protectory, and all the rest of their lives they're never able to live that down. And do you know what happens to men like Mr. Munson? If he was some kind of a day laborer he'd be put in prison."

"Oh, that's what it is," said Marjorie. *"That's"* why you had Mr. Truesdale here. Well, if you do anything to Ralph, I'm in it too."

"Indeed you are."

"I know you're not going to have me sent to the Protectory, but you could do something to Ralph like have him lose his job. If you do that, Mother, I'll leave this house."

"You wouldn't get very far—not that I'm so anxious to keep you here. You've shown how much respect you have for a good home. I suppose you're thinking of going away with Mr. Munson. But I wonder how enthusiastic he'd be about that? Can you picture him going to some strange town and getting a job in a bakery, with an eighteen-year-old girl, not his wife, tagging along?"

"He knows all that."

"Oh, then you've discussed your predicament?"

"Yes."

"And what did you decide, may I ask?"

"You'll soon find out."

"I want to find out now. You're not a child any more, young lady. Let's not have any childish bad temper. What did you and your Mr. Munson decide?"

"He's leaving town."

"I should—say—he—is. And planning to take you with him, I suppose?"

"No."

"Oh, leaving you here."

"Yes."

Sara considered this for a moment. "Where is he going?"

"I don't know. Out West somewhere. He's told them at the bakery that he's resigning his job and leaving at the end of the week."

"Do you propose to join him?"

"No. He's going away and not telling me where. But if you do anything to get him fired, keep him from getting a reference, I'll go away. Even if I don't know where he is. I won't live here another minute."

"When did you, or he, decide all this?"

"Last night."

"At the hamburger place?"

"We didn't go to the hamburger place."

"Where did you have your rendezvous?"

"At the bakery."

"At the bakery! The bakery? How did you get there, for heaven's sake?"

"Roger took me. Roger Bell. What does it matter who took me there? I couldn't invite Ralph to my party——"

"No, you can have him in your room, but not to your party. That's the kind of a love affair this was. Even you can see that."

"Yes, I saw that, and so did he, and that's why he's going away. And I never expect to see him again, so does that satisfy you?"

"I must say you don't seem very upset about it."

"What's the use of getting upset about it?"

"Well—you couldn't have loved him very much after all."

"I didn't, and he didn't love me. Who would love me?"

"What?"

"That's what I said. Who would love me?"

"Marjorie, what a terrible thing to say."

"Yes, isn't it? How could my daughter Marjorie say such a thing, and everybody talking about her? That's supposed to be the excuse. Love. Why should I have to love anybody? Nobody ever loved me. No I don't love Ralph Munson, but he was nicer to me than anybody else ever was. Except Roger. But people like you, and Herbie Ingersoll—you were ashamed of me."

"Thank you not to put me in the same class with Herbie Ingersoll."

"Why not? You wanted me to be one thing and Herbie wanted something else, but you never cared what I wanted."

"As far as I know, as far as *I* know—as far as I know you were never deprived of anything. And as to your relations with the opposite sex, I just don't understand how you could cheapen yourself. I couldn't believe it possible, even when I could practically see it with my own eyes. On my own doorstep. In my own *house*. Well, the first thing is to see Dr. English."

"What for?"

"Don't *tell* me you aren't aware of the consequences of your behavior."

"Oh, you mean pregnant. You don't have to worry about that. I'm not pregnant."

"You're sure?"

"Of course I'm sure. Nobody gets pregnant if they're careful. We're not living in the Dark Ages, Mother."

"Well, that's a relief. I'm sure I don't welcome the prospect of taking you in to see Dr. English. And I won't have to take you out of school. But when you go back I'm going to write a letter to Miss Crowder and make sure you stay on the school grounds. In other words, you're going to have to change your ways—here at home, and at school, and everywhere else. You think you know so much, with your talk about the Dark Ages, but you haven't even learned self-control."

"And having Miss Crowder lock me up is your way to teach me."

"Yes, and seeing to it that you associate with the right sort of boys."

"Like Herbie Ingersoll? All the mothers considered him the right sort of boy."

"You don't intend to change your ways, I can see that, but you're going to find that it'll do you no good to defy your mother. You won't have a cent till you're twenty-five, and if I went to court I could prevent you from getting anything even then."

"Yes, but you wouldn't do that. The notoriety."

"You're wrong. It can be done very quietly. In fact, Marjorie, those sort of things usually are done very quietly, especially when all the judges are personal friends of mine. It wouldn't be in a courtroom, you know. That kind of thing takes place in the judge's chambers."

"You'd have to say I was insane."

"No, I wouldn't. Just enough to convince the judge that you weren't ready to administer your own affairs. Financially. You wouldn't have to be certified as insane. We won't even *talk* about *that*. I'm only telling you now what can be done without any notoriety, and hope it will serve as a warning to you. There are lots of other things I can do. I can take you out of Miss Crowder's and put you in a much stricter school. I could send you abroad, to Switzerland, a school that handles difficult girls. And if you refused to go, or ran away, then I could do something more drastic, because a girl that runs away has proved that she's difficult. If you ran away now, for instance, seven years from now I could tell the judge that that was what you'd done when you were eighteen, and that would be a black mark on your record. I hold all the trump cards, and any false move on your part is going to count against you in the future as well as the present. So don't attempt anything foolish."

"That's what Ralph said, and he didn't even know you," said the girl.

Marjorie was coming out of this inquisition unscarred, and Sara knew it. She could not compel herself to be more severe than she had been thus far, with her threats of restrictions at school and vague hints of financial pressures and court actions. But neither could she force herself and Marjorie into an open, candid discussion of the girl's intimacies with men, the heart of the matter. So long as they skirted the topic, the conversation remained just that, a conversation, and Sara could already see that she was getting nowhere, that Marjorie's ways would not be changed. But if the only way to effect a change was by probing more deeply, the result was not worth the discomfort and unpleasantness it would cost Sara. In a sudden burst of futility and renunciation she said, "Well, it's your life. Make a worse mess of it if that's what you want."

The abruptness of the statement took Marjorie by surprise. "May I go now?"

"I don't know what else I can say. Yes, go," said Sara. She spoke with weary solemnity, but as soon as the girl closed the door behind her Sara experienced a sense of relief that started in her abdomen and leapt strangely to the back of her neck. She recognized the cause of this relaxation of tension: she had done everything, absolutely everything, that she could do, and now it was up to the girl herself.

And so it was, just as Sara had foreseen, and rather much as she and Marjorie had wanted it to be. The atmosphere had been cleared of particles of love, and nascent hatred was gone too. What remained, or was substituted, was a formal arrangement, a modus vivendi that functioned extremely well. Having no love to give, Sara was no longer obliged to simulate love or the giving of it; having had no love, Marjorie, under the new arrangement, was not obliged to accept her mother's counterfeit of it. She obeyed her mother's household rules that governed her hours, and she brought no one to the house, surreptitiously or otherwise, who did not meet with Sara's approval. Away from the house she behaved wholly on her instincts, and she became a convenience for thwarted men. Their number did not increase, but their age level was raised. They were husbands. At the country club, in the shopping district of the town, Marjorie's progress was frequently and momentarily halted by men who urgently wanted to see her but were reluctant to hold lengthy conversations with her in public. A man would stop her on the street or follow her from one room to another, and while making a pretense of casual conversation he would mutter, in some degree of desperation, "When can I see you? Same place, five o'clock tomorrow? Quick, Marjorie. Here comes Mrs. Hofman." She had forbidden them to call her on the telephone, and they were dependent on such chance encounters.

Their need of her gave her a special strength that enabled her to ignore the cold hatred that she saw in the faces of their wives. It was a cold and special hatred. The women knew she was not out to break up their establishments, and they would not permit themselves to recognize this faceless body as a declared enemy. Marjorie was not even a rival whom a woman could discuss with a friend, and she became in consequence the object of unexpressed and individual hatreds. "You're a menace to society," said Jap Wilson, one of her few bachelors. "One of these days you're going to wake up with your throat cut, and they won't know who did it. Too many suspects."

"Just so they get the right one," said Marjorie.

"Aren't you ever afraid of them?"

"No. If they really loved their husbands I would be. But all they care about is having a house on Lantenengo Street and their charge accounts and being Mrs. So-and-so."

"Not all of them, Marjorie. Betty Langdon isn't one of those."

"If I were as pretty as Betty Langdon I wouldn't worry about

Marjorie Allanson. But that isn't all there is to it. How would you
like to be told that you were a pansy?"

"Is that what Betty told Ben?"

"Told him, and almost had him convinced of it. Something
she read sounded like a description of Ben, and pretty soon he
couldn't get interested, if you know what I mean. For over a year
she had him in such a state that every time he went near her it got
worse. That's one marriage I could have broken up. Ben would
have married me. Anyway, now you know why Betty hates me.
I showed her up. She *wanted* Ben to be a pansy so she wouldn't
have to sleep with him any more, and now I guess he sleeps with
anybody."

"You guess?"

"Not with me. He went and told Betty about me, so I told him
that he and Betty were just right for each other. And they are. I
think some married couples get as much of a thrill out of quarreling
as anything else."

"Some do, I guess."

"Those I know about seem to. I wouldn't get married for anything. I'm *never* going to get married. When I'm twenty-five I'm going to move away from Gibbsville and live in New York. I'll get
some kind of a job, maybe work in a settlement house or something like that. And when I get to be forty or around there I'll move
to Italy and settle down with those elderly Englishwomen you read
about. Widows and old maids. Have a garden, and tea every afternoon. I'm always reading about them in books, and it sounds like a
nice life. They all have something in their past, but they mind
their own business, and they're polite to each other. Some of them
turn Catholic and the priest is practically the only man they ever
see. I don't know about that part of it for me. I've never met a
priest, but Agnes, our maid, talks about her priest as if he were a
saint, and I just don't believe it. It's going against nature, and I
just don't believe it, especially Italians. My goodness, I knew a
girl at Miss Crowder's that spent a year in Florence, and American
men are bad enough, but those Italian men must be a hundred
times worse. But I guess when I'm forty I'll be safe. I'd just like to

think that in my old age I could have a nice little villa and a few friends to talk to if I felt like it, and if I wanted to stay home and read and not see anybody, I could do that. Some of them take up painting. I wouldn't be any good at that. I probably wouldn't be very good at gardening, either, but they say anything grows over there, the land is so fertile. Genteel old maid. Can you see me as a genteel old maid, you genteel old bachelor? Kiss me while I'm young, Jap. I won't talk any more, I promise."

She was twenty, and a year out of school. She had not tried very hard for the colleges that were acceptable to her, and tried not at all for the others. In anticipation of her twenty-first birthday she was given a Chrysler convertible coupe, which she drove badly and continually. She took golf lessons and played dutifully in the lowest sixteen; she went to the movies with her friend Blandina Tuckerman. She had her hair done. She enrolled in a business college for a course in shorthand and typing, and dropped it halfway through. She continued to read a lot, novels and magazines, not for stimulation or for entertainment but purely for the consumption of time. She never, for instance, would mention a book to Blandina for the purpose of a discussion of it. Blandina was her companion rather more than she was her friend; a small, thick-ankled girl whose father owned a shoe store, whose mother was a Christian Scientist, whose brother was studying to be an ornithologist. The Tuckerman family were lost in mediocrity and bound by such respectability that they were unaware of Marjorie's special notoriety among the country club set. There was no way in which the gossip would have reached the Tuckermans, and Marjorie confided nothing in Blandina. Marjorie was the bright spot in Blandina's life, and if love can exist in a vacuum, Blandina's feeling for Marjorie was love. Marjorie, of course, was not unaware of the drabness of Blandina's life—the brick house in a row of brick houses, the father's devotion to his business, the mother's hypochondria, the brother's preference for birds over all human beings, and Blandina's own unimaginative spirit—and she was not ashamed to use Blandina in a quid pro quo relationship. Blandina did not question the fairness of the arrangement: she rode around in a pretty car, she was waited on by the Allanson servants, she

never had to pay to see a movie, and twice a year she was taken
to the country club, where her father and mother never had been.
Sara Allanson made no effort to understand the relationship, but
she approved of it. As dull a girl as Blandina could do no harm,
and she even, by her dullness, suggested a certain conventionality.
Sara reasoned that no one would look upon Blandina as an evil
influence or a partner in misconduct—and no one did.

In a few years Marjorie Allanson became a fixed figure in
the town. She was a young woman who was known to be immoral,
and yet there was no dramatic evidence of her immorality, and as
time passed there was a more moderate judgment of her misconduct. She was not invited to the small parties of the younger set,
where misconduct was not exceptional. Consequently her name was
left out of the minor scandals of her contemporaries, and her reputation, though bad, was static. The old label was there, but it was
old. One indeterminable day it became a fact that several years
had passed since Marjorie Allanson had been involved in an episode worth talking about. It was no secret that Jap Wilson took her
to hotels down country, but there was not much interest in Jap
Wilson's amours. He was well in his thirties, a bachelor, and was
said to have been turned down by every marriageable girl in town
since his graduation from State. The prevailing opinion was that
Marjorie Allanson had quieted down or was being extremely discreet, and in the absence of a spectacular incident it did not matter
which. She was also putting on a little weight, and the voluptuous-
ness of her figure had ceased to be alarming or startling. It would
not be long before she was actually stout, and she was getting
close to twenty-five.

Then one morning the town learned that Marjorie Allanson
had eloped with Chester Tuckerman, and the sensation could not
have been greater if the man had been one of the husbands who
had been her lovers. "How did it *happen?*" was the common question, and first to ask it was Sara Allanson. Along with the rest of
the citizenry she had not known that Marjorie had ever had five
minutes alone with Blandina's brother. The young man's name had
never come up even during the times when Sara was present at
lunch with Blandina and Marjorie, and Sara would not have rec-

ognized Chester if she saw him on the street. She did not, indeed, recognize him when Marjorie brought him home with her from Elkton, Maryland. "Mother, I want you to meet Chester Tuckerman, my new husband. We were married this morning."

"Yes, the paper called. How did this happen?"

"Well, aren't you going to welcome us home? We're married, Mother."

"Yes, of course. How do you do, Chester. I take for granted that you're Blandina's sister. I mean brother, of course."

"Yes, ma'am. My father owns the shoe store."

"Yes, and what do you do? How old are you? Tell me something about yourself."

"I'm twenty-six years old and I'm working for my master's degree at Bucknell."

"Bucknell. Then are you a Baptist?"

"No. My father is a Reformed, and my mother's a Christian Scientist."

"Oh, yes, I believe I did know that. There aren't many Christian Scientists in Gibbsville, are there?"

"Two hundred and fifteen, but my mother says the Scientists are getting their own church next year. Now they meet in Odd Fellows Hall."

"And you're at Bucknell. That's up near Sunbury, isn't it?"

"Lewisburg. I guess we're about fifteen miles from Sunbury. I go through Sunbury on the way home."

"Marjorie has cousins in Sunbury. Judge Doerflinger is my first cousin. That ran for State Attorney General several years ago? At least he ran for the nomination."

"I don't know many Sunbury people, unless they went to Bucknell."

"Well, Cousin Will is a graduate of Dickinson," said Sara. "Then you plan to finish your education? How long have you got before you get your degree?"

"Till June."

"And then what do you plan to do?"

"I have a job next fall, teaching science at Swedish Haven High."

"Oh, science? That must be interesting. Does that include chemistry and physics?"

"Yes, I'll have to teach chemistry, but biology is my field."

"Biology. Oh, yes. I took physiology in school, but I guess biology is much more advanced. Do you expect to support yourself and Marjorie on your teacher's pay?"

"No, but I'll work in the store during the summer. That's three hundred extra, and my mother's going to give me a thousand dollars for a wedding present."

"Marjorie of course will have her own income fairly soon. I suppose she told you that."

"Yes, I guess that'll come in mighty handy."

"But what are you going to do in the meantime?"

"Marjorie, I guess you better tell her that," said Chester.

"Yes, I haven't heard much from you, Marjorie," said Sara.

"You will," said Marjorie. "First of all, I'm having a baby."

"That doesn't surprise me. I was surprised when you eloped, but not by this piece of news. Looking at your figure, I almost asked you."

"You'd have been wrong. I just found out, and the baby isn't due for seven more months."

"Approximately," said Chester. "We're not quite sure about that. Marjorie is very irregular, and the—"

"Oh, be still," said Sara. "I want to hear what my daughter has to say."

"Your *daughter* is his *wife,* Mother. And I was the one that proposed, because I want to have a baby."

"You didn't do this deliberately, I trust," said Sara.

"No, but when I found out, I decided I wanted it. I could have put a stop to it. I know doctors that do it for other girls in town. But Chester was willing to marry me, so we eloped."

"I wasn't just *willing* to marry her, Mrs. Allanson. I'm very fond of Marjorie. She's always been very nice to Blandina, and she isn't stuck-up, like some of the girls in this part of town. In fact, I always admired Marjorie, although I never knew her very well."

"Till recently, let's put it," said Sara.

"Well, yes," said Chester.

"As they say nowadays, you made up for lost time. Well, I still don't know what your plans are. For instance, when do you begin to support your new wife?"

"He can't support me now. He only has enough money to finish at Bucknell."

"And I live in a fraternity house. I guess I could take my mother's thousand dollars and we could board in Lewisburg, but Marjorie put her foot down on that."

"Why should we live in a boarding-house and there's this house with all the empty rooms, and servants and conveniences?"

"Don't you want to be together, like most newly married couples?" said Sara.

"He can come down on weekends. It isn't far."

"I can get a ride nearly every weekend. There's over two hundred boys and girls from Lantenengo County, and four Lambda Chis live around here. Lamba Chi Alpha, that's my fraternity."

"Marjorie's father was a Phi Kappa Sigma."

"They're good. Older than we are."

"So he can come down weekends," said Marjorie. "It isn't a question of money, Mother. Mr. Truesdale said if I ever needed money I could always borrow on my inheritance."

"It isn't exactly an inheritance, you know. I hope you made that clear to Chester. You'll have the income, but you can't touch the principal. This new child of yours will get that, and share it with his brothers and sisters."

"What does it amount to, the income?" said Chester.

"Well, I suppose it's all right to tell you, since you *are* Marjorie's husband. This year it comes to a little over eight thousand dollars."

"A year?"

"Yes. If the stock market comes back it'll be more. It used to be more," said Sara.

"I don't see why Chester can't take my car to Lewisburg and then he won't have to depend on other people to come home weekends. I don't want to drive till after I've had the baby. If I want to go anywhere, William can take me."

Sara was silent.

"Do you object to that, Mother?"

"No. I was just thinking it'd be nice if you'd *ask* me to do all these things. Instead of which you're just informing me that this is going to be so, and that is going to be so. I have no voice in any of these matters."

"Would you rather I lived with Mr. and Mrs. Tuckerman?"

"Where do they live?"

"Oh, Blandina would love that," said Chester.

"No. Mrs. Tuckerman is a Christian Scientist, and they don't approve of doctors," said Sara.

"I wanted to be a doctor originally, but my father said it would kill my mother. They had fights enough over Blandina and I."

"No, you stay here, Marjorie, and tomorrow first thing we'll have Dr. English come and see you."

"Don't have him. Have Malloy," said Tuckerman.

"Dr. Malloy has never been in this house and if I have anything to say about it, he never will be. Some things, Chester, that you're going to have to leave up to me. Don't be so hasty your first time in the house."

"Pardon me," said Chester.

"Marjorie, will you tell Agnes where you and Chester want to sleep? She can get William to help her move the furniture," said Sara. "And I was wondering whether your mother and father would like to come here for dinner this evening. What would you think about that, Chester?"

"Well, I don't know. I guess that'd be all right. I mean *sure.* I guess the two families might as well get acquainted."

"What is your telephone number?" said Sara.

"Three-nine-eight-four Jay. It sounds like a party line but it isn't. I don't know why they have the Jay there."

The announcements went out, the presents began pouring in, and the social amenities were observed to the extent that Marjorie was guest of honor at an older ladies' luncheon and another luncheon for younger women. The temporary absence of the groom in Lewisburg provided Marjorie's lifelong acquaintances with a good excuse to postpone mixed parties until the fall, and it was firmly understood by them and by Marjorie that the postponements would be permanent. No one had the slightest intention of giving a dinner dance for Marjorie Allanson Tuckerman and her bird-loving husband. The nut dishes and bread plates were duly acknowledged and, when not engraved, exchanged for credit; and Marjorie stayed out of sight as her pregnancy grew more noticeable. Her baby was born on the dot, according to Dr. English's prediction, or two months prematurely, according to the explanation by Sara which no one paid any attention to. And Chester was awarded his master's degree.

Now, with a husband and a baby daughter, Marjorie vanished as completely as though she had moved to Florence, Italy. She and Chester rented a house in Swedish Haven, four miles away, but a thousand leagues removed from the people she had always known. All reports on her life had to come from Sara. "Marjorie's all wrapped up in that little girl, and I can't say I blame her. Chester's brown eyes and curly hair. They both try to keep each other from spoiling that child, but I'm not sure how well they're succeeding. I'm so pleased with Chester. He's brilliant, you know. They won't be able to hold him very long at Swedish Haven High. He's already turned down several offers from *colleges,* but he's going to stay at Swedish Haven to get experience, and besides he'd given them his word. I hope he does stay, because I couldn't bear to have them take little Robin away. I go there every Monday afternoon, but if I had my way I'd be there *every* afternoon. By the way, did you know that Chester's family are descendants of William Penn? They were an old Pennsylvania family before Gibbsville was ever thought of. I just happened to find that out when they were deciding what to name the baby. Some of these upstarts at the country club are in for a rude shock when they hear that. Chester got in, of course, but I had to laugh when I heard of some of the people that were trying to keep him out. Not that he cares. They never *go* to the club. But as I said to Marjorie, her father was one of the founders of it and one of these days she might have a son and I'm going to turn over Frank's bonds to Marjorie's son. Can you imagine somebody like that Harry Reilly questioning Chester's right to be in the club? If he knew how close he came to being kept out, and it was Frank Allanson that spoke up for him. I wish we had a college in Gibbsville, that would keep Chester here. He's a brilliant young man. Brilliant. I gave him a microscope for his birthday. It was the only thing he wanted."

Marjorie's second child was a son, and he was named Frank Allanson Tuckerman. "Such a chubby little fellow, and his initials are f, a, t. Just like his mother," said Marjorie.

"You're not fat. What they call pleasingly plump," said Chester.

"Well, I'm not as fat as I was. God, I was big this time. A hundred and seventy. Dr. English said that was too much, and I think we ought to wait a while before we have another."

"Suits me," said Chester. "If we have any more we're going to have to look for a bigger house, and I like this one."

"I love it. Why don't we buy it? It's so silly to go on paying rent, money down the drain."

"I'm against mortgages. I can pay the rent here, but I couldn't scrape up the cash to buy it."

"But I can, and you're so popular with Mother, she'd lend you the money in a minute."

"Yes, but I could get unpopular with her, too."

"Not any more."

"Besides, I may want to get out of Swedish Haven. That would make me unpopular with your mother, and we'd be saddled with a house. You don't know how long it'd be before we could sell it, and we'd be paying taxes and the mortgage on this house and paying rent on some place else."

"Yes. Well, I love this house, and if we move away I hope we can find one exactly like it."

"With certain improvements. If we bought this house we'd want to spend some money on it. The wiring should be done all over again, it really isn't safe. And I'll never buy a house that doesn't have oil heating. This furnace is a darn nuisance. Just because we live in the coal region. My father's always saying we sell shoes to the coal miners, therefore we have to use coal."

"My father said the same thing," said Marjorie.

"Well, maybe I'll get a job in Oklahoma and we'll *have* to get an oil burner. Or maybe out in the western part of the State. I filled in another application today. Spring Valley. It's a good little college. Better than a lot of them. The money's about the same, but I'd be willing to take less at a college as good as Spring Valley. I don't want to give up my job here for less money unless it's a good opportunity."

"When will you know?"

"Oh, not for a month or two. These things take time, and I'm not the only applicant, you can be sure of that. There'll be Ph.D.'s applying for this particular job. I'm not very hopeful."

"Chet, why don't you get your Ph.D.? When I have the money it's so ridiculous for you to go on teaching in a high school. Is it Mother?"

"Well, only partly. It's my mother, too. She says I'll be principal here and make as much as a college professor, and she's right. The principal of Swedish Haven High makes as much as some full professors. She looked it up. But I don't put all the blame on them. I have to take some of it. I like it here."

"Well, if you like it that much, we'll stay. We can buy this house and spend some money on it."

"You're so impulsive. It'll take me about two more years to finish my book, and then if that gets accepted I'll get better offers. I won't need my Ph.D. And this fat little fellow won't have to move till he's almost three years old."

"All right, but then let's buy this house. Let's *own* it for three years. I really want that, Chet. Our own house. We can get it for twelve thousand."

"Well, let's see what I hear from Spring Valley."

"You just don't want to be pinned down."

"Probably," he said. "How would you like me to pin you down?"

"It's too soon. Another two weeks or so."

"All right, two more weeks. But then I start looking."

"You'd never do that to me, would you?"

He rubbed his nose with the back of his forefinger. "No, I don't guess I ever would."

"I couldn't endure that, Chet. I mean it. The only person I ever really loved."

"Well, that goes for me too. My father, and our kids. But nobody else. No girl, no woman."

"I don't even like to have you joke about it," said Marjorie.

She was far more afraid of what her own reprisals would do to her than of the seriousness of Chester's threat, and this fear was some measure of the insecurity of her new life. She had forsaken all others, and—with the exception of a single half-hearted overture by Jap Wilson—they had abandoned her to her high school teacher. She was as happy as anyone she knew, proud of her children, content with her husband. But the three years of marriage had not yet made her ready for any such test as a casual infidelity on the part of Chester. She no longer entertained herself with a contemplation of a far-off Italian villa in a far-off future. She did not need to be strengthened by other wives' cold hatred of her or by the uncritical devotion of Blandina Tuckerman. And her present relations with her mother were reasonably satisfactory. She knew that Sara could not resist the impulse to take possession of Chester through flattery and offers of financial help, but after a certain point of skepticism Chester was a naïve man in his relations with Sara, and he simply did not believe that Sara's patronage was obsessive. Since he did not recognize Sara's motives, Marjorie did not see fit to educate him. Instead she rationed Sara's visits and made sure that her mother was given no opportunity to take advantage of Chester's naïveté.

The Spring Valley application was turned down; the college took a man who had already had five years' teaching experience in a large university, and Chester did not even get as far as a personal interview. "Let's face it," he told Marjorie. "I made my mistake when I didn't stay at Bucknell. By now I'd have put in four years as a college teacher. I'd be an assistant professor, and I'd most likely have my Ph.D. All of a sudden I'm a middle-aged man as far as teaching is concerned. I mean it's too late for me to change. I'm a high school teacher, and that's that. So from here on I'm going to *be* a high school teacher, not a frustrated college professor."

"All right," said Marjorie.

"George Beck is going to resign, and when he does they'll offer me his job. He's had a good offer from Tech High, in Fort Penn, and his wife's from around there. He's going to recommend me. He told me so, and the only thing they'd be afraid of is if I took the job and then up and left two or three years from now. Is that all right with you?"

"Yes."

"I'd have to promise the board to stay five years."

"You don't hear any objection from me. But there's one thing I do want."

"I know. You want to own this house," he said.

"Yes. No more putting it off. We'll buy it tomorrow."

"Tomorrow? All right. Tomorrow."

"Good! We can give them a cheque tomorrow, and the next day we can have the electricians out to look over the wiring. Next week I'm going down to a place near Philadelphia and talk to a man about putting up a hedge. I have his name in my desk."

"A hedge? A fence'd be a lot cheaper."

"But not as pretty, and the hedge will keep the kids from straying off, even better than a fence. Also keep stray dogs out."

"Then you're pleased? I mean, you're not disappointed in me?"

"Chet, you know how I've wanted to own this house, and tomorrow night we'll be able to say it's ours."

"Well, if you want to know how I feel about it, I'm glad we didn't have to move to Spring Valley. I must be getting set in my ways."

They bought the house during the noon recess on the next day, and when Chester got home after school Marjorie had filled every vase with flowers and she handed him an unopened bottle of Canadian Club whiskey. "Where did you get *this?*" he said.

"I stole it. It was in my father's private stock, and I just went and took it."

"You went to see your mother?"

"I went there, not to see her. She was out. But I wanted to get this bottle and to ask Agnes if she'd mind the children when I go to Philadelphia. I didn't see Mother, and I didn't say anything about buying the house. I'll tell her some other time. This is just us. Our own private celebration in our own house. Would you rather I'd stolen some champagne?"

"To tell you the truth, I've never had champagne. I've never had this, either, but I've heard about it. And it's pre-Prohibition?"

"Open it, and we'll drink a toast."

"Now, or after supper? You know my capacity, and on an empty stomach."

"Let's have one drink now, and we can save the rest for when company comes. I didn't mean we should get tight, but I suddenly remembered all that liquor Father stored away, and how it would be nice if we used his whiskey to toast our new house. Not Mother's. His. And I'm certainly entitled to one bottle."

"All right. Here's to our new house. Do we have to drink this bottoms-up?"

"Here's to our new house, and the happiness you've given me in it."

"That goes without saying, as far as I'm concerned. To you, Marjorie. My wife."

"And to you, the father of my lovely children."

"I guess we'll have to drink it bottoms-up for all those toasts. Bottoms-up!"

"Bottoms-up!" she said.

"Oh-ho-ho-ho," he said. "That's the real thing all right. You can feel that going down all the way. I've got tears in my eyes, and it isn't sentimental."

"I'd almost forgotten how much I like the taste."

"The taste, or the kick?"

"Both, I guess. But I always liked it. The taste as well as the effect."

"When did you acquire a taste for it?"

"Oh, on dates, you know. Some boys always had a flask or one of those flat bottles."

"You're probably more of a booze hound than I am. I used to chip in and buy a bottle after a football game, but that was just

showing off. You never went around much with those girls like
Virginia Stokes. I used to hear about how she got slopped, and
Annabella Ingersoll."

"I have to get supper. No, I never went around much with
them. Are you going to have another?"

"Not unless you do," he said.

"No, I have to put the potatoes on," she said.

"Where's Robin?"

"They're in the kitchen. She's having her supper and he's in
the crib."

"Marjorie! I smell smoke."

"So do I. *No! No!*" She ran through the diningroom and
pushed open the swinging door, and as she did so a blast of
flame leapt into the diningroom before the door swung shut again.
"Chester! Chester!" she screamed. He ran to the swinging door,
pushed it open and was blasted with flames. Marjorie was picking
the baby out of the burning crib, and he did not immediately see
Robin. Then he saw her roasted body on the floor. He wrapped
her in his coat and carried her to the front room, and Marjorie
came in with the body of the baby. Marjorie's dress was burning
and her hair was on fire. He pressed his hands on her head and
extinguished the flame, and lifted a small rug from the floor and
smothered the flames on her burning dress, now nearly gone.

"Put the baby down," he said.

"No, no. Go away," she said. "Oh, Robin. Robin, is that you,
Robin? Chester, your shirt's on fire."

He beat out the fire on his sleeve. "Put the baby down, Marjorie. It's no use."

"Call Dr. Straub. Get somebody," she said. "Is that Robin? Is
that Robin, Chester?"

"Yes."

"Aren't you going to call the doctor?"

"Yes, but it won't be any use. Marjorie, let me take them out
on the lawn. The whole house is going up in a minute, and you need
a doctor."

"Are they dead?"

"Goodness, yes. Thank God."

"Thank God?"

"Look at them. You'd pray they were dead."

"Look at your hands. Chester, you're burned."

"Please take the baby out on the lawn, and I'll take Robin. You must get out of here. Do you hear me. Look at the diningroom. Marjorie, get out of the house for God's sake."

"Do you want me to take the baby out on the lawn?" she said.

"Yes, please. Hurry."

"All right. Will you take Robin?"

"Yes, I'll take Robin. Come on, Marjorie. Come with me."

"I'll take the baby out on the lawn, Chester."

"That's a good girl. You take the baby, and I'll take Robin."

"Is your baby dead, Chester? My baby is."

"Yes, they're both dead. And the house is ready to go."

"You be sure and take your baby, Chester."

"Yes, I will, dear."

"This whole house is going to go. Unngg, that smell. Isn't that an awful smell?"

"Yes. You go first, Marjorie."

"And you follow me," she said. The front door opened. "Oh, hello, Mr. Hartman. Did you come to help us?"

"Good God," said the neighbor, Hartman. He turned his face away.

It always takes a little while to get to know Mrs. Frank B. Allanson, a somewhat unusual trait in an American lady. To some degree her seclusion may be attributed to Miss Tuckerman, her paid companion, a bouncy little woman who speaks very little Italian—nouns, mostly—and takes it upon herself to suggest that Mrs. Allanson's callers restrict themselves to two or three innocuous topics and to visits lasting less than an hour. Miss Tuckerman is hardly ever successful, but not for lack of trying. A lady whom Mrs. Allanson herself has invited to tea will get a surprise visit from Miss Tuckerman in advance of the appointed day. "I hope you'll pardon this intrusion," Miss Tuckerman has been known to say, "but Mrs. Allanson has been a bit under the weather, you know. She gets these chest colds and they hang on and hang on. So she tires easily. And at seventy-six. She doesn't look it, but she is. So when you come for tea on Tuesday, don't be surprised if I walk in and tell her it's time for her to rest. Otherwise she'd go on for hours."

"I think you can count on me not to outstay my welcome," the lady—sometimes a noble lady—has been known to say.

"Of course. But then there's this other thing is even more important. I'm referring to subjects to talk about. Not to talk about, is more like it."

"Very well, what are they?"

"First of all, you don't want to say anything about fire. A house on fire. That kind of a fire. Or grandchildren. You don't want to bring up the subject of grandchildren. Avoid that like the plague, because most of the ladies here do have grandchildren and naturally they're liable to say something about them."

"Yes, I have six of them."

"You see what I mean? And do you have anybody in your family or some friend of yours named Marjorie? Because if you do, I'd appreciate it if you didn't bring the name up."

"Isn't it a fairly common name? I should think it'd pop up quite frequently. But go on, please. Any more?"

"Well, the name Chester."

"As a place name, or as a wuddiacallum Christian name? We have a Chester, you know. Rather picturesque town."

"I meant as a man's first name."

"No. No, I don't believe I know a Chester. Chester and Marjorie. Fire and grandchildren. Extraordinary. I know a woman can't bear the very mention of snakes. I'm not too keen on the filthy things myself. But have I got it right now? One, two, three, four. Chester and Marjorie. Grandchildren and fire. Yes, four. Any of these things is apt to set her off, I take it. Oh, well. Thank you for coming, Miss Tucker, and you'll show yourself out?"

From an inner compulsion or a less excusable motive many of the forewarned women lose no time in bringing up the topics on Miss Tuckerman's proscribed list. To some it is a relief, to some a disappointment, to discover that Mrs. Allanson is apparently undisturbed by the introduction of the forbidden names or references to fires and grandchildren. If she is upset at all, it does not show.

Her outward composure is wholly ladylike, and the contrast between Mrs. Allanson's dignity and Miss Tuckerman's effervescence
has led some of the ladies to suspect that of the two it is Miss
Tuckerman who needs watching.

Mrs. Allanson never goes beyond the garden walls. Her villa
is four stories high, of which the bottom two stories are backed up
against the side of the hill, and the third story is on the level of
the road. Miss Tuckerman's small Fiat is usually parked outside
the third-story main entrance to the house, and Mrs. Allanson's
older acquaintances have learned to wait until Miss Tuckerman
has driven down to Florence before entering the house. Nothing
comes of a visit to Mrs. Allanson if Miss Tuckerman is hovering
about, in and out, interrupting the conversation. Miss Tuckerman
has no friends of her own, and to some of the ladies it seems as
though she tried her best to prevent Mrs. Allanson from having
any. But there are a few ladies who call on her, one at a time,
perhaps two or three times a year, and keep her from being lonely.
And there is no doubt, from the stories she tells in Miss Tuckerman's
absence, that she is lonely. She has had a very sad life.

"She finally confided in me," Mrs. Jessop, her nearest neighbor said one day. "I had a *devil* of a time getting that Tuckerman
woman out of the way, but I was determined to find out all
about Mrs. Allanson. She interested me from the start. Lovely hair
and eyes. Imagine she must have been quite striking-looking in her
younger days. They were here, I guess about two months, before I
ever met her. I could *see* them from my garden, and at first I
thought they must be English. But when Dr. Rossi told me they
were Americans I decided to go call on them. So I fixed up a little
bunch of my hyacinths and took them down to her place, and left
them with a note. One American welcoming another. That sort of
thing, and I was on my way back up the hill when I heard this
voice calling 'Yoo-hoo, Mrs. Jessop,' and it was the Tuckerman
person. She came stumbling along after me on her fat legs and
when she got her breath she introduced herself and thanked me.
Asked me to come for tea, and then proceeded to instruct me on
how I was to behave. I didn't get that much preparation when I
was presented at court. But they were new, and I know how it is for

an American here, especially if you don't speak the language, and they didn't.

"So I had tea with them, and I was quite surprised to see how quickly Mrs. Allanson had made herself at home. You'd have almost believed that she'd been here all her life. She talked about *her* view, and I didn't bother to point out to her that my view was just a little better. And *her* servants. I kept quiet about that, because she'd hired that Anna Valenti, who's a terrible thief but threatened a friend of mine with a carving knife when she caught her stealing. Her villa. Her view. Her companion, Miss Tuckerman, who turned out to be a friend of her daughter. 'And where is your daughter?' I said. 'Passed on,' she said, and I thought I was going to be in for it, but Miss Tuckerman firmly announced that it was time for Mrs. Allanson's rest, and I took the hint.

"Miss Tuckerman came to see me a couple of times to ask my advice on one thing or another, and once again I was invited to take tea with Mrs. Allanson, but at the last minute I couldn't go, and the next day I got a crazy angry note from Mrs. Allanson. I wish I'd saved it. But the gist of it was that I had snubbed her and who did I think I was? She had some strange thing in it about her connection with William Penn, that I couldn't make any sense out of. Something about her grandchildren and William Penn. But since I'd been practically ordered not to mention grandchildren in front of her, I was completely at a loss, and nobody'd said a word about William Penn. Then I realized that Mrs. Allanson was like quite a few of the ladies that come here to live. We come here because it's first of all cheap, and the climate is good, and mostly because we don't want to spend our last years at home. In my case, Chicago, in her case a little town in Pennsylvania. And usually there's something sad or unpleasant behind it. Nothing particularly tragic about my coming here. My husband simply told me that he wanted to marry a snip that was younger than our youngest child, and I agreed so quickly that I took his breath away. That fixed him. He had to marry her, then. But there was nothing like that in Mrs. Allanson's history. She'd been a widow for many, many years.

"Naturally I was curious about her grandchildren, because of what the Tuckerman person had told me and the thing in Mrs. Allanson's note. It centered around her grandchildren.

"Well, Blandina, Miss Tuckerman, again asked me to call on Mrs. Allanson, apparently unaware that she'd written me that angry letter. And I went. And I was fascinated by Mrs. Allanson's behavior, because she never gave the slightest indication of having written me at all. There was only one thing, and that was just before I was getting ready to leave. We were both standing up, and Blandina was out of the room, and Sara Allanson said she'd had a letter from Marjorie but please not to tell Blandina. I knew that Marjorie was the name of her daughter, but what was this business about Marjorie's having passed on? She couldn't say any more because Blandina came back in the room with my coat.

"The next thing was to see what I could extract from Blandina. But all I could get out of her, in answer to a direct question, was that Marjorie was dead, and her eyes filled with tears. I had a nasty suspicion that Blandina turned on the tears to keep me from asking any more. But I did notice that from then on she saw to it that I was never alone with Sara. I had a devil of a time learning the whole story, until I did some detective work and discovered that Blandina drove down to Florence three mornings a week. And then it was so easy that it was like taking candy from a baby. Not only because she left Sara all by herself, but Sara herself wanted to talk. It poured out of her, and she made me promise not to tell Blandina that I went to the house.

"The grandchildren were burned to death in a fire, sometime back in the early Thirties. It was a terrible thing, because the daughter, Marjorie, and her husband, were drunk. They'd left the children in the kitchen, all by themselves, and Marjorie and her husband were so drunk that they didn't even know the house was on fire until a neighbor came to help. He could see the whiskey bottle on the table, and he had to testify that Marjorie and her husband were obviously drunk. A schoolteacher, the husband was, and very pleased with himself, but the kind of a hypocrite that would never be seen in a speakeasy but made Marjorie steal the liquor from her mother's cellar. But Marjorie had a terrible punishment. Not only the horrible death of her children, but she'd apparently been a beautiful girl. Strikingly beautiful. And *she* was badly burned in the fire and disfigured for life. Not that she lived much longer. She underwent some skin-grafting that wasn't at all successful, and she wouldn't let anyone see her. Only her mother. Not even her husband. Yes, one other person. Blandina, the Tuckerman woman. She visited her in the hospital as often as she could, and that's why Sara gave her the job as companion after Marjorie jumped out of the hospital window. Sara didn't want to talk about the husband, and she gave me some rather conflicting stories about him. One time she told me that he was teaching at some little college in Pennsylvania. Another time she said he moved to Canada after Marjorie killed herself, and spent all his time studying the habits of birds. Of course I don't accept everything Sara told me as gospel, but I remembered having gone to school with a girl from Gibbstown or Gibbsville, Pennsylvania, and I wrote and asked her about the story. And most of it appears to be true. She sent me a clipping from an old newspaper, and it was all there about the children and the fire, and Marjorie being badly burned. I hadn't really known the girl very well, and she only sent me the one clipping, but it confirmed the story Sara told me.

"Interesting, you know. I mean Sara's reaction to it all. It all happened a long time ago, and you can't go on living if time doesn't help you some. But Sara's reaction is quite unusual. It seems to me that only a very remarkable woman would have her courage. Almost as if she took as much pride in her tragedy as some women do in—oh, I don't know. In other things. It was a *terrible* tragedy, but it was *hers,* if you know what I mean. And Blandina must be a trial to live with."

THE PIG

Lawrence W. Candler, age fifty-five, said goodnight to his secretary, to the receptionist, to the elevator man, and to two young men who had recently come to work for the firm. He had interviewed them while they were still in law school, and they seemed to know that his reports on them had been extremely favorable. They were always expectantly respectful, always interrupted their conversations and waited for him to greet them in the elevator, in the corridors. They were at that stage of their careers where they believed that he could perform some miracle that would get them partnerships at thirty-two instead of thirty-five. They were eager, hard-working, well-educated, and young, and at the moment he could not think of their names.

He could not for the life of him think of their names, and he did not try very hard. He hoped that they were not headed for the Biltmore Bar, but even if they were he was not going to invite them to have a drink with him. And they would have sense enough to keep their distance.

"The usual, Mr. Candler?" said the barman.

"No, today I'm going to change, thanks. Give me a double Scotch and water in a highball glass, please."

The barman's impassive acceptance of the order was almost as telling as a wisecrack would have been. Usually this barman began preparing a weak Scotch on the rocks as soon as he spotted Candler in the doorway. He made this drink strong, and quickly waited on the next customer. Not a word to Candler until Candler finished his drink, paid for it, and left a fifty-cent tip. "Thank you, Mr. Candler. Goodnight, sir," said the barman.

"Goodnight," said Candler, unable to remember the barman's name.

He stopped and bought a paper on his way to his train, folded the paper and tucked it under his arm, and took a seat in one of the coaches. In a few minutes the train was under way, and the trainman said, "No bridge game, Mr. Candler?"

"No, not today."

"The others were waiting for you," said the trainman.

"I may move up there later."

The trainman moved on. Lawrence Candler had never known *his* name. The conductor, yes; he had known the conductor's name and the names of several other trainmen through the years. As a rule he was good on names. Once, years ago, he had won a bet that he could come within ten names of reciting the roster of his college class. There was no special trick to it; it was just something he could do. One of his friends made a small joke about it. The friend said it was a knack that would come in handy when he went to work for Miles, Coudray, Witherspoon, Chartress and Ulrich, which was now Miles, Coudray, Ulrich, Candler and Beckwith. Occasionally in the past he had surprised himself by rattling off the names of the first ten players in the U.S.L.T.A. rankings, which he had not intentionally memorized. And he was never given full credit for his ability to recite the names of all the Supreme Court justices since 1900. As a lawyer he was expected to know that— but he was the only lawyer among his friends who could do the complete list in ten minutes. They all left out Lurton, of Tennessee, probably because he had served only about four years.

Their names were Alfred Charles Stephano and Wilton No-Middle-Name Snodgrass, the young men who had come down in the elevator with him. Stephano was a graduate of Roxbury Latin, Dartmouth, and the Harvard Law School. Snodgrass had gone to Exeter, Yale, and the Yale Law School. Both young men had done their military service in the army, and Snodgrass was married to a niece of Channing Chartress. If you relaxed a little it all came back to you. The barman's name was Bart. It was important to relax. It was important not to panic, to do things like forgetting names and ordering an unusually large drink. It was equally important to adhere to his regular habits—and with that thought he rose and went forward to the club car.

"Where the hell were *you?*" said George Adams. "Look who I have to play with. This guy just made a little slam and we only bid four. I showed the son of a bitch my aces, but he stopped at four."

This guy, Harold Liggett, said, "Hello, Lawrence. You can have my place, if you like. It's yours anyway. And let me point out to you, Mr. Adams, if Mike had returned John's heart lead we'd have been set four tricks. Which, doubled and vulnerable, would have cost us plenty. Mike had the ace of hearts by itself."

"Keep your seat," said Lawrence Candler. "Hello, Mike. John."

"I phoned you at your office this morning," said Mike Post.

"I was out all day," said Lawrence Candler. "I got your message just before five o'clock, and I thought I might be seeing you on the train."

"We can talk about it later," said Mike Post. "You can come to my house or I'll go to yours. Is Ruth meeting you?"

"No. You can take me home and we'll talk about it on the way. I gather you heard from the Fidelity?"

"Yes. It's all set. I'll tell you about it later," said Mike. "Whose deal?"

"The blue cards, it's your deal," said George Adams.

"Sure you don't want to play, Lawrence?" said Harold Liggett.

"No, I want to read the paper," said Lawrence Candler. "But thanks."

It had been a mistake to avoid the club car. Among his friends, in the familiar atmosphere, he immediately got a feeling of security that would soon vanish, but that was good to have even for a few minutes. He realized now that his memory for names had returned to him simultaneously with his decision to go forward to the club car. The decision released him, temporarily, from terror and removed the memory block. He loved these men. George Adams, loud and profane, was the gentlest man of them all, but you had to see him with his semi-paralyzed daughter to discover that. Harold Liggett, thin almost to emaciation, had been given the Silver Star as a marine lieutenant on Guadalcanal. John Reese was a Phi Beta Kappa at Brown, who was in the advertising business instead of on the archeological expeditions where he belonged. And Mike Post, Lawrence Candler's closest friend, and a man to whom only big things seemed to have happened—big popularity, big unpopularity, big financial successes and losses, a big love affair that ended in a big scandal, a big airplane accident in which thirty-eight men and women were killed and Mike emerged a big hero. These were the men whom Lawrence Candler saw most often; twice or once a day, five days a week, ten months of the year counting vacations. He would miss them—or, more realistically, they would miss him. And he knew they would miss him. This was no time for spurious abnegation, for a rejection of the proven warmth that was in these men. When George Adams heard Lawrence Candler's news he would weep; Harold Liggett would smash something; John Reese would get drunk. In a few minutes now he would know without conjecture what Mike Post would do, because Mike Post was the only man he was going to tell.

John Reese, dummy, looked out the window and at his wristwatch. "Make it fast, gentlemen. Four minutes to finish the hand," he said.

"Okay," said Mike Post. "I can't eat your king of clubs, George. I'll get over there with the spade, those diamonds are good, but I have to give you the club trick."

"Do you want to play it out?" said Harold Liggett. "My partner may not know his king of clubs is good." The others laughed; it was small revenge for George Adams's relentless criticism.

"I make it six-forty apiece," said John Reese. "Anybody want to carry it over till Monday?"

"Unbreakable rule," said Mike Post. "All accounts must be squared on Friday."

"All right, all right," said John Reese. "On the week, you're the big winner, Mike. Then comes Lawrence. Here are the figures. Next week you have to have a new accountant. I'm going to be in Detroit Monday, Tuesday, and Wednesday."

They all stood up, and money changed hands. "Where's your car, Mike?" said Lawrence Candler.

"Across the street at the garage. Left it there for a wash and polish. I trust you don't mind walking that far," said Mike.

"I'll make it," said Lawrence Candler. The train stopped, he said goodnight to the others, and he and Mike left the station platform together.

"We're all set with the Fidelity," said Mike. "Hunter called me this morning, just after I got in. They had their lawyers go through the whole thing all over again, from top to bottom. They found everything in good order."

"I should hope so," said Lawrence Candler. "We've been working on those contracts since last October."

"I got the feeling that if you fellows wanted to lure Fidelity away, you wouldn't have much trouble getting their legal business."

"Well, thanks for the tip, but we're not looking for any new business right now. We have just about all we can handle and do a halfway decent job," said Lawrence Candler. "Also—we're losing one of our senior partners."

"Oh, really? Who?"

"Me," said Lawrence Candler. "I'll tell you about it in the car."

Mike looked at him. "I knew there was something on your mind. I didn't say anything to the others, but I caught a glimpse of you sitting back in one of the day coaches. There, the boy's bringing my car."

The largest convertible in the Chrysler line jumped to a halt in front of them.

"Testing the brakes, son?" said Mike.

"Huh?" said the young man.

"It's a good thing those brakes work."

"You're always kiddin', always putting me on," said the young man.

Mike Post and Lawrence got in the car. "Gentle irony doesn't work with that type. But if I said what I think he'd put a little hole in the gas tank, or drop a bit of sand in the oil spout."

"Then why say anything?" said Lawrence.

"Because I've never learned to keep my mouth shut."

"You kept your mouth shut about seeing me in the day coach," said Lawrence.

"That was different," said Mike. "I can keep quiet when some-one else is involved."

"Yes, I know you can," said Lawrence. "Let's go to your house and have a drink."

"Fine. We won't be disturbed there. Madge won't be home much before eight. She's at some cocktail party."

"Ruth's at the same party, but I'd rather talk at your house," said Lawrence.

"Start spilling whenever you feel like it," said Mike.

"Well, the hard news—hard in more ways than one—will only take one sentence," said Lawrence. "I have about six months to live. Maybe seven. Maybe eight."

"Christ. I'm sorry," said Mike. "It's foolish to ask this, but I have to ask it. *You're sure?*"

"I have cancer of the pancreas. You know Sidney Devlin."

"Sure. He operated on one of my sisters. Is he your doctor?"

"No, but he was called in, and I've known him since we were in college. He was a fraternity brother of mine, back in the days when we took those things a little more seriously than they do now. I made him tell me the truth, more as a friend than as a doctor. I told him that I had to have the truth now, because depending on what he told me, I was about to make certain financial commitments. Tying up money in a way that would be all right if I could count on five more years, but would be very awkward for Ruth and the children if I was going to be around less than that."

"Yes, I think I know what you're talking about. The thing George is so sold on."

"That's the one," said Lawrence. "I've never said yes or no to George, and he won't have any trouble raising the money without my share. He spoke to you about it, too."

"Oh, yes. But I like faster action with my money. The thing can't miss if you can afford to be patient, but it'd be at least five years and maybe more before you begin getting anything back. I understand your position perfectly. You have your income from your law business, but I suppose that stops when you die. In other words, they don't keep on giving Ruth your full share?"

"They certainly don't. And they shouldn't. We're not set up that way."

"I didn't think so. Knowing nothing about law firms, but just as a guess," said Mike. "And that's how you wormed it out of Sidney Devlin? Some doctors wouldn't be so candid."

"Well, with cancer of the pancreas, as soon as I knew that, the rest was more or less a matter of how long."

They were at Mike's house. They left the car in the driveway and went to Mike's study. "I'm going to have a drink," said Mike. "What about you?"

"No, I had a big one before I caught the train."

"I suppose you shouldn't, although I wouldn't tell you not to," said Mike. He poured a large whiskey on the rocks and sat down. He had a couple of swallows of the drink. "What is there I can do, Lawrence? You have a very orderly mind, so you must know how I could be useful."

"Well, of course you're being very useful now," said Lawrence. "I haven't told anyone at the office, or anywhere else."

"When did you find out?"

"Today. I spent most of the afternoon with Sid. Well, actually I was only with him a little over an hour. Then I went back to my office and held myself incommunicado. It wasn't difficult. I sat at my desk and an hour passed, but when I looked at my clock it was only ten minutes. Then ten minutes later I looked again and an hour had passed. That was how I spent the afternoon."

"Are you in pain?"

"Some, but I've gotten more or less used to it. That comes later. Which leads me to one of the things I wanted to discuss with you."

"Good," said Mike.

"When shall I tell Ruth?"

"I knew that was coming," said Mike. "I knew it, and God

damn it, I'm not ready for it. As far as making up your mind for you, Lawrence, I'll never be ready for it, and you don't expect me to be. What you want to do is just talk it out with me, right?"

"Yes, but with complete frankness," said Lawrence. "You see, Mike, I have a theory that when you know with the certainty that I have that you're going to die, you ought not to put it off too long."

"You mean suicide?"

"Yes, but let's don't get into suicide for the moment. I watched my father die, or rather I watched my mother watching my father die. I could have been watching myself, too. We knew he wasn't going to last long. He had Bright's disease, as they called it then, and he was in the final stages of it. But he hung on and hung on. He'd have a bad night, then a good night, and that lasted for weeks. I was just out of college, living in Waterbury and getting ready to go to law school. But as I say, my father hung on, and I began to notice what it was doing to my mother. I wasn't bright enough or possibly honest enough to notice what it was doing to me, but as the days went by and he stayed alive, my mother got tired of him. That's putting it very coldly, but I think it's an accurate statement of what was happening to her without her knowing it. Almost but not quite saying, 'Good God, if you're going to die, die.' "

"And she didn't want to see him suffer," said Mike.

"That's what she told herself, and that's what she always believed. But I don't believe that. She simply exhausted her emotional resources—or he did, by hanging on. And now I'll tell you something else. When my mother was dying, about seven or eight years ago, *she* hung on. She had heart trouble and she was condemned. There was no chance that she would ever come downstairs again. And that was when I began to understand what she'd felt about my father. Because I was secretly saying, 'Mother, if you're going to die, die.' "

"Oh, I understand that, Lawrence. Someone that's been active, and reasonably healthy, we can't bear to see them any other way. It isn't anything to be ashamed of, unless you're going to profit by the person's death."

"Most of us do profit financially by a parent's death, or by the death of a husband or wife. Ruth will profit by mine, at least to the extent that she'll have more than she has now, and be able to spend it as she pleases. However that's a matter of almost no interest to me since I had my talk with Sid Devlin. On the contrary, I care so little about money for myself that all I want is a few dimes for phone calls and newspapers."

Mike smiled. "Rather gruesome joke, but you *have* changed."

"I have. If we didn't have to use money—dimes and quarters —I wouldn't touch it again. I'm practically light-headed about it. But that leads me to another problem. You know, I'm not a normal human being any more. I'm not one of *you*. I have different standards now, different from what I started the day with. And yet I'm a creature of habit and very conventional habits at that, as you well know. I would like to go around giving away money, but for instance if I had obeyed the impulse to empty my pockets for that nasty kid that brought you your car, I would have infuriated you and I wouldn't like to do that. In my present state of mind, as a lawyer I could have myself certified, declared incompetent and have a guardian appointed. I wonder how many people who saw me on the train would believe that they were looking at a totally irresponsible man. Do you believe it?"

"I believe that you believe it, momentarily. That you're temporarily in a state of shock. But that your conventional habits will prevail. That raises a question, though. Which is, if *I* had anything to say about it, would I want you to go the one way, or the other? Back to conventional habits, or on to complete light-headedness?"

"Thanks, Mike. That is understanding."

"Well, don't forget, I've always been somewhat unconventional. Done things more or less my own way."

"Yes, and there was nothing you ever did that I hadn't at some time or other restrained myself from doing. In my heart I thoroughly approved of your affair with Maude. You rather disappointed me when you went back to Madge."

"If you had told me that then—if anyone had said anything the least bit encouraging, I never would have gone back to Madge. But now I'm glad I did. I wouldn't want to have Maude around when I get *my* bad news, the kind of bad news you got today."

"Why not?"

"Because there wouldn't be any doubt about what she was thinking. Your father never knew that your mother was wishing he'd die—and anyway that's only a theory of yours, Lawrence. You could be wrong about that. But I know that when I get my stroke, or the doctor says I have this or that, I can count on Madge just as much as you can count on Ruth."

"Count on them for what, Mike?"

"Well, for one thing, to *be* there. Maude would run from a thing like that, but Madge won't run, and neither will Ruth. You *could* tell Ruth this afternoon, if you wanted to. I don't say that's the answer to your original question. There may be reasons for not telling her right away, but I feel sure you could tell her and she'd—adjust."

"The only real reason for not telling her right away is that I'd like to give her a few more weeks of not knowing about it. It's not a secret I'll be able to keep very long. I'm going to have to resign from the firm. I'm going to start having more pain. An operation. Et cetera. Ruth has all the time in the world, but I haven't, and I want to give her some of my time, so to speak. When I die, I want you to tell her about this conversation. I want her to know that I made her a present of these few weeks."

"All right," said Mike. "I'll tell her."

"And be sure and tell her that the most important part of the present was in postponing the time when she'd start to wish I would die. I think she'll understand that, even if you don't."

"I can understand it. I just don't happen to believe it," said Mike. He freshened his drink. "What about that other thing? If you seriously contemplate that, you're not going to tell Ruth, I hope."

"I seriously contemplate it. If I decide to do it, no, I won't mention it to Ruth. I'll just make my plans, and then go ahead and do it. It'll be clean and orderly, unmistakably what it's intended to be. No shooting or anything like that. Ruth had a cousin, married to a guy I never met. They lived in Pennsylvania somewhere. But he had the right idea. You close the garage door and turn on the car engine."

"I'm not going to try to talk you out of that, any more than

I'd tell you not to take a drink," said Mike. "By the way, will you change your mind and have a drink?"

"Yes, I believe I will. A weak Scotch and water. On the rocks."

"How weak?"

"Oh, not too weak," said Lawrence. "I don't have to be quite so careful any more. I gave up cigarettes a year ago, but I think I'll start smoking again. Or maybe I won't. Ruth stopped when I did, and if I started again she wouldn't be able to resist them. God, those first two or three weeks were just about the worst period in our entire married life. I'd never want to go through *that* again." He looked at his friend, who was handing him a drink and laughing.

"I'm sorry, Lawrence, but I can't help it," said Mike. "You have no idea how funny that sounds. Maybe I have a twisted sense of humor."

"You have, and thank God for it," said Lawrence.

"As you know, I was in the infantry, and a guy in the infantry develops a peculiar sense of humor. Either that, or he goes animal. Sometimes both. I didn't have much of a sense of humor before I went in the army, but I think I began to develop one soon afterward. There I was, in my late thirties, and back in prep school. Bed checks. Discipline. Being told where I could smoke and couldn't. Having to be at a certain place at a certain time. And trying to study. Just like prep school, except that I had a seat on the Stock Exchange, married twice and actually had a son who *was* in prep school, and in some respects had more freedom than I did. It just struck me so funny, the whole thing. I didn't go around laughing about it all the time, but I couldn't fail to see the irony of it. Then when I went overseas I got a field promotion to captain the second week in combat. Why? Because my captain got his head blown off and I didn't. When we went into action we really went into it. We learned all about war in two days. I honestly didn't know much more about it after two years than I did after two days, but I came to rely on my sense of humor, and I became a pretty good officer. What my sense of humor did for me was to teach me to be fatalistic, not to count on support, or replacements, or the accuracy of our artillery, or supplies, or anything. Even on being killed. A couple of times, in Italy and in Germany, things got so bad that I thought the only thing left was to get killed, and guys that got too animal or had too much of a sense of humor did get killed. The sense-of-humor guys would get careless, and the animal guys got too brave. I probably was somewhere in between. But when I got out of the army I retained this sense of humor, which was part fatalistic and part cruel. I laugh at things I never used to laugh at before the war. And when you just said you'd never want to go through a couple of weeks of giving up smoking, I had to laugh. Here you are, a guy facing death, and you say a thing like that."

"Yes, in the circumstances it was a funny thing to say," said Lawrence.

"I was probably animalized, too, if there is such a word. For a long time after the war I couldn't force myself to feel any real sadness when anyone died, even anyone close to me. Now I do, but not as much as I ought to. At first all I cared about was the competition in business, especially when it involved knocking off another guy in a deal. And women. Till I finally met my match in Maude. She was in competition with every woman in the world, and every man. And most of all she was in competition with me. It took me about four years to fully understand that I was attractive to her because I was as tough as she was, and she kind of gave me a look at myself. And I didn't think I was a bit attractive. That was really why I went back to Madge. She was the opposite of Maude, and the opposite of me. It's only since I've been back with Madge that I've been able to think of myself as as nice a guy as I was before the war. But I'll never be quite as nice a guy. I'm not as helpful to you as I'd like to be. But if there's anything you want me to do, I'll do it."

"I never heard a shot fired in anger," said Lawrence. "They yanked me out of the infantry and put me to work reading contracts. I was in the army for four years, and just before I got out, an old-timer, a warrant officer, told me I didn't even know how to salute. He was right. I still don't know how to salute. I could tell you how much it cost the government to build several big camps, but that's about all. You got something out of the army. I didn't. Not that I was terribly anxious to get the Purple Heart, but if I'd been shipped overseas I might be better able to get through the next six months. For weeks at a time I was commuting, just as I am now, and I used to be embarrassed to wear the uniform. I'd get on the train and see those kids on their way to New London, to the submarine base, carrying their duffle bags and covered with ribbons, and I'd want to give them my seat. But of course a major doesn't give his seat to a j.g. Rank has its privileges."

Mike smiled. "R.H.I.P.," he said. "I'd forgotten that old expression. But I don't know if you'd be any better off if you'd seen action. Dr. Devlin has told you what to expect, and it seems to me you're facing up to it very well. My instinct would be to get drunk and stay drunk. Your instinct is the opposite. You won't even smoke a cigarette for fear that Ruth would start smoking again. Lawrence, while I've been prattling away about the army I've been thinking about you and Ruth."

"It wasn't prattling away, Mike."

"Well, anyway, what I've been thinking—I think you have to tell Ruth, and tell her right away. Don't, in other words, make her a present of those few weeks of silence. Make her a present of those extra weeks of closeness. Later on she's not going to want to think back and remember that when you needed her most, she was going to cocktail parties and playing golf, oblivious of what was happening to you. She has a right to know now, and not be kept in the dark even for a few weeks."

"What made you change your mind? You were inclined to agree with me about giving her those weeks."

"A little, because you'd mentioned suicide. But I don't think you are going to commit suicide. I think you're going to stay alive as long as you can, and if you're going to do that, you want all the help you can get from Ruth. I'm going back again to the army. I had a young guy named Pignelli, from some town outside Chicago. Pig, they used to call him. Before we were shipped overseas he was hopeless. Always out of uniform, buttons undone, hat on crooked, dirty equipment. But once we got overseas—maybe being in Italy had something to do with it—but whatever it was, he became the most reliable soldier I had. We were the best outfit in the whole army. We were this, we were that. He did more for morale than a letter from home. Besides which, he was the perfect combination of sense of humor and animal. I made him a sergeant . . . Well, we got into a situation where the Germans had us completely cut off by mortar fire, pinned us in a kind of a gully, with behind us a hill too steep to climb and on both sides they were giving it to us with their mortars. There wasn't a man in the whole company that didn't know what had to be done, which was get to those mortars. Well, to make a long story short, Pig came to me and said, 'Who's it going to be, Captain? Me and who else?' And I said, 'You, and any two others that will go with you.' He took off some religious medal he had around his neck and said it was for his mother. 'But if I ask you to give it back to me,' he said, 'I want another medal to go with it. A nice Catholic-looking medal, the D.S.C. Don't try to give me no Silver Star.' I regret to say that I put in for a posthumous D.S.C. for him but all they'd give him was the Silver Star. He didn't get close enough to put out the mortars, but the other two with him did. What has this got to do with Ruth?"

"Yes, I know you're not just prattling away," said Lawrence.

"Simply this. That people you count on *want* to be counted on. The Pig knew perfectly well that I was going to have to ask him to volunteer, and while I was figuring out how to say it, he saved me the trouble. The analogy isn't perfect, but it's good enough."

"So I must tell Ruth today?" said Lawrence.

"Tonight," said Mike. "She'll be pleased."

"Pleased?"

"The highest compliment you could ever pay her," said Mike. "That you need her, and need her so much that you had to tell her right away. That you need her every minute."

"Since you put it that way," said Lawrence. He reached for a cigarette, then dropped it back in the box. "This fellow, the Pig Pignelli. He sounds like quite a guy. Do you think you could accidentally, casually, tell Ruth about him?"

"Not casually," said Mike. "As far as I'm concerned, he won the war."

SCHOOL

The father had dressed that morning with the greatest of care, knowing that the son would notice every item of clothing; knowing, too, that the son would make a mental note of everything for unfavorable comment later on. The son would write letters to his mother and to his girl, and he would say: "The Old Man arrived here looking like he was on his way to the Maryland Hunt or something. He was wearing his hound's-tooth jacket that he got from Anderson & Shepherd's in the year One and that green hat with the goat's whiskers in the hatband. Naturally he was also wearing his fruit boots. He would never think of going anywhere in the country without his fruit boots." The father knew all that, knew that the son would look at his clothes with a condescending smile that made him want to slap the son's face. But, ah, he also knew that if he appeared at the school in a plain business suit and black shoes the effect would be even more undesirable. The son would then think that he had somehow intimidated him. "Hey, Pa, what's with the black Peals? No fruit boots? You're all dressed up for a directors' meeting," the boy would say. On this mission there was no useful purpose to be served by giving Bud any advantage whatsoever. It would only take that much longer to slap him down again.

The first stop was a courtesy call on Spike McFadden, who was generally believed to be next in line when the Head retired. Stillman had not written to prepare McFadden for his visit, and he half hoped that McFadden would be teaching one of his classes in Greek and English. Spike did not have Bud in any class this year, but of course he had heard the rumors that he was practically a shoo-in to succeed the Head—if indeed he had not originated some of the rumors. A very smooth politician, Spike McFadden, and had been one all his life. As luck would have it, he was in his office in Rensselaer Hall. He already rated an office, and it was only three doors away from the Head's.

McFadden released his pipe from his teeth, put it down on the desk carefully, and extended his hand to Stillman. "For God's sake," said McFadden. "Hyuh, guy. Why don't you let a fellow know you're coming? Something going on here I don't know about?"

"Hello, Spike," said Stillman. "No, nothing going on. Just a family matter, that is. I wanted to have a talk with Bud, and I didn't want to make a big thing of it. So I took a day off and drove up."

"A day off from what? Backgammon with Chubby? I hear you pay all your dues and house charges with what you take from Chubby. You must have been taking lessons."

"Hell, you know Chubby. He'll take any double. A real pigeon, but he's better off losing a few bucks to me than masterminding the stock market. He says so himself. Says I save him money."

"I'll never understand you rich bastards," said McFadden.

"Don't put me in the same class with Chubby. I never had that kind of dough. And let me remind you, *I* go to *work* every day, five days a week."

"Oh, sure. Sure," said McFadden. "How's Nina?"

"Nina's just great," said Stillman. "At the moment she's trying to decide whether to divorce me in Reno or in New York. That's what I came up here for. I want to give Bud my side of it. Not that I'm going to get anywhere, mind you. But I want the kid to hear my side of it from *me*."

"This is his last year," said McFadden. "I hope this isn't going to throw him for a loss. Of course you know he has no chance of getting into Yale. You know that. Even if you had Chubby's money I doubt if they'd stretch a point for him."

"I don't give a damn about that," said Stillman. "I *do*, but not as much as I would have twenty years ago. He'll be the first in four

generations that didn't get in, but it's not the Yale you and I went
to, and Bud himself couldn't care less."

"I think you're wrong there, Sam. He does care. He cares a
lot. I've talked to him about it. It's been my experience that they
do care, but they have to pretend to their fathers that they don't."

"Isn't *that* a damn shame? I suppose he gives you that stuff
about not being able to communicate. With me, that is. He can
communicate with you, all right, but not with me."

"Don't get yourself all hot and bothered about it, Sam. It's a
situation we run into all the time."

"I'm sure it is," said Stillman. "I don't know a single father
of my age that hasn't heard that word communicate. Did you communicate with your father?"

"Very much so. We didn't call it that, but we were very close,
my father and I."

"He was a minister," said Stillman.

"In a small town in Ohio, then Pennsylvania, then upstate
New York. I couldn't have gone here otherwise. I probably could
have got through Yale all right. As a matter of fact, I did. But I
couldn't have gone to a school like this if my father hadn't been a
clergyman. He and I did everything together. Camping. Canoeing.
He was a great outdoorsman, a real lover of Nature. We never had
any trouble communicating. But of course everything is different
today. We have a boy here now, as a matter of fact on the same
scholarship that I had when I was here. His father is a minister at a
church on Long Island, no better off financially than my father was.
But they both complain about not being able to communicate with
each other. The boy's a real problem. His marks are way down,
and theoretically if he doesn't maintain a 'B' average he's dis-
qualified from the scholarship. However, we're not so insistent on
that any more. If we have to let him go it won't be on a basis of
his low marks, but a question of attitude. Toward his father, toward
the school, toward the whole world."

"In other words, a jerk," said Stillman.

"Well, unfortunately in my racket we're dealing with boys
that are going through their worst jerk period. If we had to give up
on every jerk we'd soon be out of business. It lasts anywhere from

a year to two or three years. Usually by Sixth Form most of the jerk's been worked out of their systems."

"I'm afraid it hasn't in the case of my son and heir."

"No, possibly not. But I guess that goes back to what you just told me about Nina and yourself. I'm sorry to hear that, although not exactly bowled over."

"You'd heard rumors up here?"

"Not rumors. But in talks with Bud I gathered that there was something. In my job you get so you recognize the signs."

"Don't rely on your signs, Spike. The trouble between Bud and I goes back further than my difficulties with Nina."

"If she's thinking of divorcing you in New York State, the only grounds there, even an unsophisticated schoolmaster knows what they are."

"I repeat, though, Bud and I were pretty far apart before he ever came up here. The other thing only began about a year ago."

"I see," said McFadden. "Well, would you mind telling me what you're going to say to Bud? Broadly, that is. I don't have to know the details, but I'd like to have enough information to be ready when the big blowup comes."

"What big blowup?"

"Usually when there's some trouble at home, of this nature, we can more or less anticipate that the boy is going to explode in some way or other. Destructive. A boy will break up all the furniture in his room. Get into fights. Run away."

"I understand there's a lot of that anyway, without any excuse."

"There's always something behind it, if we dig deep enough. If the parents will cooperate we send the boy in to Boston, to a psychiatrist, and sometimes that helps. But this isn't the kind of school where we can have a boy in deep analysis and expect him to keep up with his studies."

"I should hope not."

"Well, oddly enough some of the boys agree with you. Just the threat of a couple of sessions with the school psychiatrist, the man in Boston, that's enough sometimes to straighten a boy out. They hate it just as much as you do."

"I didn't say I hated it. It probably does some good in some cases. But half the time it's just passing the buck. The school is passing the buck. The individual is passing the buck. And that's a God damn dangerous habit for a boy to get into in prep school."

"Yes, it is."

"And a lot of parents pass the buck when their kids start acting up."

"Indeed they do, and thank you for saving me the trouble of reminding you of that fact."

"Have I passed the buck? I don't think I have. I've always laid it on the line with my kid."

"That can be a form of buck-passing. Parents dump a lot of ugly facts in a sixteen-year-old boy's lap, and expect him to cope with them as an adult would."

"Bud is eighteen, and he has a few ugly facts of life of his own. He's plenty tough. I'm sorry, Spike, but what I'm up here for is going to have to be between Bud and I."

"You know, Sam, you make me shudder when you say 'between Bud and I.' Why can't you say 'between Bud and me'? It was drummed into you when you were here. A thing called the objective case."

"I'm afraid it's a little late to change my bad grammar. And anyway that's not what I came up here for."

"I know," said McFadden. "You want to see Bud." He took a chart out of his desk drawer. "At this precise moment, your son is in Mr. Brissac's custody. French class. A subject in which your son has excelled. At least to the point of the Gentleman's 'C' all the time he's been here."

"That's his mother. Nina spoke French to them from the time they were born, he and his sister."

"I'm sorry about you and Nina, Sam. I was hoping that that was one that would last," said McFadden. He put the chart back in the drawer. "Brissac is in Room 4, in McNaughton. Class will be over in seven more minutes. Then they make a beeline for the Jinx."

"They called it the Jinx when my father was here."

"If you want to take Bud to the Inn for lunch, I suggest you wait for him outside McNaughton. He has to be back for a one-twenty class."

"Whatever the class is, I'm sure he'll be looking forward to it."

"Will you be coming back here? Unfortunately I have a meeting at one-thirty that's going to last most of the afternoon, but if you'd like to take tea with Judith and me, I know she'd be delighted to see you."

"I didn't even ask you how she was. Remember me to her, will you? Your daughter's at Vassar?"

"Both of them. A junior and a freshman."

"Do they communicate all right?" said Stillman.

"You better get going or you'll have a hard time finding Bud," said McFadden.

"I had to get that in. So long, Spike. Keep punching," said Stillman.

The lawns were grizzly, dried mud; the trees not yet coming to life. Everything was always at least a week later up here than in New Jersey. There were even some lingering patches of snow in the corners of McNaughton and behind the tree trunks where the sun had not reached them. But everything was pretty much the same as it had always been. The only exterior sign of life was the school truck, a half-ton Ford from which a man was unloading packages at Bishop. The truck was fairly new, but Stillman recognized the man. He could not remember the man's name, but he was unmistakably the same very tall, very thin Yankee who had been here thirty years ago and was never known to have spoken a word to any student. Pretty soon now he would be retiring, and no doubt the Head—maybe it would be Spike McFadden—would have the man at his refectory table some Friday night. Just before dessert the Head would shake the little silver bell and call for order. He would get to his feet and make a speech about the man's years of devoted service to the school, in token of which the absent trustees wished to present this shotgun, or this fishing rod, or this leather chair. (The silver humidors and cigarette boxes were reserved for retiring members of the teaching and administrative staff.) The man would get up and thank the Head, make some attempt at humor with a reference to the Jinx, which would be over-appreciated by the teachers and by the boys of the First, Second, and Lower Middle forms. The man would be momentarily stunned by his small success as a humorist, and he would have to be rescued by the Head, who would ask for a long cheer for the man. That done, the man would sit down and return to oblivion at half pay for the rest of his days.

Outside the entrance to McNaughton, in the noonday glare, Stillman could hear the simultaneous shufflings of chairs on the classroom floors and the piercing signal of the electric bell. There was a lump in his gut. The first boys out of the building were on the run, the next wave were walking fast, and then came the others. Stillman saw Bud before Bud, coming out into the glare, could see him. He was in earnest conversation with another boy. The other boy was Morton Fuller's son, from St. Louis. Unfortunate. It meant that Stillman would have to have some polite conversation with young Fuller so that he could report to Morton when he saw him two weeks hence.

"Hey, Bud," said Stillman.

"Huh?" The boy was exaggerating his surprise. "Pa? Say, hey. What are you doing up here? Fuller, you know my father? Pa, this is John Fuller. I believe you know his father."

"Hello, John. Yes, I'm seeing your father on the twenty-second. Have you any message for him?"

"No sir, I don't guess so," said Fuller. "Well, nice to've seen you, Mr. Stillman."

"I'll tell your father you were looking well."

The boy went away.

"Wish you hadn't said that, Pa. He's sensitive."

"About what?" said Stillman.

"On his chin, where he's all broken out. He'll think you were being sarcastic."

"Oh, nuts," said Stillman. "We're having lunch at the Inn. Do you want to go to your room for anything first? I understand you have to be in class at one-twenty."

"Well, I'll either have to go there now and get my books for afternoon classes, or else how long is this going to take?"

"How long is this going to *take?* I'm not going to cut your leg off," said the father. He looked at his wristwatch.

"That's good. I'll need it tomorrow. We're playing Belmont Hill."

"We should be all through by one o'clock. That ought to give you time to get your books. So what's it to be?"

"How do you mean?"

"Get your books now, or later?"

"I thought that was all decided. We'll have lunch first," said Bud. "Do we walk? You drove up, didn't you?"

"Would you like to drive to the Inn?"

"I'm not supposed to drive a car within five miles of school."

"Oh, all right, then I'll drive. I don't feel like walking. I got up at six o'clock this morning, and it takes it out of you, this drive. Not to mention the fact that I have to go back again this afternoon. You said you were playing Belmont Hill. What in?"

"Baseball."

"I thought you weren't going out for baseball this year. That's what you told me at Christmas."

"I know. But about the only damn thing I've been able to do at this place is get letters in baseball. I have two, so I decided to make it three."

"There's the car."

"I see it, yeah. Surrounded by my cohorts. God, you'd think they never saw a Bentley before. How's Uncle Chubby? I hear he's going to give the school a new gym."

"He's offered to, but they'd rather have the money and use it for something else."

"God, how stupid can they get? Typical of this place. They'll finally end up getting nothing."

"Very smart of you. I think you may be right."

"Not that I would have got anything out of a new gym. I'll be God knows where by the time one would get built. But it's just so typical of this place." They had reached the car. "All right, you guys. Get your filthy grubby hands off my car. Go on, Eckstrom, get lost. Williams, didn't you ever see a Bentley before?"

"Hey, Stillman?" said a boy.

"What?" said Bud.

The boy made the rudest possible noise.

"The same to you," said Bud.

Another boy approached them. "Hello, Mr. Stillman. I'm Tony Lucas. I visited your house last summer. You knew my mother. Was Marjorie Hartman, from Philadelphia."

"Oh, sure. I remember you, too. Didn't you have your arm in a sling?"

"That's right, sir. I had a broken wrist."

"All recovered now?"

"Yes sir. Well, just wanted to say hullo. Hyuh, Bud."

"Hello," said Bud. "All ready, Pa?"

"Remember me to your mother, Tony."

"Oh, well she died, you know," said Lucas.

"I'm sorry to hear that," said Stillman.

"Two years ago, don't you remember, we talked about her?"

"That's right, we did. I do remember, of course. Well, are you ready, Bud?"

They got in the car, and a silent, admiring group of boys watched them leave.

"Why don't you like Lucas? He seemed like a darn nice boy."

"Oh, let's not go into that."

"Well, *let's* go into it," said Stillman. "Why do you dislike a boy that you had to the house last summer? Didn't you like him then?"

"No. I never liked him. I didn't really invite him to our house. He practically invited himself. He was determined to meet you and see what kind of place we lived in. Ever since I've been here he's been asking me all about you. I guess his mother must have talked about you. He isn't my half-brother by any chance, is he?"

"No, he is not your half-brother."

"Thank God for that, anyway. There's a guy in my class that does have a half-brother in school. Illegitimate."

"Come off it. No matter what you think of the place, I assure you there are no illegitimate boys accepted."

"I don't mean that kind of illegitimate. These are two boys that have the same father. The one boy's father isn't his real father. In other words, Jack Mountley's father is also Charley Rensinger's father."

"That's an old, old story, Bud, and I never believed it. You come up with some very tired gossip, I must say. The fact of the matter is that Mr. and Mrs. Rensinger are still married, and if you knew the first thing about Stanley Rensinger you'd know he wouldn't have stayed married if there'd been any truth whatsoever to that story."

"Mrs. Rensinger has the money."

"That's what I mean about your not knowing Stanley Rensinger. That wouldn't have made the slightest difference to him."

"Charley Rensinger believes it," said Bud.

"Then *he's* a jerk. He believes it because he wants to, because the Mountleys are more social than the Rensingers."

"Oh, boy, are *you* wrong. Charley's about as un-social as anybody in school. You should see him."

"I don't want to see him. Anybody that would rather have Jack Mountley for a father than Stanley Rensinger."

"I thought Mr. Mountley was supposed to be a friend of yours."

"Mr. Mountley is a rich boor. Not a bore. A boor."

"I know the difference."

"He's getting to be a bore, too. But he was always a boor. Our fault. We let him get away with it for so many years because he was so *God* damn rich, and a good-time Charley, and everybody liked his father. Well, the hell with the Mountleys. We haven't got all day, and I have a lot to talk to you about. I'll be in the diningroom, if you want to wash. Or do you want to order and then wash? It'd save time."

"Can I have a steak?"

"Sure you can have a steak. How do you want it?"

"Medium rare. And a glass of milk. Real milk, not that watery stuff we get."

"All right. I'll see you in the diningroom," said Stillman.

They were the first and quite probably would be the only luncheon guests. The Inn was now a member of a hotel chain. The menu did not identify the Inn separately from the others, and

Stillman presumed that he could go to any of fourteen hotels and the bill of fare would be the same.

"Yes sir?" said the waitress.

"Good morning," said Stillman.

"Good morning," said the waitress, and could have added, "If you insist."

"I'm ordering for two. My son will be along in a minute. He wants a steak, medium rare. And a large glass of milk. Whole milk. Not skimmed. I'll have a club sandwich and coffee."

"On the steak, do you want the regular steak dinner? Number Four? That's the five-fifty, including choice of super-appetizer—"

"What is a super-appetizer?" said Stillman.

"Soup *or* appetizer. *Or.* Like it says. Tomato juice, V-8, soup da djoor. The soup da djoor today is—I'll have to find out. I just came on. Then with the steak goes choice of two vegetables, and the mixed green salad."

"I suggest you bring him a cup of soup and order the steak, and get the rest of his order when you bring the soup."

"You don't want to give me the whole order now?" she said.

"I'd dearly love to, but I don't know what he wants."

"All right. And you just want the club sandwich. If you order the Number Eight you're entitled to appetizer, dessert and beverage."

"Just the sandwich and coffee, please. All white meat, by the way."

"Oh, well that'll be extra."

"The sky's the limit," he said, and for some reason, or no reason, his remark made her laugh. "And now I'll be excused," he said.

"Taking turns, huh?" said the waitress.

"Very well put. What's happened to Mr. Colby? I didn't see him on the way in."

"Retired, I guess. I only been here since January. You mean the Colby that used to be the manager. Yes, I think he retired. Mr. Chickering is the new manager now, but he's not in today."

"Probably visiting the Steinways," said Stillman.

"I don't know. I don't know who his friends are. You *know* Chickering?"

"Through the Masons and the Hamlins. Here's my son. He can complete his order," said Stillman. He got up and went to the men's room, unable to explain to himself the silliness that had come over him, the kind of light-headedness that he had some- times experienced in his skiing days and sometimes when a day at the office had been especially exhausting. It came out today as petulance turned to a good-humored ribbing of the waitress, but he wondered how long the good humor would last.

Bud had finished his soup and was eating heavily buttered saltines. "You ought to see the skinny little pieces of butter they give us," said Bud. "Even when they give us baked potatoes, Wednesday night, the same little slice of butter that isn't enough for a piece of toast."

"Here, have mine. I'm having a club sandwich. I won't need it."

"Thanks," said Bud. "What is it, Pa? My marks?"

"That I came to see you about? No. I think I've exhausted that topic in my letters. *I* have. Not you. You've written me twice since September. No, I didn't come to talk about your marks."

The waitress arrived with a large tray. "I inquired about Mr. Colby," she said. "The chef said he understood Colby got a job at some factory, running the cafeteria. It's some address in North Carolina. Do you want me to get it for you?"

"No thank you."

"Medium rare, the steak. All white meat, the club sandwich. That's thirty-five cents extra, the all-white meat. Homogenized, the milk. The sky's the limit today, hey?" said the waitress.

"Sky's the limit," said Stillman.

"Nothing too good for the younger generation," said the waitress. "I'll get you another pad of butter, young man. They love to eat butter. I can always tell one from the school. *They* don't waste any butter."

"Thank you, Lillian. You're doing fine," said Stillman.

"Saw my name on the pocket, hey? Only I'm not Lillian. I'm wearing Lillian's uniform because mine didn't come from the laundry. My name happens to be Lucille. Starts with an L and has the same number of l's in it. There was some mixup at the laundry. Your friend Colby was very lucky. The new job pays more than what he was getting here, and I guess the weather in North Carolina's an improvement over what we have generally. I'll bring the younger generation an extra pad of butter."

"Never mind, really, thanks," said Bud.

"Whatever you say," she said, and left them.

"Christ, what did you do? Pat her on the behind?" said Bud.

"I don't pat waitresses on the behind. Do you?"

"Well, not that one anyway," said Bud. "If I felt like it I probably would, but not that one."

"The fact that you suspect me of making passes at waitresses, leads me to believe that your opinion of me has changed recently. Has it, and if so, why?"

"Is that what you came to talk about?"

"The general area," said Stillman.

"I thought so. If it wasn't my marks. You mean about you and Mother?"

"Yes. And you. I would like to know why you told your mother that I was having an affair with Mrs. Connor."

"True, isn't it?"

"You answer my question, please. I'm curious to know why a son would want to make trouble between his mother and father. Outsiders passing along gossip, I can understand. The world is full of such people, especially when they see a marriage lasting as long as ours did. Envious people. I dismiss them. There'll always be that kind, there always have been. Read your Shakespeare. But I never knew a son before that did what you did, and it's very important for me to know why."

"I had my reasons," said Bud.

"All right. Let me hear them. That's why I'm here," said Stillman.

"I don't want to talk with my mouth full."

"Since when? All right, finish your steak. How is it? Is it done right?"

"It's a little too rare, but I'll eat it."

"The bacon in this isn't crisp enough, either. I should have told her. Lucille." Stillman sipped some coffee and lit a cigarette. "One of the first shows I ever went to was called *La La Lucille*. I don't remember a damn thing about it. Except one tune. 'Nobody But You.' By George Gershwin."

"That's all I want," said Bud.

"How about dessert? You have your choice of—"

"No thanks. I'm laying off the sweets."

"Do you want some more milk?"

"Nothing," said Bud.

"Then let's get started again," said Stillman. "I could have written you a letter about this, but your record for answering letters isn't very good, except when you want something. Now it's my turn to want something. A straight, honest answer to my previous question. What prompted you to go to your mother with your prep school gossip?"

"I thought she ought to know."

"You did? It never occurred to you to come to me first?"

"You would have denied it, naturally."

"Nevertheless the honorable thing to do would have been to ask me if it was true. You'd never heard any such talk before."

"Maybe not, but that doesn't prove you never played around before. For all I knew, you'd been playing around all your life. This just happened to be the first time I ever heard about it."

"So you promptly went tattling to mummy. Jesus Christ."

"Not promptly. I thought about it. I thought about it a lot."

"And convinced yourself that the righteous thing to do was to add a little fuel to the fire. Well, you did. If there was any chance of your mother and I working something out, you plumbered it. As she said, if our son knows about it and feels so strongly, what's the use? That was the clincher. After that, after you went blabbing to her, all bets were off. But why? What do you get out of it? Is this your way of getting even with me?"

"For what?"

"For times that I've had to punish you. Times I refused you things."

"That's not why I did it."

"Then for Christ's sake tell me why you did it," said Stillman. "I'm glad to hear there's some reason, whatever it is."

"I didn't think you were good enough for her," said Bud.

"I see. When did you come to that conclusion?"

"A long time ago. I never liked the way you treated her."

"Be specific. What did you object to?"

"I knew you were going to ask me that," said Bud.

"And you don't seem to have an answer. Well, we can rule out the usual things. I didn't beat her. I wasn't a lush. I wasn't mean about money. And I didn't go on the make for her friends. Those are the usual complaints, but in this case they didn't apply. Or do you think they did?"

"Not as far as I know, they didn't."

"Well, let's go on to Phase Two. The less obvious. Was I disrespectful to her?"

"Not exactly."

"Not exactly. But sort of?"

"Yes," said Bud.

"How?"

"Well, this woman you're playing around with in New York."

"Now wait a minute, Bud. We were talking about way back. A long time ago, you said. You came to the conclusion that I wasn't good enough for your mother a long time ago. That was years before you had any knowledge of my interest in another woman. How was I disrespectful to your mother a long time ago, that finally resulted in your turning fink, I believe you'd call it?"

"Oh, lay off. You know you weren't respectful to her. I don't have to tell you *how* you weren't. You just weren't. You were always putting her on. You and that waitress. She told me you were a great kidder. That's the same way you used to treat Mother, as if she was some waitress."

"That's your version of it. Why don't you come out with a straightforward answer? Why don't you tell me that you don't like me and haven't since you were about fourteen years old? Why do you kid yourself with this pious nonsense about my disrespectful treatment of your dear mother? My treatment of your mother had nothing to do with it. It was just you and I, Bud. The usual hostility between father and son. The rest is hypocritical nonsense."

The son did not speak.

"I knew this was the way it would be when I started out this morning," said Stillman. "But I had to make the trip, to see if you had anything at all to say for yourself. And you haven't. Well, you're eighteen years old. Not a kid any more. Old enough to make trouble, and you've made it. Your mother is divorcing me. I suppose you knew that."

"Yes."

"The harm's done. Not all by you, but you did your little share. I won't be up for graduation, which shouldn't surprise you. In fact I never expect to see this place again. Not even when Mr. McFadden becomes the Head. As far as that goes, I won't be seeing as much of *you*. You'll be living with your mother, and I guess you'll be going to college somewhere."

"Not New Haven. You knew that."

"I knew that. Then you'll have to do your army. So there's no telling when I'm likely to see you again. However, let's hope something can be salvaged from this trip, from this whole damned thing. As far as you and I are concerned, I don't see much of a future. But maybe you'll learn to keep your trap shut. I know I wouldn't like to go through life knowing I'd helped to break up my parents' marriage."

"Is that all?" said Bud.

"Yes, that's all," said his father.

"Then I think I'd like to go back to my room."

"Got some letters to write, I suppose," said Stillman. He laughed.

"What's so funny about that?"

"Private joke," said Stillman. "Goodbye, and good luck."

"The same to you, sir." The boy left without shaking hands, and the father waved to the waitress.

"May I have the check, please?"

"The boy not coming back?"

"No, not coming back," said Stillman. "Do you suppose I

could have a room for a few hours, to take a nap? I have a long drive ahead."

"As far as I know, there's only three rooms occupied. Tonight there'll be more, but today's very quiet. Even the manager took the day off."

"I know. Mr. Chickering. Is he upright, Mr. Chickering?"

"Oh, *is* he?"

"That's grand," said Stillman. "Lucille, did you ever know that the square of the hypotenuse of a right-angle triangle is equal to the sum of the squares of the other two sides?"

"Oh, sure. Everybody knows that. You better get your nap. You're getting light-headed," she said.

THE STARING GAME

It was not only that it took hours now that it used to take the same number of days to get to the same place. Six or seven hours now, where in the old *Rochambeau* you had a week. Three or four days it used to be by way of the Broadway Limited and the Santa Fe Chief. There was nothing really new about how little time it took to get to France or California. You said that more than twenty years ago, when you could fly across the country, and the men said it during the war, when they were ferrying bombers to England night after night. Lee would come home on leave and she would ask him where he had been, and he would say something like "Now really, old deah, one doesn't awsk that sort of question, does one? I meantosay, awfter all. A slip of the lip may sink a ship." And she would be glad to have him back for a few days, long enough for him to relax, to sleep once around the clock —and then for the tension and discontent to start setting in once again. He would say very little, but he said enough for her to know that he hated what he was doing. The Canadians had women doing the same job, for one thing; and for another, when he got to England and saw the men who would be flying those bombers over Germany they would ask him to deliver messages or presents to their girls and wives back home, and they did not have to be more explicit about what they thought of his job. It didn't matter that you were just as dead if you went in the drink a hundred miles east of Iceland as the man who got it over Hamburg. There was a theory that you lasted not more than six minutes in the water at those temperatures. That was five minutes and fifty-nine seconds

too long, considering that you never fired a shot or had been fired
at . . .

How did she get into that? Oh, yes. How it was during the
war that Lee and the other men got so used to cutting a six-day
voyage down to six hours. How he had done it so often—thirty-
some times—that that part of it, the *brevity* of the trip, was commonplace. And because it was commonplace—but not only because it was commonplace—he had not wanted to talk about it. It
was a phenomenon of time and space that became a part of our
lives without our getting much chance to wonder at it. It was as if
someone came to your door and told you that they had just passed
a law that made it unnecessary to take so long to get somewhere.
It was a brand-new law that you had had nothing to do with, for or
against, and you said all right; and you thought nothing much
about it until you saw a travel ad and you were reminded of the
trip in the *Rochambeau* in the summer of 1927. The *Rochambeau*
going over, the *Paris* coming back.

But there was something else. Oh, yes. It was not only that
you measured travel time in hours now instead of days. There was
something else, and it had to do with time but not travel time. It
had to do with all kinds of time, or one kind: time itself. What was
happening to time? What was happening to her time? There was
still sixty seconds in a minute and twenty-four hours in a day, but
it was whizzing by without her being able to slow it down. The last
ten minutes on a train were still very long in passing; when the
dentist kept her waiting a half an hour, the wait seemed endless;
a few seconds' delay during a telephone call was just as irritating
as it had always been. But time, time, time was going so *fast* and she
had no control over it. She hated it for its speed, and since it was
all speed, she hated time. She hated, hated time. It made her
want to cry. She did not want it to go backward, oh, backward in its
flight and make her a girl again just for tonight. Ridiculous nonsense, that must have been written about a man who wanted to
make love when he was too old to. Some poem her grandfather
used to quote. Always quoting some poem to show what nice
thoughts he had. Forever quoting Longfellow and Wordsworth
and Shelley, to try to make people disbelieve what they believed

about him, which was that he was a hypocritical, lecherous old man. And now she herself was just about the age he had been when she had first begun to hear the stories about him.

Why was she thinking about her grandfather all of a sudden? Oh, yes. Backward, O, backward, turn Time in your flight, and make me a boy again just for tonight. Time. And speaking of which, if she didn't get a wiggle on she would be good and late for Mary Barrow's luncheon. Get a wiggle on. Would any of the Jet Set know what she was talking about if she told them to get a wiggle on? No. They would thing it had something to do with the Twist. That awful Twist. The Mashed Potato. The Slop. The Twist. The Mashed Potato. The Slop. When she was a girl she laughed at her elders who talked about the Bunny Hug and the Turkey Trot, and now she was scornful of the Twist and the Slop. But think of actually calling a dance the Slop. The Bunny Hug was probably some awkwardly innocent thing, like the Camel Walk, which she *could* remember. Or the Toddle. She could remember that very well. "Stumbling." You did the Toddle to that tune. Boys were always coming down heavy on the first note and the first word of "Stumbling," and getting out of the rhythm. It took a good dancer to maintain his beat and still emphasize that first note and that first word. Lee could do it. Like so many other big boys—and big girls—he was light on his feet. Or was then, when he was at Mercersburg. An excellent dancer, and had a surprisingly sweet singing voice. Dear one—the world—is wai-ting for the sun-rise. The thrush—on high. He would get so serious while he was singing. There was a secret sweetness about him when he sang, a secret between him and singing and not between him and anyone else. There were some boys who performed when they sang, who would use their singing to make themselves popular. But Lee had never done that. He had never sung to anyone, not even to her when they were creating something new called love. Just singing was enough for Lee; it did not have to have anything to do with performing or wooing. And Lee did not know how different he was when he sang. She had never told him, no one had ever told him. You could not say to a boy, "You are transfigured when you sing." Transfigured was a word she had never used in conversation and never used at all except in one song. Glory, glory, glory, glorious. One keg of beer between the four of us. Thank the Lord there is no more of us. And then someone would start, "I'll sing you a song of college days, and tell you where to go. Johns Hopkins for your knowledge, Cornell to learn to row. To Harvard for your dainty dudes. Old Eli for your men. To Bryn Mawr for your pretty girls, and for hard luck go to Penn." Why Penn for hard luck? Well, why Bryn Mawr for pretty girls? Mary Barrow was a Bryn Mawr girl and she had been an *attractive* one, but *pretty?* Not unless you called Katharine Hepburn pretty.

Mary Barrow opened the door. "Good morning, Madame Seltzer, and how are *you* today?"

"A little late, I'm afraid. I'm sorry."

"It doesn't make the slightest difference, Kitty," said Mary Barrow. "It's just you and me. Margaret ratted out on me, and took Ann with her. At the very last minute they got tickets for some play that they'd been trying to get tickets for. A cancellation, I guess. So there'll be just the two of us, and no bridge unless we can scare up two others."

"No bridge? What do you mean, bringing me all the way out here under false pretenses?" said Kitty Seltzer.

"I know, isn't it awful? We'll just have to sit and talk," said Mary Barrow.

"Instead of sit and listen while Margaret tells us how we should have played the last hand. Fond as I am of Margaret, I can do without her at the bridge table."

"She *isn't* all that good," said Mary Barrow.

"She could be Goren himself and it'd be no excuse for those volunteer lessons. I was playing bridge when Margaret was still playing pinochle."

"So was I, but let's face it, when Margaret puts her mind to a thing—is that new?"

"The stole? It isn't new, but it's new for me. Lee's aunt. We went visiting her last Sunday, our annual pilgrimage. She said I could have it but not to expect a birthday present. Considering the type thing she usually sends me for my birthday. Last year it was an umbrella. If it cost her fifteen dollars they must have seen her coming. But this is real sable. I wouldn't have worn it just for you. I thought Margaret was going to be here and she'd know real sable when she saw it, not like you, you dumb thing."

"How would I know real sable when I saw it? I haven't got any rich aunts."

"Well thank God Lee has Aunt Toddy. I shouldn't say that, of course, but it's awfully nice to know that your husband has a rich aunt with nobody else to leave it all to. I must take you there sometime."

"What's the name of the place?"

"Seaversville, what else?" said Kitty Seltzer.

"I *did* know that."

"It's in Lehigh County, to the north of Allentown but not on any main road. It's a real farm. That is, it has barns and animals and tractors. That's for tax purposes. Old Judge Seaver used to own trotting horses, and when he died Aunt Toddy got rid of them, but her lawyer advised her to keep up the farm."

"Kind of lonely for an elderly lady."

"Lonely? Maybe during the week, but every Sunday she has callers. When you have all that money, you can entertain, and she has six to eight people for Sunday dinner all year long. Not to mention all those good Lutherans that were disappointed when the judge left everything to her. Did you ever stop to think of how many Lutheran colleges there are, and orphanages?"

"Why should I? I'm an Episcolopian."

"Well, there are a lot of them, I promise you. And as Lee says, they're out there feeling Aunt Toddy's pulse every Sunday. They come from as far away as St. Louis, Missouri. I told Lee, I said we ought to be feeling her pulse a little more often or some seminary is going to rook us out of our share. 'What do you consider our share?' he said, and I said about ninety-five percent. Let's not be greedy, I said."

They were at the luncheon table. "Why particularly would I be interested in visiting the old girl?" said Mary Barrow.

"Oh, because she's a character, and you like characters. And the place itself. You have some Stiegel, for decoration, but she has hundreds of pieces. She keeps her teeth in a Stiegel tumbler, and she has another set that she serves drinks-on-the-rocks in."

"Another set of teeth?"

"No, you dumb thing," said Kitty Seltzer. "Set of Stiegel glasses."

"Does she drink?"

"Oh, she drinks. She has her two ounces before every meal. The doctor told her it would be good for her, so I guess he'll be mentioned in the will."

"Rooking you out of some of your share," said Mary Barrow. "By the way, I never offered you anything. Would you like some sherry with your soup?"

"It's too late now, but I'll remember it when you come to my house the next time."

"No, really, Kitty. I'm terribly sorry. I just never thought of it."

"I notice a lot of my friends never think of it when I go to their houses."

"Quite by accident, I'm sure," said Mary Barrow.

"Oh, sure."

"But you can have something if you want it. I'm offering it to you now, so don't be silly."

"Listen, I know Lee told you not to encourage me to drink. I could even tell you when he told you. He told everybody at the same time. A year ago February."

"Well, yes. I didn't know he told anyone else. I thought it was just me he told."

"No, he told Margaret and Ann and two or three others. Gwen Bader. That was the only one I really minded. Gwen Bader. She's not even a friend of mine. That hurt, telling Gwen Bader to go easy on the drinks when I went to her house. Why did he have to say anything to her? He should of known she'd go right to Henry."

"Henry Bader isn't the kind of man that that would have made any difference to."

"Maybe it didn't make any difference to Henry, but it made a lot of difference to me. You remember Henry and I."

"Yes, of course I do."

"Well, would you want the first person that you were ever in love with to go around thinking how lucky he was he didn't marry you?"

"But you were never in love with Henry. Not really. You told me that yourself. You could have married Henry, but you married Lee instead."

"But Henry was in love with me. And he stayed in love with me long after I married Lee."

"In a way, I guess he did," said Mary Barrow.

"In a way? He didn't get married till he was well in his thirties. *Well* in. Closer to forty. And then he picked a girl from out of town."

"No he didn't," said Mary Barrow.

"You're crazy. Gwen came from Phoenixville. Born and raised there. If that's not out of town I don't know what is. And she was close to forty when he married her. A widow with two children. You know, Mary, sometimes I think all this reading books and stuff you do, you don't pay enough attention to what's going on around you. You play golf. I grant you that. So I can't accuse you of sitting inside all day and reading one book after another."

"That's the impression I give, though, isn't it?"

"Well—that, and playing golf."

"But it could be a wrong impression. Like the one that you sat home and drank too much."

"That was a dirty mean thing to say," said Kitty. "You didn't have to say a thing like that. I did drink too much and I admit it, but I've always been a good wife to Lee and I raised two children to manhood and womanhood. I think that remark was entirely uncalled for. Really I do, Mary. I got tight, and I did some things that I wasn't exactly proud of. But I never hurt anybody."

"Well, now, damn it. You did."

"Who, for instance? Who did I ever hurt? Name one person. Just name one."

"I'd have no trouble naming three, and then I could add two more. And then two more."

"You think I hurt Lee? Well, ask him. I made a good home

for him. Careful of money. And if it's any of your business, I've never been unfaithful to him. Never."

"You've been unfaithful to him for thirty years, or however long you've been married to him."

"That's a God damn stupid lie, and why it's stupid is because you know it's a lie. The passes that were made at me, and there isn't a man living or dead that can say he ever got to first base. And you *know* it, Mary Barrow. If there's somebody that circulated the rumor that he ever slept with me, I'll meet him face to face and call him every kind of a liar I can think of. Face to face, and with I don't care how many people present. Who was I supposed to be unfaithful with, may I ask?"

"Henry Bader."

"Oh, come off it. I was a virgin when I married Lee. I have two people to prove that. Well, one of them is dead. Doctor Fink. But Lee could prove it. And I never even kissed Henry Bader after I got engaged to Lee. You really ought to have your head examined, Mary Barrow. Sitting here in this crummy old house and inventing stories about your friends. I'd like to call Henry right this minute and straighten you out on this whole thing, because Henry would never say a thing like that. Henry would be the *first* to tell you he never even kissed me, all the years Lee and I were married. What have you got against Henry that you want to start a rumor like that? Never mind, don't answer." She put down her napkin and rose. "I'm leaving. I'm beginning to think you just got me here to torture me."

"Maybe I did. I'm not at all certain that I didn't," said Mary Barrow.

"I think you ought to have your head examined. They talk about *me* being sick. All I ever did was drink too much. What about a person that deliberately invites one of their oldest friends to lunch and starts accusing her of a thing like that? This is the end of our friendship, Mary Barrow, you can rest assured. What wonders me is why you pretended as if you were a friend of mine all this time."

"If you're going to go, go. Don't just stand there."

"I don't feel well," said Kitty. "No, I don't want any help. Stay away from me. But I have to sit down a minute. Just leave me alone for a minute. Couldn't drive the car."

"All right. Go sit in the front room. Do you want an aspirin?"

"No," said Kitty. She walked slowly to the front room and sat in the first chair she saw. Even to get that far required all her strength, and the moment she was securely in the chair she felt a slight dizziness that turned immediately to sleep.

When she awoke she knew where she was but not how long she had been there. Mary Barrow was leaning against the far wall, her arms folded low beneath her bosom. Kitty started to get up, and discovered that she had no shoes on.

"Now will you take an aspirin? I have one here," said Mary Barrow.

"How long have I been here?"

"About a half an hour, I guess. Time enough for me to do the dishes and put things away. What happened? Did you pass out, or just take a nap?"

"Where are my shoes?"

"Under your chair," said Kitty. "Do you want me to get you a taxi? I don't think you should drive your car."

"When did you come in?"

"Five minutes ago. I heard you snoring."

"Too bad I didn't have a heart attack."

"I knew you weren't having a heart attack. I've seen people with heart attacks. My mother died in this room with one. What do you want to do now, Kitty?"

"Put my shoes on and go home."

"I don't think that's very sensible. You haven't got diabetes, have you?"

"No. You know that."

"I don't know everything about you, and people develop diabetes at our age."

"No, you don't know everything about me, that's true. You just think you do."

"We won't go into that. Just tell me what you want to do, but I don't think you should drive your car."

"What do you care what happens to me?"

"Frankly, I don't. But there are other people on the road besides you. How would it be if I called Lee? He can come and get you. He can take a taxi out here and drive you home. That's probably the best way. What's his office number?"

"He's in Norristown, in court all day. Why don't you call my lover, Henry Bader?"

"Your lover!"

"That's what *you* said."

"No I didn't. I know better. If you weren't such a stupid, self-centered pig you would have listened more carefully. I said you were unfaithful with him, but you didn't let me finish. What I wanted to say was that it was all in your mind. You slept with Lee, but you held on to Henry and you wouldn't let him go and you wouldn't let him go."

"Oh, now I begin to see. *You* were in love with Henry."

"You're beginning to catch on. Yes, of course I was in love with Henry."

"Then why didn't you marry him?"

"And have you calling up at all hours of the day and night because you had to talk to him?"

"Me call him at all hours? Is that the story he gave you? You're not as intelligent as I gave you credit for, if you believed that. Ask him about the time during the war, when he called me up at two o'clock in the morning and Lee answered the phone."

"Ridiculous."

"Ridiculous? All right, have Henry come here, right now, and watch his face when I tell that story. Just watch his face. Do you know why, Mary? Because Lee beat him up, and he'll never forget that. Do you want to know all about Henry Bader? Maybe if you get that out of your system you'll be better off. But you can't face the truth. Answer me one question, if you have enough courage."

"I'll match my courage against yours any time."

"All right. When you were in love with Henry, did he mostly call you up at night? Late at night? After midnight?"

"During the war? He had to. I was never here in the daytime."

"Never mind about the war. After the war, when we stopped doing war work. Did he call you a lot at night? The truth, now, Mary. Just that one question."

"I play golf nearly every day, and you know it."

"You're evading the issue. Did he or didn't he mostly call you late at night? Not at six o'clock, when you got home from the club, but eleven, twelve, one or two o'clock in the morning. Even later sometimes. By the way, does he still call you late at night, if Gwen's away?"

"No."

"Why, you're lying to me. It's written all over your face." She reached down and put on her shoes. "You don't have to worry about me any more. I can drive the car."

Mary Barrow took a chair. "Wait a minute," she said.

"What for? You don't want to listen to a selfish pig, that you don't care what happens to them. A *stupid* selfish pig, and you're so bright, with all your books. The graduate of Bryn Mawr College."

"Please wait a minute, Kitty."

"You won't like it. You're going to ask me about Henry, and every word I'll say is the truth. Regardless of him lying about me."

"All right. What is the truth?"

"I don't know where to start. How far back do you want me to go? Kindergarten? Dancing school? Mrs. Woodward's? He was in your class at Mrs. Woodward's, not mine."

"Later. Start with when he was in love with you. What happened on the *Ile de France?*"

"I was never on the *Ile de France*. It was the *Rochambeau*. What did *he* tell you?"

"I want to know what happened, not what he told me," said Mary.

"I and three other girls had a cabin together. It was the first time I ever went to Europe and we were all on the same tour, I guess you'd call it. Some woman that taught school at—God, I forget where. She had sixteen of us or twenty or I don't know. And Henry was the only boy from around here on the boat. His first trip, too, and I sort of took pity on him because he wasn't making friends with anybody. He was in a cabin with three other boys, but he didn't know any of them, and they were drinking and everything and made Henry feel out of it. Well, I was popular and I liked Henry. From my home town and knew him all my life, and he was nice-looking. Oh, this is such a long story, I'll try to make it short. I got a crush on Henry and we used to neck, and then one night we were all at the dance and I went to our cabin to get something. Lipstick or I don't know. And there was Henry in the bunk with one of my roommates. They had all their clothes on, but Henry was trying to rape her. I blamed her at the time, because he told me she invited him down to the cabin. Oh, some excuse. He told one story and she told another. But I believed Henry. Maybe he was telling the truth then. But when we got home that summer, my parents didn't like it when Henry would call up at ten or eleven o'clock at night and I was out on a date with another boy and he'd keep calling till I got home. You remember, I had a lot of dates with boys, but my father wouldn't allow me to get serious with one, although for quite a long time I liked Henry the best. The modern slang for him was a creep, I guess, but I really loved him in a way, because he'd try everything with the other girls but we never even heavy-necked."

"You didn't have an affair with him on the boat?"

"I never had an affair with anybody except Lee. Not what a grownup man and woman mean by an affair. The limit. Did he tell you we had an affair?"

"Yes."

"Yes, he told somebody he'd had an affair with the girl in our cabin, but I know for a fact that he didn't. It doesn't surprise me that Henry thinks he had affairs with girls that he didn't have affairs with."

"Why?"

"You must know better than I do."

"Oh."

"Yes, oh. What's more, Mary, I wouldn't be surprised if he never had an affair with anybody till he did with you. I could ask *you* a very interesting question."

"Don't."

"Yes, I will. I took enough from you today. Did you have an affair with Henry?"

"Of course I did. I'm not ashamed to say I did."

"No, that's not what you're ashamed of, Mary. You're ashamed that you didn't. That you never did. That it was all in your mind, because with Henry that's the way it had to be."

"That's not true. He's married to Gwen."

"I don't know a damn thing about Gwen, and I don't want to know. I don't like her. She had her own good reasons for marrying Henry. But you know and I know that those reasons weren't sex."

They stared at each other. "You want to see how long you can keep it up, Mary? It's going to be much harder for you. I'm stupid, but I'm telling the truth and you're not."

"Childish," said Mary Barrow. "I could always outstare you."

"You could always outstare everybody. But I'll bet you won't this time."

Mary Barrow ran her fingers through her hair and looked up at the ceiling. "I'm not giving up. Just bored."

"Oh, sure," said Kitty. "I'm still looking at you. I haven't even blinked. There, I just blinked."

"I'm sure you must feel much better."

"Oh, I could have lasted all afternoon," said Kitty. She stood up and gazed about the room. "Taking a last look at this crummy old house. It was never any fun to come to, even when we were kids. The Barrows always thought they were better than everybody else. Always thought they were so superior."

"They were, and they still are," said Mary.

THE VICTIM

One night Leonard J. Kanzler was on his way home from work—he was a pharmacist at Smith's drug store and it was his turn to close up on Tuesdays, Thursdays, and Saturdays—and a man stepped out from behind a chestnut tree and blocked his path. "Put up your hands," the man said.

"Put up my hands? What for? You robbing me?" said Kanzler.

"You're damn right I am. Back up against the tree, and don't try anything. This is loaded."

"You won't get much from me. A couple dollars at the most. My watch and chain."

"Come on, Kanzler. The money from the cash register."

"Oh," said Kanzler.

"Yes, oh. Your inside coat pocket. Put it all on the ground and then start walking as soon as I tell you."

"I think I know who you are," said Kanzler.

"You don't, though. So just put the money on the ground, and your diamond ring. You can forget about your watch."

"Yes, I think I know who you are. Are you J.M.?"

"No, I ain't J.M., and quit stalling. You don't know me, but I know you."

"Yes, I guess you do. All right. There's the wallet, and on top of it my ring. That's a Masonic ring, you know. Won't do *you* any good to wear it, because *you're* not a Mason."

"Who said I was gonna wear it?" The man, who had a handkerchief over the lower half of his face, reached down and picked up the wallet and ring.

"Now what do I do?" said Kanzler.

"Wait till I have a look inside of the wallet."

"The money's there. Two hundred and eighty-six dollars. Is that enough to go to jail for? If you're who I think you are, you wouldn't shoot me."

"You better not count on that, mister."

"Mister? I guess you're *not* who I thought you were."

"You wouldn't know me from Adam, bud. So don't take any chances. Now you can start going, but walk slow. If you start running I'll give you a bullet in the back. Just take it easy."

"Now?"

"Now."

"How did you know I—"

"Saturday night, you always take the money out of the cash register, and Smith comes and gets it from you Sunday morning. See, I know."

"As soon as I get home I intend to call the police."

"Sure. And tell them to go looking for J.M."

"No, I don't think you're J.M. any more. I'm glad you're not. He's in enough trouble as it is."

"Get going, Kanzler."

"No, you're not J.M. You're not from around here. You don't pronounce my name right."

"Do I have to root you in the tail to get you started?"

"I'm going," said Kanzler. "It's Con-slur, not Canz-lur."

He walked slowly to his house, which was up the hill in back of the Court House. His wife was in nightgown and bathrobe, her hair in curlers, and she was sitting at the kitchen table with a *Delineator* spread out before her. "Len? Will I put the coffee on?"

"Be with you in a minute."

"You going to the toilet?"

"Making a phone call."

"Who to at this hour of the night?"

"Come and listen," he said. He picked up the receiver. "Get me two-two-oh-jay, please."

"Who's that?" said Leora Kanzler.

"Hello, Police Headquarters? This is Leonard Kanzler speaking. Oh, hello, Jack. You sound like you had a cold. Well, there's a lot of it around. Come in tomorrow and I'll give you something for it. Or no, I won't. I'm off tomorrow. No, every other Sunday. Well, to tell you the truth, I got held up and robbed. Five minutes ago. On the way home. I'm all right, but the store is minus two hundred and eighty-six dollars and I'm minus my diamond ring. Young fellow with a pistol. A revolver. Came out from behind a tree on North Second, the 400-block. You know where that row of trees are. I had the night's receipts in my wallet. We never leave them there over Saturday night. I bring them home for safekeeping and —no, I thought I recognized him at first, but it was somebody else. This fellow was a stranger, an out-of-town fellow. Say about thirty maybe, medium height and build, wore a handkerchief for a mask. No, I'm all right. I wasn't even scared at the time, but now since I'm home I think he would have used the gun."

"Good heavens," said Leora Kanzler.

"I'm home. No, the wife and I usually have a little lunch on Saturdays that I'm not opening up the next morning. If you send anybody tell them not to make any noise, will you, Jack? We don't want to wake up the whole neighborhood. No, they're both away visiting their grandmother in Shamokin. They won't be back till Tuesday."

"Wednesday," said Leora Kanzler.

"Wednesday, my wife says. Okay, Jack. I'll be waiting for them. No, I don't keep a gun in the house. We have one in the store, but I don't even think it's loaded. It's not mine. Right." He replaced the receiver.

"Good heavens. Right here on Second Street? Are you all right? Are you sure?"

"That was Jack Riegler. Sounds asthmatic to me. No, I'm all right. But I wouldn't like to repeat the experience. As long as I was talking to him I wasn't worried, but all the rest of the way home I began thinking if he put a bullet in my back. I could lie there and bleed to death by the time somebody found me."

"Two squares from home."

"Or even less."

"I'll get you a drink of whiskey."

"No, some coffee'll be all right. I don't want any whiskey on my breath when the police come."

"They're coming here? The police coming here?"

"I'd rather they came here than I go there," said Kanzler.

"Yes," she said. "You sure you're all right, Len? I'd die if anything happened to you."

"We're safe and sound. The last place the holdup man wants to be is this neighborhood. I told him I was sending for the police."

"What kind of a man was he? A thug?"

"Well, I guess he is a thug. He had a gun, and he would have used it. A professional criminal, I'd say. Studied our habits at the store. Knew I brought the receipts home Saturday night. Got close enough to me to see my ring. Very little he didn't take in. Probably in and out of the store a half a dozen times, studying every move. One thing, it should teach Harry Smith a lesson. I told Harry three years ago, I said leave the money in the cash register and hang a light over it, an ordinary six-watt bulb, that you can see it from the street. He said that'd be a temptation, an invitation, but what he was thinking was the waste of electricity."

"Instead of the waste of maybe a man's life."

"Well, I did that for the last time."

"I'll say. Don't you ever risk your life for Harry Smith. I'd die if—"

"Gives me a good chance to get some other things off my chest."

"A raise," she said.

"No, I never had to ask him for a raise. That much I'll say for Harry. In another year and a half I'll be getting sixty, and that's as much as any other man in town gets, unless he graduated from P.C.P. But they start higher, the P.C.P. graduates."

"But you have your license, Philadelphia College of Pharmacy or no Philadelphia College of Pharmacy. More doctors depend on you than the college men."

"That's because I'm used to their writing. I have to admit, the college men got training I never got. When it comes to the U.S.P.,

I don't have to take a back seat to anybody, but—uh oh. That'll only be the police." He went to the front door. "Oh, it's Tom Kyler."

"Evening, Len. Understand you had a little trouble."

"Come on in, Tom. You all by yourself?"

"Norm is down waiting in the car. Norm Ziegler."

"You got here quick."

"Well, you know we have the blinker on the pole down at Main and Scandinavia. Soon as we see a certain signal we call headquarters. Jack said you had an armed robbery. You all right?"

"Fine and dandy. Not saying he wouldn't have used his gun on me. At first I didn't think so, but he was a cool customer. Have a cup of coffee with the missus and I. Tell Ziegler."

"Thanks, we just finished a little lunch at the Greek's. But all right, I'll have a cup of coffee while you describe the suspect. Evening, Mizz Kanzler."

"Oh, they have you a detective now, Tom," she said.

"On night duty I don't wear the uniform. It gives you away. Well, Len, tell us all about it. You's on your way home with the night's receipts. That was two-eight-six, Jack said. Then somewheres in the 400-block on North Second, about how far from the corner of Pine would you say?"

"I'll tell you the whole story from beginning to end," said Kanzler.

"First can I use your phone? Have to tell Jack we're here, then you can tell me your story," said Kyler.

"Under the hall light," said Kanzler.

"Tommy Kyler," said his wife. "I had him in seventh grade. More than once I whacked his little behind, I'll tell you."

"Shush," said Kanzler.

Kyler returned from his telephone call and sat stiffly in the kitchen of his seventh-grade teacher. As Kanzler told his story, Kyler would interrupt with pertinent questions, and whenever he did he could not keep from glancing at Leora Kanzler. She would nod and smile approvingly at her old pupil, but Kanzler was irritated. "Tom, you better let me tell it my own way or I'll lose the thread," he said. "Let me tell it through, then you come back with your questions later."

"Tom's an expert at this, Len. Don't tell him how to run his business," said Leora.

"Listen, the two of you act as if I couldn't tell it without your help. I'm the one this happened to, not you or Tom. Let me tell it my own way, while it's fresh in my mind."

"I just want to get a few details before you forget them," said Kyler. "You say the fellow sounded like he didn't come from around here. What do you mean by that? Did he talk southern, or something on that order?"

"Didn't talk southern, didn't talk northern, eastern or western. He didn't talk like a New York salesman, and he didn't talk like an Irishman from up the mountain."

"Was he disguising the way he talked?"

"Now, Tom, what kind of a question is that? Was he disguising. If I knew that I'd have to know what he was disguising, wouldn't I? There was the one thing gave him away, and that was how he pronounced my name. My *last* name, before you go asking me questions about it. He said Canz-lur. Now how does everybody pronounce our name around here? How do you pronounce it?"

"Like everybody else, I guess," said Kyler.

"Say it," said Kanzler. "What's my last name?"

"Con-slur," said Kyler. "Oh, *I* see. Canz-lur. Con-slur. Therefore you figured out he was from out of town." He wrote in his notebook and accompanied the writing with the spoken words: "Out, of, town."

"See how careful he is? Puts everything down. That's why he has to ask you those questions," said Leora Kanzler.

"He puts it down, but it's a lucky thing I noticed it or what would he have to *put* down? I've been doing a little detective work of my own, don't forget."

"How's that, Len?" said Kyler.

"Well, now, you take here's a fellow knows my name and my habits. But doesn't know how to pronounce my name. So he doesn't know me. Personally. All the same, he's been in town long enough to study my habits and find out that Saturday nights I always bring home the receipts."

"You told him all that before," said Leora.

"Will you please, Leora? Please? So therefore this fellow must of been in town a couple or three weeks at least."

"More than likely," said Kyler. "More than likely."

"Well, if I was in your place," said Kanzler. "What I'd do, I'd go around to all the hotels and rooming houses and find out if they had a fellow answered that description. Medium heightth, medium build, and somewhere around thirty years of age. If such a man took a room in the last two or three weeks you could get a complete description from the landlady or the hotel manager. His name. Fingerprints. Everything. He most likely told them he was some kind of a salesman."

"There's a lot of men answers that description," said Kyler.

"Yeah, but there's a lot more that don't. All tall men, all short men, all fat men, all skinny men. All Italians. All colored. All men that were raised here in Gibbsville. All one-legged men. All every kind of man except medium-heightth, medium-built men around thirty years of age. You'll soon narrow it down, just as soon as you find out what hotel or boarding-house he stayed at."

"Uh-huh. That's what they call routine police work," said Kyler.

"Routine common sense, that's what it is," said Kanzler. "But the thing about common sense is that it's so uncommon. If you'd listen to me instead of both of you interrupting, maybe we'd get somewhere."

"Now, now. Now-now-now," said Leora.

"*I* could probably catch this fellow, if he's still in town," said Kanzler.

"Maybe I ought to ask the mayor to have you sworn in, Len. Put you on the force."

"You don't have to get sarcastic, Tom. I meet a lot of people in my business, maybe just as many as you do, and I have to be a student of human nature. You know, people come in the store and they hand me a prescription, all folded up. I look at it and see what it's for and I just say to come back in a half an hour. But that person has just told me things about himself, if his friends knew, or his boss, or sometimes his *wife*—if I ever said a word about that prescription, entire families would be ruined. *Ruined.* And some of the most prominent people in this town, believe you me. Tonight I was thinking when this fellow held me up, first I thought I recognized him, and I said to him, I asked him if he was So-and-So and mentioned two initials. The initials of a certain young fellow that comes in to get prescriptions filled. They cost a lot of money every refill, and he'll be coming back for a long time. That's who I thought was holding me up. But the more I talked to the robber, the more I knew it wasn't the certain party, and I was glad it wasn't, because this party has trouble enough as it is, without robbing people at the point of a gun."

"Who did you have in mind?" said Kyler.

"It wasn't him, so I don't intend to tell you."

"How can you be sure it wasn't him? He was wearing a handkerchief over his face," said Kyler.

"You can ask me till you're blue in the face and I won't tell you. It wasn't him. What you ought to do, Tom Kyler, you better concentrate on the hotels and boarding-houses. This fellow that held me up, he won't be satisfied with any two hundred and eighty-six dollars and my diamond ring. I wouldn't be a bit surprised if he was robbing somebody else right this minute. He has to. He got two hundred and eighty-six dollars and a diamond ring from me, but now you police are looking for him. The question is, where does he strike next?"

Kyler looked at Leora Kanzler. "He's right," he said.

"Do you think he is?" said Leora.

"I know he is. He has it all doped out, and he has the right dope," said Kyler. "Earlier tonight we had a report of an armed robbery at Schlitz's. You know Schlitz's, the grocery store all the way out West Market? They stay open late Saturday night."

"Paul Schlitz's, sure I know them. Didn't I used to live at 1844 West Market?" said Leora. "They were held up too?"

"Not a whole hour before Len was held up. Paul and his wife, they closed up a little after nine. Shades down. A knock on the side door. They wouldn't of opened the front door, but the steady customers know about the side door. Paul went and opened the door and there was a fellow with a handkerchief over his face. A .32 or a .38 revolver in his hand. Pushed Paul out of the way, went right to the counter where him and his wife had the money in little piles. Close to four hundred dollars. Saturday's when a lot of their customers settle up so it may be more. They have to go through their ledgers to make sure."

"Were they injured?" said Leora.

"She fainted, but nobody was hurt. The robber put all the cash in a paper bag and then he took a meat cleaver and hacked the telephone wire. That was when she fainted, when she seen him pick up the cleaver."

"I would too," said Leora.

"Yeah. We didn't get the call on that till around a quarter to ten. Schlitz had to go next door to phone the doctor. I guess she had some kind of a heart attack, so we were late getting the call."

"Was it the same fellow that held me up?"

"Well, it sure sounds like it."

"Funny Jack Riegler didn't mention anything to me."

"Well, I guess he wasn't sure it was the same fellow, and it don't pay to get people excited. But I guess you're right, Len. First the fellow robs Schlitz, out in the West End, then he can be on North Second in five or ten minutes. He has around seven hundred dollars on him, in small bills and silver. He won't be satisfied with under a thousand."

"Exactly the way I doped it out. Small bills. Now where else would you go for small bills on a Saturday night?" said Kanzler.

"The speakeasies. Only there he'd be liable to run up against some opposition. Drunks, full of Dutch courage. Too many people. This fellow is too smart for that."

"Well, all the stores are closed by now," said Kanzler.

"Yeah. Nothing open after eleven o'clock, except the speaks. Where there's any money, that is."

The telephone rang. "I'll bet that's for you," said Kanzler "Jack Riegler."

"All right, I'll answer it," said Kyler. He went to the telephone, and the Kanzlers stood in the hall to listen. "Kanzler's," said Kyler. "Yeah, Jack, it's me. Uh-huh. Yeah? Yeah? For Christ's sake. I'll be a son of a bitch. I didn't know he had it in him. Wuddia want us to do, Norm and I? No, they're all right. Well, maybe shook up a little, but we been talking. Yeah. I think he wants to be a cop. Ha ha ha ha ha. Okay, Jack. We'll get over there right away." He hung up the receiver and turned to the Kanzlers. "Got him. Got your man."

"Arrested him?" said Kanzler.

"No *sir*. Charley Paxton, old Charley, shot him dead as a mackerel. Four shots. I didn't think old Charley could shoot that good, but I was wrong."

"What *happened? Where?*" said Leora.

"Well, remember we were trying to figure out where there'd be cash at this hour of the night?"

"Uh-huh," said Kanzler.

"We forgot the Armory. They have them dances there Saturday night."

"What dances?" said Leora.

"Big dances, every Saturday. Gents seventy-five, ladies a half a dollar. They get good crowds."

"Oh, *public* dances," said Leora. "Yes, I've seen the ads."

"Your stick-up man seen the ads too. I guess. Anyway, he went out there to the Armory, and Ted Haggerty, he runs the dances, he was in the booth where they sell the tickets from. The ticket window was down, and he was getting the money ready to pay the orchestra. Knock on the door, and I guess he thought it was the fellow from the orchestra. He let him in, but it was the fellow with the gun. But this time he wasn't so smart. They always figure it out wrong. He told Haggerty to put the money in the satchel, and that was the last thing he ever said. One, two, three, four. Old Charley Paxton was sitting there in the booth, half asleep most likely. And he just took out his gun and he fired four straight shots and hit the guy with every one of them. Old Charley Paxton, getting ready to be retired. You sure have to hand it to him. Just quietly pulled out his .38 and one, two, three, four. Guy was dead before he hit the floor. Three in the body and one in the head."

"You would have thought the fellow'd know Paxton was there," said Kanzler. "I would have made sure of that."

"Surprises me, too. Only I guess maybe he didn't think old Charley was a cop. Well, he's a cop all right. I'm proud of him."

"For killing somebody? Tom Kyler?" said Leora Kanzler. "I'm ashamed of you."

"That was his duty. You wouldn't like it so much if the same fellow killed Len. I gotta be going."

"As I look at it," said Kanzler. "This young desperado was clever, very smart. He studied me and my habits, and did the same thing with the Schlitzes. Also the Armory. Had it all figured out to the last detail, including Charley Paxton. I don't agree with you that he didn't know Charley was a cop. I'm sure he knew he was a cop. But he probably saw Charley out there, half asleep or half intoxicated. Everybody knows Charley gets intoxicated, Tom. You don't have to cover up for him. Charley only had so much longer to go before they retired him, and he's been celebrating all winter. Was Charley wearing his uniform?"

"No," said Kyler.

"No. Because about two months ago he wasn't exactly suspended from the force, but they furloughed him. Isn't that correct, Tom?"

"Well, what they did, they didn't suspend him because he only has a little while before he's retired. They took him off regular duty and had him on standby. Like tonight, being a Saturday, he was on special duty. Saturday's our busy night, and those dances at the Armory draw a rough crowd, sometimes. All the same we can't spare a man unless it's somebody like Charley, but he was as good a cop as anybody else tonight."

"Because he killed a man?" said Leora. "Is that what he was there for?"

Tom Kyler patted his hip pocket. "I carry this in case I have to use it, Mrs. Kanzler. I'm supposed to protect life and property."

"I never thought I'd hear one of my pupils say they think it's all right to kill a man."

"Be fair, Leora. Be fair," said Kanzler.

"I don't understand you, either. The things *you've* been saying tonight," she said.

"I'll go now," said Kyler.

"Yes, I guess you have to, if you don't want to listen to a family argument, Tom. Goodnight. You know your way out."

"Goodnight, Len. Mrs. Kanzler," said Kyler, leaving.

"A while ago you would have died if anything happened to me, so you said," said Kanzler. "Well, just stop to think that if we didn't have the Tom Kylers and the Charley Paxtons—"

"Oh, I'm familiar with all that. But you, all of a sudden I don't understand you at all. First you put yourself in the same position as a robber and it was uncanny, your mind worked the same as his. Then you turn around and defend a drunken policeman for killing a man."

"Well, maybe I don't understand myself, either. But I was never robbed before. Never had a man point a gun at me and take my wallet and my ring. That's an experience that doesn't happen to me every day."

"I hope it never happens again, if it has this effect on you."

"What did you used to whack his behind for—Tom Kyler?"

"What do you want to know that for?"

"I guess you never thought about it this way, but you used to be a kind of a policeman."

"Go to bed. You and your customers and prescriptions and human nature."

"No, I'm going to stay up awhile. This makes my third cup of coffee. But you don't have to stay up, Leora."

"I don't intend to. Will you be sure and turn all the lights out?"

"Uh-huh. I wonder what his name was."

"Whose name?"

"Oh, the fellow tonight that didn't know how to pronounce my name."

"The sooner you start forgetting about that," she said.

"Shouldn't be hard. I don't have much to remember," said Leonard J. Kanzler, pronounced Con-slur, in Gibbsville, Pa.

WHAT'S THE GOOD
OF KNOWING?

The social evening was at an end and Mr. and Mrs. Young got in their car and went home. Beatrice Young stayed in the car all the way into the garage; she and her husband got out together. He lowered the garage door, and in the driveway he looked up at the sky and said, "If it wasn't the wrong time of year, I'd say we could expect snow."

"Well, we don't get snow in September. Have you got your key?"

"In Wyoming they get snow in September," said Albert Young. "Yes, I've the key. You mean the kitchen door key?"

"What else would I mean?"

"Well, you could mean the garage key, or the front door key."

"Since when did we start locking the garage door? I don't remember it ever being locked."

"I used to lock it during the war, when we had gas rationing," said Albert Young.

He unlocked the kitchen door and they went inside. "Want a bottle of beer?"

"Good heavens, no," she said.

"Good heavens no? Don't make it sound like a crime, Beatrice. You *asked* for beer at the party."

"That doesn't mean I'm going to sit up drinking beer all night, does it? I'm going to bed. Goodnight."

"Sit down, Beatrice. Just sit down and tell me what the hell's the matter with you?"

"All right. I won't sit down, but I don't mind telling you how disgusted I was with you tonight. You, and George and Archie and all the rest of you."

"I knew that was it."

"Did you? Do you have any idea how you sounded, a bunch of older men suddenly talking like prep school boys."

"I guess we did," said Albert Young.

"And believe me, I wasn't the only one that was disgusted. There wasn't a woman there that didn't wish her husband would shut up."

"No, I guess there wasn't."

"Even the ones that haven't always lived here. Edith Morgan, I could see her mentally thanking God her husband never knew Sadie Carr. He probably would have been just as bad as the rest of you. How on earth you ever got started on the subject of Sadie Carr, I'll never know."

"Well, I'll be glad to tell you if you'll listen."

"I don't want to listen," she said.

"Sit down and listen, for Pete's sake. It'll do you good."

"Do me good? Well, I like that."

"It'd do you all good if you'd listen," he said.

"Thanks just the same."

"Sit down, Beatrice. We talked like prep school boys, but you're pouting like an eighth-grader. I'm going to get myself a beer, and you can sit or stand, but I'm going to have this out with you." She sat at the kitchen table, her chin up, her gaze fixed on the wall straight ahead. He opened and poured a bottle of beer, taking his good time about it.

"We were sitting out on the porch," he said. "You women were all upstairs so you didn't hear the beginning of it. I'm not sure whether it was George or Archie or who it was that first brought up Sadie's name, and I don't even know why. But I know the first time I heard her name I laughed, and that's the same reaction the other men had. We all laughed except the men that didn't grow up here. Then they wanted to know what we were laughing for."

"I can imagine what came next," she said.

"And there you're absolutely wrong, because you *can't* imagine. Sam Morgan said who was Sadie Carr, who *was* she? And there wasn't a man there that volunteered the answer. Not a one of us. Finally I spoke up and said she was a girl we all used to know."

"It would have to be you, of course."

"It had to be me because I just happened to be sitting next to Morgan. Morgan pursued the subject. He would. He wanted to know why we all laughed when her name was mentioned and then suddenly shut up about her. What was she? Some kind of a town tart?"

"A very good guess on Sam's part, I must say."

"You can say what you like, but I'll tell you this. There wasn't a man there that wanted to say anything derogatory to Sadie. We all did laugh, that's true, when her name came up. But after the original reaction we all wanted to—we didn't want to say any more about her. I think we were all thinking the same thing. That Sadie never did anybody any harm, that she didn't have a mean bone in her body. I doubt if any of us had even thought about her for years. That's why we laughed at first, because when we were younger we used to make jokes about her. But she's been dead for over thirty years, and maybe we realized as we got older that Sadie was really quite a sweet girl."

"Oh, for God's sake."

"All right. What did *you* know about Sadie? Actually *know?*"

"Well I'm sure I was glad to take your word for it, all of your words, you gay Lotharios. None of us girls knew her to see hardly, but you Don Juans hinted at plenty."

"Mm-hmm. Hinted is right," he said. "Always hinted that more went on than actually did."

"All right. Point-blank. Did you go all the way with her?"

"Yes."

"Did George?"

"I don't know."

"Did Archie?"

"He certainly did. He wanted to marry her. He gave her his fraternity pin and had her up to State for one of the proms."

"Well, he's a sap anyway. But at least two of you in the same crowd had intercourse with her. And what about Mr. Codway that she worked for?"

"All right, maybe he did."

"You realize of course that it's just coming out, about *you* and this quite-sweet little girl, and we've been married thirty-six years. Why were you so protective about *her?*"

"I don't know. I just didn't tell you. I don't know why. Any more than I know why the other fellows there tonight were protective, as you call it. I guess George slept with her, too. I'm not sure he was one of those that laughed tonight. He was at the other end of the porch away from me."

"He probably did. You and he were the ones that disgusted me the most, trying to pretend that she was a kind of a harmless innocent that you all had fun with. Good clean fun. Ha ha ha. Well, now it comes out, and if that's all, I'm going to bed. I'll leave you to your tender memories of Sadie Carr."

He remained in the kitchen but did not finish his beer. He rinsed out the glass and the bottle, and he was in his bed before Beatrice was in hers. He was asleep before she was, and in the morning he was gone before she got out of bed. There was a new engineer at the factory, a young fellow named Robert Stannard who looked promising but in this, his first week, was suffering from shyness. The simplest way to overcome that was to spend a lot of time with him, show him the equipment and let the personal relations take care of themselves. "Now about this boiler," said Albert Young. "This isn't going to be one of your problems. We're getting a new one. Of course the job of installing the new one *is* going to be one of your problems, but at least you know now that you're not going to be saddled with this one."

"It has seen better days, all right," said Stannard.

"Yes it has," said Albert Young. "But it was a good one. I'm going to introduce you to Eddie Thomas, foreman of our steam-fitters. Eddie helped to install the boiler and he's kept it in good shape ever since. I suggest you spend an hour or so with Eddie. It won't be a waste of time. Get Eddie talking about this boiler and that way you'll find out more about Eddie and he about you than any other way I can think of. He's a good man, but he's a Welshman and they can be hard to know. I'll make myself scarce while you two get acquainted."

He took Stannard to lunch at the hotel. "Next week I'd like to make a suggestion, after you and Mrs. Stannard are more or less settled in. It's just a suggestion, but it's worth thinking about. Namely, get into the habit of once in a while—not every day, but once in a while—bring your lunch to the factory. Most of the time you'll eat it alone, because one of the worst things you could do would be to try to be pals with the men. Their lunch hour belongs to them, just as yours and mine belong to us. But an engineer is something like a doctor. He has no hours. And if the men get used to seeing you around like that, they'll separate you from the sales department. Do you see what I mean?"

"I think so, sir."

"You don't have to do the things the men are paid to do, such as crawling inside the boiler, or climbing up on top of the water tower. Actually the men resent that. Our men know their jobs, for the most part, and what they say you can rely on. For instance, you'll find that some of them have a lot of theoretical knowledge— metallurgy, electricity, things like that—that may surprise you. When I came here I had an engineering degree, and even though I'm the third generation to own the factory, and had worked here part of every summer, I made the great mistake of underestimating the practical men's technical knowledge. Luckily my father'd made the same mistake, so he saw to it that I didn't repeat it. He put me in the hands of a man named Jacob Carr, one of our foremen, a man who only got as far as eighth grade in school but came here to learn his trade when he was about fourteen or fifteen. He was apprenticed to old Matthew Logan, a master mechanic that had started out with my grandfather, and Jacob Carr was just as tough on me as I imagine Matthew Logan was on him. It was quite an experience, you know, getting slapped down every once in a while by a man that hadn't finished eighth grade. He'd say things like, 'What is two-eighteen point eight?' "

"That's the boiling point of oxygen," said Stannard.

"Of course, but Jacob Carr—Mr. Carr, I always called him— he was testing me to see how much I learned at State."

"And showing off a little," said Stannard.

"Yes, he was showing off, but doing it for a reason. My father had told him to put me in my place, and he did. Every day for a year I reported to Mr. Carr at seven A.M. And by the way, I had to be shaved. 'I shave before *I* come to work, so you come shaved too,' he said. My, was he strict, and my father backed him up in everything. At the end of that year I was cut down to size, but I knew more about the factory than I would have learned in five years, or ten, if I'd gone right into the office. My second year I was transferred to the accounting office under Henry J. Ingalls, and I had more of a knack for that work than for the manufacturing end, but I missed Mr. Carr. I asked my father to put me back on the floor, but he wouldn't. He finally told me why—oh, five or six years later. He said that Mr. Carr had told him I'd never make a real floor man. I didn't have the real mechanical turn of mind, he said, and he was right. I could follow everything, but I didn't look at a problem and lose myself in it. I was, in other words, an office man. That was before we heard so much about the word executive. I've often thought that Mr. Carr was just as disappointed as I was—or would have been, if my father had told me I didn't measure up. He didn't tell me that until after Mr. Carr died. Was killed, actually."

"In an accident at the factory?"

"Yes," said Albert Young. "Yes, he was."

"How?"

"How? Well, this was before you were born, so I guess it's all right to tell you. From a teetotaler, not even a glass of beer, Mr. Carr suddenly became a heavy drinker. So much so that he began to bring a pint of rotgut to work with him in his lunch-can. My father found out about it and fired him, hoping that would knock some sense into him. And it did for a while. He went on the wagon for a month and came and saw my father, and my father was only too willing to give him his job back. But the reform didn't last. He didn't bring the booze in his lunch-can any more, but he still brought it with him and had it hidden somewhere. One day he'd been hitting it a little more than usual, because some of the men said later that he was obviously drunk. One man told him to go home, before my father caught him in that condition, but Mr. Carr told the man to mind his own business. Then a little while later he went into the generator room, where he had no business to be, and went behind the switchboard and fell against a bus bar. Twenty-two hundred volts. A.C."

"Yes, D.C. might have knocked him away."

"He knew that, Bob. I didn't want to say anything to my father. He was upset enough. But Mr. Carr grabbed hold of that bus bar. It was no accident."

"Sounds to me as though he'd found out he had cancer," said Stannard. "Something like that."

"He'd found out something," said Albert Young.

"Did they call it accidental death?" said Stannard.

"Oh, yes. The insurance company wasn't very happy about that, but the coroner's jury wasn't made up of insurance people, and the insurance company couldn't go against their verdict."

"So naturally the family was taken care of," said Stannard.

"The widow and two daughters. One of them named Sadie. The other one—I think her name was Peggy. Or maybe it was Betty. Doesn't matter."

"Dessert for you gentlemen?" said the waitress. "Mr. Young, we have the first punkin pie you asked for last week."

"Just coffee for me, Mildred, but Mr. Stannard might like some. Bob?"

"Yeah, I'll try the punkin pie."

"You want the whipped cream on it? It comes with or without. In other words, you don't have to have it with," said Mildred.

"Without, then," said Stannard.

Albert Young lit a cigarette. For some unaccountable reason he was disliking this young man—and then he knew it was not this young man he disliked. It was the remembered image of himself that he had succeeded in obliterating for nearly forty years. He wondered if enough time remained to hide himself again. What the damn hell had brought the Carrs back into his life?

He took young Stannard to the factory and left him in the draughtsmen's room; he had no wish to be with anyone so young. In his private office the afternoon dragged on because he knew that at five o'clock he was going to the club in the hope of encountering George Watson, and yet he could not count on seeing George or make an appointment with him. It was going to be enough of a surprise to George to see him at the club at that hour of the day.

He was lucky. George was there, sitting in the bar with Sam Morgan. "Sit down, Bert. Take the load off your feet," said George.

"I had a slight hangover today. Did you fellows?" said Albert Young.

"I told you years ago," said George. "Moderation is no good for anybody. You didn't drink enough last night to bother anybody, except one of your moderation addicts. Have a good stiff snort. Have a boilermaker, for God's sake."

"No. I'll have a bourbon on the rocks."

"All right, but don't say I didn't warn you. Moderation. Moderation."

"It's not that I drank any more than usual last night. But it seemed to hit me."

"I didn't notice anything—except I did notice that you got sort of reminiscent there about Sadie Carr. My God, if you have to go back that far."

"I was talking about Sadie Carr?" said Albert Young.

"You wouldn't stop. Right out of nowhere you started talking about her."

"No," said Sam Morgan. "Bert wasn't the one that brought her name up. It was Archie. Archie said that the young girls nowadays all take some kind of a medicine that keeps them from getting pregnant, and then he said what a godsend it would have been for Sadie Carr. Naturally I didn't know who that was, and I asked Bert. It wasn't Bert that brought her into the conversation."

"Well, maybe not, but he kept talking about her," said George.

"So did you, George," said Sam Morgan.

"Well, I didn't say anything derogatory," said George.

"Far from it," said Sam. "The only derogatory thing was Archie's remark about the godsend if they'd had that medicine then."

"Oh, well I didn't hear that," said George. "If I had, I sure as hell would have lit into Archie. He had no cause to make disparaging remarks about Sadie. Him least of all. Bert, were you ever favored with Sadie's tender ministrations? I don't seem to remember you being on her list."

"If you think a minute, you'll remember, so there's no use my lying about it. Yes."

"By God, you did. I remember now. It was some picnic or something out at the old Park. Didn't you have some fight with some Irish boy? Fellow, his father used to own the marble yard on the East Side. Mc-Something. McCahill. McCahill. The Irish were having a picnic. The Knights of Columbus. And there was a dance. Some big orchestra. Was it Paul Whiteman? I think it was Paul Whiteman, or maybe it was Vincent Lopez. Anyway, she went out with you at intermission, and then when you came back McCahill —no, I'm wrong. That was Archie. I remember now it was Archie, because he had a shiner. But there was something about you and Sadie. I'll think of it."

"Don't wrack your brains. I admitted it," said Albert Young.

"Poon-tang," said George. "A little piece of poon-tang, that was Sadie. All the same, she was a hell of a good kid. I never knew what she wanted out of life. Not money. You wouldn't think of offering her money. Never occurred to me to offer her money. Her father was a—hell, he worked for *your* father, Bert. In fact he was killed in an accident out at your factory."

"Yes he was," said Albert Young. "Electrocuted."

"And Sadie always worked. She had a job there with R. D. Codway when I knew her. Codway was an optician, had a place on South Main. He was a widower or maybe a bachelor. Single, anyway, when he came to town. And what went on between him and Sadie I never knew for sure. But she had to look presentable, and she did. She had style about her. Always very *neat,* wasn't she, Bert? So was her father. They were very clean-looking people. I never knew her mother. But their house was very neat and tidy. I was inside the house several times. Do you remember their house, Bert?"

"I never got inside."

"I never understood about the Carr family. I used to call for

Sadie to take her out. Eight o'clock. Ring the doorbell. Sadie'd let me in, and there wouldn't be a sign of anybody else. And you wouldn't hear anybody moving around. Not a sound. She'd tell me to wait in the front parlor and I'd sit there and all I'd hear was the clock ticking. I don't know whether her father and mother went to bed right after supper or what. But she'd come downstairs with her coat and hat on and out we'd go. Maybe the father and mother were in the kitchen, I don't know. But they stayed out of sight. Strange. Those kind of people, I guess they were anxious to get their daughters married off. Some of them of course were very strict, but some of the mothers gave the girls plenty of leeway, and that must have been the case with Sadie. Didn't seem to make any difference what time I got her home, just as long as it was before daylight. I was the one that caught hell from my family for staying out late. Two, three, four o'clock in the morning."

"Did she finally snag a husband?" said Sam.

"Sadie? No. She died. What was it she died of, Bert?"

"Appendicitis. Peritonitis."

"An abortion, maybe?" said Sam.

"No," said Albert Young. "Malloy was their doctor. He was a big Catholic surgeon around here in those days, and he wouldn't touch that kind of a case. He could always send a woman to another doctor, but he was the one that operated on Sadie. She never came out of the ether."

"And even before that she'd begun to go downhill," said George. "I think her father's death was a great shock to her. She began to lose her looks, and I think it was her father."

"Had a lot to do with it, all right," said Albert Young.

"Well, even today you can't fool around with a ruptured appendix," said Sam.

"No, I guess you can't," said George. "I had mine out when I was sixteen."

"I've never had any trouble with mine," said Sam.

"Now they have them up and walking around the next day," said George.

"Yes, I remember when Beatrice had hers out, she was home

from the hospital in just over a week," said Albert Young. "And that was a good ten years ago."

"They still don't know what the hell it's there for," said George. "What good it does."

"Well, unless you want to take into consideration a lot of Cadillacs and mink coats," said Sam.

"You mean doctors' wives got the mink coats," said George.

"And the doctors got the Cadillacs," said Sam. "Gentlemen, I have to head for home. George. Bert." He rose and departed.

The two friends said nothing for a little while. "I don't know, Bert. We're getting on."

"Yes, we are," said Albert Young. He waited, without knowing what he wanted from George, for he had never known.

"When I get a little stitch in my belly, I know it can't be appendicitis, because I've had that out. But I'd just as soon not know, wouldn't you?"

"I suppose so, George."

"It's going to make damn little difference whether I know or I don't," said George.

"So in other words, what's the good of knowing? I think you're absolutely right, George."

"And if you'll just tap that bell, I'll let you in on the secret of eternal life and connubial bliss and good fellowship and all the rest of it. The magic formula, my friend."

"Right you are," said Albert Young, and tapped the bell.

THE WHOLE
CHERRY PIE

Spider Nicholas commuted between Short Hills and his office in
Radio City. In the summer he went to East Chop. Jack Norgate
lived in Stamford and worked in the financial district. His summer
vacations were spent in Manchester, Vermont. The two men, in
other words, would arrive in New York at about the same time
every working day, put in the same eight and a half hours, leave
the city more or less simultaneously, and never see each other
from one year to the next. There was nothing particularly remarkable about this except to the men themselves, who after
thirty years had not got together until a few weeks ago.

"It just isn't possible that it's been that long, Jack," said Spider.

"I know," said Jack Norgate.

"When was the last time we talked on the phone, do you
remember?"

"I'm not sure. Could it have been when your son was born?"

"It couldn't have been that long ago. Peter is twenty-four."

"I think that's when it was, though," said Jack Norgate. "Yes.
You called me up from some bar. Celebrating. And you wanted
me to join you but I was taking a train to I think it was Chicago.
Probably Chicago. That was when I used to go to Chicago once a
month. Yes, that would be it. In '39."

"And you mean to say that was the last time we actually had
a conversation? What the hell happened to us, Jack?"

"Well, I guess what happens to a lot of people in this rat-race."

"But you and I weren't a lot of people. God, we were Damon
and Pythias. That's what the Yearbook said."

"With striking originality," said Jack Norgate. "Bud Williams wrote that, I guess. Do you ever see Bud? He lives out your way, doesn't he?"

"He did. He cooled about a year ago. Don't you read the obituary columns? Come to think of it, though, a lot of people didn't know about Bud. If you die on a Saturday people don't seem to read the obituaries in the Sunday papers. I don't know why that is, but it's true."

"Maybe that was it. Actually, of course, I was never very great buddies with Bud. He was a wisecracking type that I did my best to stay away from. A gladhander, always promoting Mr. Vance W. Williams. He was one that I made up my mind I was never going to see when we finished college, and I never did. That's not literally true. I did see him, ran into him at the theater, restaurants. But if he didn't see me first I kept out of his way."

"I hope you never saw me anywhere and ducked me," said Spider Nicholas.

"Oh, come on. You know better than that."

"I know, Jack. I'm not being touchy."

"Neither one of us has any right to be touchy. As I see it, we're damn lucky."

"How so?"

"Well, now for instance whenever I think of college I naturally think of my old friend Spider Nicholas. The good times we had together. Do you know something I often remember about you? This may surprise you."

"What's that, Jack?"

"You were the only man I ever knew that bought a whole pie and ate it."

"What do you mean by that?"

"You don't even remember," said Jack Norgate. "But I often think of it as one of the greatest things a man ever did. I remember we were walking down the street one afternoon. Junior year, it was. Suddenly you said, 'I feel like having a pie.' Not a piece of pie, but a pie, meaning a whole pie. So we stopped in at the bakery and you bought a cherry pie. Thirty-five cents. You asked me if I wanted one, and I said no, I might have a piece of yours, but you said no, you were going to have the whole pie for yourself. You'd buy me one, too, but I had to eat my own. You were determined to have a whole one to yourself. And by God you did. You had them cut it into four quarters and we went and sat on a bench while you ate the whole thing."

"Funny I don't remember that at all."

"It was sheer inspiration. It must have gone back to your boyhood days, when we never got enough pie. But I never knew anyone else to act on such an impulse. It only cost you thirty-five cents, but it must have been one of the great satisfactions of your life. I've never forgotten it. To do something you've always wanted to do. You know, I admired you more for that than if you'd earned a varsity letter. Phi Beta Kappa. Anything."

"I don't remember a damn thing about it."

"No, I don't suppose you do. But I do. Just think of getting rid of a frustration so easily, for thirty-five cents. Tell me, do you ever eat pie nowadays?"

"Occasionally. Mince pie at Thanksgiving, Christmas. But as a general rule I don't order it, and we don't have it very often at home. Go in for lighter desserts."

"Well, that's because once in your life you ate a whole cherry pie."

"That's what you remember best about me," said Spider Nicholas.

"Many other things, but that still stands out."

"I wonder what I remember best about you."

"I'd be interested to know," said Jack Norgate.

"There is one thing. It wasn't anything like eating a whole pie. It was something you said. Something you told me that had to do with women. Girls, although we called them women. You were always more successful in that department than I was. I don't say you were more aggressive, but you were certainly more successful. And I remember one time we were driving back from Poughkeepsie. I'd gone there with you on a blind date, and the girl I had a date with wasn't the usual blind date. She was exceptional. Very pretty. Good figure. Her name was Minnie Jordan. She came from Milwaukee, Wisconsin."

"Oh, sure. I remember her very well. She *was* a good-looking girl."

"But I got absolutely nowhere with her. She was polite, friendly, but when I made a pass at her she gave me no time at all. She just wasn't interested, and said so. And yet she seemed to like me. I know she did. Anyway, on the way back to college I told you I'd got nowhere with her, and I told you I couldn't understand why. And you had the answer."

"What was it?"

"It was a piece of wisdom that impressed the hell out of me, and I followed it in later years—with some success, I may say. You said never to forget that if a girl was attractive to me, she must have been attractive to other guys before me. An attractive girl is an attractive girl. She knows she's attractive. She's been told so. And when a guy meets her for the first time and acts as though he'd been the first to discover her, he's practically insulting her."

"Well, that's true, although I don't remember saying it in so many words."

"Well, you said it to me, on the way back from Poughkeepsie one night in our senior year."

"It was such sound advice that I didn't always follow it myself."

"I did, and it changed my life. Ever after that, whenever I met an attractive girl I always made a point of finding out what kind of a guy she was in love with. Your theory was that every attractive girl was in love with somebody besides yourself, actively in love with him or just starting to be, or just breaking off. So you have to treat every attractive girl with that in mind, that there's another guy. None of that 'Where have you been all my life?' As though she'd been waiting for you to come along."

"Yes. Then they think of you as a very perceptive man, very understanding. How did that change your life?"

"Well, I got so God damn understanding that for the first two or three years out of college I was one of the worst chasers in New York. And I married the wrong girl and had one hell of a time shaking loose from her when I finally met the right one."

"Oh, yes. That first marriage of yours. I heard about that

from various people. I guess I may have been a little sore at you because you never introduced me to her."

"That accounted for your not asking me to be an usher when you got married."

"Yes, I suppose it did."

"Well, we've finally got that cleared up," said Spider Nicholas.

"Yes. I'm glad we did."

"So am I. I really am," said Spider Nicholas. He looked at his friend. "What are you thinking?"

"What was I thinking? I'll tell you what I was thinking. I was just thinking that if either one of us were to eat a whole cherry pie today, he'd probably drop dead. Can you imagine eating a whole cherry pie?"

"No, I can't," said Spider Nicholas.

"I wouldn't even want to, would you?"

"No."

"But I *wish* I wanted to. That's the awful thing," said Jack Norgate.

"So do I," said his friend.

"I wish I did want to eat a whole cherry pie," said Jack Norgate.

ZERO

It was so cold that no one was out. At the top of the hill, sitting in his car with the motor running, Dick Pfeister could see all of Main Street to the south, and in more than an hour not a soul had ventured forth on foot. Once in a while an automobile would come along, usually an out-of-town car on its way through. Once in a while it would be a truck, likewise on its way through and carrying five to ten tons of coal. Town people were staying in. The Orpheum had not even bothered to turn on its lights, and Richard Arlen and Carole Lombard, who were probably sitting in the sun in Southern California, or anyway had been doing so a few hours earlier, could not complain if their fans chose to stay home on such a night. The trolley from Gibbsville, due at eight-twenty, was reported two hours ago as stuck halfway up the mountain. The track was clear of snow, but something had gone wrong with the lubricating system and the trolley was just sitting there and the passengers had to wait until they could be transferred to a relief.

According to the information Dick Pfeister got from the traction company office, the trolley came to a halt and then the wheels would not turn. The motorman then had to walk down the track a couple of miles to the nearest emergency telephone. He was a brave and strong man, the motorman, to risk freezing to death. The thermometer outside the traction company office registered eight degrees below zero, and what it must have been like on the mountain was anybody's guess. The motorman was going to try to walk back to his car, which was at least better than sitting down and falling asleep. Meanwhile the passengers in the trolley had light and some heat, and help was on the way. They could have been a lot worse off.

The repair car, followed by the relief, had passed by about an hour ago on their way southward. The relief, with the passengers from the stalled trolley, should be along any minute now. Ordinarily the entire trip from Gibbsville took only fifty minutes, but this was not a night on which schedules were being observed. Tomorrow's papers would carry items giving the temperature in other Pennsylvania towns, like Snowshoe and Clarks Summit, and no doubt it *was* colder in those towns than in Mountain City; but it was cold enough to kill you here, and you died just as dead at Mountain City as at Snowshoe.

Down at the end of town a beam of light appeared, and Dick Pfeister watched it until the source of the beam, the relief car, came into view. He checked his fuel gauge; the tank was a little less than half full. He switched off his motor and got out of the car and went to the street corner where the trolley would stop. He stood in the doorway of Hutchinson's furniture store for protection from the cold wind. It was strange that no one else seemed to be meeting the trolley—and just then two automobiles came from different directions and stopped at the corner, apparently having heard at the last minute that the relief trolley was on its way.

The relief stopped at the corner, and three passengers got out. The first was a middle-aged woman with her arms full of bundles; the second was a man whom Dick Pfeister recognized: John J. Flaherty, the lawyer, who rode to and from the county seat five days a week. Flaherty was being met by his son; the woman by a man whom Dick Pfeister took to be her husband. The third passenger was Eva Novak. She was carrying a black imitation-leather hatbox and a heavy suitcase. She looked around, but Dick Pfeister did not come out of the doorway until the middle-aged woman and Flaherty had been taken away in their automobiles.

"Hey," he called to her.

She saw him, but she did not speak.

He went to her and picked up her luggage. "That's *my* car, across the street," he said.

"Okay," she said. "Where we going?"

"I'll take you to your sister's."

"I didn't have anything to eat. Is it all right if we get a sandwich or something? I didn't eat anything since I left Philly, only a milk shake in Gibbsville."

"Can't you get something at your sister's?" He opened the door of the car and she got in, and he put the luggage in the back.

"I'd sooner get something at the diner. I'll pay for it. I don't want to go to my sister's and the first thing I ask her for a meal. It's eleven o'clock at night, and she won't even be up at this hour."

"I'm not sure the diner's open," said Dick Pfeister.

"He's *always* open. You can see from here. Listen, if you don't want to come in with me, that's all right, but I gotta have a plate of soup or something. The last two hours all I could think of was a Yankee pot roast at Joe's diner."

"All right," said Dick Pfeister.

"You don't have to eat with me, if that's what you object to. You don't even have to let on you know me."

"It isn't that," he said.

"Yes it is. You don't want anybody to see me with you. Well, maybe I feel the same way, but first of all I'm hungry."

"Maybe there won't be anybody there."

"Don't be too sure of that. They're liable to come in. The best thing is you take me there and I go in alone, then you come in a couple minutes later. We don't have to leave together."

"It'll look fishy, you going in there alone on a night like this."

"Listen, Dick, I didn't ask you to meet me at the trolley. That was all your idea."

"What if I got a couple of hamburgers and a container of coffee? Would that satisfy you? I can't go in the diner with you, and that's all there is to it. And you can't go in there by yourself, not on this kind of a night."

"For Christ's sake then, get me a couple hamburgers and some coffee. Just so I get something or I'll faint dead away. Then you'd have to take me to the doctor's. I'm still weak. I only been walking on my two feet since Monday. You have no idea."

They drove to the diner and Dick Pfeister got the hamburgers and coffee. He put them in her lap. "We'll drive out toward your sister's."

"Did he put sugar and cream in the coffee?" she said.

"Both."

"The container's hot. That's good," she said. She took the wax paper off one of the hamburgers and commenced to eat as they headed for the edge of town. She finished the first hamburger before they reached her sister's neighborhood of company houses. "Now I can have some coffee," she said. "It is hot. Do you want some?"

"I'll take a sip," he said.

"There's a quart of it, I don't want it all. You want a bite of hamburger?"

"No thanks," he said.

"So much the better," she said. "I shouldn't eat so fast. It isn't polite, but what do I give a darn about politeness? Do you have a cigarette? We smoked all ours on the trolley. Everybody ran out of cigarettes. I only had enough to last me to Mountain City, then I was gonna get another pack, but I shared mine with a fellow sitting next to me. First we smoked all his, then we smoked all mine. He just come from burying his uncle in Gibbsville."

"What was it like on the trolley? Were you scared?"

"I wasn't. What was there to be scared of? I was worried for the motorman. He walked a couple miles to phone the trolley company, to say we were stuck. If it wasn't for him we'd be there yet. He bundled up warm. Two pairs of gloves, two mufflers around his head. But they had to give him first aid. He passed out as soon as he got back in the trolley. He was in terrible shape, the poor fellow. He was on the trolley I came in on. They were taking him to the doctor's. They said he had frostbite and might lose a couple toes. I don't know. That's what some person said. I know you *can* lose a foot if you get a bad frostbite. It happened to a buddy of my uncle's, worked at the Madeline Colliery. He got drunk and couldn't find his way home, a night like tonight. Stanley Bolitis. You probly noticed him, with the crutch."

"Yes, I know him," said Dick Pfeister. "What about you, Eva?"

"Oh, they told us we shouldn't worry. The electricity was connected up, so the lights were on and we got some heat."

"I didn't mean that."

"Oh." She took a long drag of her cigarette. "They said I wasn't supposed to take a job that I had to stand up all the time. I'll have to look for work that I can be sitting down. I thought of a telephone operator. They train you, and you don't have to have a high school diploma. They don't pay much to start, but they're all right to work for. I don't have any money left. I only had enough to get home."

"How much more do you need?"

"Well, that's up to you. Look in my purse, there's only a little over four dollars. I'll have to pay my sister board and room."

"How much did you tell her?"

"Oh, she guessed. She didn't tell her husband, or he wouldn't let me stay there. He'd put me out. He'd say be a girl in a house, but I can't even be that for a while. Not that I want to, but I couldn't if I wanted to."

"I don't have much money either. I brought fifty dollars with me you can have, but that's the last I can lay my hands on for I don't know how long."

"Well, I never said it was all your fault. It takes two. But this way is better than if I had the baby and I had to tell who the father was. That would sure be the end of you, Dick."

"I know that, for God's sake. You don't have to keep reminding me."

"No, but you don't have to act as if you were the one that was doing all the favors. *I* went to that crummy hospital, and I was the one that took a chance on dying. You pleaded and begged me, but since then you act as if you didn't have any responsibility. As soon as I can get work I don't care if I never see you again, the same as you feel about me. I'm going to save up till I have enough to go some place else, and then believe me, Dick, I'll get out of here so fast. I'm suppose to take it easy for two months, but I start looking for work tomorrow. Or anyway as soon as this cold spell lets up. I can't walk that far in this weather."

"Where do you expect me to get more money?"

"You work in a bank, you're suppose to know."

"Are you suggesting that I steal it?"

"That wouldn't do me any good, if you got caught stealing. I have enough to tell in confession without that on my conscience. No, don't start stealing on my account. But you have to get the money somewhere, till I find work."

"What if I can't get any more? Just can't?"

"Don't say you can't when you can. You can sell your car, borrow money on your house. Ask your father and mother."

"You might as well tell me to get it from my wife."

"Well, if she'd give it to you. You're doing everything to protect her, but what's she entitled to more than I am?"

He slapped her. It was not a hard slap, from his somewhat cramped position in the car, and it barely glanced off her face, but her left cheek received some of the blow. She put her hand to her cheek. "Wud you do that for? That was a lousy thing to do."

"I'm sorry I did it," he said.

"Yeah," she said.

"But you don't have to bring my wife into it."

"Bring her into it? She's in it whether she knows it or not. You can't keep her out of it. She's in it. Maybe she doesn't know it, but she is, and sooner or later she will know it. *Because you'll tell her.* I can keep quiet, I showed you that. But you'll tell her, if she don't find out for herself."

"Not me. I won't tell her."

"Yes, you. I got to thinking a lot about you, Dick, in that crummy hospital. I went in there and I signed my name Evelyn New. Evelyn New. As soon as I did that I was alone in the world, because if I died they didn't know my name. I couldn't have any visitors, I couldn't talk to anybody. They even said I couldn't have the priest if I was gonna die. All alone, see? So what I did was think, and I sure did think about you, Dick. All right, you were paying for it, but on account of yourself, not on account of me. I'm not surprised you slapped me."

"I apologize for that," he said.

"Apologize. That's just a word. If you thought you could get away with it, you'd murder me. Maybe you don't know that yet, but you would. That's why I wasn't surprised by you slapping me. You didn't only want to slap me. You wanted to murder me."

"That's what you figured out in the hospital?"

"Yes. When I thought you were in love with me I couldn't of figured that out, but down there I knew you weren't in love with me. That's all right. I wasn't in love with you any more, either."

"That sounds as if you wanted to murder me, too," he said.

"No, not murder you. I was doing enough killing for one person. Maybe the baby would have been another Paderewski, somebody famous like that."

"Paderewski? You mean the piano player? What made you think that?"

"Well, he'd of been only half Polish, so I guess not Paderewski. I don't know. Was there anybody famous in your family?"

"No."

"Well, maybe only a basketball player. That's when I got stuck on you, when you used to play bastketball. You wouldn't even look at me then. I didn't know when I was better off."

"Oh, I looked at you, but you were too young."

"You only thought I was," she said. "Thank God for that, or we'd of been in worse trouble. Then my father was still alive, and speaking of murder he would of murdered you. If I had any brothers they would of murdered you. But instead of that you want to murder me."

"Ah, the hell with all this talk about murder. Nobody's going to murder anybody. That's all your imagination, because I gave you a slap in the face. I'm sorry for that, but I'm not going to keep on apologizing all night. I have to take you home or my alcohol will evaporate and the car'll boil over."

"All right. You said you had fifty dollars," she said.

"Here it is."

"Thanks. But don't forget, Dick, I'm gonna need some more."

"I'll try to get you another fifty next month, but I don't promise."

"How will you get it to me?"

"I'll mail it to you in cash."

"All right. Four weeks from tomorrow I'll be expecting it. Fifty cash. But don't put me off. Some of it has to go for medicine."

"I'll do the best I can, and whatever you do, don't you come in the bank. I don't want anybody to see me talking to you."

"It's no pleasure talking to you, either, Dick."

He moved the car closer to her sister's house. "Can you carry those bags all right?"

"Oh, sure. Those delicious hamburgers gave me my strength back."

He kept the motor idling until he saw the door open at her sister's house, then he drove home and put his car in the garage.

One lamp was burning in the kitchen in the otherwise dark-ened house, but he knew that Emily was still awake. As soon as he opened the kitchen door he knew she was awake. The house was still; she was not moving around upstairs; but from her to him came a hostile greeting. He put his overcoat and hat and arctics in the hall closet, making no sound. He went to the cellar and made sure that the furnace was all right for the night. When he returned to the kitchen she was sitting at the table in her blue flannel bath-robe and smoking a cigarette.

"I tried not to make any noise," he said.

"I was awake. I heard you come in."

"It's bitter out. Must be over ten below," he said.

"It's fourteen below outside the bathroom window," she said. "You want to tell me where you went to?"

"You mean after the meeting?"

"There was no meeting. Phil Irwin phoned to say it was called off."

"Yes, I found that out when I got there. There was a notice on the door of the gym. Alumni Association meeting postponed, account of severe weather. Phil didn't show up, but some of the others did, so we went over to the Elks and had a few beers. Jack Showers, Ed McGraney."

"Always Jack Showers and Ed McGraney," she said.

"They're on the athletic committee."

"And you never see them any other time. *I* never see them at all."

"Well, why should you? Got any pie or anything?"

"Pie on top of beer? You'll be yelling in your sleep all night. Why don't you have some pretzels?"

"Don't tell me what I'm hungry for, will you?"

"No, I won't tell you anything. You don't tell me anything but lies. You never went near the Elks tonight."

"I can prove it."

"Who by? Jack Showers and Ed McGraney all over again?"

"They were with me. Where do you think I was?"

"That's what I'm trying to find out. Listen to me, Dick. I know there's something funny going on, and I'm going to find out what it is. I'm not going to let you make a fool out of me. Whoever it is, it isn't one of my friends because I keep tabs on them. Norma. Elaine. Especially Norma. But it couldn't be her, because when I was checking up on you and her I found out she has another boy friend. But whoever it is, you might as well prepare yourself. I'm going to make trouble."

"Make trouble for yourself. That's what you're doing right now. And keep your voice down or you'll wake the kids."

"Oh, isn't that rich? You showing consideration for the kids. I like that, all right. It's all right to make a fool out of me and go whoring around, but we mustn't wake the kids. That's rich, that is. Go on up and wake them. Tell them where you were tonight, with some whore."

He slapped her. "Shut up," he said.

She drew away from him. "Don't you do *that* again, don't you *ever* do that again. I'll *kill* you first, Dick. I swear I will."

"Go ahead, you'd be doing me a favor," he said.

The strange, simple words shocked her. Whatever else he had said to her, these words she recognized as the truth; at this moment he wished to be dead and free, but not only free of her. More than to be free of her he wished to be free of the other woman. She could think of nothing to say, but she knew that no words of hers could threaten this man with trouble. She was looking at destruction, and she had had no part in it.